ASCENSION

Y DDRAIG [THE DRAGONS OF BRYTHON] - BOOK II

Gwendolyn Beynon

Dark ^PAges Publishing

Gwendolyn Beynon/Dark ᴾAges Publishing
www.yddraig.com.au

Book Layout © 2016 BookDesignTemplates.com

Ascension/Gwendolyn Beynon -- 1st ed.
ISBN 978-0-9943527-3-6

Dedication

For our dragon, Gus. Miss you every day.

And to our newly Ascended boy, Nigel.
Welcome.

Acknowledgements

To Karen, Birra-Li, Anita, and Bel—thank you for your enthusiasm and the early impressions that helped me shape *Ascension*.

To Dan, as always, thank you for your friendship and support—I love that we get to do this together.

CONTENTS

Glossary of Characters & Terms

BRIEF PRONUNCIATION GUIDE

f - pron. as hard 'v'

ff - pron. as a soft 'eff'

ll - The Cymraeg 'll' consonant is like a soft 'thl' or a 'cl'

w - a vowel sound closest to 'oo'

dd - pron. a hard 'th' [as in lithe]

y - pron. 'uh' alone or within a word or 'ee' on the end

c/g - 'c' is always hard and interchangeable with a hard 'g'

GWANAELLE [*gooan-eye-thl*] The daughter of a noble family in the North, she fled her father's weak ways and lived wild until she stumbled upon Melangell's valley ("Sacrifice", book one). When the Dragonling emerged from the Creil, Gwanaelle kept her wits about her and, in the simple act of reaching a hand out to it, became the Dragonling's new carer and mother.

EIFION [*eye-vee-on*] Second-in-command to the High Chieftain's exiled brother, Cai, and now in exile himself, Eifion took the Dragonling and Gwanaelle from the yew valley when the darkness came. He has lived in a neighbouring valley with them ever since harbouring a dark and devastating secret.

NYNEVE [*nun-ave*] The child who emerged from the Creil. A Dragonling, unascended. She has lived for fourteen years in ignorance of her true heritage surrounded by the love and protection of Gwanaelle and Eifion.

BLEHERIS [*ble-hair-is*] A traveller in song, silver of tongue and hair. Bleheris is a bard, well-schooled in the politics of the land. And of *y Ddraig*.

GWALCHAFAD [*gwolk-a-vad*] Once squire to his illustrious older brother Gwalchmai (known in Artwr's company by the epithet 'Gauwain') Gwalchafad fought his way out of his brother's shadow and became a warrior in his own right. Now thane of Trellech. Known in the language of the Angles as 'Gaheris'.

ARTWR [*ar-toor*] High Chieftain of all Cymry, has fought for decades against the Angles and Saxons invading from the east. Relocated his stronghold to Caerllion when a dragon destroyed the one at Caerwent. Surrounds himself and his Queen, Gwenhwyfar, with warriors there.

Y DDRAIG [*uh thr'eye-g*] Drake or Dragon. Amongst the oldest creatures on the islands of Brython, survivors of endless invasions from across the seas. Have lived in increasing seclusion since men first wrought iron against their forests. Revered and feared equally, *y Ddraig's* magic is universally coveted.

CREIL [*cray-el*] The dragon's egg, y Ddraig in senescent form. Hunted for its power—political and actual—it offers the sight to those who can master it.

CYMRY [*cum-ree*] The Romano-Brythonic people south of those lands held by the Picts and the Scoti. Until the 17th century, *Cymry* referred to the people as much as the land and borders shifted and changed with the people inhabiting them.

Author's Note: The language in *Y Ddraig* borrows both from known Brythonic phrases common before the adoption of 'Old Welsh' and brings forward the creation of the classic Welsh consonants 'll' and 'dd' into the 6th century for consistency. In other cases, I have simply *imagineered* elements of language to suit the tone of the story.

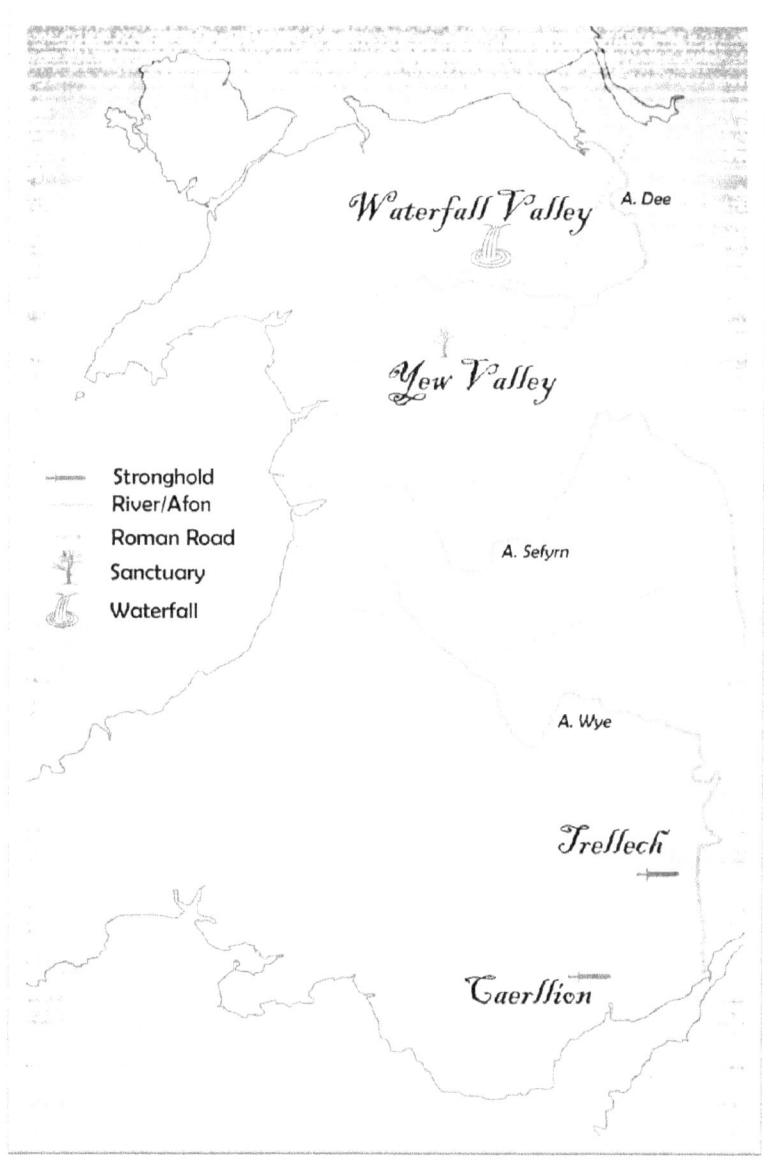

Waterfall Valley

A. Dee

Yew Valley

Stronghold
River/Afon
Roman Road
Sanctuary
Waterfall

A. Sefyrn

A. Wye

Trellech

Caerllion

PROLOGUE

THE QUARTER MOON blazed high in the sky as *Makepeace* yielded to the time of *Song*. Two nights had passed since the Creil's crusty outer breached and the dragonling long-nurtured within had scrabbled her way out on human limbs. She did not eat the fish Eifion caught for her, nor the hare, nor the stripped flesh of a goat, though she did tolerate sheep's milk mixed with water but only in tiny amounts.

Nowhere near enough to sustain her.

She hungered and suffered through her first days in this world and everyone in the little yew-filled valley suffered with her, Gwanaelle especially. The child had begun well the first day, on emerging, still fed by whatever magic lingered from her time inside the egg, then she had taken to loud, raucous protests at the absence of food in this new world. The following dawn had seen her slacken, pining for something none of them could provide and, as the day wore hungrily on, her loud protests fell away to a miserable whimper.

'We cannot let this creature perish,' Melangell murmured. 'An entire people died to give it life.'

Gwanaelle scowled, tucking the listless infant against her belly and rocking her gently to ease the stiffness in her sinews. 'She is a child, not a creature. Not an "it".'

'We do not yet know what it is,' Melangell corrected, 'no matter how like a human babe it looks. Only that it is dying.'

Beyond them, Eifion jogged into the clearing, returning from his hunt for new types of food; something that the dragonling might find acceptable. *Anything.* He carried a struggling moorfowl by its legs and a string of dead furred creatures over his shoulder.

'Perhaps one of these?' he said, raising them up as he drew near.

Gwanaelle breathed a quick word of thanks to the Drygioni for the sacrifice of so many of their upland creatures and boosted the suddenly restless child higher against her shoulder. Perhaps she could smell the fresh meat.

'Give it the rat first,' Melangell instructed. 'We have not yet tried a burrower.'

Eifion bled the rat before skinning it and the dragonling immediately twisted in Gwanaelle's hold. She soothed and rocked her, and grew ever more anxious when nothing seemed to lessen her distress. The tighter Gwanaelle held, the more the child writhed and turned in her grasp with vigour she just should not have.

'It seeks your breast,' Melangell realised, her keen eyes narrowing. 'Perhaps it feeds like a normal babe?'

The child issued her heartbreaking whimper again—too weak, now, to cry proper, but she gnawed heartily on the thumb Gwanaelle slipped into her little mouth to give her some peace.

'Surely dragon maidens could not conjure milk at will?' she said in despair. She had as little to offer the child as the barren Morwyn Ddraig must have.

Melangell uttered, once again, a phrase that Gwanaelle was growing heartily sick of hearing.

I do not know.

What kind of a tradition was it of Melangell's people that the most important knowledge was held over until the very end of a Morwyn Ddraig's training, when it could be laid waste by any of a score of untimely interruptions? They knew all to do with the slumbering egg but how could so much about a *living* Ancient One be unknown to the Mathrafal?

Did the Old People truly expect the dragon to never hatch?

The whimpering grew more eager and Eifion moved on to the moorfowl, killing it and plucking it urgently, sending feathers flying in a way that was uncharacteristic of the prudent warrior who never wasted anything, but the dragonling only seemed to sense his urgency and her cries escalated.

'Give it your breast, Gwanaelle,' Melangell ordered. 'Perhaps your flesh can silence it as your thumb no longer can. At least for a moment.'

The thought of those bony gums clamping down on the sensitive meat of her breast scarcely appealed, but the infant's squawking drove straight to her heart. She glanced briefly at a distracted Eifion amongst his feathers and then loosed one breast from her wears as privately as she could. The babe immediately nuzzled along it and closed fat little lips around her pinkest flesh. Not well fit and not precise, but eager and instinctive.

Silence in the valley after days and nights of loud distress got everyone's attention. As the child awkwardly suckled at nothing, Mair emerged from her tree hollow to look, Eifion paused his plucking and glanced up, and even aloof Cai ceased the grinding and oiling of his blade, stood to his full height and stared toward them across the yew circle.

Gwanaelle winced, both from discomfort at the unfamiliar sensation on her breast and at the scrutiny of such an intimate act undertaken so publicly, but the babe in her arms settled as its mouth learnt what it needed to do and her heart softened as the Ancient One's sinews gradually did.

'Peace, little one,' she murmured.

If a mouthful of empty breast brought that, so be it.

But the peace did not last, and the inexperienced and fruitless suckles soon grew more urgent. Those sharp gums pressed down on Gwanaelle's flesh until her winces became cries of pain, but lifting the infant did not detach her, and trying to remove her determined suck only stretched her flesh uncomfortably.

And then it happened…

She'd been raised in the middle of five siblings and she'd watched the youngest grow from a babe. The first of her brother's tiny year-teeth had broken through Thelwn's gums over the space of a fortennight and the second came similarly; so that was how Gwanaelle knew the teething to work…

Gradually.

But nothing happened slowly with the dragonling. Its first four teeth erupted as flat and tiny as her brother's had, except in an instant it seemed—between one wince and its fellow—and the very next clamp drove them deep into her tender flesh.

Her pain brought everyone to their feet.

'Gwanaelle!' Eifion leapt first, crouching at her side and laying hands immediately on the child, ready to assist, but the discomfort quickly diminished and the suckling returned to a less fevered rate.

Then, disturbingly, the dragonling appeared to swallow.

All in the valley held their breath.

'Melangell?' Eifion finally murmured, nodding meaningfully toward Gwanaelle's bare flesh and drawing the Lifebringer's gasp.

Gwanaelle stretched her neck and peered downward around the babe to find what concerned them both so much, and then saw it—a dribble of bright red blood emerging from the corner of its pursed little mouth. Eifion scrambled to pull it off, but it was the first time since she'd first picked the child up that her suffering had eased and her pained cries ceased.

She twisted away from Eifion's efforts to detach the babe. 'No! She feeds at last.'

'You can't—'

'She's *feeding*,' Gwanaelle insisted, begging understanding in eyes the colour of dug earth. 'After days of starvation.'

A dark kind of fury filled Eifion's normally placid face and he leaned back on his haunches, watching her intently, monitoring the suckling child, glancing helplessly at Melangell in between. Still the babe fed, pulling from her breast in long, deep draughts and her tiny body grew less tortured with every tug. Soon, Eifion stopped even looking at the infant and simply watched Gwanaelle's own eyes for any signs of distress. Compared to being witness to the death by the hour of this unready, frail infant, feeding it with some of her blood was nothing. If that's what it needed.

It seemed only a few breaths had passed when Eifion's hands on her shoulders jerked her to sense and she found herself half-toppled in his hold. The valley around him spun wildly.

'Enough.'

He twisted back to the floppy moorfowl he'd been plucking, snagged it up and returned to her side. Within a moment, he had drawn his leg-blade across the thing's scrawny neck and upended the sodden wound against her chest. Warm blood ran down over the curve of her breast, over her nipple, over the child's greedy lips, which immediately shifted focus, detaching from her breast and searching for the new flow. As soon as Gwanaelle's ruined flesh plopped free of the child's mouth, Eifion stole the dragonling up into his own arms and pressed the fowl's neck open at her tiny mouth. She searched around for a fresher source of food but, finding none, settled for draining the just-dead fowl of its essence.

Melangell tucked Gwanaelle's bloodied breast back under her wears and pressed her hand against its wounds, sending Mair to fetch witches-weed from the waterfall pool.

Their uncertain gazes met.

'I'd almost forgotten what she was,' Gwanaelle croaked, panting as the pain returned.

Melangell laid a second hand at her back and pressed it toward its mate, staunching the blood flow from her breast with firm but not unkind pressure.

'She is an Ancient One, Gwanaelle. We can never forget.'

They sagged against each other and watched the bundle in Eifion's arms drain the death from the moorfowl. Her hungry lips slurped and sucked until, eventually, she fell into a deep, sated sleep. Eifion dropped the leached carcass, let his cramped knee go free under him, and buckled to the ground with the tiny dragonling curled content at last in his arms.

For the longest time, none spoke.

'I suppose we should name it,' Melangell eventually breathed, never taking her eyes off the infant Ancient One. 'Now that it is going to live.'

Gwanaelle's lids fluttered open again and fell on one of the two people in this whole world she loved best cradled securely in the powerful arms of the other.

'Nyneve,' she whispered. 'She will be called Nyneve.'

Part I

I

547 A.D.

NYNEVE'S TAXED ARMS trembled in violence and the nails of her fingers threatened to tear away at her dangling weight. Breath crouched, trapped, in her throat just as she needed it the most. She tried to discipline her scrabbling legs—swinging only made her blood-slippery fingers lose whatever purchase they'd managed—and felt along the face for a crevice for the big toe of one bare foot and then the other. Far below, their little valley spun enough that she dared never to look down. Height had ever been her enemy and nothing in the world was higher than this cascade.

Least not the small world that she knew.

She paused a moment, took a breath, her body frozen in the most unnatural of shapes, then she pushed up—hard—with legs almost too weak to obey, and she crept herself that tiny bit further above the valley floor. She'd never before climbed beyond the toad-shaped stone—if the toad had been especially deformed—but now it first pressed against her cheek, then she rested her chin on it, then a weakened shove hooked her ribs on it so that she could take some burden from her suffering legs. Just for a moment. She ignored the stinging of her knee as she scraped yet more skin off it pressing herself further up the waterfall's spray-slicked surface. It tore like leaves, these days, and it scarcely needed the rough corners of rocks to rend it. She would have climbed closer to the centre where the stones had been beaten to soft roundness by the river thundering down the valley wall if not for the self-same water that would pummel her bones to powder. Never mind the bone-shattering sarsens laying at its foot that cried out for some unwary child to tumble down onto them and nourish them with her blood.

Nyneve lifted her eyes to the ridge far above, blinking away the sweat that stung into them. One day she would make it to the top and she wasn't entirely sure what would happen when she got there. She just had the strongest sensation that reaching the top mattered. A great deal.

But that day was not this day.

She'd learned the hard way to leave herself enough vigour for easing herself back down to the ground and while she might wish she had the gift of the birds who could just glide back down and alight there with grace, her only gift were the two scrawny things dangling from her hips. And they could only take so much.

'How far did you get?' Eifion murmured as she slumped down next to him much later where he sat carving pegs for Gwanaelle.

'The toad,' she grunted.

'Good progress.'

'I've been trying once a se'nnight since I could walk,' she said, striving to keep the self-pity from her voice lest it disappoint the man who was as Father to her.

'I know. I've been watching you since then.'

She caught his gaze. 'Should not I have done it by now?'

'Not everything in this world can be conquered,' he said, mildly.

She glared. 'Mother foolishly believes you were a mighty warrior, once. I see no evidence of it.'

If he felt the barb of her words, he didn't react to it and, as always, he refused to answer her invitation to demean Gwanaelle. 'A good warrior knows whether to stage a battle over a se'nnight or a moon.'

Or entire winters. More of them than her slim fingers could count. Nyneve sagged fully on the damp dirt, her face turned to the sky and the earth's coolness soaking into her heated flesh.

'You might help me,' she grumbled.

'When you have the fortitude to climb the waterfall alone,' he said, mildly and not for the first time, 'you'll have the fortitude to explore what adventures lie beyond this valley.'

The awful cloistered sensation returned in a flush. Of being compelled inward, curled into herself, her face pressed against something cold and smooth. Breathing and secure but…buried alive. Like she'd lived a dozen lifetimes like that already.

She wasn't about to live a single one more.

'Nothing lies beyond this valley,' she muttered. Just endless, empty hills.

Eifion halted his work. 'Melangell's yew circle and her new risen church both stand outside of it. You travel there regularly enough.'

Nyneve snorted. 'Out of one waterfall-hewn valley and straight into another, every *Gathering*. That is scarcely adventure.'

He scooped up a handful of dark, rich soil and sought her gaze. Imprisoned it. 'The dirt of this land is nourished by the corpses of those who would give anything for a safe valley and life of low adventure.'

She threw herself back onto that land with dramatic arms. 'Ugh. No more tales of Angles and Artwr and the battles for Cymry.'

'Which is to be Nyneve—adventure or no adventure? You will need to decide.' All those creases at his eyes' corners managed to soften his rebuke.

She tugged at the wears cloying at her throat. Climbing always made her especially hot, but it was always worth it. Sometimes—for just a moment—she would get the sense that she could push off from all those uncomfortable rocks and just...float...to the top. As effortless as breathing. Sometimes it was all she could do not to try.

'War is not adventure,' she grumbled. 'War is just angry men sticking swords into each other.'

Eifion wielded silence just like one of those swords. It never failed to shame her. She yanked distractedly at her sleeves.

'Is it bad today?' he asked, gently.

She shrugged, knowing that pouting diminished her in Eifion's eyes. Wishing to be more like Mother—poised, reflective, enduring; beautiful despite her age—but unable to while such furious heat burned at her from within.

'Come on.'

Eifion stood, stretched a large, rough hand down to her and pulled her to her feet. He led her back to the waterfall and waited while she completely disrobed. He used to do that too, as did her mother still, but he'd stopped since her body started to change. Growing curved where once it was lanky and straight. Some days she could almost feel the changes happening under her skin. Now, Eifion simply hiked up his brecs as high as his thick legs would allow, and removed his wools and tunic before wading into the pool after her. This waterfall was the largest for a three-moon's march, and its thundering waters were cold and pure and, according to Mother, the only thing that could ease the fire within when it began to burn. Eifion positioned her under the hammering pressure and then waded back out to collect the timber slathe set on a rock at the water's edge. He used it to stir the dark bottom of the pool and then hauled one large scoop of mud out and placed it on a nearby rock.

'Nyneve.'

That gentle, matter of fact voice never failed to calm her, even in the midst of the worst burn. Eifion was the only person who had ever treated her like a regular person, right from the earliest. Her mother still thought she was a child. Nest and Elen insisted on playing with her like she was a doll for the two fortennights that they saw her every Sun's March; dressing her up and weaving flowers into her hair. Melangell studied her like a curiosity. Cai glowered at her more than not and kept his sword handy as though he were expecting something to burst forth from within her flesh at any moment.

She stepped out from under the thunder and stumbled, water-blind toward Eifion's voice, standing meekly under his mild touch as he slapped thick mud over her nakedness.

'Why are we here?' he murmured beneath the suck and slurp of mud.

The first easing always came as a sigh. It was impossible not to when the dreadful heat she lived with stopped so suddenly with the application of the frigid mud. Better than weeping with relief as she'd done when she was a child.

'Because the waters help with the Searing,' she groaned.

'And what is the Searing?' *Slap* went the mud.

'A sickness of my blood.'

'And will you die of it?'

'No.'

Slap. 'And will you master it?'

'Someday.'

'And until then?' *Slap* on her back.

She rocked with the gentle pressure of the slathing. 'Until then, I have you.'

The slapping stopped—the gorgeous smear of mud on her skin by rough hands stopped—and she relented.

'Until then, I have the waters,' she sighed.

He turned her and smiled into her eyes, studying them closely as he always did. 'Good. Arms up.'

No matter how pleasant she found it, Eifion always approached the slathing like every other job he undertook—thorough but detached. Having slapped wads of mud across her body, he smeared them all into each other until she was more slime than skin.

Until the Searing stopped.

For as long as it *could* stop.

Short of living permanently under the waterfall, she could not be free of it for long. She'd had it as long as she knew but last winter it had grown more unkind; hotter, vengeful. As soon as she rinsed the mud off and crawled back into her wears, the heat began re-kindling. Sometimes she went an entire se'nnight without giving in and seeking the slathe again. Sometimes relief only lasted a night or two, but Eifion or her mother was always on hand and willing to bring her back in here and cover her. No matter the hour. No matter their activity.

Eifion was her preference because he sat and talked with her after easing her down onto a rock to wait for the mud to dry and begin its good work. Like he had no more important task to be doing. Her mother usually sat, too, but there was little conversation between them now.

Some days she missed it. Some days she loathed it. Her inner emotions blazed and changed as fiercely as the Searing.

'Was it bad?' A soft voice spoke from behind them.

The waterfall's thunder made sure they rarely heard anyone's arrival, let alone the hare-footed Gwanaelle.

'Bad enough,' Eifion grunted, disguising the brief flare in his eyes by dropping his gaze to the water. As was his wont around her mother.

'I made it to the frog, today,' Nyneve said, for something to break the uncomfortable silence.

'Good.'

But her mother's smile did not reach her eyes, and she did not approve. Instead, she struggled and failed to mask her stricken expression at her daughter's accomplishment. If she had her way, her timid mother would keep her here in this valley forever. Never to discover the world, never to discover her purpose. Never to discover the mystery of men, just because *she* had not and now she was too old for any of it. Thirteen winters had passed in which Eifion could have laid with her if his interest lay in the same direction that her mother's obviously did. Instead, he took himself out of the valley regularly and sought satisfaction elsewhere while Gwanaelle remained a maid.

Not that Nyneve had a particularly clear idea of what "satisfaction" actually meant. Her knowledge of the relations between a man and a woman came from a single example—Melangell and Cai—during *Gathering*. If they were to be believed, men and women twined together a dozen times a week, loud and wild and wherever the mood took them yet never, ever created new life. So what was the purpose? Perhaps it was just another one of Melangell's obscure, otherworldly demands.

You will never know what she sacrificed for you. Her mother's voice in her memory demanded respect. Yet, how could she know when nobody would tell her? She knew that Eifion was not her true father. Neither was Gwanaelle her true mother. She knew that they had all lived together once, before Gwanaelle had swaddled her tight and followed Eifion into seclusion in this remote valley when the long Darkness came. She knew she was not of their people because everyone save Eifion looked at her like such a curiosity. Because Nest and Elen made such a fuss about her eyes.

Because none of *them* ever Seared.

So what was she…? An orphan waif from a remote people? A fugitive like everyone else in Melangell's valley? Discarded because of her blood sickness?

Her eyes lifted to the tree line, to some shadow she kept seeing there but could never find. Nothing but the same moss and charcoal colours as far as her eye could see.

'How do you feel?' Eifion murmured, drawing her eye from the wood and bringing her closer to the tumbling waters.

Mercifully, the Searing had ebbed to almost nothing. Just a few tingly patches. Though she feared she'd be back in mud soon. Or being roughly scrubbed over with sop-weed. It was getting shorter between episodes, and hotter.

'Better. Thank you.'

'Rinse off,' he murmured. 'I'll take you hunting.'

Hunting meant moving to the fringes of the valley since most of the wildlife in it knew not to come too close to their camp, and the edge of the valley was almost—almost—out of it, and given she could walk there without climbing anything or shedding skin or blood or tearing off a nail, then hunting was almost as welcome a reprieve as the mud.

Fortenyear

GWANAELLE WATCHED from under her lashes as Eifion dragged his feet out of the muddied pool below the waterfall, gathered up his wears and marched barefoot and bare-chested back toward his shelter.

He was no longer the compact, muscle-packed young warrior he'd been when a brutal Lord had first chased her into Melangell's valley, but even as silver began to invade his dark hair still nothing had changed about his easy, unconcerned talent with vulnerable girls. He'd used it on her when she was young, and now he worked the same kind of magic on Nyneve.

The child who liked no one.

The passage of many winters had transformed him into a lean, sinewy survivor, since the day they had fled the yew valley and found this place. Not as pretty and not as ancient as Melangell's *Dragon's Rest* but their valley was small and deep and safe, and it had fed them through the Darkness. Artwr credited the gloom to his God joining him in war against the Angles whose creeping advance halted for two entire marches of the diminished sun, but if that was true, then God also went to war with the woods and every living thing in them. None could thrive when there wasn't enough sun even to cast a shadow. Month after hungry month. winter on winter. The creatures starved, the plants starved where they struggled to grow, and Melangell's valley began to fail. So much so, that Eifion had taken her and Nyneve from the yew circle to lessen the numbers trying to exist on the valley's meagre growings. He'd found this place, claimed it, and they'd never left it since, first scraping a lean living out of its untouched earth and then turning it to comfortable profit.

So it was that Nyneve spent the first years of her life believing everything was always that dark. When the sun first began to shine again, Nyneve's body heat began to rise and they took to the damp cave behind the waterfall to ease her, but the sun was not to blame as it turned out. It was her dragon blood coming to the fore. In the many winters since, only the waterfall kept the girl at a temperature she could survive and so they rarely left the waterfall unless it was to go somewhere with another one.

'I'll keep her busy until the sun touches the uplands,' Eifion murmured, moving closer and shrugging back into his tunic. 'Will that be long enough?'

Gwanaelle quietly mourned the absence of his exposed flesh. 'I will raise the shelter.'

A fortenyear gift for the ungrateful.

Eifion had insisted on secrecy, but Gwanaelle feared that Nyneve would receive it as she received everything new these past few winters—without a hint of grace. Though, given her own shelter would see her freed from sharing one with the mother she believed she no longer needed, perhaps *this* gift would be more welcome.

Eifion nodded and picked up his leather bag filled with makeshift traps and weapons, but he stopped and turned back before he'd taken two steps.

His brown eyes blazed into hers. 'She suffers, Gwanaelle. In ways we cannot comprehend.'

'Has she confessed to you?'

'Can you not see it in her unearthly eyes? She is in agony. All the hours of the day. That would make the strongest man brittle.'

Never mind a young girl trying also to become a woman.

With a dragon imprisoned within.

'I fear that coming of age might be a disappointment to her,' Gwanaelle murmured, glancing Nyneve's way.

Eifion grinned. 'Wasn't it for all of us? I can't begin to tell you the depravities I imagined waited on the other side of my fortenyear.'

The heat that suffused her whenever Eifion grinned at her like that surged through her as always until she wondered whether Nyneve's Searing had begun to spread. What depravities she would gladly deliver him if only he would—

'Girl!' Eifion shouted, turning for the edge of camp. 'Sunset holds for none of us!'

A freshly rinsed Nyneve scrambled into the last of her wears and jogged after Eifion as he powered out of the camp and beyond the valley's thick trees.

She is in agony. In ways we cannot comprehend…

Gwanaelle comprehended something about enduring agony. She'd been in love with Eifion since she first gave him her trust, yet he'd loved Melangell for three winters longer than that.

That wasn't without its pain.

~

The new shelter took longer to raise than Gwanaelle might have hoped. Eifion's neatly carved pegs and secretly twined ropes and the animal skins she'd scraped herself hidden away in a distant corner of the valley were all there, yet none wanted to cooperate under the pressure of the sinking sun. Nyneve and Eifion would be back any moment and would find her swamped and tangled amidst a half-ruined shelter. Not how she preferred to be discovered by him. She'd been through a lot over the years but her mother had raised her to be proud and some lessons could never be unlearned.

She forced a peg through the chewed sinew on a determined cry, hammered it into the ground with a stone before packing the earth in around it and, this time, it held. As did the six after it. Still, she had barely laid out two winter skins within the erected shelter when the low trees at the edge of the camp rustled and Eifion and Nyneve pushed through.

Gwanaelle staggered upright and tried in vain to smooth her damp hair from her hot and dirty face. Eifion marched toward her with his eyes only slightly alarmed at the closeness of disaster her dishevelled state indicated.

Nyneve couldn't have been less interested in what she looked like.

'Wh—?' The girl skidded to a halt in front of the new shelter; a startling new arrival in a valley that had scarcely changed in thirteen winters. 'Is this for me?'

Ah, the absent humility of youth. 'It is your fortenyear,' Gwanaelle said. 'Eifion and I wished to—'

She got no further, Nyneve shrieked like one of the pegs had pierced her very flesh, threw herself at Eifion, then flung herself away from him again and dove into the shelter.

'It has a flap!' she cried from within.

Gwanaelle caught Eifion's eye. 'If we'd known something as simple as a door would make such a difference to her humour we should have done it earlier.'

Because it was true, Nyneve had only grown difficult as her winters in this world could no longer be counted on two hands. Before that she was a delight.

Eifion smiled down on her again and his gaze flicked over her dishevelled appearance. 'Did it trouble you?'

'It was not as easy to do alone as it was to do together,' she said, referring to the last shelters they had risen. 'But I managed.'

'As I knew you would.'

And there it was again. The softening he sometimes got. Impossible to know whether it was pride, amusement or affection—or some mix of all three—but whenever he did it, the look sent her heart into a flutter. Like this one. She fought to keep her hand from wiping the rivulets of sweat from her brow. All she had in these moments was dignity. And in that small regard she understood Nyneve's excitement at having her own tent. She'd had her own matting in her parent's long-hall long before her fortenyear, and long before her father's intimate attentions drove her away.

This shelter was the gift of dignity in a single gesture.

'Thank you,' Nyneve said, emerging again. Her glance to her mother might have been brief but it was there, at least. 'Why do we mark the Sun's March today, particularly?'

Gwanaelle visualised the intricate stitching on the skin she kept folded in a secret crevice in the cave behind the waterfall. It was the mirror of her father's bronze peg board and it allowed her to keep the nights and seasons in order out here in the wilderness. It also helped her to track Nyneve's changing behaviour across the three-score months that comprised a full skin. Only one winter to go and she would need to unstitch the whole thing and start over.

It also allowed her to mark the Christ days that had been important to her mother, bringing the longed-for woman secretly closer. She liked to imagine what her mother would be doing on those days, and on those days her own work always suffered. If Eifion noticed the pattern he never said.

'You were born on the night when *Makepeace* became the time of *Song*,' Gwanaelle said. 'And that is tonight. When the sun rests in the west and the east moon is born.'

Nyneve's expression grew still. Her clever mind began its work. 'The night I *arrived*, you mean?'

Eifion caught Gwanaelle's glance in his and covered her careless slip easily. 'The night you first shared a fire with us.'

Born... Arrived... Shared a fire. All true. Yet none of them the whole truth. Soon-time they would have to tell her the whole truth, but, for now, Nyneve was content to accept Eifion's word. As was she ever.

'So this is my...fortenyear?' She stumbled over the unfamiliar phrase.

'It is,' he nodded. 'If you were a boy you would leave your family, travel to your Chief's stronghold and prepare to be an armsman.'

Her riven eyes flared with the imagined adventure. 'And if I was a girl?'

'If you were a girl,' Gwanaelle said lightly, 'you would prepare to be mother.'

Nyneve blinked, unimpressed. 'How happy, then, that I am neither.'

She jested, but every now and again words spilled from Nyneve's lips that reminded them both what creature she came from. The creature she would someday—somehow—become, and the precious foresight that she had harboured for all those years slumbering within the Creil's crust. That power did not leave the shattered egg with her, but the tiniest threads still remained and they emerged in subtle ways. Never on command.

'So...I might sleep in here from tonight?' Nyneve checked.

'Or you might not,' Gwanaelle murmured, struggling to give up the beautiful, loving child she'd raised. How she would sleep alone in her furs tonight without Nyneve's roasting heat to snuggle up to... 'It is up to you, now.'

'Why have you never before spoken of the magic of the fortenyear?'

Eifion chuckled. Perhaps to her, freedom was a kind of magic. 'Because awaiting it would have been pointless and painful cruelty.'

This girl who already waited for—and pained—so much.

She glanced from man to woman and the two colours in her brown-green gaze glittered with intelligence. 'So... I am no longer a child?'

Gwanaelle took a deep breath. 'No longer.'

May all the old gods save them.

Nyneve chose her next words with precision. 'And I might do anything at all that I like, from now on?'

'Yes.'

'Including leaving?'

Gwanaelle's chest caved beneath the disguise of her wools.

'If you don't wish to live long,' Eifion said, just as carefully.

That brought split eyes around to him and she murmured. 'You have so little faith in me, Father?'

She used the word seldom, but she knew exactly the effect it had on him. Little weaver of trouble.

Eifion's regard softened. 'I have little enough faith in what's out there.'

'If you stay,' Gwanaelle took care to explain, 'you assume the work of an adult. You contribute as much as you are able. In return, you earn equal say in our choices.'

The idea that she should ever be equal seemed as impossible to her as grasping the water that tumbled down from the uplands into her hands.

She looked from one to the other, mouth agape. 'I…'

Gwanaelle held her breath. This child she had protected and raised from an infant was not ready to face the world. Not when the world wished her such harm, and not before she knew what she really was. Except how did they tell her than when they barely knew themselves?

'I will consider your words—' Nyneve began, holding herself as tall and noble as any Queen ever had. In that moment it was easier to see the Ancient blood rushing through her body, making her more woman than child. Then she ruined it by breaking into a wide grin and squealing as she darted back beyond the skin flap. '—in my own shelter!'

~

'She will have to come out to dig a hole, at least,' Eifion murmured, shoving at the fire coals with a stick and glancing at the darkened shelter. 'Her body will force her out.'

Knowing Nyneve's fierce determination, that was not necessarily truth. She was as likely to dig a pit for her bodily issue right inside her shelter rather than emerge and risk losing it to the fates.

'She has never had anything of her own,' he reminded her. 'She will be drunk on it.'

I would rather she grew drunk on fermented wildberry.

He lifted his long stick from the coals and poked harmlessly across the fire at the furs she wore. 'You cannot will her out with your stares, Gwanaelle. Leave her.'

That forced her gaze back to his, and, as it always did, that steady regard drew her inmost secrets out.

'I have not slept alone since the yew tree hollow in Melangell's valley,' she murmured. 'It will feel so...'

Wrong. Unnatural.

Lonely.

The thought of still laying alone when she was grey and loose-skinned loomed like the darkness that had brought them here.

'Remember how we cramped in together when we first came?' he asked, quietly. 'In the cave. With little Nyneve pressed between us.'

Remember? She was scarce two years past her own fortenyear and she was in love. This valley that had been so strange and unfamiliar by day became a kind of heaven by night. A babe curled at her breast and Eifion's protective arm tossed over them both. His strong body curled around her. The memories had burned into her very skin. She'd worked her hardest to make him hers, but the memory of Melangell shone too bright.

'I remember how long we thought it was *us* making *her* hot,' she said, so that she should not say what she was actually thinking.

'It is right that you should miss her, Gwanaelle,' Eifion murmured. 'But it is right that she should not miss you.'

She nodded, and a tear splashed into the fire and sizzled in its death. 'I was younger than she when I left my family.'

Eifion glowered. 'You had little choice.'

She grew hypnotised by his dirt-packed fingers on the firestick—strong and long and worn. Nothing like her infatuated father's fumbling, smooth ones. The fingers she had fled.

'If Cai had not been riding with his Prince that day...'

She was small and pretty and she'd had the narrow hips of a child. She never would have survived the frenzied attentions of the lascivious Prince Brychwel, and she would not be sitting here, now, by a fire, a grown woman. A free woman.

A maiden still.

And mother to an Ancient One.

Not what she had imagined her life to be like when she had crept out from under her father's heavy arm and taken a pack of food and a final, desperate kiss from her distraught mother by the wood's edge. Her first miserable se'nnights amongst the trees were numb and confused and unbearably lonely, and she'd grown convinced that she was being banished—punished—for her father's lack of resolve, but in the moment that the dragonling curled its tiny, sticky hand around her thumb a fortenyear ago this night, Gwanaelle had seen the truth as vivid and rich as if it happened right in front of her. Her mother's utter, utter heartbreak on discovering her bonded-man turned to their own daughter. The two younger mouths she yet had to feed. The gut-churning moment her mother realised that the one to be exiled could not be her weak Lord and provider.

It was the only Sight Gwanaelle ever had—gifted by the last magic of the Creil in the moments after Nyneve had burst out of it—and she had told no-one, but it was enough, and it had healed her, as only understanding could.

It had also forged an obligation between herself and the Ancient Ones that she would never, ever forsake. They had given her back her mother. She would be sure to give them back their daughter. Whatever may come.

As they sat in silence, fat droplets sent from the clouds blanketing the sky fell into the fire and onto the earth around them. Like the tears she longed to shed.

'On the morning then,' she said suddenly, wanting this moment over with. She'd survived months of seclusion in the woods before she found Melangell, she could surely survive the time it took mother moon to track across the dark sky. All she had to do was lie there, after all. The sun would rise eventually.

Eifion stumbled to his feet but not quickly enough and she left him, half risen, by the fire.

Her shelter was cold after the warmth of Eifion's fire and company but she made herself strip down to her underdress and crawl in amongst the furred skins within. Her favourites were gone, gifted to Nyneve who always snuggled more deeply in the thicker, larger furs, but that left her with Nyneve's thinner furs and as Gwanaelle pulled them up around her and the rain hammered on the skins of her shelter, the girl's subtle smell filled her breath and eased the ache in her heart.

Parting

'I HAVE DECIDED,' the child said as soon as all had risen with the gloomy light, her breath puffing as mist around her words. Gwanaelle straightened painfully over on his right. Looked like mother and daughter both had had sleepless nights but for very different reasons.

'Decided what your contribution should be?' Eifion said, to slow this down. 'Good. I look forward to no longer hefting wood.'

Nyneve ignored him and spoke louder, as was her habit. She had yet to learn the brutal power of a woman's silence. 'I have decided that I would first like to leave the valley. For one night. To see.'

'Leave? Alone?' Eifion felt Gwanaelle's fear without having to witness it.

'Just one night. Two days. Eifion does it often and he returns unharmed.'

'Nyneve—' he began, but Gwanaelle beat him to speech.

'Eifion is a warrior. He wields a sword.'

His eyes fluttered closed. Had a mother ever understood a daughter so ill?

Nyneve immediately pressed her feet more firmly into the sodden earth. 'It is my fortenyear and you said I was equal in making decisions.'

'Not foolish ones—'

'That right is earned,' Eifion said. Gods, had negotiating with the enemy ever been this fraught? 'Not demanded.'

'How shall it work then?' she insisted. 'One day outside of this valley for every day I toil within it?'

'We hadn't imagined that the very first thing you would do on reaching your fortenyear would be to escape the people who love you.'

His grief birthed the same in her sweet face. Tears washed over both the colours in her eyes. 'I do not *leave* you. I just want to look.'

'Then I will take you,' Eifion offered.

'No. I need to learn myself.'

'You don't understand—'

He caught Gwanaelle behind his arm before she could get much closer to Nyneve.

'No, *you* don't understand,' the girl cried. 'I long for my freedom, and you have given me a waft of it but no more?'

'Just not today, Nyneve,' Gwanaelle begged. 'Not before…'

'Before what?'

Gwanaelle found his eyes beseechingly, hunting for the right way to say to the girl what they could not. 'Before you know how the world works.'

'And how can I discover that from here?'

Certainty sat in his gut like ill-risen bread. She was going to go. No matter what they said. Two days was better than a fortennight. Or a moon's path. Or…Gods…an entire Sun's March.

'Do you have food?'

He might as well have plunged his sword into Gwanaelle's belly. She turned her horror to him. 'Eifion!'

'She is going whether we like it or not,' he hissed and Nyneve looked as triumphant as his sword-brother, Cai, ever had. 'Better that she goes safely.'

Gwanaelle lost all speech.

Nyneve opened her hipfold—*his* hipfold, actually; when had she taken that?—and showed him the dried foods within. Not freshly picked but she'd gathered them with her mother originally, it seemed only just that she be allowed her share, now. She looked at him with the same hunger for his respect that she always had.

'Do not go to the uplands.' She was nodding before he even finished speaking. 'Swear it.'

'I swear.'

'Eifion!'

'One night only, Mother. One day out and the second day back so really it's only one day's march from home.'

Gods, she was her mother's daughter. With sense like that. Gwanaelle clung to the barest sinew of hope. 'Can't you wait—?'

'I have waited my whole life,' Nyneve said, more gently than usual. 'And then I waited all of last night until I nearly burst. I need to do this, so that I know I can.'

Whether it was Nyneve's heartfelt supplication or because Gwanaelle knew that she had survived much longer than two days in the woods herself when she was much younger—or whether she simply knew that she had no further right over the actions of a fortenyear old woman—Gwanaelle seemed to sink back into herself, to shrink, and she nodded.

Just once.

Triumph blazed in Nyneve's riven eyes and she hiked her bundle up onto her shoulder as she'd seen him do ten-score times before leaving the valley.

'Wait,' he ordered and then crossed to the fire where his staff lay. 'Take this. Use it as I've shown you.'

'If I need to?' Once again she was looking to him for any sign that he respected her capabilities.

She had no idea what she was, and they had no idea what might happen if she found herself under threat. She could probably defend herself better with teeth and nail than any of them could with a weapon. He'd just never imagined that she would be alone when they found out.

'If you need to,' he agreed.

He wanted to hug her, desperately, but that's not what she needed from him now. She needed his confidence.

'One night. Then I'm coming for you.'

'Two days,' she nodded. 'You won't need to come for me. I will return.'

After that, there was nothing more to be said and an uncomfortable silence fell. Nyneve broke it by smiling, raising her small hand and turning away from them. Neither of them said a word as she walked, calm and confident, to the edge of the clearing. When she reached the tree line, she seemed to hesitate, turned back and lifted her small hand in parting.

'Eifion, I beg you—'

Gwanaelle did not look around as she hissed her plea and he did not look at her. They each rose a single hand in farewell, but Gwanaelle had always been so stoic, so practised in the art of disguising her thoughts from her voice. To hear the tremble of fear in it now… It was almost unbearable.

He didn't protect just one person in this valley.

Together, they watched Nyneve disappear beyond the tree line, alone. For the first time ever. He turned, forced his hands up into the hair either side of Gwanaelle's white face, and found her eyes.

'She will not see me,' he pledged. 'And I will not leave her.'

He blazed his vow into her until she nodded, curls the colour of sunrise bobbing weakly.

It went against everything that he was to leave Gwanaelle unprotected in their little valley but she was surely more prepared to defend herself than young Nyneve was. He turned and jogged straight for the place that the girl had disappeared into the woods, tracking already, but before he could get halfway across the clearing, Nyneve re-emerged, backwards, stepping back into the footfalls she had just laid, his own staff brandished in front of her defensively.

A man followed her into the clearing; relaxed, heavily robed, grey of hair and tall of build. Easily as tall as Cai, though stooped. Not at all interested in their camp or its occupants, his attention solely fixed on Nyneve.

Traveller in Song

'BLEHERIS,' THE MAN SAID by way of introduction, without taking his piercing gaze off hers. 'I seem to have come at a parting. Apologies.'

No. This man was not sorry, and his arrival was no accident. Nyneve knew that truth as easily as she knew the feel of the dirt under her feet. It just...was. Every instinct said she should run back across the clearing to Gwanaelle, but it was bad enough to have come scuttling back into camp at the first sign of a stranger without also humiliating herself extramuch.

'Who—?'

Eifion saved her the trouble, appearing behind her and carefully relieving her of his long staff. 'Who are you?'

'Bleheris,' the man repeated. 'A traveller—'

Lie.

Again, she just knew it. His pale eyes seemed to flash at her from under the skin-folds cutting across them but then they redirected to Eifion.

'—and a Bard,' he went on, and nothing inside her objected to that. 'Travelling late in the time of *Song* and seeking a fire to earn myself a meal.'

'We have nothing for you,' Eifion said, drawing Nyneve behind him with a strong arm. 'Apologies.'

Lie. Eifion was no sorrier for sending the stranger away than the stranger was for arriving. The old man stepped forward and she remained bonded to Eifion's back.

'Do you have no interest in the happenings beyond this lovely little valley?' the stranger asked.

'Unless you herald a second Darkness or the end of warring between Artwr's chieftains and the invaders, then no. Our interests are few enough.'

'And would you send away a man who has not felt the warmth of a fire for more than a se'nnight?'

No, you would not, Second.

Nyneve shot around as the voice sounded from behind her, only to find it absent of anything but morning mist. In the distance, Gwanaelle wrung her hands in front of her.

Eifion paused before finally speaking, but when he did, he did not sound convinced. 'No. I suppose not.'

Nyneve turned to stare up at him. Since when did a Second from the army of Artwr the Hewer capitulate that easily on any matter? Even if he had been out of the host for longer than he was in it. Bleheris was the first visitor to this valley, ever. Eifion had worked diligently to ensure that no-one ever came here. Did this man's arrival not warrant more care? Suspicion was live on the younger man's face even as he turned aside and let the man into their camp. Their sanctuary.

'I would hope that someone would offer you a fire if you needed it,' Eifion murmured to her as he passed. 'I cannot do less.'

Lie, but she couldn't quite tell if he was lying to her or to himself. Or both. Still, she followed him back into camp, all thoughts of leaving the valley abandoned in the face of such a new and exciting development. Ahead, Gwanaelle shrunk back away from the newcomer who entered, paused in the middle and turned a full, slow circle, frowning as if baffled by what he found.

'I have something for your table, Mistress,' he said at last, reaching beneath his leathers and pulling out a long flatbread.

Gwanaelle's suspicion easily matched Eifion's as she stared at it.

'There are no hearths within three days ride of this valley,' she murmured. 'How is it that your bread has the tarnish of only fire on it?'

Nyneve understood, then. The man was on foot. Bread from any hearth he could have come from should be coated with green-yeasts.

'I baked it myself,' he said, simply, both hands held out in a conciliatory gesture. 'In the rich earth of these magic hills.'

'Yet you have not felt the heat of a fire in a se'nnight?' Eifion said, tight.

The man turned slowly and locked eyes with him. 'Anyone can coax a flame from twigs. By far the greater warmth of a fire comes from those assembled about it. Company is what warms me.'

'Your bread is welcome, stranger,' Gwanaelle said, easing the tension a little. Nothing about her guarded expression said the man was at all welcome in their camp. 'As are you.'

Nyneve stepped out from behind Eifion. 'Does this mean I cannot go?'

Gwanaelle winced. 'Not while we have a guest, Nyneve.'

The silver-haired face turned her way and tilted, just slightly.

Put your things away and return, child. We have much to discuss.

Nyneve gasped before looking first at Gwanaelle and then at Eifion to see what they made of the unearthly murmur. Neither so much as blinked.

Eifion stepped closer. 'Nyneve?'

'I... You are most welcome, sir,' she said to the man as though Eifion's use of her name was a mere reproval for her poor manners. Something deep down inside her urged her not to acknowledge the whisper in her mind 'I will just...'

On that barely convincing utterance, she turned and scuttled back to the privacy of her shelter.

~

'Where have you come from?' Gwanaelle asked brightly, carefully drawing the old man's attention off the departed girl. She had a way with people that Eifion could only admire.

'I am of the Cornuvii originally.'

'But not lately?'

'My master visited the great fortress of Cornovion in my fortenyear and brought myself and a newling infant out into these lands where I have since spent two-score-and-three years.'

'So long from your home,' Gwanaelle murmured and Eifion saw, not for the first time, the glimmer of longing for her own people. He didn't like any common ground between her and the stranger.

'Wherever my teacher went was my home,' Bleheris said. 'He was as father to me.'

'And what of the infant you travelled with?' she asked. 'Did he become as a brother in your travelling family?'

Pale eyes glanced his way, briefly. 'As a brother, yes, but not to me.'

The old man lowered himself onto a trunk near the fire and let his pack slide off his shoulder on a grunt. By the moment, Gwanaelle grew inured to his strangeness. The traveller-in-song was gifted, indeed, to seduce her with such simple conversation. He had not even begun to sing, but, then, the man spoke of family and such talk struck hard at the heart of a woman torn from her own.

'You studied your whole life?' she asked.

'The ways of the Bard are intricate and abundant. Our craft is precise. It takes near as long to master as the ways of the Druid.'

That was no casual mention. This stranger tested their beliefs.

Eifion stepped forward and said what would be expected in a God-fearing, *Artwr-fearing* family. 'You sit in our camp, accepting our hospitality and insult us with talk of the pagans?'

'No insult, friend,' Bleheris said, easily. 'Likening vocations, merely, for comprehension. Becoming an adept soldier takes a few breaths by comparison.'

Gwanaelle glanced at Eifion's balled fists, reminding him to disguise them behind the folds of his wools.

Bards drew information from strangers as skillfully as a poultice drew infection. It was essential to their craft as wielding a sword was to his, but what did this man search for here? Amongst isolated peasants who could know nothing of the world? Or should.

Gwanaelle slapped a slathe of morning sop onto the iron fireplate to warm it along with chunks of the stranger's flatbread then called Nyneve back to break her fast. She stumbled as she laid out the only vessels they had.

'Take mine,' she offered the stranger.

He glanced at the three bowls with much curiosity. 'You have no spare vessel?'

Instinct told Eifion to lie—a normal family would have visitors sometime.

'It cracked,' he blurted, artlessly. 'Our guest's dish. My careless work in seasoning the wood. I have not yet replaced it.'

Eifion doubted Bleheris believed him any more than he believed the sincerity of the Bard's smile.

'I wouldn't last long as a travelling man without this.' He smiled, producing a small, tidy bowl from his own pack. 'This will happily serve.'

Gwanaelle honoured him with the first slide of hot morning sop off the edge of the fireiron and into his bowl and he was reminded again of the instincts she had retained from her childhood. 'It is not much but it will be improved greatly by your bread, sir.'

The man eyed her closely. 'That is no peasant's upbringing…'

But his words were interrupted by the return of Nyneve who eased herself down a careful distance from the stranger on Eifion's other side. He glanced at her to see whether her earlier anger was going to vent over the fire, but there was no anger in her gaze, only confusion, and curiosity.

'Not the meal you had planned to have on this morning,' Bleheris guessed, at Nyneve's silence. 'Where were you going as I arrived?'

'Away, sir,' she murmured. The girl could be wilful, but they'd raised her to have courteous manners, at least, even as they'd wondered if she would ever need them. 'I have entered my fortenyear.'

Bleheris smiled and said simply, 'Yes.'

'Just to see what's out there,' Nyneve muttered. Disappointed perhaps at his lack of amazement at the fact.

'I have travelled my whole life, Nyneve,' Bleheris said. 'Can I perhaps tell you a story or two to recompense for the delay my arrival has caused?'

That brought her eyes up to meet his directly. 'Travelled where?'

Eifion tensed. This close, the stranger couldn't fail to see the girl's riven eyes, the two colours that made up each eye, but when the Bard's gaze met Nyneve's, Bleheris didn't react at all. A kindness to his hosts, not to shame their daughter for her disfigurement.

A hint of gratitude leached, unwilling, out of him.

'Everywhere. From one sea to another. Mountains. Valleys. North to the Pictish lands. Even the very gate of Annwfn.'

Nyneve sat up straighter. 'Tell me.'

He chuckled and glanced at Gwanaelle. 'It is ever Annwfn. Has any place ever been more mysterious than the Otherworld?'

He was asking permission, Eifion realised, and his gratitude swelled. Even as he resisted it.

Gwanaelle saw it, too, but still answered with care. 'I'm sure we would all enjoy hearing of mystical Annwfn.'

'A faery story it is, then.'

He scooped sop onto a bread crust and took his time chewing and swallowing. Nyneve used the time to settle in and focus and, in this girl, silence was miracle enough. It was not hard to imagine the same trick working in Artwr's very court to hush his drunken lords. Except this man had no trace of Artwr on him. Or if he did, it was artfully disguised.

'I was in Glyn Cych,' he began. 'Travelling with no host for protection. Warriors warred up ahead and so I left the path and took to the trees. It was slow going, picking my way down through the fallen branches and tangled bracken but eventually I stumbled out onto another path. Wide, like it was travelled by kings' parties. Dappled in the richest of light. Quieter than the last and empty of any life at all save mine.'

Nyneve and Gwanaelle both sat suspended within Bleheris' thrall. Eifion flicked his eyes between them lest the magic of the story-land should somehow spill out and swill around them dangerously.

' "How could this road exist?" I wondered, even as one foot set after the other. I trudged, lost and confused but drawn ever onwards as the road led me deeper into the wood. Lower into the trees.

'Down it went. Down I went. The light grew thinner as it struggled to breach the many trees stretching tall for the same breath of sun's air. Yet greener, unaccountably. A magical kind of hew to everything. The pathway became rumbled with their reaching roots and I stumbled and nearly fell repeatedly. I couldn't imagine how that King's party could have traversed the way as I did unless it had been older than the trees themselves,' he paused for affect. 'Or untroubled by the same laws of nature that I suffered.'

'The picture grew in my mind,' Bleheris went on, 'of a party carrying a great, portly King. Stumbling as I had on the roots, and their King tumbling out of his seat and rolling ahead of his party down the steep pathway. I laughed aloud at the thought and—I swear—the trees laughed with me. High and tinkling and not at all like you would imagine a wood to sound.

'Down, ever down, I tramped, and the trees on the side of the path grew larger, wider. Older. Covered in thick moss they were, twisted and split with age revealing the trees innermost flesh. When I looked at them, I saw old wood—the sort you might have made your staff out of, Eifion—but when I looked away, that wood twisted to life in the corner of my sight and leaned out of the fissure in the tree like a gnarled maiden, to peer after me, giggling.'

'What manner of road was it?' Nyneve whispered.

If nothing else, perhaps the Bard's stories might make her think twice before marching off into the woods alone.

'Ask not *what* the road was, girl, but *where*.'

Her eyes widened and glittered in the way only hers could. 'Annwfn.'

It had been so long since they'd enjoyed the company of little Nyneve—the excited, interested young girl she had not been for so long—Eifion couldn't help but smile at her now. Adorable child.

Bleheris nodded. 'I approached one of the ancient entrances to the Otherworld, and the very trees and earth around me came to life as I passed, to wonder at the sight of this foolish man treading steadily to his doom. Sure none else could have been there in an age judging by the roughness of the road and the thickness of the forest. Perhaps it did not even exist for anyone else save me that day.'

'And then, of a sudden, I stumbled out into a small clearing, far at the bottom of a steep valley, deafened with the roar as capacious and thundering as your own cascade, but theirs split into three parts—three ever was a favourite of the Fae—and it could be nothing less than one of the watery entrances to Annwfn.'

'What did you see?'

'Sight is no friend to you in Annwfn, Nyneve,' he said, earnestly. 'Rather hark your instincts and the pebbling of your flesh. My eyes knew nothing but a pretty and unearthly waterfall. The next I knew, I was waist-deep in the water, pressing deeper between the slippery, black walls of the fissure like a man easing into his first whore—'

Eifion glanced at Gwanaelle, then, and a furious heat stained the pink ridges of her cheeks.

'Deeper I pressed. Higher the icy water rose. Until I stood half drowned in the purest water, tangled in the wet roots that stood sentry at the entrance to whatever majesty lay behind the waterfall.'

'Did you enter?' Nyneve squeaked.

He gifted her question with a stern gaze. 'If I entered, I would not be here with you today, foolish girl.'

'Then what happened?' she demanded, entirely un-chastened.

'A voice stayed me.'

Gwanaelle burst forth. 'Whose voice?'

How long had it been since he'd seen that look in Gwanaelle's eye? Such colour in her pale face? So enthralled was she in Bleheris' story she had forgotten to maintain her usual soberness. The distance that kept her safe from all the world. Now she looked as her borrowed daughter did—charmed and equally heated by the Bard's story, arms open to whatever mystery was to come, but on Gwanaelle it wasn't sweet or adorable.

It was stirring.

She was no longer the girl he'd first met, she was a woman, rounded and ready, and her flushed heat did nothing to diminish the image. He forced it to bay.

'A child's voice,' Bleheris said, and Eifion forced himself to attend. 'A boy's voice. Calling my name.'

'A child of Annwfn?'

'No, Nyneve. A child of Glyn Cych's forests. His warning cry pulled me out of the thrall, redrew me to my senses so that I could struggle free of those cloying sentinels that pulled me under and turn to flee. I remain ashamed of the scene that he beheld, me flailing like a drowning sheep, my mouth agape in terror, surging against the clawing glug of the water. That should not be the lasting memory of a novice for his master.'

Nyneve gasped. 'He was your apprentice?'

'He was from that day forth. In return for saving me from the determined lure of the Otherworld.'

'Whence did he come?'

'I did not know and he could not tell me. It was years before Lailoken uttered another intelligible word to me. I had to teach him to speak our language.'

'Yet he spoke your name? Did he not?'

Bleheris looked steadily from one woman to the other and waited just the right amount of time to keep his hook well-baited with intrigue.

'Of all the mysteries in that magical place,' Bleheris finally finished, eyes bleeding conspiracy, 'that is perhaps the greatest, yes? *How* did the boy know me?' He looked between the two women. 'How?'

Eifion glanced from Gwanaelle to Nyneve and back again in the enchanted silence that followed. This man would be dangerous if he came here with a more wicked purpose than to ply his trade in return for comfortable passage through winter. Either woman would be naked before him in moments.

Bards were the most notorious scoundrels in the land.

Second only to warriors, perhaps.

Nightfear

OH, HOW NYNEVE fought all attempts to give Bleheris her new shelter. Her good humour lasted only as long as the traveller's exciting stories did not require her to give up her comforts. After that she would have been as happy for him to sleep in the fork of a tree.

'He is nearly three-score winters old,' Gwanaelle had whispered. 'Yield your shelter and come back in with me where there's space.'

And warmth.

And welcome.

Compassion failed as badly as an expectation of common sense. Instead, Nyneve thought it appropriate for *her* to share with the stranger. Or for Eifion to.

'You would disrupt everyone in this camp to get your way?' Gwanaelle had hissed, all patience gone. 'You are fortenyear. Act like it.'

But Nyneve's equal say constituted a mad dash back into her shelter and a loud call from beyond the held-shut flap. 'It is up to you who you share with, Mother. I am not moving.'

Bleheris had pretended to overhear none of the loud dispute as he packed away his lyre under gathering skies and Eifion had roamed the shadowy fringes of camp, furious at this girl who sometimes called him father, but when the sun fell fully behind the valley walls, Eifion had had no choice but to vacate his small shelter and throw a few extra skins beneath Gwanaelle's larger one.

'We have managed before,' she reminded him, with a glance at his still angry face outside the open door to her shelter, and surely there had to be many worse things than sharing with her.

Surely.

'I will be small as a mouse,' she murmured. 'You may sleep as comfortably as ever.'

His grunt needed no translation and Gwanaelle crawled into the shelter, first, stripped to her underdress and snuggled into the skins there as far to the side as she could without bursting the pegs holding the shelter's edges down. That left the wolf's-share of the space for Eifion and his temper. After a few moments, the shadow that was him entered, barely disrobed and crawled in beside her.

'Nyneve has to grow sense sometime,' she murmured to the broad back he gave her.

'I think of you at the same age; stoic and silent and all-seeing...' he muttered from the darkness. Then paused for several heartbeats. 'You are like completely different creatures.'

'We *are* different creatures,' she chuckled. 'Perhaps Ancient Ones take longer to become adult.'

'How long?' he grumbled.

'I do not know.'

As ever. There was so much they did not know.

His chest rumbled. 'I will speak to her in the morning.'

'Don't,' Gwanaelle urged. 'You are important to her. She needs your confidence, particularly.'

'How can I be confident in such a...child?'

'We gave her rank in this family. We cannot then be sour because she has exercised it.'

Her inability to see his prone form only made her more sensitive to the anger fairly pulsing off him.

'I could easily have been a child of no sense,' she reminded him. 'You are just lucky that I had such a serious young head. I would have driven you mad out here alone.'

His silence practically glowed. 'Wrap tight, Gwanaelle.'

Oh, she would. Lest her arms creep out and find their way to him in the night.

'Wrap tight, Eifion.'

~

Nyneve's nightfear came sudden and in the middle of a vastly more peaceful dream about the Otherworld and woods full of tinkly laughter. It forced its way between the trees and over the face of Bleheris' apprentice boy who stared at her out of the dream with the same kind of curious intensity that the traveller himself had.

Fire, at first. Though not the sort that burned pleasantly upwards from a circle of wood and warmed her hands and roasted her food.

This fire came straight at her, with massive force as though flung from a sinew-and-stone or spewed out over the high edge of their falling water cascade. Then it *became* the cascade, fire tumbling down only to explode in a molten storm in the pool below. Nyneve climbed the falls as she did every se'nnight, but the falling flames hampered her less than the falling water always did, the hot air buffeting up from the pool below almost lifting her. Giving her wings. Easing her climb. It burned, but there was no pain. Her skin scorched but it troubled her not.

Up she crawled, through the blazing torrent. Up...up.

She paused near to the top, knowing what Eifion had described from his journeys up there. Expecting the flat uplands and a wood like their own. The great lake that spilled over and down to them in the valley below. But, when she hooked one singed arm up over the edge and pulled, tearing away the scorched flesh of her arm, it was not woods that she saw.

Beasts.

Three of them, coloured more vibrant and other-worldly than she'd ever seen. Two warring with each other lazily on the edge of the lake as the third took its pleasure in the deep waters. Long necks poised to strike, smaller front legs lifted slightly off the ground as their back ones took their massive weight. Blazing wings as fine as weavers-web spread vast behind them. Bursts of fire from the biggest catching on the lake waters and setting it ablaze.

They were terrifying.

And utterly beautiful.

There was no harm in them despite their war-games and as Nyneve tugged her crisped body up onto their shelf, the one in the water turned, surprised, and began to bob her way, massive ripples peeling out to either side of it.

She looked down at her ruined flesh but felt only curiosity at how her sinews could have brought her up here when so little but coal was left of them. Below the char, a glimmer caught her eye and she picked at the wasted skin with nails grown long as the flesh at their base shrivelled and withdrew from the fire. Great chunks of ashrock broke away from her limb and the surface beneath was smooth, shimmering the same green as the lake, patterned like one of the crawling creatures down in the valley.

She chipped more away...and more...

A watery chuff brought her gaze back up. The approaching beast was near, its bobbing head bigger than a whole horse.

Nyneve, its voice said. Rich and warm like Eifion's only more powerful, and resounding deep inside her head. *Nyneve...'*

She stumbled back at its approach, knowing only that the surge caused by its massive body rushing toward her would push blazing water up over her and beyond to the pool below, and, from here, she could never survive the long fall. She'd been falling off that waterfall all her young life. She lowered herself, cringing, back below the cascade's protective lip.

When you are ready, the thing promised from above, calling directly into her head, *we will meet.*

The flaming waterfall turned wet again, shrank back into something smaller and darker and took her with it. She clung to the roots tangled over the entry to Annwfn just as Bleheris had with flesh restored to health.

And as she clung, she heard a voice behind her, calling her name. She struggled to peer back over her shoulder until she saw him again—Bleheris' apprentice—standing in the distance, obscured by the tumbling water. He had the figure of a boy, but the voice of the beast.

You are the reason I am come, Nyneve.

Her eyes fluttered open.

~

The high moon reached its tendrils through the gaps in the shelter's roof when Eifion sat upright, the trailing remnants of a dream on his lips. Gwanaelle pushed to her elbows next to him, and he tried to ignore how close to each other they'd shifted in the night.

The sort of wood you might have made your staff out of, Eifion...

'The traveller,' he answered her little mewl of question. 'He used my name.'

Her sleep-crumpled face could make no sense of his concern.

'Before we offered formal introductions,' he clarified.

'Magic and mystery are his trade,' she slurred, drunk with sleep, placing a small, reassuring hand on his chest. 'Sleep, Eifion.'

But rest was over for him for tonight. His mind was already winnowing through the facts. He flopped back down into the skins and barely noticed as Gwanaelle burrowed into his side, close and warm and immediately returned to slumber.

The traveller's tale. The boy who had saved him from the Otherworld. Except in Bleheris' tale the question glowed with a residual green magic instead of with Eifion's dark suspicion.

But they were the same words.

How did he know me?

~

Gwanaelle stirred, as was her habit, just before the first reach of the sun into their valley, but, unlike her habit, she did not immediately crawl out of her shelter, wrap herself in wools and begin her day. She woke curled into Eifion's side. Not draped across him—thanks to the merciful gods—but neither had she maintained the dignified distance she would have preferred.

'Eifion?'

His short breathing meant he was awake, and for a moment she cringed that he should have been held captive here by her clinging presence, but his murmur, when it came, was not unhappy.

'She wakes.'

His words were more breath than speech and they gave her legs tremendous heft. Far too much to move. She was warm, she was rested and she was half-burrowed into Eifion's strength. The smell and feel of him swamped her. If her heartbeat stuttered to a halt right now, she would be quite content.

A vague memory of him waking in the night returned. Something about Bleheris. She crept her head up. 'Have you slept?'

'Not since the dream.'

Probably started by the traveller's tale of magic. The fact that a warrior could still have nightfears only worsened her softening. She peered at the first hints of light raining down from the gaps in her shelter.

'There's still time before mistrise,' she murmured, much as she had to Nyneve all her young life when the child could not rest. 'None shall harm you while I stand as guard.'

She felt his smile in the gentle shift of his stiffened body. 'I will enjoy the sleep of the dead in comfort of that knowledge, valiant little Gwanaelle.'

He resettled himself more restfully, and carefully withdrew his right arm from between their bodies before passing it over her and tucking her more closely into his side. He did not mean it for anything more than the embrace of a brother, but the air in her chest caught, regardless. Yes, sleep would definitely come like this, and when they next awoke the sun would be high over the valley edge.

Though, perhaps she would not want to rise even then.

This was the cave, again. With warrior Eifion and quiet young Gwanaelle bundled for their lives in the dark damp. Except there was no mewling infant tucked between them, now.

Nyneve had always been there, between them, one way or another but she was also the reason they were here, together in this valley, at all. Eifion would never have left Melangell if not to ensure the survival of the dragonling, and where Nyneve went, Gwanaelle went. So the dragonling had brought them together and the dragonling had very naturally and easily kept them apart. Enough that winter after winter after winter after winter had gone by. She had chosen a Mother's path the day she reached her finger out over the ruptured Creil for the infant Nyneve to grasp to, and Eifion had chosen the Protector's path when he had guided them out of one valley and into the security of another.

Alone.

Except Nyneve was now in her fortenyear. She no longer needed a mother, and soon she may not need Eifion's protection. And then what—would Eifion turn to her at long last, with no reason not to, or would he leave and return to the lady and lord that he had loved so well? Would she never know his touch, even when she was free to?

She was no Melangell, perhaps, but she was here, and she was willing.

Gods, how she was willing.

'Gwanaelle?'

She froze on a breath at Eifion's murmured word. He reached a cool hand over and pressed the back of it to her blazing cheek. 'You are afire to rival Nyneve. Do you sicken?'

How much simpler that would be. She could boil up some kind of healing tea or pack a poultice over her ailing heart and be well again.

She struggled to her elbows against him, her cheeks flaring further at being so betrayed by her flesh. 'I am quite well, but, I think I will rise. Sleep on if you can, I can as easily guard you from without.'

He loosened his arm, releasing her, and she tugged a long, trapped length of sunrise-coloured curl out from under him before rising and crawling out of the shelter into the dawning light, dragging her wears along with her. She donned her wools in haste in the cold morning air and then set to making a fire to warm them all.

Eifion ap Gwilim had had more winters than fingers in which to bed her if he wished it. He would have found a way, some fast, private moment up against a crag or hidden in the trees while Nyneve slept.

If he wished it.

She would never be Melangell, but surely she was readier—and cheaper, gods knew—than the village whores he trudged three days there and three back for.

Surely.

V I

Myrddyn

BLEHERIS EARNED his place by their fire with much more than just songs and stories, though those were as warmly received as before. His contribution despite the great number of winters he had seen shamed Nyneve into becoming far more fruitful and useful. Together, they finished the work of *Gathering* shortly after the season began.

Nyneve grew more adult in the fortennight he was with them than the same number of winters before it.

'Do you not need to leave soon?' Gwanaelle asked of him one day. 'If you are to make the roaring fire of some Lord's great hall before the passages ice over?'

It was no hint and Bleheris did not take it as such.

'Roaring fires hold little interest for me when they must be shared amongst scores. Your fire is both easier and warmer and far less crowded. Nothing like wintering in some great-hall to remind you how the time of *Smoke* got its name. I would gladly trade a few goose-pimples for the fresh air.'

Gwanaelle stared at him. If he did not leave now then he would not be leaving until winters-end.

'You will stay right through to *Rise*?'

'If you can bear me.'

Fortennight after fortennight sharing a shelter with Eifion...

Gods. One had been challenging enough.

'What will you do?'

Though it occurred to her that very old men, much like very young women, had to settle where best they could—not quite beggar-folk but with fewer options than regular people. Even Bards.

'I thought I would—' His light brows dipped as he spoke more carefully. 'I hoped, I might teach Nyneve.'

Gwanaelle simply stared. 'Teach her what?'

'Whatever she seeks to know.'

Confusion thickened her speech. 'What could the girl seek to know that a man is better placed to teach her than a woman?'

'She is a woman newly-born. She has interests. Questions that none have been able to answer. Or willing,' he finished, poking at the fire calmly.

The criticism burned as hot as those coals. There was much about Nyneve's heritage that they had not yet told the girl but it was not obstinacy that delayed them.

Bleheris did not fail to notice her vexation. 'You know the vast education that Bards receive. Why shouldn't the girl benefit from that? In return for the safe passage of winter.'

'And what do you imagine she will do with this...education? Use it on the mice and birds and fish in this remote valley?'

Bleheris turned to look at her, hard, until she felt bruised. Then he shrugged and creaked his neck and, in doing so, his entire demeanour seemed to shift and change. A score of winters sloughed off him like a snake's skin. The white of his hair streaked with pewter and the raven-foot of creases around his eyes smoothed to just a few.

Ice surged outward from Gwanaelle's core as she stumbled back from him. She reached out fast with her heart to discover where the people she loved were. Nyneve, with a basket, over by the far trees where the yeasts grew. Eifion, carving a pike on the far side of the waterfall.

Neither of them would reach her in time, but neither of them were at immediate risk, either. One or both would be able to flee into the woods at her scream, and this man could only hunt one of them at a time.

'Who are you?' she whispered.

'Bleheris,' he affirmed, carefully. 'As I told you. Traveller in Song. Master of the silver words.'

The hidden fist around her throat squeezed so hard it made breath almost impossible to use. 'And what else?'

His narrow shoulders heaved and his pale eyes grew wary. 'And Myrddyn.'

Horror pushed her to her feet even as desperate air forced Eifion's name loudly from her lips. She knew he would be running even now, knew that he would watch her die before his eyes if this man worked his easy magic.

The Myrddyn were Cunning Men. Seers and intimates of kings.

'Artwr!'

She threw her panicked voice toward the trees. Melangell had once foiled *Artwr the Hewer* in his attempt to secure the Creil's magic for his own use. Did he now seek to exploit the creature born of it instead?

'I am not here to hurt her, Gwanaelle,' Bleheris hastened. 'Or you, and I am not here in the name of Artwr Pendragon.'

She scrabbled back from him. 'You are his man.'

'My master was his man,' he corrected, his hands raised afront of him—but whether to calm her or curse her she could not tell. 'I took my leave of him and his war-mongering.'

Eifion could move like the wind when he had to and as noiselessly. Where in the gods was he? But Bleheris careful rise and outheld hands told her he neared. She spun, saw him silhouetted against the low light of summer's end, his pike raised in defence of her.

And in that moment she knew only death would ever part them.

'Be calm—' Bleheris said as Eifion approached.

'He is the Myrddyn!' Gwanaelle cried.

'Behind me,' Eifion ordered, his voice not quite steady.

'She is no safer behind you, Second,' Bleheris said, reasonably. The fact he could be so calm while all around were in chaos was strangely reassuring. As though he had faced this moment many, many times. 'Both of you are closer connected to Artwr than I.'

'Not true…'

'You are Eifion ap Gwilim,' he went on in his rich Bard's voice. 'Once a warrior in Artwr's army, Second to the King's own brother Cai ap Cynyr.'

That was far more than ever he'd been told by them.

Bleheris turned his gaze to hers. 'You are Gwanaelle ferch Eiludd, fled of a father closely tied to a northern Chieftain, and once a dedicated sheep in the flock of Artwr's God.'

Eifion glanced at her, but it was impossible to know whether it was her past connection to a northern Chieftain or to God that surprised him more.

'And she,' Bleheris said, tossing his head back over his shoulder toward the far side of the valley without taking his eyes off Eifion's pike, 'is kin to neither of you.'

Questions clamoured amid the fear, demanding voice, but Eifion beat her to it. His weapon lowered a little.

'Why do you hunt us?'

'I do not. I sought Nyneve. Imagine my consternation to discover her living here, with you. *Y Ddraig* never live with people beyond puberty. It's too dangerous.'

She glanced at Eifion. They had never thought to hear that name from lips other than their own in this valley.

'They live with Morwyn Ddraig,' Gwanaelle risked.

'You are no Morwyn, sweeting.'

Embarrassed heat flooded her face. They could not each be Melangell. 'I have had some training,' she defended.

'You must have to have survived this long—'

One leathery hand shot up to silence himself mid-sentence. He frowned, and then pressed two tanned fingers to the place his jaw met his ear and slowly rotated his head. Gwanaelle glanced at Eifion for certainty.

'Ah,' Bleheris said, ceasing the twist of his head. Instead, he grinned. 'Someone seeks our attention.'

Gwanaelle looked beyond his shoulder, to the far side of their camp where Nyneve no longer collected yeasts. Instead she stood, legs braced, Eifion's sinew-and-stone fully drawn and loaded, pointing it very clearly at the back of Bleheris' head. Even at this distance she would knock him senseless. The girl had a connection between her eye and her hand far superior to either of them.

'How did you know?' Gwanaelle murmured.

Grey eyes rose to hers. The eyes he hadn't needed to know what Nyneve was doing.

'Because she told me to stop frightening her Mother.'

Y Ddraig

'HE HAS BEEN speaking to me regularly for a se'nnight,' Nyneve murmured as her mother held her close. 'But I had not replied until today.'

Until he threatened the people she loved.

'How do you hear him when he does not give voice?'

'I thought at first I must be touched.' She was still not convinced she was not. Her beast dream still troubled her. Though Bleheris' voice and the beast's were not at all the same. 'I kept glancing around for another stranger, but then I realised I was hearing it inside.' She tapped her head. 'Not outside.'

Gwanaelle stared at her, winnowing the most important part free. 'And what has he said to you so secretly?'

She frowned. 'Small amusements. Sometimes he would add a line to a finished conversation, merely, or the middle.'

Gwanaelle glanced at Eifion then back to her. 'He poked. To see if you could hear him.'

'I poked back,' Nyneve said. 'To see what he would do when I did not.'

Eifion squeezed her arm. 'Clever, girl.'

As it always did, Eifion's approval warmed her through, but then she looked from him to her mother. 'You cannot hear him, then?'

They shook their heads.

'Then how can I?' She hated how small her voice sounded but it was impossible not to give voice to the fear that flooded her the moment Bleheris heard her in *his* mind. 'If it is not his talent then it must be…mine.'

'There is much we need to tell you,' Gwanaelle murmured. 'But there is much more that we cannot answer.'

'And Bleheris somehow knows?'

'He says so.'

She looked at the two faces she'd loved since she was small. 'What is the Myrddyn?'

Her mother paled. 'He is a man that knows things. Many things.'

Nyneve considered this and then straightened from their kneeled huddle, glancing over to the fire where Bleheris sat, utterly unconcerned. Confident in his ability to defend himself against anything they might try.

'I haven't Seared since he came,' she confessed just before they stood, and they all three looked long at each other.

'He's been taking her pain,' Gwanaelle finally whispered.

But Eifion was not so affected.

'Which means he can return it at any time,' he warned. 'Remember that.'

Nyneve walked on light feet toward the fire, toward the man who, even now, whispered in her mind, but she ignored him. Who was he to demand such intimacies?

Her resistance only served to amuse him.

'From the beginning,' Eifion demanded of him as they each sat and, inside her head, Bleheris laughed at his impertinence.

The fox kit yips at the bear.

Loyalty to Eifion brought a furious heat to her face but she refused to reply again. She did not enjoy being wrought by this devious smith.

'The beginning of all things or the beginning of this story?' Bleheris said. 'One will take vastly longer to tell than the other.'

'We have all winter,' Gwanaelle pointed out archly. 'Begin with your birth.'

His eyes grew thoughtful. 'No. That place is too strange. I will begin somewhere a little more familiar and weave my way back there.'

He scanned the little group and waited for silence as was his way as a Bard, then his lids closed and when they reopened his voice grew enthralling.

'When I was little more than a sprout,' he began, 'a man named Seisyll arrived in the woods of the Cornovii. He was old, and mysterious, and he was tangled deep with the Chieftain of those lands. Seisyll worked a knot that I would not understand for many winters to come, but a child had resulted from that work. It was on his path to retrieve the child that he also collected me—a boy not quite at my fortenyear—from my home in the woods. I thought he must have bought me from my mother, though I never saw the price. She did not cry as I left her. If anything, she looked…relieved. Like she had been expecting him. I assumed my sale had been negotiated long before.'

'We trudged north, foot after foot together, through Rise and the time of Brightness, and he taught me of many things until, finally, we turned toward the sunset and trudged a full moon more. None troubled us on that journey, none begged food or fire and Seisyll never fell short of precious items to trade. I had never travelled afore and so I did not know, then, to wonder at that endless supply, but then I had never met a Myrddyn afore, either.

He took a long breath. 'We did not pause our journey until we came to a gloomy stronghold in a beautiful, lake-hewn valley, but we did not get to enjoy its waters. Seisyll delivered the babe to the stronghold and we left that same day continuing north.'

Eifion glanced at her mother.

'You know this tale?' Nyneve demanded of them.

'We three know someone who does,' Eifion muttered. 'That stronghold was the birthplace of Cai ap Cynyr.'

Melangell's Cai? Giant, vigilant Cai? Then didn't that mean…

She'd heard the story ofttimes but from Cai's point of view. So many times… 'That babe was Artwr the Hewer?'

Her eyes returned to Bleheris. *He* had travelled with the infant Artwr and delivered him to the stronghold of Cynyr Forkbeard?

'That fat little babe grew into a fine boy, then a strong young warrior and, soon after, a mighty Chieftain—the most mighty if a little unprepared—but I knew nothing of all that. I was deep in the mountains far from my home learning the ways of the Myrddyn at the foot of my master.'

'Seisyll would leave me often, in those days,' he said. 'A night at first. Then se'nnights, fortenights. Once, he was gone from one moon until the next off immersed in some intrigue or another. I foraged. I practised the tasks he left me. I grew and became proficient until, one day when I had seen one-score-and-five winters, Seisyll failed to return at all. I waited for him in that croft a year-and-a-day—as is the custom—and then travelled south to Caermyrddyn to record myself there as *Myrddyn Bleheris*. Then I returned to my solitary studies.' His eyes grew soft. 'Although I had none, now, to learn from bar the land itself.'

'You did not replace your master at the King's pleasure?' Eifion challenged.

'I did not. Nor was I invited to. The young Chieftain was greatly absorbed with an alternative source of power, then and did not feel the absence.'

Again, Eifion and Gwanaelle looked at each other sombrely.

'What took you so long to learn in the north?' Nyneve asked. 'So very many winters.'

Bleheris passed a glare between Gwanaelle and Eifion as if it were their failure to have not given her this information in the past.

'The Myrddyn are conjurers,' Gwanaelle stammered to rectify. 'Seers. Intimates of nature and cunning in all arts—'

Bleheris threw his arms up dramatically. 'Commanders of goblins and workers of night wonders.'

Defence of her mother surged forth. *She* may make a fun of her mother's stammers but this man was not welcome to.

'You are not those things?' Nyneve challenged.

'We read the stars, yes, and interpret them, and we are skilled in the way of numbers and language and nature, but not through some fae-given gift. They can all be learned given the passage of enough time.'

'Even conjuring?'

He waved a casual hand. 'Performance merely. Like our songs. To enthral and entertain.'

'You knew our names,' Eifion cut in, unimpressed. 'Our history. That was no conjure.'

Long, worn fingers steepled in his lap as Bleheris considered his next words. 'We are gifted with a talent for…divining truth, but that is all.'

Lie. It came as hard and fast as it had before. Nyneve locked eyes with the old man. 'No. You are a seer.'

Yes, and the talent for truth spills over when we are close, his voice in her head chuckled.

'My dear, you are the only one in this circle with no experience of the Sight,' he condescended aloud. 'It is not so exceptional as you imagine.'

Nyneve looked to her parents for their denial but neither of them could. Colour rushed up her mother's jaw.

'Nyneve—'

'What sight?' she demanded.

'Let us explain in—'

'What sight, Mother?'

Gwanaelle's pretty, dark lips thinned. 'I have had only one…'

Eifion stared at her then, disbelieving.

'Wh— When? How?' Nyneve asked.

Gwanaelle straightened her wears and folded her cold-chapped hands in her lap. Gods, that slow manner of her mother's drove her mad. Always so considered. Always so…soft.

'The *when* is the day you were born. When first I laid hands on you, but the *what* is between me and my own mother. A private thing. I took it as a gift.' She leaned in, appealing. 'A gift from you.'

Nyneve slumped against the log at her back and grasped the most graspable part of that tale. 'You were there when I was…born?'

The word felt so foreign on her lips. They'd so seldom ever used the word. Always *arrived*. That's why she thought she'd been delivered to them much as everyone else in Melangell's valley had arrived—blindfolded and on Cai's horse. Or likely swaddled, in her case.

Ever her mother's protector, Eifion spoke up.

'We all were there, Nyneve. When we lived in—' he glanced at Bleheris and changed his words '—the other place.'

'You both saw me born?' She split her confusion between them. 'Then you must also have known my first mother?'

The two most important people in her life glanced at each other nervously.

'We've both seen her,' Eifion hedged. 'But we cannot say we knew her.'

A lie, surely, even if her blood didn't tell her so. The opportunity to learn more about her mother was too good to spoil by picking at their deceit and so she did not.

'What was she like? How did she look? What happened to her?'

'We only saw her from afar, Nyneve.' Gwanaelle glanced at Bleheris but he offered no aid. Indeed their discomfort seemed a kind of sport to him. 'But she was…beautiful. Breathtaking, really.'

Her instincts said that was truth but…how could it be? 'If you touched me as I was born,' she pressed, 'wasn't she right there? In front of you?'

Her mother's face dropped, long curls falling either side of her heated cheeks and she echoed Eifion out from behind them. 'We only saw her from afar.'

'Then you didn't see me birthed!' she cried.

Nyneve recognised her own petulant tone from her past few years but was powerless now to stop it. Gwanaelle she might have expected deception from, but Eifion…

Father…

'You were not birthed,' he said now, 'so much as—'

It was his turn now to glance to Gwanaelle for assistance. She was more use to him than mute Bleheris was. He just sat there, smirking at their suffering.

And at her own.

'—you emerged.'

She stared at the both. 'Of course I did. Squeezed from between my real mother's thighs.'

She leaned extra-much on the word 'real'.

'Nyneve—' Bleheris finally interrupted as Gwanaelle blanched. 'Calm yourself. Everything in good time.'

'No,' Eifion ordered. 'We will not let her suffer longer.'

The deep affection in his gaze helped calm her a little. As it always had.

'Please,' she murmured. 'Father…'

Eifion shifted in his seat. 'You understand that you are not of the same people as mine. Or Gwanaelle's?'

'Yes.'

'And you know that you have features that are…unique amongst us.'

'My eyes, yes. My sickening blood…' Bleheris gaze grew sharp, then, and it distracted her for a moment. 'What of it?'

'Those features belong to your own kind.'

Her *kind?* She would have expected such condescension from lofty Gwanaelle but not from good Eifion. He was the most fair-minded person she knew. Not that the number of people she knew was particularly great.

She glanced between them again. 'You know who my people are?'

Why had they never said?

They are saying now, child—

She rounded on Bleheris before remembering not to give him the satisfaction. 'You! Silence!' Then she gave him her back and returned to Gwanaelle. To Eifion. 'Tell me.'

Man glanced at woman and Gwanaelle dipped her head, deferring to him as she so often did.

'There is a creature—'

Gwanaelle choked a little and he glanced at her then corrected himself, beginning again. 'There is a *people* known as *y Ddraig*. Scarce seen in modern times but still in this world, hidden away, underground...'

Underground? 'Like dwarves?'

'No,' Eifion gritted. 'Not dwarves. They are larger.'

'Normal sized, then,' she guessed.

The shake of his head was almost imperceptible.

She glanced between them again and whispered. 'Giants?'

She could hardly come from giant stock. Would she not be taller? But Eifion's dark glower said that wasn't right either. She sat up straighter.

What was bigger than a giant?

'Dragon,' Bleheris blurted, annoyed, 'you foolish girl. A dragon is bigger than a giant.'

She turned her confusion to him.

'You didn't even *teach her* about dragons?' Bleheris half-roared to her parents.

Gwanaelle sprang to her feet. 'How could we without—'

'Nyneve!' She forced her roaring head to focus in on Eifion's voice, which eased her. 'A dragon is a mighty creature, with wings and a long tail and a coat that sparkles like sunlight on water.'

The dream beasts...

'And their young hatch out of eggs.'

In her confusion, she was slow to make the connection. 'Like the birds?'

'Yes. Except bigger. Large enough for me to carry in two arms.' He slipped one of those arms around her shoulders and pulled her close.

Really? He needed to be holding her for what came next?

'You emerged from such an egg, Nyneve,' Eifion murmured.

The cloying press of hardness against her skin. The cramped, uncomfortable curl of her body. The endless, eternal cold wait. It all rushed back familiar and real. And terrifying.

She laughed, thin and brittle. 'No, I didn't.'

But Gwanaelle's pale face said it was truth.

And Bleheris' silence said it was truth.

And that new thing inside her concurred.

Truth.

'Your mother had eyes riven like yours,' Eifion went on. 'Melangell described them—"each one as green as the treetops on one side and brown as earth on the other".'

She had her mother's eyes. To this day, Nest and Elen still stared curiously at them. Mighty Cai always kept his sword loose in its sheath when she was around. Melangell's constant scrutiny...

She had her mother's eyes.

'And dragons have a great heat about them, through their whole body. Like yours,' he went on.

'No, I have a blood sickness...'

Except that was just another lie. She saw it now. How many she been told. How much of her life was an untruth?

'You are *y Ddraig*, Nyneve,' Bleheris said quietly.

Fear skittered up the knotted bones of her back. 'You cannot be certain...'

Except that her mother had watched her *hatch*. People did not hatch.

'Melangell protected you in your egg for five winters,' Gwanaelle murmured. 'And her teacher for a score-and-ten before her. The Mathrafal for many lifetimes before that.'

'I thought the Mathrafal were ruined?' Or so the stories of Melangell's people went.

'Recently ruined almost to death, but they've protected the young of the Ancient Ones for an eon.'

Her heart hammered. Ancient Ones. Dragons. Beasts.

Do you not feel the truth of it, Nyneve?

She ignored Bleheris, still too afraid to have him in her mind. 'How is this tale related to the Sight, then?'

'Your...egg,' Gwanaelle began, 'was a protective crust. It kept you safe within, but it carried a kind of magic. It offered the Sight to those who held it.'

'That made it very important,' Eifion added. 'And hunted by those who sought power.'

She knew this story. She'd heard it around Melangell's fire many times. The Creil. Artwr had sought it. A war had been fought over it. They'd only just escaped with their lives, but no-one had ever said whence the Creil came.

Or what came from it.

Cold certainty rushed in and it tightened the cords of her neck. '*I* was the Creil?'

'No.' Eifion urged. 'The Creil was your crust. It was no more *you* than this wooden bowl is the sop that it holds.'

'What happened to it?'

Bleheris stared off into the distant trees as if all talk of such simple truths was tiresome to him.

Lie—interest practically hummed off the Cunning Man.

'Gone,' Gwanaelle murmured. 'Destroyed during your birthing.'

Eifion shoved the fire, sending sparks up into the dim air and studied it closely.

Nyneve recalled his earlier words. 'You carried me in your arms? So you've had the Sight, too, Father?'

Darkness flooded his face. Always so reliable. Always so knowable. 'Yes.'

'And is what you saw as much of a secret as what mother saw?'

'It is no secret,' he murmured. 'Melangell saw it first.'

Her interest in his vision fell second to the fact that Melangell also knew of this secret. Melangell who'd always judged her so harshly. 'Melangell has Seen, too?'

'And Cai,' Gwanaelle gently offered.

'And you've seen?' she accused Bleheris.

'I see without the aid of an egg, Sweeting.'

Nyneve shot to her feet. 'So I truly am the only one here who cannot See past the trees rimming this valley?'

One day you will beg for blindness, tiresome child, Bleheris admonished, in her head.

But aloud he said, 'The mind and heart of a young dragonling is ill-prepared for the limitlessness of the Sight. On emergence, the talent goes into the same torpor that has seen your body through eons within the confines of the Creil.'

All three of them stared at Bleheris, wide-eyed.

'It…sleeps only?' Eifion murmured.

'It waits.'

'For what?'

'Ascension. When *y Ddraig* are mature enough to accept the secrets of all time.'

Gwanaelle's pinched face looked like she wanted to ask more but Nyneve's patience was as fractured as the egg out of which she had apparently tumbled.

'So… These glittery, giant, winged beasts lay eggs and leave them in the care of a now-ruined people and when they hatch they are not little beasts, but…people?' She glanced down at her body. Apart from her riven eyes and the heat of the Searing, it worked the same as anyone else's. 'How can that be?'

'We do not know,' Gwanaelle murmured. 'That's why we are here, sequestered in this valley. Until we *can* know.'

It came to Nyneve then, so clear and vivid that it almost was like the Sight Bleheris assured her she did not yet have—Eifion had not taken them away from Melangell's valley to help spread meagre resources after The Darkness came, and he had not taken her away to protect her…

He took her away to protect *them*.

'Until some creature claws its way out of my flesh, you mean? And feasts on whoever is closest?'

Gwanaelle blanched. 'It won't be like that—'

'How can you know!' she cried.

'I am come.' Bleheris pressed to his feet, and his voice seemed to come at them from all corners of the valley at once. 'That is how.'

Nyneve's chest heaved her fury.

'I am come to teach you what you need to know,' he said, milder.

'You came to *teach* me?'

Lie.

Old eyes had never seemed younger. 'I came to…meet you.'

Still a lie, but she could not divine the truth. It lurked behind a kind of fog.

'I expected you to be in the care of a Morwyn Ddraig,' he urged. 'I expected you to have been raised with some knowledge of your kind. I never expected this…ignorant family.' He waived his hands around them at the fire, around the whole valley clearing. 'It is beyond extraordinary that you have lived.'

Gwanaelle bristled. 'You think that we would not have taken good—'

'I speak of you and Eifion,' Bleheris snorted. 'You have seen the deadly training of the Morwyn Ddraig, yes?'

'Used in protection of the Creil,' Gwanaelle said, past thinned lips.

He snorted. 'Used in protection of *themselves*. What purpose a warrior's skills in seclusion?'

Eifion gaped.

'A poorly trained Morwyn would not last a moon with an un-Ascended Ancient One,' Bleheris confirmed. 'Yet I arrive here, and pass the only trained Morwyn for a fortennight ride living in carnal, chargeless comfort three valleys over while two unprepared peasants have care of a fucking *dragonling*.'

'Melangell's training was incomplete,' Gwanaelle confessed. 'Because of Artwr's war, and she did not...'

She caught her own words.

'She did not like me,' Nyneve blurted. 'Just say it. She has never liked me.'

'She did not understand you,' Gwanaelle soothed.

Lie.

'It is not the Morwyn's privilege to like or not like their charge. They have a calling. She should be here. Instead you are, Gwanaelle ferch Eiludd. Why?'

'She was just a babe—'

'A babe who fed on blood,' Bleheris interrupted, paying no heed to Nyneve's horrified gasp. 'She must have or she couldn't have grown to health. You still thought her *just* a babe?'

'She had no-one else...'

'She had a Morwyn Ddraig, pigheaded though she may have been...'

'She chose *me*—'

Nyneve turned her dismay to Gwanaelle. 'I did not choose you!'

'You curled your chubby little hand around my finger and have never let go since!' Gwanaelle challenged. It was so rare that her mother cast off her placid demeanour, her passion silenced them all.

'Regardless,' Bleheris finally murmured, 'it is only by the grace of the Gods that the two of you yet live. I would know how you managed the girl to adulthood.'

'Another day,' Eifion ordered, watching Nyneve closely. 'We have learned much today and need to think on what has been said.'

'We have all winter,' Bleheris agreed, but as they rose to depart to their shelters he raised his voice just slightly, speaking so all could hear.

'And we will need it.'

The Creil

EIFION SAGGED onto one knee as he hauled himself up and over the steep valley edge closest to the hollowed out crag. It was impossible to see from the valley or from the uplands, disguised as it was behind a tangle of thorns, and anyone who hadn't torn their skin squeezing into its small slit would have no idea that it opened out just beneath the protective blanket of earth. Enough that a man could get in. Enough to hide away their treasures from any who might seek them.

He turned and surveyed the wilds all around him to make sure none followed, then craned his neck to peer back down into the valley in search of signs of life. The sun was high enough to provide light sufficient for this task but low enough to disguise his passage as he moved under the cover of tree to tree up the valley-side. Still, he wanted to be sure that none gazing up at the right moment had seen a flash of him climbing the valley side.

Nothing.

He tugged his hood up, shrank his forearms back into their long sleeves and began the tight squirm beneath the thorns, twisting and pressing with his face to the earth, dragging himself forth on powerful elbows.

Had any babe ever struggled as hard to crawl back into the womb?

Finally, he smelled the familiar whiff of damp earth and pressed on into the dark. The little cleft parted for him and he tumbled down and into its fusty stink. There, he struck spark into the tinder from the folds in his woollen cloak and used the little puff of flame to light the brand that waited here, before wedging it into the damp earth. Gentle light filled the dark little space. Enough to see that his treasures were secure. Three sharpened swords, a purse full of old kingdom coin, and one last bundle, stuffed back in the shadows of this already shadowy place, carefully folded in skin and bound in the hard leather bridle that had once born its full weight.

The Creil.

Its remains, anyway; one crooked half and a score of odd-shaped blades of thick, grey shell. The remains everyone believed he'd buried when he bundled them up and took them out of Melangell's valley a fortenyear ago. He'd taken them, aright. Out of their valley and into this one, in the smallest, darkest, safest place he could find. It was how he knew of this valley to bring the toddling Nyneve here just a few years later when The Darkness came.

He dropped to his haunches in front of the bundle and tugged carefully at the skins, exposing a slab of grey crust. The Creil had never offered them visions on command but, right now, it was the only tool he had to discover Bleheris' true purpose here. Everything in him cried out that Bleheris had come for these shards.

Or worse. For the dragon child they had contained.

He flattened his hands on the cold surface of the Creil's largest shard—almost half the curved egg, big enough to act as a cauldron—concentrating his mind on Bleheris. Waiting for what secrets of him the Creil would reveal.

Immediately he was back in that place, a glinting blade pressed against a soft, feminine throat, the pain as he severed the throat from ear to chin with a trembling hand and bled all life out was as vivid as if he'd plunged it deep into his own chest.

A trembling hand…

You will slay one whom you love dearest, Melangell had prophesied all those winters ago, fuelled by the Creil's sight. They'd both expected it to be her when they'd fled together into the yew-filled valley to hide the Creil from Artwr. But he had never loved Melangell except as a sister. Not in any way that would make his blade-hand tremble. Five more came in the winters before Nyneve was born— some as damaged women, some as brutalised girls like Gwanaelle, and six more made their way in the two winters after they'd bested Artwr's army and word of Melangell's sanctuary spread.

Soft, female throats every cursed way he'd looked.

And so he'd fled from that female-filled valley and left them all to the protection of the Chieftain's warrior brother as he'd spirited Gwanaelle and Nyneve away to this valley. If he'd had a clue what to do with an infant girl he might have reduced his burden to zero and taken the dragonling alone.

Still, one was easier to harden his heart against than eleven. Even if it was the sweetest and most gentle young woman he'd ever known. He was a man—and he had made bigger sacrifices in the past. It had worked. In the score of winters that had passed since he betrayed Artwr and fled with Melangell into the woods, he was yet to lay a hand on any woman in violence or otherwise. Except for the village whores, and he never looked at them as he fucked them or did it twice with the same one from the same village in the same year.

That way, there was no chance he could come to care.

If he didn't care, they wouldn't die. Not by his hand.

Near twenty winters without the intimate touch of any woman not paid to apply it...

He squeezed his eyes more tightly and concentrated on Bleheris— his face, his long fingers, the specific pattern the lines in his face made—and tried to imagine what the man was truly doing here in their valley. Yet still the Creil only showed him the slash of his blade over a vulnerable, female throat. Over and over and over. And not with any blade he recognised. It had taken him four winters to discover that.

The blade was not his. Though the trembling hand was.

'Gods...!'

Eifion shoved the shards back into their skins and away from him, sagging back onto the leathers of his brecs and letting the unsettling vision fade from behind his eyes. It was not going to help him with Bleheris. Either the Creil couldn't see the Myrddyn or he was somehow blocking its sight. Who knew what Cunning Men could do?

He could not believe that Bleheris was here for anything but ill.

It took no time to pack everything away, douse the brand and hoist himself back out into sunset's ruddy spill. Compared to the dark of his climb out, the sun's last reach was almost as daylight.

He turned and eased his way back down the valley face taking care to tear his skin no more than he already had.

~

Nyneve returned to sleep with her that night—not because she had surrendered her shelter to Bleheris, after all, but because she was still a child at heart, and because this child was in chaos. Her emotions churned and burned as much as her blood and though she would never admit it, she still needed her mother's touch sometimes.

Eifion—if he slept at all—must have done so in Nyneve's shelter because he did not return to hers. More likely he stood guard against the danger they'd let into their valley. The place that had been so safe for so long.

Bleheris had sat all afternoon and evening by the fireside, calm as you like, to make himself easily available for the approach of any of them to continue their discussion, but his efforts went unrewarded, none of them dared step nearer to him than the cold demanded. He sang them a song—uninvited and unwanted—of the earliest peoples of this land. The ones that came after the old gods had all passed into Annwfn. It was sonorous and epic and Gwanaelle had to fortify herself against the interesting tale until, finally, she took a silent Nyneve and withdrew within the skins of her shelter.

In it, they huddled together, though Nyneve lay tight and long in the determined circle of her arms.

'I will start from the beginning as I know it,' Gwanaelle murmured, low. Nyneve thought them liars for having kept the truth from her. In fact, they were cowards, but neither was much to be proud of.

'First there was Melangell,' she began, her lips pressed up to Nyneve's ear. Though given the Myrddyn could speak straight into Nyneve's head was there any point in whispering? Perhaps he could hear any of their thoughts at any time? 'She was trained as a Dragon Maiden—a Lifebringer—to care for the Creil, for you,' she stammered, 'as an egg. Melangell was taken by Cai for the Pendragon, Artwr, who wanted the Creil, and where it went, the Morwyn Ddraig went. But Artwr meant you harm and so they fled with Eifion into the valleys to hide. For years they existed there, content enough, but Artwr's reach finally ended their secrecy and he sent soldiers. I was there by then, I saw what happened in defence of you.'

Scores of lives lost.

'But he did not only send men, he sent his prisoner-dragon to end our days. You knew it when it came,' she said, gently, 'and by touching you Melangell then knew it, too. It was your mother.'

The girl had begun to tremble and her voice grew tiny in the silence. 'She was a creature of Artwr's?'

'She suffered his brutality. She came to do his bidding, but then she saw you and she knew that you were in our care. So she betrayed him to you. And in doing so she saved us all.'

And died in the betrayal.

'We curled around you for days,' she went on, 'warming you to life, and Melangell had nothing more to do than tell us the whole story of what happened up on that valley side. Your mother wanted you to live, Nyneve. She knew you were hers and she chose to defend you.'

'But she chose not to stay. With me?'

'It was winter's end before Eifion travelled out and discovered the truth of what had happened after we saw her fly from our valley. The dragon returned to Artwr at Caerwent but she did not give herself back into his captivity, instead she razed that stronghold to the ground and melted the mortar holding the foundations fast. Half of those slumbering there died that night. Soldiers, women, children, horses, goats. Artwr fled with his warriors and women to another stronghold nearby but he did not pursue us again.'

'He surrendered?'

'Artwr believed his own brother killed in that battle, and in his arrogance, he'd sent into the fray both the men who knew the location of our hidden valley. Your mother breathed them both to ash along with the rest of his host, and so none knew exactly where we were hiding.'

Nyneve considered her words, long. 'And so I was born.'

'You had slumbered long, Nyneve, but either the violence of the day or the loss of your mother sparked your wakening and you were born after just a few days, and none of us knew what to do.'

'Even Melangell who knows all?' Nyneve snorted.

'Oh, she does not know all, you angry girl. She knew how to care for you as Creil, and some of that she'd had to guess after she was thrust unready into the role of your protectoress. None of us knew what was going to happen when you emerged.'

'Yet here I am.'

'We guessed at much, but it was enough.'

'Bleheris said I was dangerous. That you should not be alive.'

'I cannot think what he means. You have never once tried to harm us.' Even as she'd fed off blood as an infant—hers and Eifion's in rotation if they could not find another source. Until she grew big enough to eat raw meat. She preferred it bloody to this day. 'But we will find out. He has come to teach you.'

'You believe that?'

'I believe he can teach you,' she hedged, because, no, that was not why she feared he had come. 'And so we will use this opportunity to learn what is ahead of you.'

'Will you make me leave this valley?' she whispered.

Gwanaelle pushed up on her elbow to stare down into eyes that were almost too dark to see. This child who had wanted so desperately to leave the valley of her home one short night ago.

'How can you believe that?'

'You took me from Melangell's valley. Why, if not to protect them all from me?'

'I took you, Nyneve, somewhere where there was enough live meat to sustain you. You could not thrive on the roots and diggings that were left to us when The Darkness came. We needed our own place, with our own hunting until the sun returned.'

Suspicion stained her voice. 'And your own warrior? Was he to make sure I did not hurt you?'

'Eifion had been protecting you for five winters, he was not about to let you go without him. He gave up a lot to be with you,' she chided, gently.

The lord—and the lady—that he loved best, and his king afore that.

Nyneve lay silent in the darkness but the energy of her fevered thought pulsed off her in waves that Gwanaelle needed no supernatural senses to feel.

'If it is up to me,' she went on, to be as clear as she could, 'you and Eifion and I will grow old together. Whatever we discover at the Myrddyn's side we will discover—and face—together. No-one is going anywhere.'

She stroked Nyneve's damp brow. 'If for no other reason than winter is upon us.'

Cunning Man

'ONE OF US must always be present,' Eifion ordered, glaring toward Bleheris in the distance. 'We cannot stop them from speaking to each other, but we can be on our guard.'

'Perhaps he truly does simply wish to teach her.'

'He is a Myrddyn,' Eifion growled pulling his end of the sinews tighter for Gwanaelle to twist hers around more firmly. 'And you imagine he's stopped whatever intrigues he's sunk up to the neck in to come here and teach a young girl about her parentage? No. He wants something.'

'He is nearly three-score,' she reminded him, twisting, 'and she is almost still a child.'

'I do not claim that he has come to bed her,' Eifion growled, 'but he is here for something more, I know it.'

Her hands paused. 'He claims no friendship with Artwr.'

'He can claim whatever he wants. I will judge him by his actions, Gwanaelle.'

She followed his intense gaze toward the traveller and then brought her concern back to his greyed features. 'You cannot stand watch by night and work every day, Eifion. You will be no use to us slumped, senseless, on the ground.'

He remained unmoved.

'He need only put his voice in her head if he has something he wishes to say to her,' she pointed out.

Or do. What other cunning gift did this man possess?

'And that does not trouble you?'

'Do you remember our first winters with Nyneve?' she asked, pulling back against his strength to twine her rope. 'How we ever watched. How we feared? How she first drank of blood and then ate her food raw, but we grew used to that. Then came the Searing that terrified us at its start, but it is now just a normal part of loving her.'

Eifion grunted.

'Well, now her mind is open to the probing of a cunning man. Just another of the mysteries of *y Ddraig*. I am more troubled by what he might say than how it is that he says it.'

'I do not trust him.'

'I do not think he expects us to, Eifion. Or cares of it. He is not here for us. He would be well pleased were we to leave this valley entirely, in fact.'

Eifion glowered across the clearing where Bleheris and Nyneve sat across the fire from each other, staring intently at one another and speaking—presumably—in their heads. The Myrddyn sought to build up her skill for it. Doubtless, so he could enter her head whenever he chose. Nyneve had promised her that she would work, untutored, on also learning how to bar him out.

'He does know her kind,' Eifion allowed, pinning the sinew between his teeth to free up a hand to tug his woollen wears closer around his throat against the cold.

And that wasn't a small thing. None of them—not even Melangell—knew much else about Dragon-kind than how they slumbered before birth. None other could teach Nyneve what she needed to know to survive, and the way the Searing had come again and again each time sooner than the last...

As though it were preparing itself for something.

'We can only do as we have done these past se'nnights,' she said, knotting her end of the sinew twice over and pulling it firm. 'Trust, but watch.'

'I cannot trust him.'

'Not him,' she murmured, sliding her hand over his briefly as he folded the now thick sinew into her hold. 'Nyneve. Believe that she will tell us if something is not right.'

Though she was still such a child. Fortenyear was more than old enough to breed her own child, make a home and defend it, but she had grown up so protected, she knew so little. *Could* they trust her to do right?

So distracted was Eifion by the silent conversation happening across the clearing he did not immediately withdraw his hand as would normally be his way. Gwanaelle ran her thumb over its strong, calloused peaks. To bring him peace, and to torture herself. Her skin sang where it touched his.

He pushed to his feet without noticing her brief caress—or without recognising it *was* a caress—and took up his staff.

'I will take myself away since I seem unable to think of anything else while I am here. Perhaps my suspicions will be better employed against a moorfowl or two.'

Two, yes. One that she and Eifion could cook until it was charred and then share, and one that Bleheris could share with Nyneve since he seemed to favour his meat as ill-cooked as she did. Or perhaps that was just another kindness he extended her to make Nyneve feel less…beastly.

~

'*Y Ddraig* and the first Men shared the woods as easily as any other of the woodland creatures,' Bleheris intoned over the fire that evening. The cadence of his voice and the mystery in his words and changeable face made ordinary words magical. 'But Man grew. He spread like the plagues that he brought. He birthed alchemists into this world who, in turn, birthed something cold and hard and world-changing. Iron.'

Nyneve groaned. 'Not another story about swords…'

Hadn't she heard quite enough of the tales of Artwr and the Angles and his warriors from Eifion?

Bleheris managed to look impatient and tolerant at the same time. 'Something much more dangerous than swords, child.'

His eyes flicked to each of them in turn as they each imagined what could possibly be more deadly than a newly forged sword. 'The axe.'

Nyneve flopped back onto the earth. 'Farming!'

'As far as a man could walk in his lifetime, the woods of Brython fell. For fire and shelter and fortification. To brace the hillsides and to blaze the furnaces in which evermore iron was born. To lay paths in the mires between village shelters and to make weapons with which to defend them. Men pushed deeper into the thick trees that once blanketed these lands and built humble shelters inside dragon territory. Then less humble ones. Then they enclosed the lands and filled them not with woodland beasts but with their own—beasts for food, for labour, but the dragons were used to hunting the woods for their food. They did not always discriminate between the wild creatures and those belonging to the Men. Nor between beasts and Man, always.'

He glanced at Nyneve's now rapt attention. 'Do not look amazed, Nyneve. Put any people into too small a space and conflict will eventually rise…'

Nyneve tried hard not to look at Gwanaelle.

'Soon, these children of the gods were feared as much as they had been revered. Men pressed their faces to the earth and sacrificed within the weathered circles of their ancestors to plead for the gods' help in ridding them of the beastly blight. Never knowing where they stood,' he went on. 'Never knowing that those same stone rings were the petrified trees that once formed the dragon's own resting places.'

'Gwely Ddraig,' Gwanaelle gasped. Just like the yew circle in Melangell's valley. Formed on the site a dragon took its last breath.

Bleheris nodded. 'Just like the ones they'd felled with their iron.'

'They truly didn't know?' Eifion grunted.

'They were Men, warrior,' Bleheris said. 'With Man's arrogance. They assumed them to be tributes to their own gods.'

'What happened then? Did they return to peace with *y Ddraig*?'

'They might have, child. Enough of them began to realise that they cut the very heart out of their land.'

'But they did not? Why?'

'Emissions,' Bleheris pronounced and then fell silent for moments. 'Men discovered that the swords they used to slay dragons never after broke in battle, they were stronger and more invincible. What sprung from their veins, what leaked from their eyes, what drooled from their fang—all of it could be put to use, and from there it did not take long for Men to discover that it changed *them* just as greatly—down beneath their skin where they could not see.'

Gwanaelle glance at Eifion. Were they both remembering Melangell's healed feet?

'It changes men?' Nyneve said, annoyed that there was so much she did not know, perhaps.

Bleheris snorted. 'How did Man think the first Giants had been created, foolish creatures. Sprung from the earth, merely? More dragons died in that greedy age than in all the ages before it combined.'

'Men killed them?'

'Like so many pigs, and so the dragons retreated—to the mountains and lakes and what few patches of thick cover remained. Some opted to commence the long sleep and may still lay in slumber

ASCENSION - *Y Ddraig [The Dragons of Brython]* 71

even now beneath our feet.' He glanced about at the high valley tops surrounding them. 'Those left above ground communed only with the Men who revered them—the Druids.'

'Communed?' Eifion queried. 'How?'

But Bleheris was not telling this story at his audience's pace. 'They became friends, of a sort. *Y Ddraig* even trusted their young to the care of the Druids.'

Gwanaelle gasped. 'The Creil?'

Bleheris paused. 'Do you truly know so little about how *y Ddraig* create new life? What was your Morwyn Ddraig doing when she should have been attending to her lessons?'

Gwanaelle burned to defend her friend and teacher. 'The Mathrafal did not teach their Morwyns how the Creil's came to exist, only how to care for them once they did.'

Bleheris paused and all gathered knew that his tale would divert, here, but he was a skilled traveller in song, and they knew that it would return to this place, too, without misstep.

'The breath of *y Ddraig* can burn a man to dust,' he began and Gwanaelle let her eyes drop at the awful memory of watching Nyneve's massive mother turn three-score of Artwr's army to ash with one flaming belch. 'It can render woods into vacant moor, and it can melt the very rock beneath our feet.'

'This country is pocked with dragon burrows,' he went on. 'Though most Men do not realise what they are. When she prepares to lay an egg, *y Ddraig* presses her mighty snout to the ground and scorches a hollow down to the deepest part of the earth. Until the flames are quenched by the water on which this whole land floats, and up it bubbles.'

Gwanaelle blinked. 'You speak of wells?'

'In the language of Men, yes. Did you imagine they were cut by the gods? Or by the very waters themselves?' His scorn brought heat to her cheeks. 'Once they have forged their blazing earth-burrow, *y Ddraig* deposit their egg deep into the frigid waters within, there to slumber until it is time to emerge.'

Gwanaelle looked to Eifion then back to Bleheris. 'The Morwyn do this, too. Though not burn them, of course.'

The Myrddyn snorted. 'As *y Ddraig* advised the Druids, and the Druids advised the first Morwyns to do. Or did you think they decided that for themselves?'

Eifion's low voice rumbled. 'Druids taught the Mathrafal?'

'Tsk. It is like educating children,' Bleheris wearied. Pewter eyes fixed on Eifion firmly. 'It is no accident that the responsibility fell on the oldest people in Brython. Since the time before our time they have guarded the young dragons and helped them to maturity.'

Gwanaelle's head ached from so much astonishment.

Bleheris paused for effect. 'But then the red tide washed over Brython.'

Nyneve glanced at Eifion whose own ancestors trudged up from a land far to the south. 'The Imperium?'

'The red cloaks recognised none of the signs of dragons all around them, but they felled more woods and widened the old roads and pushed north into the mountains with their great travelling armies. Well, now, didn't the mountains push back? The people of these highlands were still loyal to the old gods who fought through the Druids, and the Druids fought with *y Ddraig* behind them.'

'Do you say it was dragons not the people that made it so hard for Rome to succeed in the mountains?'

'I do say it, because that is how it was. They freely gave of their blood, their eye and mouth waters. They did for the Druids what they'd done for Man's iron, and Rome did for Brython what had not been done for an eon before it—it reunited Men and Dragons. They became Cymry's greatest secret. The red cloaks never knew from whence the vast power of the Druid's really came.'

'Then why did the dragons forsake them?' Eifion asked. 'If the Druids had protected *y Ddraig* through the ages?'

Bleheris turned hard eyes on him. 'It was not a forsaking.'

'But they—'

'The Druids protected the dragons,' he marched on. 'As they always had. Death could not change that. To have fought back meant exposing *y Ddraig* to the might of rapacious Rome. Can you imagine what the Empire would have done with the power of *y Ddraig* in their thrall?'

'But they were slaughtered,' Gwanaelle breathed.

'And took the arcane knowledge of dragon-kind with them. All that yet remained was the duty and knowledge of the Morwyn Ddraig. Knowledge that was diluted with every new generation. Until, it seems, so little remains.'

They all fell to silence as the great import of Bleheris' words sank in.

'How did they commune?' Nyneve asked, finally. 'The Druids with *y Ddraig*?'

'Us,' Bleheris said, simply. 'The Myrddyn interpret between peoples.'

'Then but not now,' Eifion clarified.

Pewter eyes glanced at Nyneve. 'Do we not?'

She leaned forward. Gwanaelle could not help but follow. 'You speak with dragons? Even now?'

'Those few that remain. One in particular.'

'Who?' Nyneve urged.

'A hoary, frail, sequestered beast. She might have been your grandmother.' Nyneve straightened immediately. 'No, child. I said "might". This beast lingered and aged because she had never fulfilled her function. She never reproduced. She is nobody's grandmother.'

'Do they die, then, after they reproduce?' Like the winged creatures of their valley.

'No. They may blaze a dozen such burrows to nest a dozen Creil in.'

Nyneve stood, suddenly. 'I might have a sister? Or a brother?'

'Sisters most assuredly. A brother perhaps...though you would never know him.'

Her eyes widened with something that looked a lot like pain and Gwanaelle wondered whether the Searing had returned.

'And how old am I?'

His eyes grew soft. Almost kind. 'Impossible to know. How long had the Morwyn Ddraig been watching you?'

She turned to Gwanaelle. Gwanaelle turned to Eifion.

'Generations,' he murmured. 'Melangell could not trace the names back beyond eleven Assumptions before her own.'

'Eleven?' Nyneve gaped. 'I was trapped in there for eleven lifetimes?'

'You slept, Nyneve, you were not—'

But the girl ignored her and turned instead to the Myrddyn. 'Bleheris?'

More heat billowed up under her furs.

'It is possible.'

'So my...people...could all have lived their lives and died by now?'

'Or they may not yet have emerged. It depends.'

'On what?'

Bleheris studied her seriously. 'On so much. Too much to tell in what is left of this small fire. Sleep now, serious child, we can resume at Mistrise. You have much to think on.'

But as Bleheris pushed himself to his aged feet, his voice almost whispered deep in her mind.

And you have many questions I cannot answer out here.

X

Star-Fire

GWANAELLE FEIGNED sleep as Eifion ducked into their shelter and burrowed swiftly under their mingled skins. Her eager ears had heard him return from his last patrol, glance into Nyneve's shelter before tinkering a while at the fire to lengthen its life. Only the rain brought him in here, she guessed. If he hadn't stood guard all of last night and the one before it, he'd probably have watched them all again tonight. The fact he'd come in at all said something about his exhaustion. Eventually, his breathing grew steady and then deep. Gwanaelle lay there for an age, waiting for him to fall into that fathomless place where gods lingered, but once he had, she moved closer to his warmth, turning into it and freeing one hand to reach out and explore the place they fit together. Eifion's body may no longer have harboured the great strength it had when he was wielding battle weapons from mist-rise until rest, but his flesh spoke of the many hours of hard work he still did here in their valley. Her fingers crept out and pressed against his warm skin, stroked it shyly, glancing at him in the shadows lest he come awake and fling her out into the cold.

But it would take the heaves of the earth to wake this weary man.

Beneath her touch, every muscle interlocked with another, and her fingers skittered up and over each one like a fine horse speeding over upland and down valley, mapping him. Knowing him. Where she rested her horse-fingers, his skin slid slightly across the firm flesh beneath it. All of him must be thus—hot and soft and hard at once.

But the intrigues of his form were not her purpose here tonight and she shifted into a more comfortable position against him. She had wanted to do this since they first lay together in the cave a fortenyear ago.

She had wanted it every single night since then.

She tugged at the split throat of his nettle undershirt and tugged it down as she'd grown breathless dreaming that he would someday do to her, exposing the dark hair of his chest, the hard breadth of his breast. Then, as she settled more comfortably next to him, she paused her long fingers over that flat strength—right over his heart— twitching with indecision.

Would he wake? If he did, what would he do? What would she do? Scuttle back to her side of the shelter, or look him in the eye, smile and continue her exploration?

Gods, how she wished she was brave enough for that.

He was a man. Surely any man who woke to find a woman discovering his flesh would seize the opportunity to return the favour.

Then again he was Eifion.

Before she could think better of it, she lowered her fingers down on the flutter of her lashes. Beneath the furred strength of his breast, his strong heart beat heavy and sure and she immediately recalled those long nights in the cave. How safe that steady thrum had made her feel against her back. How sure the heavy fall of his arm.

Cherished, if not loved.

Protected, if not wanted.

Never quite wanted.

Now, the forbidden touch robbed her of the breath she needed to keep on living and the longer she went without air, the lighter her head became and the easier it seemed to just die right here in Eifion's arms, but even as she had the thought, her body made the decision for her and she gasped in a lungful of air spiced with his scent. Desire, deep and urgent and impossible to ignore surged through her blood, heating her just as Nyneve's blood Seared. It crunched low in her belly, twisted in the tangled hair between her thighs and it pulled.

Gods, how it pulled…

Is this what years of loneliness had done to her? Turned her into the kind of woman that used to roam the woods, approaching men for coin? Or food? The kind of women Eifion visited in the village? Could a maiden even *be* a whore?

Her mouth could— she knew that from her father. He'd forced her to use that before her mother sent her to safety.

And so if her mouth had not been a maiden for winters…

Her tongue crept out to wet lips suddenly dried and, once started on a journey it seemed ill-inclined to stop. She leaned in closer, pressed her mouth against all that hot skin and tasted him. As though she were discovering any new meat for the first time, she pressed him once with her lips first, then licked them to get a sense for his flavour. Then she parted her lips against the hard curve of muscle and brushed, gently back and forth. Her mind swum with the pleasure, but it was not enough. Never enough. She dragged her lips upward, placed it right over the hardest point on his chest and curled her tongue around the circle of dark flesh there as it pebbled to a hard point.

Her heart beat at her chest like the drummers at the front of a warring host, and she imagined Eifion's matched it beneath the cage of his ribs. That he was as eager to feel the gift of her mouth as she was to deliver it.

And so she closed her teeth around the hard point.

Eifion's exclamation was more choke than cry, but his powerful muscles drew his chest upright and cast her back into the skins beside him.

'Gwanaelle?' Slurred and alert in the same breath. Completely confused.

Scurry, little mouse. Far away.

It was excellent advice, but frightened little mice never amounted to much, did they? They scurried their whole lives until, one day, they were not quick enough and they made a meal for something bigger. Something braver. And then that was their time on earth over with.

She was not leaving this earth without at least reaching for something she wanted.

'Eifion…'

One big fist came up to rub at his eyes, trying to force himself awake. It was at once strong and completely vulnerable. Immediately she had a flash of Eifion as a boy, all small and dark and serious…

'Sleep,' she murmured. 'You're so tired.'

'I…' He glanced down to the place his shirt gaped open and his flesh still prickled. Then back to her.

'Perhaps you were dreaming?' she hedged.

Confusion chased across his expression and everything in her sung that he considered dreaming of her touch an actual possibility, but that wasn't fear making her heart beat, it was anticipation. Tasting him had been rousing but getting caught was making her breath tight.

'Or perhaps I was trying to help you sleep,' she risked, her voice low. Failing terribly at Melangell's flirtatious tone.

His hands fumbled with the ties of his shirt and his laugh was weak. 'Like that?'

She pushed herself upright. 'Or perhaps I just wanted to see what it was like.'

His dark stare grew wary. 'Biting me?'

She smiled but it was as slow and gluggy as her blood was beginning to feel. 'Yes.'

'Gwanaelle—'

'Lie back down, Eifion,' she murmured. 'I will ease your weariness.'

'No,' he dragged one strong arm behind him and began to push up. 'I should go.'

'Why?' she asked curling her hand in his shirt and stopping his rise. 'To get an early start on your journey to some village?'

His chest rose and fell deeply. 'Gwanaelle...'

'You are the only man that I see,' she pressed. 'Ever. I'm the only woman near you for the best part of any Sun's March. Why do we not...engage in...'

His eyebrow lifted. 'In?'

'In anything. You waste days trudging to the village in search of comfort when I am right here.'

'We are not—'

'*Why* are we not?' she urged a bit louder than was sensible given how closely Nyneve slept, and Bleheris. She dropped her voice. 'Why?'

'Because we're...not... You are as a sister to me.'

A knife, bright and sharp sliced through her gut, but she did not lose courage. 'You would hardly be the first brother to teach his sister the ways of men. Someone has to do it.'

Wasn't that the very excuse her father had used?

'Gods, Gwanaelle—'

'Or shall I ask Bleheris for his tutelage?'

A dark gaze slashed her. 'Why do you need to know the ways of men if I'm the only one you ever see? What will you do with all this know-how?'

His logic was infuriating. 'Perhaps I wish to know the ways of women, then. There is much I don't know about my own body.'

Talk of her body seemed to force him into action. 'Enough. I'm—'

'What is wrong with me?' she asked before she lost her chance, and her nerve.

He paused and looked back. 'Nothing, Gwanaelle, you are...lovely.'

'But she is so much more lovely?'

Confusion creased his face. 'Who?'

'Melangell. Does she hold your heart so tightly?'

'I do not love Melangell,' he frowned.

He was scarcely convincing. 'Then why can't we be together?'

'Because I do not love you either.'

The knife from earlier made a return slash across her gut upward toward her heart, but she was no green girl any longer. She was a woman. About time she learned what that meant.

'Have I asked for your love?'

'Gwanaelle...' His voice grew soft in the silence. 'You have been asking for it since that first winter we met.'

Just as well it was dark in here because she feared the look he might otherwise be giving her. Humiliation caused a heat so roaring he would surely have to feel it whether or not he could see her.

'Well,' she croaked. 'Then that is long enough, don't you agree? Now it is something else I want from you. Something I had hoped you might find a little easier to give.'

'Stop...'

She pushed to her knees. 'Nyneve will leave us, Eifion. She will come into her dragon...self...and she will go. Then it will just be you and me. I will grow old here, in this valley with a man who chooses to take his pleasure elsewhere—to travel far away and pay for it—rather than lie with me whenever it suited him, for free. I will die a maid and I will never know why it is I was not good enough for you.'

'Gods, Gwanaelle—'

'Do I not have the right parts for the task?' she begged. 'Surely I am at least assembled better than the worn, toothless whores you visit. Or are you roused only by women with fae-features—'

'I do not love Melangell...' he repeated, harder this time.

'Then what is it?' she almost cried. 'Please just tell me so I can understand.'

The silence simmered.

'I cannot love you, Gwanaelle.'

'You do not love the whores and that does not seem to stop you being able to...'

'To what?' his rich voice challenged.

She sucked up all her courage. 'To toss them on their backs and impale them.'

Gods what she would give for one good thrust of that sword...

'Don't,' he urged. 'Those words on your lips. It is not right.'

'Is it not?' She'd never felt less like laughing, yet one coughed up out of her. 'Is it right that I should never experience what every other woman in this land has the opportunity to? To feel what it is like to have a man's weight bearing down on me. His strength inside me? I heard Melangell's muffled screams when she was with Cai, yet it was a pain she craved. Demanded even. I would understand that pain.'

Dark eyes pinned her. 'You want me to hurt you?'

I want you to love me, but that was not going to happen.

'I want you to know me. I offer myself with no expectation of more.'

'Gwanaelle,' he groaned. 'No.'

The man had the resistance of iron. She pushed up and tugged angrily at the ties of her undershift. It had been a long time since she thought of her body critically but she hoped that her flesh was as toned and firm from hard work as his, and that it might somehow please him, if for no other reason than it was so close. She stretched her arms to either side displaying herself without dignity.

Because this is what I am become.

'I am not yet thirty winters, Eifion. Will you truly allow me to simply wither because you cannot muster enough vigour to tumble me on my back even once?'

His head dropped in the shadows but his eyes slide sideways, looking at her pale flesh between lengths of his long, dangling hair.

'You do not know what you offer.'

She brought her hands in and cupped her own breasts. They spilled over. 'The Gods meant these breasts for hands bigger than mine, Eifion ap Gwilim.'

He groaned and tipped sideways, the rest of his big body following his hanging head, coming to rest against her naked torso and, for a moment, she regretted bringing this fine man so low, but then the whiskers of his beard rasped against the unmarked skin of her breast and blood began coursing wildly through the channels of her body.

She brought her hands to his head, forked through his thick hair, pressed a cheek to the top of his head and entreated him.

'If not because you desire me then because you at least care for me,' she murmured. 'Do not condemn me to death as a maiden. Please. As my only friend…'

Those words marked the end of his resolve and his resistance. He turned his face into her skin and breathed there for moments. Then he dragged his lips across her throat as she'd done on his chest. One hand replaced hers on her breast and the other drew her close, held her close. Just as she'd always imagined. She folded her arms around him, keeping him close as he mouthed, lathed, and bit her throat, her shoulder, the mounded curve of one breast. She dragged his hair back away from his face as he discovered her, hungry to do the same. The only part of him she could reach was the shadowed place behind his ear and so she pressed her lips there. Hard on the beat-echo of his heart.

Eifion gathered her up in his arms and pulled her across the furs still in his lap, laying her out more comfortably, but he did not look at her, pressing advantage instead to circle the screaming peaks of her breast and suckling there as Nyneve once had. She twisted her legs out from under her and stretched a free hand down to bunch her undershift up around her waist, cooling the fervent burn between her thighs and hoping to entice him to more than just the worship of her breasts, but he would not be led, and he gave first one breast his full attention and then the other before mouthing his way back up her throat, along her jaw to her chin.

And then he was there.

At her mouth.

His pressed into it hot and wet and he forced hers open with a strong tongue, even as one of his hands explored down along her belly and between her thighs. There, his fingers did to one hot, wet place what his tongue did to another.

She arched against him, into him, as a confusing fog swilled around her, then reached out for his free hand and threaded her fingers through his. 'Eifion…'

'This is how you wanted it,' he warned, against her mouth, forcing her hand down against the furs and pinning it there even as his body pinned hers with its weight. 'Fast and hard. Like the whores.'

He pressed his weight against her shoulder and nudged her over, onto her side, as he yanked his wears high, then let her fall back against his bare chest, into his heat. It was the cave all over again except now their flesh was bare and there was nothing—no-one—between them.

One strong hand traced from her knee up over her hip and breast to her scalp and dragged her thick hair back out of the way, baring her throat. He fastened his mouth on the back of her neck—sucked there—and returned his hand to lift her thigh up and hook it over his hip. His knuckles brushed her rump as he freed himself from his brecs and she longed to see what made him a man. She'd glimpsed it any number of times over many winters but never seen it like this—hot and angry as it felt, ready for its intended purpose.

Ready for her.

He wedged it in between the round mounds of her rump. Then he paused, stroked the length of her throat and bared shoulder with a single knuckle, ending it with a soft, feathery fingertip.

She twisted back toward him, wanting to watch his beautiful face as this happened but he collected himself, pushed her forward again, fumbling at the furrow between her thighs so she could not.

'I can't look at you,' he grunted.

Gwanaelle froze… Tightened all over. Did he even know he'd murmured aloud. She should have wept that he couldn't bring himself to even think about the woman he was plunging himself into, but as he spoke, he pressed himself against her, lifted her leg high over his hip and pushed himself forward and all thought—even the sad ones—were forced out of her on a grunt as he pushed in. Smoothly, unwavering. Like he didn't want to stop to think about what it was he was doing. Or who with, perhaps. He bit into the flesh of her nape and began moving against her, inside her, rubbing his bare chest against her back, its fur causing a delicious friction against her spine. The intrusion of his large cock inside her caused little pain thanks to her father's fumbling fingers but it stretched her flesh almost painfully and Gwanaelle realised that this was the pain that Melangell cried out over.

For.

Blazing heat focussed where their two bodies met. Eifion lowered her leg once he was buried deep and curled an arm around her belly, bending her back into him, driving against her and back again, into her and out again, but never quite leaving her. The fingers of that hand slipped into her from the front even as he pressed into her from the back. The friction first burned, then tingled and then seemed to go numb—as though someone had swathed her with Rue—but beneath all of that was a swirling tightness, slipping into grasp and then away again, but every time tightening like a twisted tourniquet.

'Eifion,' she gasped as he raised himself on one elbow, all the better to batter against her walls.

But he did not speak, and he did not breathe her name the way she had with his. He grunted and sweated and all the time he mouthed that place beneath her hair, and fixed himself there. The forearm at her belly tightened enough to affect her already strained breathing and the slap of his hips against hers grew faster and faster even as his hand pinched and squeezed the wet flesh he'd been teasing. The sensation of his strong hand without and his powerful cock within caused a rasp that grew unbearable and the twisting grew so tight she was sure she might snap, until—finally—he cried out against the flesh of her neck, muffling his oath there, and spasmed against her—inside her.

And then she did snap.

She burst from years of longing, years of wanting and waiting, and just moments of his powerful grunts. She burst into a starfield as vast as the blanket above their little shelter in summer and it stole her breath and replaced her blood with a kind of thick mead that glugged rather than ran. She fumbled an arm up behind her, curled around Eifion's neck and clung there, needing him to root her here on earth.

He sagged against her, chest heaving, body slick and loosed his arm from around her belly, withdrawing it, trembling, back down into the furs.

Then the heaving stopped dead. The languid pressure of his body ended as he stiffened against her. A half-breath later he pushed distance between their half-naked bodies.

And he was out of her.

'I'm sorry, Gwanaelle…'

'No—'

But though she spoke fast, he withdrew faster, stumbling up onto his knees and then his feet, tucking himself back into his brecs as his wears fell back down and snatching up his wools. 'I will take watch.'

And then he was gone, leaving her splayed half-naked and awkward in the furs, misery spreading down her thighs.

Was this how he was with the whores? He spent himself and then just…left?

She wasn't foolish enough to expect love, but she hadn't expected he would flee the very moment the act was done. He was Eifion, a man of honour, and he cared about her at least a little.

Or so she'd thought.

She sagged back against the furs and hauled one up over her nakedness before the cold night air stuck fast to her slick flesh. The place between her legs was tender but not uncomfortably so. Her flesh tingled where he'd sucked but she did not mind carrying Eifion's mark. Her breath still stammered from the extraordinary star-fire he'd kindled in her.

Yet she couldn't help wondering how it might else have been.

This is how you wanted it, he'd murmured.

No. Not how she *wanted* it—never that—but this was exactly what she'd agreed to, and so she wouldn't cry though she desperately wanted to, and she wouldn't judge him, though she had reason enough. And she wouldn't turn him away if he turned to her tomorrow night for more of the same.

This was Eifion—a man she had loved for most of her life. She could have his body, if not his heart, and that was already more than she feared she'd ever experience in her life.

Perhaps it would be enough.

X I

Earth Burrow

ABANDONMENT is a construct of man, Bleheris corrected deep inside Nyneve's head. *It is no failing for y Ddraig to leave their egg once laid and never see it again. It is their way, but it does not mean they do not care for their young. Look at what your mother endured to ensure your survival.*

'And is it always in a well?'

While she was learning, it hurt less to vocalise her thoughts even as she also pushed them to Bleheris through her mind, and while she was alone, she could safely do so. At least if she only murmured and so could not be overheard. She burrowed deeper into her furs and stared at the top of her shelter to help her mind focus on Bleheris doing the same across the clearing from her.

Earth-burrow, he corrected. *The chill of the earth's waters numbed you, helped you sleep. Kept you safe.*

'Was it the same magic that kept Eifion so healthy before I was…born?' Just because they did not have a well in this valley didn't mean she hadn't attended to the stories she'd been told. The folk of Melangell's valley only ever drank from their well. The well she'd been kept in as…

As an egg, Nyneve. Denying it won't make it any less so, but the water of an earth-burrow is only water until a Creil is deposited within. It did not give you your power, you *imbued it with new magic.*

How could she have once been so magical within a shell when her existence out of it was so…dull.

If you discounted the past few weeks.

'And a young dragon cannot emerge until in the care of a Morwyn Ddraig?'

Dragonlings are little more than grubs when they are emerged. Y Ddraig *may be able to nurture its spirit but they cannot fashion their claws into hands safe enough to handle it.*

What poor nature was that?

'And so, they look to Man for aid?' The Mathrafal, specifically.

Bleheris spoke with his mind so casually he could even grunt in thought. *The two species have grown rather reliant on each other.*

Nyneve turned in her warm cocoon of skins and whispered into the night. 'So she did not abandon me?'

The waves of his thought stroked her mind and brought unwanted water to her eyes.

She left you in the care of the Mathrafal for your protection. So you could sleep until ready and then grow in their care into the individual you were destined to be.

'Except that didn't happen.'

War has a way of intruding on the most careful planning...

'Are there others like me?' Nyneve whispered.

You would likely not recognise your fellow dragonlings, he admitted. *Nor they you unless you drew close enough to see their eyes. They grow fast and hard under the protection of the Morwyn Ddraig. They grow to survive. They do not much trouble themselves with conversation or cooperation.*

There. Wouldn't that satisfy Mother to know that it wasn't her bad rearing that made her the disagreeable girl she was sure they thought her.

Woman now. Girl no longer. With a woman's responsibilities.

'Yes, yes. I know all about my responsibilities.' Hadn't it been made abundantly clear?

I fear you are only starting to understand them, child.

'Child no longer...' she said smartly, thrilled for once to have outplayed the master.

But there was nothing. No agreement, no disagreement, no reply even. Nyneve fell silent, unaccountably chastened and she waited for the tingle in her mind, but, even then Bleheris did not speak. The silence punished her the longer it went.

'Myrddyn?' Nothing. Had she angered him with her wit? Had she grown too comfortable with him?

Myrddyn? she whispered, straight into his mind.

Apologies, Nyneve. I was distracted from thought.

Truly? The man who could finger a lute and sing a complex tale of intrigue while whispering something completely else into her mind? Distracted? 'What by?'

You have to ask? he laughed. *You are closer to it than I. You must be able to smell it, at least. The stink of rutting.*

His meaning took a moment to sink in, even though it wasted no time moving from one part of her mind to another. Foolishly, for a moment, she was sure he was talking about their boars. Or the valley hares, but then she disconnected her mind from Bleheris' close hold and let her other senses resume their function.

Everything in her turned to frost. There were only four people in this valley and two of them were presently engaged in discussion about the origins of dragons. So it could only be the other two making those unholy sounds, so low and urgent.

What a delight, he went on. *It is rare that I am surprised. I find I have missed the sensation.*

Pain shafted through her body. 'Well… She has finally worn him down.'

Come now, Nyneve. Jealousy belittles you. Besides, rutting with a Man would serve little purpose, except perhaps in the earning of skill.

Was it jealousy? She poked around and discovered that it was. That Gwanaelle should hold such a unique place in Eifion's regard… A place she could never go.

But I admit to being heartened at your affection for him. Good Sir Warrior is only a score of winters younger than I. Perhaps you may yet come to like me and trust me.

'Not true,' she was fast to correct, though whether she was denying her jealousy or Eifion's age or ever being able to trust the Cunning Man she was not certain.

Still, an interesting development.

Nyneve listened out again. Nothing now; nothing, at least, that stood out against the other night sounds, but soon enough she heard the familiar brush of Gwanaelle's shelter skins raising and flapping back in place. She had passed in or out of that opening more times in her fortenyear in this valley than she'd stood at the edge of the wood and peered into the thickly treed darkness, dreaming.

Whatever had just happened, one of them had ended it.

XII

Gathering

EIFION ADJUSTED his sticky cock where he'd shoved it back into his brecs with such little care, and shrugged down by the darkened fire. The tiniest glimmer of red coal promised him warmth for the long night to come—his third with little sleep.

He tossed some dried grasses onto it and then forked them to flame before adding some sticks, a broken branch and finally wood. Then he poked periodically at the coals and ensured they were evenly distributed around their fire pit.

He leaned forward and held his sword-hand, overturned, flat above the growing flames. He felt the sting of the fire's heat, smelled the singeing of the dark hairs scattered over its back.

Steady as a warrior's now. No trembles now.

It didn't mean anything just because it had quaked before.

Nights without sleep—wasn't that enough to make any man a little quake-handed? To do something he knew he shouldn't.

Bedding Gwanaelle was such a thing. Sweet, honourable Gwanaelle—raped of honour now, befouled by his gluttonous cock. No matter that it had been by her own request.

He was the only man who had ever treated her with gentle hand. Her father had betrayed her where he should have protected her, and Cai had been a party to the terror that brought her first to Melangell's valley—she'd long forgiven him his role but had never quite forgotten—and so *he* was the only man who had ever cared for her, protected her as her weak father should have without asking for anything in return. He'd long recognised her infatuation but he'd never meant to take advantage of it, he'd privately honoured it. She was clearly of better blood than his—even ripped from her home the evidence of her breeding was in her speech, her walk, her gentle kindness. Only the wealthy could indulge kindness in a land at war with itself.

All the more reason that his despoilment was vile.

Perhaps he should have sent her back to Melangell, to join the virgins in her sanctuary, where she could have circled herself in the affection of their hearts if not in the affection of a body she only thought she craved.

He could offer her none—he glanced again at his hand—not if it left him trembling like that. He could not tremble for Gwanaelle, though the Gods knew she was worthy of it. Her beautiful mouth, her pale, untouched skin. The thick tumbling hair the colour of the palest part of a flame, and her eyes. The same eyes as Artwr's Gwenhwyfar as the stories went. Finer warriors than he had tumbled for eyes the colour of the blue Milkwort that bloomed along the face of Eryri.

Did all women of noble blood have those eyes? Was it what distinguished them? Gwanaelle was the only one he'd ever met up close. Yet, she would not go back to Melangell, not if it meant leaving Nyneve undefended, and so his only option was to leave *her*. Leave them all. Before it got any worse.

He glanced at his shelter where the seer slept within.

Whatever the Myrddyn was here for, it wasn't to hurt Nyneve. That much he believed. In the same way he believed his visions born of the Creil—it was just a...knowing. The Cunning Man wanted to use her, no doubt, for his own purposes, and it was as impossible to think that it didn't have something to do with their power-hungry Chieftain, but he wasn't going to hurt her as long as Artwr desired a dragon's powers, and there was only one way that Artwr would end his hunt for *y Ddraig*—by getting what he wanted.

Or believing he did.

Eifion's eyes tracked up the valley-side to the place where the Creil shards lay bundled harmlessly together in their earthy womb. It would be a matter of a mere fortennight to get them south to Artwr's winter stronghold if he used some of the Imperium coins he'd hoarded over the winters. They may not hold their original value but their smelted ore was still worth a horse or a meal at least and Brython was yet raw enough to enjoy the sight of some once Emperor or another melting to deformity in the white-fire. Added, it was now the time of *Gathering*; folk of sense would be rejoining their hearths at this time of year, not leaving them. The workers of land would have harvested their crops and collected their livestock from the woods, winnowed the fittest and slaughtered the rest so that they had the fewest mouths to feed through the brutal times of *Plenty*, *Silence* and *Frost*. The dark time of year. A certain mistake for anyone to begin travelling now.

Yet he must. If for no other reason than he would be certain to catch those he sought returned to their strongholds or close to their way there. Who knew where they'd be the rest of the Sun's March. For, once the business of harvest and slaughter was in hand, the people of this land could relax, gather together and celebrate the survival of another Sun's March, and they who warred—warriors and chieftains—had more reason than most to celebrate surviving another year, and so he should travel south in time for Old Soul's Night—the Hag Feast Melangell would have called it—when the winter began anew and the celebrating began.

But he must go now if he had any hope of returning before the ways grew unpassable. Of returning to Gwanaelle and Nyneve.

It sickened him to leave them at all but this was not a task he could pass to Cai, who all Cymry believed dead, or to Melangell whose life would be forfeit if her name so much as carried to Artwr on the wind. Yet he could not undertake this task himself and deliver it to his Chieftain's great door. Artwr would imprison any who rode up to his stronghold with a sackful of dragon egg, torture them until they confessed all—whence it had come, whence had gone the creature that emerged from it—such was his desperation for power to defeat the ever encroaching Angles. So the head that delivered the Creil to him had to be vacant of all knowledge of Nyneve's whereabouts lest it be teased out, and, preferably, beloved enough by Artwr that it would remain fast on its shoulders.

Neither of which described him.

But, while Eifion ap Gwilim was merely a lowly warrior, he wasn't without connections of his own. Men he'd come up with first as pages and then squires in the strongholds of Cymry. The best amongst them, Gwalchmai ap Gwyar and his brother Gwalchafad were sons to the sister-by-birth that Artwr had married off to a Northern king immediately on becoming Chieftain. Nephews once, now trusted members of Artwr's own force; men charged—as Cai was—with retrieving the relics of *y Ddraig* wheresoever they could.

If a kinsman and warrior of Artwr's rode up to his stronghold with what the Chieftain sought there would be no questions. No torture.

But not Gwalchmai—he might be favourite of the Chieftain but what secret could hold fast in the storm of mead that he regularly whipped up?

Gwalchafad.

Sombre little brother Gwalchafad who had measured his words and used them only to the greatest effect. Who let men think him mute or dull-witted rather than speak just to hear the music of his own voice. Serious Gwalchafad who had squired diligently for all his brothers and pledged himself to become one of the finest warriors this land had seen. Better even than Cai. *He* would carry the Creil's remains to Artwr and then Artwr would recall his Cunning Man to help him master the sight it still offered, a fortenyear after Nyneve broke out of it, and by the time Artwr had grown inured to its magic and sought something stronger—something with a beat at its throat— they would have spirited their dragonling away to some further valley, out of his reach, perhaps north to live amongst the Picts, and out of Bleheris'. For as long as that lasted. By then, perhaps, Nyneve would have come into her dragon power and would be better positioned to defend herself against Artwr's insatiable hunger, though her own mother could not.

Perhaps Artwr would finally be satisfied. Perhaps he would master the sight and conquer the Angles and would then have no need for a living dragon in the caves beneath his new stronghold.

Eifion shoved his stick at the smouldering coals to bother them to life.

And perhaps he could, himself, at last honour his pledge of fealty to the high Chieftain and undo some of the treachery of half a lifetime by giving him one of the greatest relics he sought. Now that it could not hurt anyone. He glanced at the shelter he'd once called his own, considered the sleeping man in it. Bleheris was a Myrddyn, there was probably nothing he could not defend the valley from. Unless of course it needed defence from him, but he could not take them to Melangell's valley without exposing Cai's truth to a man directly attached to Artwr. Potentially. Something deep in his heart questioned Bleheris' true intentions but the man had made no attempt to hurt anyone in the time he'd been with them.

A coal-fall sent sparks high into the gloomy night—his third awake—and he tugged his furs more tightly around him.

It was pure convenience that accompanying the Creil to Artwr also parted him from Gwanaelle for a time. Time enough to refortify his heart against her. Time enough for her to do the same. He knew what lay in that direction and he would never see Gwanaelle suffer the stinging slice of his blade. No matter how much she begged. Or seduced. Or fought.

Or hurt.

Nothing would hurt as much as waking to the cold press of his sword against her soft throat. That moment of realisation as he betrayed the great gift of a lifetime of her affection.

X I I I

Origins

HOW CAN I look like this? Nyneve demanded as soon as her reaching mind found something softer than the hard nothing she'd been skirting blindly along for half the morning. *If I am dragon?*

Those creatures she had seen in her dream… She couldn't imagine how one of them could linger in her body now, without her feeling it. Or burst from it without killing her.

Bleheris' pause was scant. *The sage moths begin their life as a grub, do they not?*

Her frown grew so tight, staring into the dark, concentrating on holding his mind now she'd found her way in, an ache grew at her temples.

Or the bald prickled little thing that looks like a man's cods when it hatches. It later becomes the glorious Tanna bird. Why should you be so different?

None of his analogies were particularly flattering.

How does it happen? she urged. *When the change comes?*

Violently? Suddenly? Would she control it or would it rip her apart right before Eifion and Gwanaelle's horrified eyes? Would she tear them asunder in the very next breath? She pressed firm fingers to her temple that now screamed.

Come to me by the fire, child, Bleheris murmured, *before your mind fractures.*

Then he was gone. The ache ended immediately and the marshy sensation hardened rapidly into the same kind of barrier she remembered from her time within the Creil. For surely that is where her earliest memories came from—the cloistered, airless place she sometimes dreamed about.

It was real.

She slipped from her shelter, dragging a fur around her as she emerged into the clearing to meet Bleheris, already seated, awaiting the rise of the sun in the light mist of dawn rain. The pinkish light seemed to swirl around him like the muds in the pool where she bathed and the pewter of his wild hair almost glowed in the fire's light. She padded closer and paused further from him than his arm could reach.

Although when a man could stretch right inside your head was *anything* truly out of reach?

'Sit, child,' he invited, shifting over.

She tightened the fur around her and eased herself down next to him. Somehow it was less frightening staring into the fire instead of into his all-knowing eyes.

'These lands were once nothing but rock and flame,' he murmured turning the coals in the fire with a long stick. 'And dragons. So many kinds.'

Nyneve slashed him a glance, but she didn't interrupt. Not when someone was about to share the secrets of the land with her, and everything in her knew that was what he'd come to do. He would tell Gwanaelle and Eifion what they needed to know but he would tell her so much more. If she but listened.

He nodded toward the glowing red coals. 'They first spawned in earth and flame. Heat has ever been their favourite.'

'They like water,' Nyneve pointed out to be clever and then remembered that her dragons were only dream. She waited for the Myrddyn's ridicule.

'Some do,' he agreed. 'Enough time has passed that dragons have grown used to all manner of dwellings, but they still need heat.'

'Or they die?'

'They sleep. Deeper than any you can imagine. Longer, too. Through ages of ice and through the rise of the water, but they need heat to live in our world.'

'What if there is no fire?'

'Dragons first take their heat from the sun.'

'Even in winter?'

'Do you know nothing of the world around you, foolish girl?' he mocked. 'The sun does not *wither* in winter, just because you cannot see it. It blazes as hot and fierce as ever. *Y Ddraig* fly up and up and glide on the raging flurries high above the gloomy blanket of winter until the sun's warmth has soaked deeply into every one of the scales on their body. Then they return to the cold ground.'

She followed his gaze up into the gloaming. 'They could be up there now chasing the rising sun high above the clouds.'

The idea of doing that now, at the start of the dark time of year, appealed extra much.

'So, *y Ddraig* have existed longer than we have, fed by the sun's warmth?'

'Longer than *Man* has, yes.'

She lifted her gaze back to his. 'And I am not Man?'

'Do not fret that,' he chuckled. 'Man's kind are nothing exemplary.'

'Why are there not more dragons?' If they'd been around for so very long. Although it occurred to her, then, that maybe there were. Just because she had not met them…

'*Y Ddraig* are patient,' he said. 'And they are wise. They would rather out-wait an enemy than fight them.'

'Dragons and Men are at war again?'

'Man and their kind are the most selfish of all creatures. Territorial like Giants but greedy like a Quickhatch. When they take land they swarm it, strip it, and do not share its bounty. That makes them enemy to dragons regardless.'

'You speak as if Man is just one of many equal creatures.'

He snorted. 'You speak is if they are more.'

They. Nyneve narrowed her eyes. Was the Myrddyn not strictly a man either, then?

'Dragons lived in harmony with Men as long as their numbers were contained. Their likeness is ground in ash into rock-faces deep below the earth from the days when even Men shared their cave networks. When men grew too rapacious, the dragons retreated.'

'To where?'

'Caverns, underwater realms, mountains, skies. Wherever Man was not at ease.'

'The world is surely large enough for all?'

Iron-coloured eyes ridiculed her. 'And how would you know that?'

She would not. Of course, she would not. The land could drop away into a blazing pit with no bottom just one day's ride from here, for all she knew.

'So dragons withdrew, and they live in peace away from Men now?'

Or should she hate Gwanaelle and Eifion as well as not belong with them?

'Man covets what he does not have,' Bleheris murmured. 'There can never be peace between them. Though there are sometimes truces.'

'Truce? Doesn't that imply a war?

'We will get to everything,' he promised. 'For now, think on what you have learnt, and be ready with questions this same time on the morrow. This fire will be your place of private learning before Gwanaelle rises for the day.'

'But you have not answered my questions!' she cried.

Most pressing amongst them, how she could she look as Gwanaelle did yet *be* a dragon. Or become one.

'You have lived amongst Men too long,' Bleheris frowned, displeased, 'and grown as greedy as one.' He pushed to his feet but Nyneve knew that it was she—not he—who would be leaving. 'When you are come into your dragonhood you will discover that the world's pleasures need to be stretched out over eons.'

He pinned her with his gaze. 'T'morrow, then.'

X I V

Ruin

'NYNEVE—'

'No! You cannot go.'

'I must Nyneve, I have—' Eifion glanced over at Gwanaelle only for a heartbeat before lying '—a pledge to honour. Besides, I have left this valley before and returned. Have I not?'

'Only for days,' she hissed. 'To the village and back. Never for se'nnights. Never for fortennights.'

A moon, easily, if he was to tell the truth. Which he was not, not to a teary young Nyneve. Gwanaelle's ashen face said that she, at least, had guessed it.

'Bleheris will remain and has offered you and your mother his protection. You do not need a rusty warrior when you have a Cunning Man.'

'I do not want him,' she cried. 'I want you. Please do not leave, Eifion. I fear it.'

'Do not. I will be back by the time of Plenty. I swear it.'

Any later and he would not be able to return until thaw, anyway, because the passages would be blocked by snow.

Nyneve started to argue but then grew suddenly blank the way she often did when Bleheris was in her mind. When her riven eyes sharpened on him again they were still awash but no longer quite so afraid.

'I will miss you,' she murmured.

It was easy to take this Nyneve in his arms—this young woman that he had cared for from a babe—and to hold her like the child she was and not the beast she would someday become. He only did what he did to ensure that happened.

'And I you,' he murmured, pressing a kiss to her dark hair.

He hiked his pack up onto his shoulder and turned to Bleheris next. 'Thank you, Myrddyn for your advice about the journey ahead.' And the valuable clues he had offered to ease his way. 'Guard these women as though they were your own.'

'As if they hold the greatest secret of our age,' Bleheris pledged.

It was difficult not to believe him when his silver eyes glowed with such sincerity.

He hiked the pack unnecessarily higher and turned, reluctantly, to Gwanaelle, who stood trying not to tremble, her hands twisting in a knot at her front. The woman he'd drained his cods into last night. The woman whose virtue he'd stolen like some drunk, callow thief. The woman who trusted and loved him above all others all of her adult life.

'Take care, Gwanaelle,' he murmured and it sounded like the hollowest farewell. Something for a stranger.

'Don't leave,' she begged, soft. 'Not because of me.'

'This has nothing to do with you.' Anger surged up under his tunic—a liar as well as a thief, now—and his words fell more impatiently across his lips than he'd meant, but they were, at least, effective.

Gwanaelle paled further and stepped back from him, curling her fingers into her furs. 'Of course.'

He could not look at her tiny, twisted hands without remembering how they had felt against his skin last night, and so he could not look at her at all. He threw a last, tight smile at Nyneve and turned from them all. It took but a moment to get to the edge of the trees. There, he glanced up at the sheer face of the valley-side and planned his next steps. He would scale that crag, visit the tiny cave and retrieve everything he needed for this journey—coin, iron and the Creil shards. He would march to the nearest village and buy the first horse that looked like it could carry him for a month even if it died in the attempt. He would visit Cai on his journey south, beg him to creep out once a se'nnight and check on Gwanaelle and Nyneve—just from some safe, high vantage point. Just to be sure they were aright.

And then he would ride south—far, far south beyond Cai's old stronghold even. He would ride dangerously near to Artwr's winter stronghold at Caerllion, seek out Gwalchafad, convince him to take the Creil shards to their Chieftain and end this destructive obsession. He would beg Gwalchafad to ask no questions, show him the Creil's power if necessary, and he would make all of this right again.

But first he had to step into the wood.

~

'You did this!'

Nyneve turned on her the moment Eifion finally disappeared into the trees, unable to contain her heartbreak a moment longer. 'Whore!'

Bleheris spun on her. 'Watch your mouth—'

But all of Gwanaelle's pain from Eifion's hasty withdrawal last night and all of her shock on discovering him packed and preparing to leave just now swirled together in a kind of alchemy of misery and her hand acted before her ears could understand Bleheris' defence. The crack of the back of her hand meeting the soft flesh of Nyneve's face and then the girl's shocked cry filled the silent valley like an echoing thunderclap.

A valley that would be silent until the day Eifion returned to them. To her.

'Where did you learn that word?' Gwanaelle hissed at the girl that had once been her daughter as soon as she was able to breathe again. Her father had called her a whore even as he'd pressed her face down into his lap. Lord Brychwel Ysgithrog who had pursued her through the woods with dogs all those years ago called her one, too, though she'd been little more than a child, on both occasions, but neither she nor Eifion had ever used the word in Nyneve's presence. Just as they'd never spoken of dragons.

Nyneve may have thought herself a woman but she was no way in command enough of her emotions for her eyes not to slide sideways to Bleheris. Gwanaelle followed their direction.

'Context, my dear…' the Myrddyn said, calm as you like despite Nyneve's betrayal. 'You were hardly—'

'Leave!' she demanded. 'Now.'

'I have just promised—'

She raised up as big as she could. 'I don't care where you go, I don't care what time you come back but in this moment you will get as far away from me as you can, Cunning Man.'

Perhaps he knew how much more it would infuriate her that he not react with fear or even surprise, instead, he just smiled and narrowed his lids over glinting eyes and murmured as he turned away from them both. 'Well, well. The little mouse has claws…'

'And you!' Gwanaelle spun back. 'You will return below your skins and remain there until you understand just why it is that I am so angry.' Though hopefully the girl would not guess exactly why. 'And why that word will never again be used in this clearing.'

Bad enough to feel like one without being named such in front of a stranger. By a stranger.

'When I am Dragon,' Nyneve roared, her young face flushed red, as she ran to her shelter and lifted the flap, 'you will be the first one I eat!'

And then she was gone, and Bleheris was gone, and—God help her—Eifion was gone.

And Gwanaelle stood, completely alone, in the middle of the clearing, her heart in utter ruins.

Part II

X V

Sanctuary

'THIS IS THE last time you leave this valley with a mount of mine, Second.' Cai ap Cynyr slapped Eifion on the shoulder and tossed the leathers at him. 'Make sure you bring this one back.'

Not exactly the regal animal that *Gwddfhir* had been, but then this pack-mare was less likely to draw particular interest from anyone he should meet on the road, and taking her from Cai meant fewer days lost to travelling to some beast-merchant before departing south.

'Worry not, Lord. This creature is far too tall for me. I will not wish to keep her long.'

'I have not been a Lord this past fortenyear, Eifion, as well you know. Here, I am merely Cai.'

From Sword-arm to the King to a man like any other. It would be a tragedy if Cai had not chosen it so himself—though it was not without cost—but if there was only one man left in this land who would extend Cai ap Cynyr the courtesy that was his birthright, then *he* would be that man.

'Perhaps I should join you on your journey,' Cai murmured. 'As *your* Second.'

'Riding into the heart of Artwr's lands with his long-dead brother for company would scarcely help me pass through them unnoticed.'

Cai's gaze shifted to Melangell across the clearing, where she crouched talking to a wide-eyed young girl. Souls in need of refuge seemed to keep arriving. 'Entire moons go by in which I am content to protect this place of peace, but when you walk in with iron slung across your back I suddenly ache for a good skirmish.'

Somewhere below their feet still lay the bones of those who had first skirmished in this valley, and the ashes of those who had come after them. Did he truly wish these women back into an unmatched fight like that one again? With sticks and stones and tree sap against iron, fire and warriors?

And a dragon.

'I would happily knock you down, Lord. In the name of friendship.'

Cai snorted. 'You would have to reach me first, Second.'

A slim form curled herself under Eifion's arm as a young Gwanaelle had once curled for protection under her skirts.

'Lifebringer,' he murmured. Once, Melangell's affection would have made him wary because of her place in Cai's heart. Now, his reticence was purely because of his vision—that knife, that pale throat—it was instinctive, but he only saw Melangell once every Sun's March. Scarce time to develop the kind of deep feeling for the dragon maiden that would make his blade-hand tremble.

Melangell peered up at him. 'It is time?'

'Past time. I need to keep moving. Though it has been a pleasure seeing you again. Brief as it was.'

He passed her off to Cai who looped his arms across her front and tucked her back into the protection of his large body. The natural manner hit Eifion deep in his gut, in the place that longed to be free to hold a woman with such a mix of love and tender care.

He finished fixing his belongings to the pad on the back of the mount and then boosted himself onto the horse and swung to sitting.

'I will return with your cob by the start of *Smoke*, Lord.'

'Be sure of it, Second.'

The horse danced a little as he lingered, off the trail for too long. 'If I do not, bring Gwanaelle and Nyneve back here. Protect them from whatever is coming.'

He hated the ripple in his own voice. It was way too close to the trembling hand in his visions.

Cai just considered him evenly. 'At *Smoke*, then.'

Eifion tapped his finger against the taut leathers and turned the cob's head away from the clearing, back into the trees. It took but a moment to sink deep enough into them that Melangell's yew circle might not have existed at all. He knew this valley like his own skin; even after so many winters he easily found the places in the woods that opened out to passable trails and in no time the sturdy mare carried him up above the valley into the uplands. He paused before stepping out of the trees and asked silent permission of the Drygioni as Melangell had taught him all those winters before.

The fair folk offered no objections. Indeed, the grasses shimmered as thought they were delighted to see him. Here, at least, he could let free with his affection.

'Come on, then,' he murmured to the gentle horse whose ears twitched back towards his voice then forward again as if marking their direction. 'We have a long journey ahead.'

It was only as he crested the uplands that he realised he had failed to mention Bleheris at all.

But by his mount's next step he had already forgotten it.

~

Nyneve swayed to and fro by the fire, rocked by the steady scrubbing with sop-weed that Gwanaelle attended on her naked body. Its oils soaked in and eased both the Searing and the patches of roughness on the girl's skin where it had begun to flake and split like the bottom of a dried stream. Unlike the swathing on of waterfall mud—which laid a thick barrier between her flesh and Nyneve's—applying the oils required direct hand-on-skin application. Repetitive. Gentle. Stroking and massaging until it had all soaked in and helped restore her skin to its youthful softness.

It was like Nyneve's earliest days anew. When the infant dragonling practically purred to be caressed. If her belly was full and her skin worshipped, she was a content child.

'He teaches me, mother,' older Nyneve grumbled, but not so annoyed she moved away from the spellbinding contact.

Gwanaelle's brows dropped. 'I'm just wondering if those teachings have to take you away from the work of this valley quite so regularly? With Eifion gone—'

'And whose fault is that?'

Gwanaelle's stomach tightened.

Hers. Almost certainly. The price for yielding to her feelings. If she had not been so weak perhaps Eifion would be here with them even now.

'With Eifion gone, there is a lot more to be done,' she said, finding patience from somewhere, 'and with you and Bleheris constantly off on your mysterious apprenticeship there is only one other to do them.'

Nyneve clucked. 'Have we yet failed to do a task, between us?'

No. She could not say that exactly. Some days she had no idea how everything got done but Bleheris always made sure that it did. It seemed that as she took an inward breath the tasks waiting to be done seemed overwhelming and by the time she exhaled again they were complete. She may not understand it but she would not complain.

Except to note that Nyneve was rarely the one to do them.

'I cannot be taxed with mundane tasks,' Nyneve waved the observation away as regally as any Queen when her mother said so. 'My responsibilities are to myself and my People, now'

The tone wheedled its way in under Gwanaelle's ribs. 'Oh, how tired I grow of hearing about *your People*. Do you know how much others have sacrificed for the Ancient Ones—for you—long before you learned of your heritage?'

'Yes, yes...' Nyneve rolled her riven eyes. 'Melangell gave up her freedom. Cai his lands and title. Father his sword. You gave up...what, Mother?' Her oil-slicked face was all innocence. 'I forget?'

It was tempting to cross that entitled mouth with a slap of bruised sop-weed, except that Nyneve's unkind question was really not that far from the truth.

What had she given up? *Her youth?* That would have passed regardless. *Her chance at love and a bondmate?* That disappeared the day she stumbled into the sanctuary of Melangell's valley of virgins. *Children?* That's exactly what Nyneve had been to her. Even if she refused to own it now that she was grown.

Truly, what had she sacrificed midst the company of those who had given up so much?

Indeed, what had she ever risked? She'd passed from her family's protection to Melangell's then directly into Eifion's. She'd battled Artwr's bloody host when she was a girl but only because the alternative was the angry point of a warrior's sword. She'd walked away from her family and everything she knew, but only because her father's ongoing violation meant she could not remain. She'd travelled dangerous fortennights through the wooded valleys of Cymry but only because her choice was starvation.

Assuming responsibility for a chubby, hungry infant was the first stout choice she'd ever made and Nyneve had scarcely behaved like a monster so how brave was it, in truth? Plus, Eifion had been with her every step.

Everything courageous she had ever borne she had borne because she *had* to. Else she had not borne it.

Gwanaelle resumed her steady, oily strokes. 'Perhaps they are your kin, but *we* are your People. Never forget that, Nyneve. You belong with us because we are a family.'

A long silence fell.

'I will have to leave one day,' Nyneve finally murmured.

'You do not *have* to. You are welcome by our fire until we no longer need its warmth.'

We. As if Eifion would have any reason to stay once Nyneve had grown into her dragon-self.

But when Nyneve curled around to look at her, silently, it was not entitled and it was not the glare of an impatient child. It was the compassion of a young woman.

Gwanaelle sighed. 'But, yes, I do understand.'

Nyneve was not hers to keep. She never had been.

'How is that?' she eventually said, rubbing the last of the sop-weed's issue into Nyneve's skin.

The girl ran her light fingers over her troubled flesh.

'Better. Thank you.'

'Thanks, is it? Gods, who is this young woman?' She wiped her oily hands on her furs and smiled. 'We will hunt stream-serpent this se'nnight. Its greases will help you, perhaps.'

'Ugh.' Nyneve had ever preferred bloodier meat. The rawer the better. 'I detest eel.'

'Perhaps this will pass soon,' she murmured. 'When the cold sets in hard.'

Because surely this girl had been through enough without adding crumbling skin to her discomforts.

'I will ask Bleheris what it is. He has seen so much of the world. Perhaps he will know it.'

Yes. The Myrddyn's stories were the best part of every evening these past nights since Eifion left. Only they could take her mind from him. Where he was. What he was doing. Whether he was in good health as he fulfilled the mysterious pledge he had sworn to. If not for the fact that it was *Eifion* of whom she constantly thought, she would have believed his pledge to be a convenient deceit—some makeshift disguise—because he was too honourable a man to speak in untruths, but then again, this was *Eifion*, who had lived with her like a sister for nearly a score of winters and so that same honour may well have taken him away from them. And now she was worse off than ever 'fore she'd weakened and pressed her lips to his. For, not only was she robbed of his touch but now even his company had been snatched from her.

This is your own doing...

How often had her father whispered that, hot against her young ear? Blaming her fairness, the seductive tinkle of her laughter for his abuses. Anything but his own lack of fortitude. But it seemed that father had gifted more than just shame to his daughter.

She was heir to his frailty.

XVI

Trellech

Over the next se'nnight, Cai's mare plodded Eifion down out of the uplands, over the old Empirium road, back through the thick dark woods through which he and Melangell had fled all those winters ago, and south past Cai's old stronghold. Where it all had begun. Where Artwr had come to collect the prized Creil and found only his empty-handed brother. Where his vengeance had been born. Another Lord had sat in Crug Eryr's seat this many winters and though both he and his mount were in need of their hospitality he pulled her head away and passed purposefully by.

He would not set foot in Crug Eryr's great-hall again whilst Cai did not sit at its table.

The lands of Ylfael he had no choice but to cross and he did so, swiftly, pushing on past his exhaustion until he hit the River Gwyr, whereupon he turned the sinking sun to his back and followed its serpentine charms east.

Scarcely the most direct route to his destination but it was the surest.

East, then, under an ever brightening moon, the hefty maid between his thighs growing slower with every hoof-fall. He passed his sixth night wrapped tight in his furs curled beneath her belly where she stood, sleeping, on the scarp of the valley overlooking the lands of the Yrgyng chieftain. Come morning, they began the long plod south. Here, the Gwyr looped back on itself repeatedly as it found the softest earth to cut through and Eifion grew infuriated at the lost time but Bleheris had given warning that Yrgyng's vast, wild woods was home to an old and territorial *y Ddraig* as well as bear, boar, and arrant thieves which made wending his way through it on his merry little pack-mare carrying the pulsing shards of a dragon's egg the least clever thing he'd done in recent memory.

Yet despite the Myrddyn's warnings—or perhaps because of them—through it he passed comparatively unmolested save for the disguised attentions of a group of howling grey wolves he never did manage to see, though his trusty mare knew to a one where they lurked and her eyes rolled toward some seeming vacant spot in the trees now and again to remind him that they were there. Beneath towering Beech and Oak coated white with snow they trudged; between Alder and Sallow, Hazel and red-budded Celyn keeping the flowing Gwyr at all times on his left. Just before the cluster of dwellings that sat like watchmen at the mouth of the Mynwy where it met the Gwyr, he forded the river to avoid them, leading the nervous mare across a beaver dam. He had no time for a village full of curious folk with little left to do now that their harvest was complete but enquire into his purpose travelling so late into the time of *Gathering*. Let them think he, like many others, was travelling to a stronghold in time for Old Soul's Night.

When at last the activity of a small river harbour grew on the forward horizon, he turned his back on the Gwyr and headed up the steep valley-side toward the afternoon sun in search of the stronghold he'd come for: Trellech—somewhere to buy food, and dry grasses for his bed and the mare's breakfast. The last place he'd heard Artwr's two nephews had wintered. One of them as Chieftain of these flatlands high above the river.

He only hoped they were as content to set in a comfortable situation as they had been as boys. A trained rider could get up beyond the Pictish lands in the two winters since they'd been here. What if they were gone that far away?

He first rode wide around the base of the slope atop which sat the stronghold, well beyond it, before circling back around for the stones he sought, the three stones that gave the village clustered below the stronghold its name and that the Myrddyn had directed him to. Each had been raised by men from the time of the Old People, Bleheris had said, but each was buried into the dark earth bowed, aligned with one of the pure streams running under the village, marking their direction. It was not hard to find them, standing like dark guardsmen against the white-covered ground in an open field. The most looming of them pointed like a fat finger toward the very place he sought.

He looped the leathers behind the mare's head and left it to pluck what sweetness it could find above the snow, and he stood his back against the biggest of the stones, orienting himself by its course.

That way.

He drew the reluctant mare from its foraging and followed on foot the course the stone had set—through trees, over mounds—until he came to the most subtle of circles, grown-in and lost deep within the wood but a formal, treed circle none-the-less, and therein he found it.

Annais' well. A Queen of the Old People. One of this land's earliest inhabitants.

To a passerby, her well was invisible, impossible to see from any of the trails that ran through this wood. To a local villager or warrior, her spring was little more than a rocky place to refill a pigskin, but the pointing stones told him different. The overgrown circle of trees told him different. The fact that it was the only body of still water not crusted with ice told him different.

Earth-burrows never froze over. Nor dried out. It was part of their magic and their protection.

Eifion glanced in all directions for any sign of curious eyes, then he knelt at the well's mouth and drank deep, testing the water for the kind of purity he remembered from Melangell's valley.

It slid like sweet air across his tongue.

He checked again for anyone watching, braced himself against the cold and tugged first his furs, then his wears off until he was naked from the waist up. The approach of winter was not the cleverest time to attempt this. He pressed one hand on the stones on the back of the spring and plunged the other deep into its waters, reaching about in the depths below the witches-weed with no small amount of trepidation searching for signs that the well was occupied by anything other than the little frogs that he sent leaping all about. His fingers found nothing, so he stretched out flat out on the freezing snow and plunged his whole upper body under. Compared to the snow-peppered earth and the brisk air above, the water was pleasingly warm protected as it was by the earth. With closed eyes, he felt out with his hands deeper into the well where it bent around toward the trees, searching.

Nothing.

Whatever dragon's egg had first inhabited this well was now long gone, and no Morwyn Ddraig worth the name would bring an Ancient

One into seclusion here at the doorstep of what was now such a busy little village. Though perhaps this had once been as isolated as Melangell's valley. Once. He burst up from the hole and sucked in the sharp air, pressing up off the snow. His winter skin blushed as rosy as Gwanaelle's cheeks where the snow had burned it with cold. He crossed to the mare and unbound his leather fold then gently lowered it to the ground, letting the sides fall open. Inside, the Creil's shards waited as ever its whole self had—patient, understanding. He took the largest of the pieces—almost a full half egg—and placed the other pieces inside it, then he turned and knelt again where Annais' spring opened to the ground.

He was not about to just walk into a stronghold of Artwr's with something so valuable tucked under his arm.

This time, he welcomed the water's warmth. He submerged the egg and let it carefully fill, then followed it as it plunged to the well's bottom, tucking the Creil half into the deepest recesses of the spring. It did not block the flow but it wedged in there happily enough. Safe. Nurtured.

Content.

The mare leapt as Eifion burst back out into the air on a curse, the skin of his belly protesting the icy violence of the snow. It had wandered over to sup the precious weed spilling at the edges of the disrupted well and it did not content itself merely with what little now lay on the water's surface. Eifion stood, trembling in the cold air, as the horse whiffled its way over his bare skin, hotly lipping up the little plantlets and drafting him clean of them, only losing patience as his mind took him back to another day, another set of soft, persistent lips tracing his skin.

He shrugged the animal away. How thrilled Gwanaelle would be to be so likened to a pack-nag.

It took painful moments to shrug his wet self into his dry wears, then layer his furs on, and longer again to jog a few laps of the tree circle, rubbing his flesh back into burning life, but it was done. The Creil shards were secreted in a place and manner they would be content with and he could contact Gwalchafad with no risk of it being taken without his knowledge. Exactly when in the se'nnight's ride he'd started thinking of the shards of shell as a living thing and worrying about its satisfaction, he could not say. Perhaps simply because it was part of Nyneve, and he'd come to worry about her satisfaction on a daily basis.

Thoughts of home swamped in where his resolve should be and he cast anxious eyes toward the stronghold whose peaks he could see just above the wood. No doubt some of its inhabitants drew their water from this well with no sense of what it actually was. Or who first blazed it deep into the earth.

Or why.

A firm nudge from behind reminded him that his mare was cold when she wasn't moving and probably very interested in something more to eat than the witches-weed she'd liberated from his flesh. He gathered her leathers and tugged her easily behind him toward the looming grey of Trellech stronghold.

X V I I

Dragonhood

'THEIR HORN?'

'Ground into the forge to render swords—'

'Not just swords, Nyneve, any weapon cast through alchemy.'

Spears, axes, shields, but not wood. Not stone. 'All stronger. All unbreakable.'

'Good. Tears?'

'Binds him in thrall who consumes them.'

'Mouth-waters?'

She sighed. 'Heals flesh. As their blood gives the strength of giants and their egg gives the sight and their eyelashes make…seafaring ships for the little Drygioni.'

Bleheris glared at her dismal wit. 'Perhaps my wisdom no longer interests you, Child?'

Child. He always used that when he wanted her to feel most like one. 'Everything you say interests me very much… The first time,' she muttered, but even the greatest tale lost something of its power on relentless retelling.

'You need to know this as readily as taking breath, Nyneve. This is your People's culture.'

'No. It's not. Weapons and thrall and warring is Mankind's culture…' And once she was Ascended she wished to have nothing further to do with Man. She would take herself to the furthest reaches of this land and there stare at the sky from sunrise until set, and she would be content. 'What does dragon horn do for *the dragon* other than give it something to scratch with? Or its tears except make its eye more comfortable in the wind of flight? Or its blood other than give its heart something to beat with?'

'It may not matter what you wish, Nyneve. Someday your life will depend on understanding what the Men who find you want from you.'

He said that like it was such a given.

'My life will depend sooner on understanding what I am, and my mother's and father's too. Can you not find something more presently useful to teach me, Bleheris? I beg of you.'

He regarded her thoughtfully, then pressed to his feet. 'Come.'

It took only as long to cross the valley floor as it took the sun's weak brightness to illuminate the mist all around them. It glowed with the soft morning light of winter, though it would be some time yet before it managed to peek its face over the high ridges all around them, but there was enough warmth in it to rouse the smallest creatures of the valley about their daily business. Bleheris paused at a hornstalk that was near as tall as she was. At its top, a solitary little fellow quivered about its business on each of the blooms there, surely the last before the long winter to come.

'Magical creatures, honey-misers,' he began. 'What do you know of them?'

She gaped at him. She wanted tales of dragons, not insects, but she knew from experience what result protesting would have.

'Slow to take offence,' she answered, regarding the busy little fellow, 'but a talented swordsman when finally roused.'

'This is no swords*man*, Nyneve.'

She looked more closely at the rotund little fur-body. 'How can you know?'

'Because they are all female. As is their Mother deep inside their comb-house preparing to sleep the winter away.'

'There must be males?'

She'd at least learned that much from her visit every sun's march to Melangell's camp. From the women there and from the breathless dance between Cai and Melangell that was impossible to miss, there. A male and a female were required. That is why such division existed at all.

'One or two, perhaps. Outnumbered more vastly than were the last Druids standing against a tide of red-cloaks.'

Nyneve blinked.

'In their world,' Bleheris went on observing the busy creature, 'males are required only to service the Mother and then only once in her life. They die in the service of their duty. It is the only useful thing they do in their otherwise idle lives. Every grub the Mother will ever produce is seeded that very day.'

Nyneve studied the busy little quiver-woman up close. It crawled all over the yellow centre of the hornstalk busily stuffing what little sweetness it could gather into a ball under its back legs. Just one moon ago she would have been held utterly rapt by the simplest of glimpses at Bleheris' knowledge. Now, she had nothing but impatience.

'Why do you waste time with tales of honey-misers?' she puffed.

'So that you know it is quite possible in the world already,' he murmured, low and even, 'before I tell you that all Ascended dragons are female...'

Her eyes rushed back to his. Suddenly that gentle little creature became the sole focus of her curiosity. *Female only.* All of them?

'...and that every young she will ever produce is similarly seeded during one single encounter.'

'Seeded by who, if all dragons are females?'

'That is not what I said.'

Ugh, that slow Bard's way of his could drive her to madness. Not all tales needed to be spun like weavers-web. 'Yes, you said—'

'That all Ascended dragons are female.'

Ascended. Come into their dragonhood.

Nyneve's quick mind raced. 'So, there can be a male dragon? Just not ascended?'

'There is no 'dragon' until there is Ascension, Nyneve. Even you are not *y Ddraig*, not yet.'

She had only just discovered who she was. She was hardly ready for it to be taken from her, so soon. 'Then what *am* I? And what are they?' Were males born Man-like as she had been? Or were they wriggling grubs like the infants that fell from a broken comb-house?

Or were they something else altogether?

Her mind grew fevered. 'So, all dragons start life looking like me, but they become *y Ddraig* if they are female?'

'And when they are ready, they lay their eggs across this wide land, and their ancestors' line continues.'

When Bleheris said 'theirs' he, of course, meant 'yours'. That is, hers.... *Her* Ascension. *Her* eggs. *Her* continuing line. There was an obvious gap in that tale—*her* mating—but she would have to wait for Bleheris to return to it. Having seen the rutting animals in the valley, she was in no rush for the details despite her curiosity.

'And they will be females? The eggs that I lay.'

'Almost certainly.'

'But first I must find some man to mate with—just once—and that will do me for the rest of my life?'

'Not a Man, Nyneve. *Y Ddraig.*'

She frowned. The idea of laying with some...beast...did not appeal, even as she remembered that she, too, would become such.

'But males are un-Ascended?'

'Yes.'

Relief filled her. Not beasts. 'So they're...boys?'

She could not bring to mind how a boy could mate with a full-grown dragon and survive but it seemed far better than the opposite. Unless he did not. *They die in the service of their duty.* Were dragons just like the honey-misers—did female dragons *eat* un-Ascended males down into the same bellies that grew fat with eggs and have it done that way?

The idea of swallowing whole some hapless boy cheered her enormously.

'You imagine they stop growing at their fortenyear just because you Ascend then?' Bleheris tutted. 'They grow to be old, Nyneve. Very old, often, though never quite as ancient as the females.'

Old, powerless Men.

'Well, I imagine that a man tastes much like a boy when you're swallowing him,' she quipped.

Bleheris frowned but did not correct her. That was a rare circumstance, indeed.

'Come,' he said, instead. 'It is time to really test you...'

Yvain

'YOU ARE NOT known here, stranger. Fuck off.'

The biggest of the guards at the gate to the stronghold had reserved his poor opinion of Eifion only for the length of time it took the messenger he sent up to the great-hall to return with their Lord's refusal, but he abandoned all pretence of courtesy now that the man standing before him was of no consequence whatsoever. The Gwalchafad he knew was too sensible and quiet a youth to have grown into the kind of man who could forget the friends of his past no matter the years passed, but his friend had always been furnished with a deviousness to rival the Fair Folk.

Eifion sighed and saw the trap Gwalchafad had laid for him. 'Tell him it's... *Yvain.*'

Every mouth in earshot twitched—those that weren't already busy sneering. The name may have been a strong one across the sea in Brittany, but here in Brython it meant something very different—that place in a woman that a man loved best, and feared most. As boys, Gwalchmai and Gwalchafad had delighted in butchering his own name in favour of it until it fasted to him like a plague sore on skin.

'If you seek to earn your way into this fortress with promise of a ripe cunt, you've picked the wrong Lord, stranger.'

As if the watchman had not given him enough reason already to put him through with a blade... He'd first heard the slur whilst buried too deep in a whore to take the proclaimer to task and while Eifion had ample memory of Gwalchafad' passions from their youth, for his own watchman to scoff at it—*at him*—so publicly...

He reached back over his shoulder.

'Stand down, Man, before *Yvain* fashions you a convenient one of your own betwixt shoulder and ear.' A pale, serious face pushed between the armsmen clustered at the stronghold's entrance, blocking Eifion's entry. It was framed by long, straight hair the colour of Gwanaelle's. Far too clean to have seen any time on the road recently. 'You never could enjoy a jest, old friend.'

The man-at-watch blanched. Had it truly only just occurred to him that the stranger might be known to his Lord? Just how shabby did he look? Eifion forced steel into his expression and stepped up closer. 'It has been a lifetime since any dared call me *Yvain* to my face.'

Around them, the soldiers' fingers twitched.

Gwalchafad snorted, utterly unconcerned by Eifion's menace. 'Nor understood how prodigiously you earned the title.'

They seized each other by the forearms and held there. 'It is good to see you, Eifion, by whatever name.'

'And you, friend.'

They turned from the guards who silently parted to allow them through as a boy appeared from nowhere to take the mare. Only the man-at-watch continued to regard him with unease; the rest returned easily to their boredom. Gwalchafad studied him as they crossed the stronghold's yarden; that intense, almost uncomfortable way he always had. Like he was looking right into his soul. 'What happened to you, Eifion? You got old.'

'And you flabby, Gwalchafad.'

'Blame Gwalchmai,' he snorted, sucking in his gut. 'He named me Thane only a few winters after Artwr brought me into his company. Now my roamings are restricted from bed to negotiating table and back again, and the greatest weight I lift is a counting block.'

A stone made itself known deep in his belly. 'Thane, is it?'

A *Thane* was not a man who could simply ride into Artwr's court, unannounced and deliver him a great prize. Not as easily as his warrior brother could...

Gwalchafad's lips twisted. 'A better use of my skills, it seems.'

There was more to that story, for certain. All he had ever wanted as a boy was to become a warrior to rival his brothers, Gwalchmai and Agrafane.

'I believed you dead,' Gwalchafad murmured.

'Not dead, as you see. I've been in…the North.' And he wasn't about to discuss Cai with anyone. Even a trusted, old friend.

'Yes, I can see.' Eifion glanced down at his wears, but he knew clever Gwalchafad well enough to doubt the casual indifference in his voice. 'And now you are not?'

He had practised this aplenty on the long journey down here. 'Passing, merely. I chanced to see if my old friends still remained in Trellech, but have I found only one brother at home?'

'Agrafane has returned to our border lands. Gwalchmai is in Caerllion for Old Soul's Night. At his Lord's side, as is expected of a Second.'

'Yet you are not?'

Gwalchafad slid him a sideways look. 'Have you been dwelling in a cave in those Northern mountains of yours?'

Eifion stopped, stared. He was so much closer to the truth than he knew.

'You must have heard… About Artwr's decree?'

A fist curled in Eifion's chest but he didn't know why.

'I was removed from Caerllion twelve winters ago,' Gwalchafad explained, as if it were nothing. 'I am no longer welcome in Artwr's Company without summons.'

With those simple words, Eifion's plans to have Pendragon kin deliver up the Creil to Artwr shrivelled to a dried currant. 'Why?'

He waved the question away. 'A…discord.'

And Gwalchmai made him Thane of Trellech so that his warrior's seat would no longer be empty in the Pendragon's great-hall. One man could not hold both positions. 'What could come so between uncle and nephew?'

Gwalchafad slashed a dark, sideways look. 'Half-uncle.'

Interesting. His plan with the Creil may have received a blow but his chances of developing an ally against Artwr just crept up. Small mercies.

Silence fell and, in it, Eifion remembered what it was that an ordinary traveller warrior should care most about. 'You will be feasting to Old Souls here, I presume,' he asked Gwalchafad. 'There will be mead?'

'Mead. Song. Any number of accommodating orifices.' His fine wrists waved. Beneath the pale skin, a dark vein beat, determined.

'Trellech may be small but it is as modern and civilised as ever Caerllion was.'

And suddenly this stronghold made a good deal more sense. Artwr would have wanted to keep his proud warrior nephew within a day's demand, but the disgraced one suitably far away from his Company.

'Then I look forward to celebrating with you and seeing more of these lands.'

That was a lie. All Eifion looked forward to was the speedy return north to Gwanaelle and Nyneve as soon as the Creil was surrendered, but a request such as that took trust and trust needed a little time to regrow—even between childhood friends.

Gwalchafad pushed through the big doors to the stronghold's great-hall. Gods, how long had it been since he'd stood in one? Yet they hadn't changed scarce at all in all those years.

'Extraordinary weaves,' he commented, scanning the room. Wherever there was wall enough, a massive weave hung there, celebrating acts of violence, debauchery, cruelty and valour. Central to them all was a massive weave featuring what he could only assume was supposed to be *y Ddraig*. It looked more like a serpent with stumpy little legs and ugly, beady eyes, breathing an indiscriminate fire at some hapless warrior that was way too big compared to it. Clearly the artist had never seen a real dragon and whoever paid richly for that weave clearly had not, either. Then again, he'd only ever seen the one. Who was to say that they did not all look quite different. If he had to choose, he preferred the beautiful proportions, glinting hide, soulful eyes and deadly flame spout of Nyneve's mother.

'My brother chooses to surround himself with his favourite aspects.'

'Yet he is not pictured?' Eifion said, carefully, sliding the sword of opportunity his friend's way.

Gwalchafad curled his hands in front of him. 'Modesty prevents him directly commissioning a weave of himself in some greatly heroic pose to hang behind the high seat of this hall. I feel its absence as, I'm sure, do you.'

Nothing in his friend's face gave him away but long-ago winters of listening to his grumbles as he squired for his arrogant older brothers betrayed him. Gwalchafad said the most when his face said the least.

'Fortunately, Gwalchmai's host are more than willing to pretend that the poems of his exploits sung by the Bards were not composed largely on their Lord's own ale. Or in a bed furnished by him with their first audience being some woman also furnished by him.'

Gwalchafad flung himself into his brother's seat with a certain amount of glee, leaving his own for Eifion to sit at. 'Tell me of *your* exploits, Yvain. what have you done since last we clashed iron? Other than grow most comfortably into your age. You must have to beat the whores back with your sword...' His brown eyes fell for the space of a heartbeat to Eifion's lap. 'It is as well Gwalchmai is not here; he would not welcome the competition on Old Soul's night tomorrow.'

It was no Beltane, but he remembered well enough the annual debauchery in the name of the dead. Or perhaps warriors and their men just found every opportunity for depravity. 'He has not taken a wife?'

Gwalchafad's eyes glinted. 'He has, and the wives of several others, asides, but neither intrudes on his full and proper respect for the dead on Old Souls night.'

Eifion lifted one brow. 'Does he imagine that your ancestors are concerned with how often he greases his sword?'

'Just as we enjoy meat and ale for the dead as they poke their heads through the thinned vale, Gwalchmai believes it his personal responsibility to enjoy a fuck for every one of them. too, and he takes his responsibilities *very* seriously.'

'He has not changed then?'

'Which of us has?'

Gwalchafad had.

Gone was the all-seeing boy who only spoke after the greatest consideration.

Grown, Gwalchafad was as fast with wit as his brother ever had been with a sword.

And both were equally dangerous.

X I X

Sight

CAN YOU SEE IT? Bleheris pressed directly into her mind. *Or feel it?*

If "it" was a darkness like the deepest cave, full of…nothing, then yes. 'How can I know what I should be seeing or feeling?'

'Females are not as finely tuned as males but you will know. It will be something that doesn't belong.'

She opened her eyes and glared at him. What did that mean?

'Just search, Nyneve. Tighten your senses bit-by-bit, the way I adjust the gut on my lute. You wanted to experience the Sight…'

She tried again, trying to imagine what tightening her senses might be. It almost certainly came with a scrunched face.

Bleheris sighed. 'Take a moment. You will weary yourself.'

Because she hadn't already? Exhaustion dogged her, much more than with any other exercises, even the difficult business of learning to speak with her mind, and along with the exhaustion, fear. Harder to explain but unquestioningly there. As though what she was doing was somehow dangerous.

'There will be something,' he murmured, and his skilled voice was like a gentle caress on her exhaustion. 'It doesn't fit here, in this valley, with me. It might not be big—a sound, a smell, a taste—but it will feel real. That is what the Sight is. Reality out of place.'

Her eyes opened. 'Could it be a fear?'

'The sensation, yes, that is possible. Since there is nothing around us to be afraid of. It does not belong.'

Nyneve clutched the sensation to her, curled her mind's fingers in it, then used them as nimbly as she worked with Gwanaelle to weave their cloth, tugging it closer to her, hauling herself toward the emotion.

'Darkness…' she murmured aloud because it helped. 'Water?'

This could simply be a memory from when she was curled up inside the Creil. Couldn't it?

'What else, Nyneve? Hunt!'

The searching was like a pain and every muscle in her body screamed with the effort. Like she'd done a weeks hard labour in one hour. That could not belong here, surely. She grasped the pain to her, too, and hauled, and as she did so she realised that it was not *her* exhaustion, nor *her* fear, nor *her* pain, but she followed it regardless…

Eifion!

She saw him then—felt him, really—bound and weakened and afraid, and wet. Like he was drowning. It was the fear that disturbed her the most.

In all her life she'd never seen Eifion truly afraid. Let alone felt it in her bones.

She spun urgently to Bleheris, startling him upright. 'This is a vision of what was? Or what is to be?'

'Or what could be right now,' he said, casually. 'As you grow in skill you will be better able to tell them—'

'Mother!' she cried out, shooting to her feet.

~

Gwanaelle knew enough of the power of *y Ddraig* to know not to dismiss Nyneve's vision as fancy, but she did check it with Bleheris, because so much was at stake.

'I'm sorry, Gwanaelle,' he said. 'The Sight cannot be commanded in that way. I cannot simply…peer in on Nyneve's vision.'

She glared at the old man. 'How true are they?'

'The visions of an un-Ascended *y Ddraig* lack reach but not faithfulness. She may not be able to see further than the few of us she already knows but *what* she sees will be truth. Whatever is causing Eifion's fear and exhaustion, it is real.'

'You will come with me,' she ordered Nyneve, mind spinning, 'and winter with Melangell while I go for Eifion.'

Wasn't it time she took a risk?

'Ugh.' The girl's anxiety for her father was never so great that she couldn't think of herself, first. 'Melangell hates me.'

'She does not, Nyneve.'

'Resents me, then.'

That she couldn't argue. Melangell had scarcely rushed to accept responsibility for the dragonling after she'd been born, having given her entire youth to the care of the Creil. Though, in fairness, none of them had understood that the Morwyn Ddraig's responsibilities even extended beyond the hatching.

Just as none of them had understood that *people* raising a dragon was a sentence of death.

Or should have been.

'You cannot stay here alone, Nyneve.'

'She would not be alone,' Bleheris murmured. 'I will protect her.'

'I cannot ask that of you, Bleheris.' In truth, she could not trust one of the land's most valuable mysteries to *a Myrddyn*, no matter how well she had begun to like him. 'Nyneve is my responsibility.'

If he knew her thoughts, he did not say.

'The girl yet has much to learn,' he urged, 'and not long to do it in. She will be a danger to herself and everyone if she ascends without the knowledge that she needs.'

Nyneve stared at him. 'I am not ascending until I know everything, Bleheris, and perhaps not even then.'

'Foolish child,' he dismissed on a puff of cold air. 'That is not in your power.'

'Fill your pack, Nyneve.'

Gwanaelle hoisted her own onto her shoulder then turned to the old man. 'You are welcome to remain in this valley, Bleheris. It is a good winter shelter.'

'I will not come,' Nyneve cried.

Gwanaelle had no further patience. 'Child! Eifion may already be in such danger…'

'Then go! Waste not a moment longer on me. Bleheris will be *my* guest.'

'Nyneve…'

'I am past my fortenyear,' she pressed. 'An equal member of this family, and this is my decision. I will stay with Bleheris and continue my learning. You should run as fast as you can to get aid.'

Gwanaelle turned her panic to Bleheris but found no deliverance.

'Go,' he urged. 'I will teach her. I will feed her. I will protect her. We two have much to accomplish while you are gone.'

Nyneve took her by the shoulders and turned her towards the trees. 'He *needs you*, Mother.'

Were any words ever designed more fulsomely to get her gone from this camp? All she'd ever wanted was a child and a man to love and protect, and here was her opportunity. Though protecting one meant leaving the other in the care of a Cunning Man…

But even as the thought occurred to her, another rushed in—bold, masculine and full of assurance—and swamped it away.

She is going to be well.

Oh. Then, what reason was there to stay if Nyneve was going to be safe?

'I will return as fast as I can,' Gwanaelle told Bleheris back over her shoulder, never thinking to second guess her own mind.

'As you need,' he said, stepping up beside Nyneve in a way that was at once resolute and proprietary.

~

'I felt that,' Nyneve murmured as they watched Gwanaelle disappear into the trees.

Bleheris did not move, did not look, but his body seemed to stiffen nonetheless. 'Felt what?'

'Whatever you just did to Mother. What was it?'

'She was going to take you to the next valley. Leave you there. Is that what you wanted?'

What she wanted to was to learn everything there was to know. The question was, why was Bleheris so determined that she should be cultivated now? This very se'nnight. This very moment.

'No.'

'There you are, then.'

'You have done this before,' Nyneve realised without knowing where the thought came from. Every time it happened she grew more and more familiar with how the Sight felt. The…rightness of it. Her inner voice backed it up.

Truth.

Bleheris did not remark on her ability to See. As though he simply expected it by now. 'Several times, yes.'

'With other dragons? Where?'

'North. Far from here. You may well be my last. I am getting too old for all this travelling.'

The idea of that was at once disappointing—that she should just be one of so many—and intriguing. She knew there must be others but to be standing next to a man who had met them…

'Who were they?'

'They are *y Ddraig*. The person they were no longer matters after their Ascension. Nor a single piece of their flesh remains.'

A thought flash came then, of a dark space, chunks of flesh bobbing on a barely moving pool.

She forced the disgusting image away.

The idea of changing into a beast was frightening enough without such graphic foreshadows. 'Do they have names?'

More usually, Bleheris answered questions with the barely tolerant air of someone who had heard them a score of times before, but that entreaty brought his head around and she recognised the brightness in his eyes.

Novelty.

'You are the first I have ever known with a name,' he allowed. 'The Morwyn Ddraig never speak to a dragonling except to teach it what it needs to know. They would not grant it a name any more than they tell it their own. They do not even hold the creature again once it can crawl on its own belly. It's how they were raised and it is how they raise *y Ddraig*. To be self-sufficient.'

'Never held?' she gasped. Imagine going an entire fortenyear without feeling the warm security of arms around you. Like some beast of the forest. Nor the quiet gift of conversation. Her own youth had been full of conversation, and learning and laughter. What would she have been like without any of it. 'Nor speak?'

'What use a skill that will expire upon Ascension? They teach the dragonling the words they will need to understand their world, but do not waste effort on teaching them to manipulate their tongue into the strangled sounds Man uses for speech. Such a stumpy, small bit of meat will be useless to them as *y Ddraig*.'

The thought again, of how her body should become a dragon's…

'Will I not be able to speak?' she asked. 'After I've Ascended?'

'You will have no need for speech.'

'But if I need to communicate. How will I?'

Like this, he pressed into her mind, but *you will not need to. Nor want to once you have found a quiet resting place to make your own.*

That might be fine for talking to Bleheris but how would she speak to her Mother? To Eifion?

How would she say goodbye?

'Will I remember?' she asked. 'After I've Ascended? Will I remember who I am and how I was?' And how life was, here in this little valley that was her whole world.

She turned and stared all about her, tried to imagine living a long, long dragon's lifetime in a valley like this one with none but her own thoughts for company. The ways of the Morwyn Ddraig might be harsh but—if nothing else—it prepared *y Ddraig* for the lifetime of solitude to come. How was she going to ever forget how *not lonely* a life could be… How was she going to mark every Sun's March without Gwanaelle to keep track of them on her skins? Or without Eifion's careful sense know just how many upland creatures they could harvest without permanently hurting their numbers?

'How will I learn?'

Bleheris slid his eyes sideways. 'The whole purpose of teaching you now is so that you will remember what you are taught. If you are to survive in a world dominated by Men you need to know about them as much as you.'

Surely that gave her an advantage, then, since she had been raised as one.

Perhaps, yes.

Bleheris turned his gaze back out to the forest where Nyneve could see nothing but trees. 'She keeps pausing. Looking back. Worrying about you.'

'She is my Mother. She will always worry about me.'

Another first. Defending Gwanaelle. Now that the valley was empty of all but the two of them, it suddenly felt much bigger. Yet tiny, too. Who was Bleheris, after all? This man who knew so much about the world and she so little. He could be withholding anything.

I am withholding much, he admitted, *but everything in good time. We have all winter.*

'No. We have only until Gwanaelle convinces Cai to go off in search of Eifion.' Then she would be back. In a se'nnight. A fortennight at the most.

The little rattle in her mind sounded and felt like a snort.

Everything in good time.

X X

Journey

THREE NIGHTS IN the forest when she should have been curled up in the rugs of her safe little shelter in her hidden little valley was more than enough to remind Gwanaelle of those awful weeks after she'd fled her family. It had been seventeen winters since she'd made that first arduous journey. Seventeen winters since she'd last been truly alone. The silence had nearly screamed. All sensible forest creatures had either fled south, by now, or were already in their deep burrows ahead of the onset of winter and so the only sounds in the forest were the heaves of her own breath as she trudged through fresh-fallen snow and the creak of the trees where they'd rubbed against each other like secret lovers.

Cai took little convincing to fly to Eifion's aid, even as Melangell remonstrated with him the risks of a *dead man* once again roaming these hills for all to see. Neither of them had any trouble at all believing that it was a vision of Nyneve's that had sent Gwanaelle running. They'd all had their share of visions from her when she was within the Creil.

'Eifion took my horse,' Cai frowned. 'I'll need to get another at the first village. You're sure he was heading south?' he checked.

'Yes. To Trellech.'

But she did not tell them who had told her that. Or how Bleheris knew. It was only the second secret she'd ever kept from her friends— the people who had saved her life—but she did not omit him because she wanted to. For some reason, she could not bring herself to mention Bleheris at all. The moment she thought of using his name her mind grew weighted, crowded, and she found that she could not say the word. She even tried other names for him—Myrddyn, seer, cunning man—but they wouldn't come either, and as she tried to talk her way around him she began to speak in riddles.

Melangell saw her struggle, but couldn't draw anything of sense from her. Instead, she just watched, suspicious.

And so Bleheris went unmentioned but Cai nonetheless gathered his sword and pack and prepared to jog south.

And that was what mattered, wasn't it?

'You cannot join him,' Melangell said now as Gwanaelle pushed also to her feet.

'I must. It is Eifion.' And so there was no question.

Compassion filled the older woman's eyes. 'What use will you be?'

'Much, I would have thought.' In truth, she'd thought of little else on the walk over here except how to ensure that Cai took her along. 'A warrior as tall and commanding as Cai travelling alone will draw attention. A noble woman travelling with a strapping sword-arm is surely more common.'

Alone, neither of them would pass unnoticed, but together...

Melangell's face crumpled with concern. 'You are scarcely a noble woman, now, Gwanaelle. Whatever you were as a child.'

So she knew. That should not surprise her. Melangell had intuited far greater secrets in her time. Not through any skill of the Creil's but through her own wit. 'I can be, once more. I will trade in a village for passable wears and the rest is in the deceit of my bearing.'

'Walk as tall as you like, Gwanaelle, it will scarcely undo the rigours of seventeen winters living wild.'

'Then *help me*, Melangell, instead of fighting me. This valley is filled with women fled from courts and villages and brothels. Put their past talents to use for one evening. Make this work.'

And so it was that Gwanaelle was scrubbed with frigid and magical well waters until her skin shone fair, her brows twined and tamed, her damp curls combed until they blazed their fiery colour, then braided and twisted into the current style by the newest refugee come to the sanctuary. The torn roughness of her fingers was rubbed through with the wax of a honey-miser's comb-house and the worn wears of her feet were exchanged for the most whole pair to be found in the valley. Much to the despair of its previous caretaker.

Finally, Melangell gave Gwanaelle the thick cloak right off her back.

'You may pin it back onto me when you return in safety,' she commanded, fixing it at her throat with Gwanaelle's own small, tarnished clasp and pressing it gently against her throat.

It was the closest she would ever hear to 'good luck' from the Morwyn Ddraig. Or approval, but she knew it for what it was and she curled her now-smooth fingers around her friend's. 'Thank you, Melangell.'

Melangell glanced at Cai, standing ready at the edge of the clearing, then crossed to him as Gwanaelle thanked each woman who had helped her with this artifice. When she was done, she moved to stand by the warrior's side, as small against him as a child. Still, that would only benefit their deceit...

'Safe journey, Gwanaelle.' Melangell said as she released her love from her grasp. 'Bring him home.'

She meant Cai but Gwanaelle was thinking of Eifion.

'We will all be back, soon enough,' Cai affirmed in that authoritative way he had. The voice of the King's sword-arm, still. When he said it, they all believed it.

His confidence warmed her more than any cloak.

With no further sentiment, he turned and simply stepped into the trees, leaving her to scrabble after him, newly polished, cleaner and softer than she'd been in seventeen winters.

~

Their first camp was a meagre shelter but with Cai's big body to break the gusts cutting up the valley-side, trees to break the snowfall and a small fire crackling, it was adequate. Gwanaelle had soaked a corner of her cloak with her own waters in order that the clasp at her throat would shine with its true nature. She'd squatted off in the trees but had no choice but to return to the fire's warmth to do her polishing.

Cai's grey eyes narrowed as her pungent scrubbing took effect on the tarnished little clasp.

'You've had that all this time?'

Through the Darkness. Through the battles with Artwr. Through lean winter after lean winter in their little valley. A fortenyear of them, and this clasp the whole time pinned close to her heart. 'It was my mother's.'

The only thing she had left of the woman that she'd loved and the comfortable life that she'd fled. The harder she rubbed, the shinier it grew. Back to its original silver.

'That delicate clasp says *noble* more clearly than any clever braids or fancy wears,' he pointed out. 'Its ore could feed a village.'

'Or buy us horses, food and comforts for our journey and with coin left over for the return.' She would snag Melangell's thick cloak shut with bramble if she needed to. 'Eifion needs it now.'

Frosty eyes regarded her for silent moments. 'You are loyal, indeed, Gwanaelle, to surrender something so treasured.'

Or foolish, depending on your view. 'Eifion has protected me most of my life. It is nothing in return.'

'You still look on him softly?' Cai murmured.

Humiliation stole her reply and so she focussed on scrubbing seventeen winters of smut off her clasp.

Cai dropped his head lower, to catch her downcast gaze. 'But he still refuses?'

The memory of Eifion's powerful body pressing her face-down into her furs as he pressed himself between her thighs... It wasn't much of a memory, but it was something. Not that it changed anything between them. Least not for the better.

'He is...indifferent.' Or he was. He seemed even more set against her after she had enticed him.

'He has given his life over to your protection. That does not speak to me of disinterest.'

'The dragonling's life. I was merely her bearer, as ever Melangell was while Nyneve was still within the Creil.'

Cai frowned. 'I do not believe that. Eifion would never have let you leave us, alone, either.'

'He is the best of men,' she affirmed. 'And thus he is welcome to the best of my possessions.'

In truth, he'd already taken that, but that was not for Cai to know.

'You know why he travelled to Trellech?'

Yes. To take himself far from her and from what they'd done. His honour wouldn't allow anything else. 'No. Only that he has gone there.'

Though Bleheris probably knew. She hadn't asked for fear of the answer and he hadn't offered.

'He has taken the Creil shards,' Cai murmured.

Her head snapped up. 'He still has them?'

'If he buried them at all a fortenyear ago they did not stay buried. He takes them now to my brother's Second. Artwr's nephew.'

After everything they had done to avoid Artwr getting his hands on the Creil... She croaked past the sudden fist grown in her throat. 'Why would he do such a thing?'

Her confusion and concern were tempered by the leap of hope that he had genuine business in the south.

'He would not have left you and Nyneve alone unless he believed he was saving your lives.'

'But we were not alone, we—'

A shriek out in the darkness drew both their focus and her speech dried up. Her mouth fell silent and shut. She frowned. They were not alone, they were with the Myrddyn; she could think it yet why could she not say it? Had Eifion not been able to speak of Bleheris either, to have not told his most trusted friend? Suddenly the Cunning Man's mysterious arts seemed far more dangerous than she'd believed. If they ever needed help against him, how would they ask for it? How would anyone, if they could not bring his name to lip?

'Did it not surprise you to hear that we *were* alone?' she tested, mostly to see how close she could go to him before words failed. 'That he did not bring us with him and leave us in your valley while he travelled south? After a fortenyear of loyal protection?'

'He seemed very set on his path.' But then Cai frowned. 'Though, it does seem amiss, now, at this greater distance.'

'And I....' She began, though even as she did her train of thought began to wander and she found herself thinking about the clasp in her fingers. The day her mother had first given it to her. The last time she had pinned it over her heart... But she forced her mind onward. Her blood thrummed hard enough to feel in her throat. 'That I have left Nyneve alone in our valley. A dragonling, unprotected.'

None had expressed concern when she arrived in the yew valley. Not Melangell. Not Cai. Nor any who knew Nyneve. Who, as far as they knew, languished alone in the valley with no protection. Cai's brows dropped, now, as he tried to grasp his mind onto that concern but could not. As if he knew he should be worried by it but could not hold the thought long enough to indulge it. His eyes flicked to her clasp and cleared of confusion.

'That silver will feed a village.'

Gwanaelle blinked and grasped on to her surprise like the slipperiest of eels. 'Yes. So you have said, Cai.'

He pressed to his feet, his long legs towering him over her, irritated to be corrected. 'I will walk the fire's circle. Ensure we are safe.'

Was this how the Myrddyn defended their own secrets? By wiping themselves from all the minds of any who would dwell on them?

But, no, not from their minds because she could think of him well enough, she just could not speak of him.

Cai grunted as he stepped to the edge of the fire's circle, amongst the trees, and he seemed to transform, then, into a shadowy memory figure—silvery, stooped—standing at the edge of the trees in their waterfall valley, watching Melangell scrubbing a naked Nyneve under the cascade days before her fortenyear. She remembered, in that moment, having seen Bleheris there days before he had arrived, too.

Her anxious gasp brought Cai's eyes straight back to her. 'But that means—!'

And as quickly as the realisation came, it was gone again.

'Gwanaelle?'

She snapped her gaze back to his and when she next relaxed her mind it was to wonder what she had been doing a moment before. Cai had been speaking of the Creil, and of Eifion taking it to Artwr. But he'd been seated at the fire, then, and now he was weaving through the trees guarding against any lurking dangers.

What had she been doing just heartbeats ago? Her eyes fell to the places that shine was returning to her besmirched clasp. When had she polished it so far?

A coal fell loose in the fire and sent up a pillar of sparks. Perhaps she'd been tending the fire moments ago? And Cai gone for fresh wood.

She glanced once again to Cai's shadowy shape and frowned at the fanciful sense that she'd seen it before somewhere.

But then the patina on her clasp drew her concern again and she resumed rubbing it with her sodden patch of weave.

'All is well, Cai.' She almost hummed. 'All is well.'

XXI

Old Soul's Night

PERHAPS THIS feast should be renamed *No* Souls Night because surely there could not be a single soul left in any village within a day's ride of this stronghold. The compound writhed with feasters, all packed in around the enormous all-fire lit in its heart to warm the dead as much as themselves.

Eifion lurked around the fringes of the space, watching Gwalchafad, watching his men—watching the disguised places they ducked in and out of the stronghold when they thought none was looking—all the while appearing to watch only the women strutting and flaunting and presenting their best assets for consideration. Of which there seemed to be an unnaturally large number. The *true* daughters of god were ahome behind locked doors on this night marking Old Soul's night privately, and so those number left here were the least Christian women in these lands. Whores mostly but not all. The challenge for the men of Trellech was to find the few that were not—more chance of coming away with some sickness of the flesh, but less chance of having to pay coin to sink into some field girl at her first Feast, and drunk men were ever short-sighted.

'Surely this number are wasted with Gwalchmai so far from home,' Eifion called out when next the stronghold's Thane passed unsteadily by.

'Women are never wasted in a stronghold,' Gwalchafad tossed back, his wispy hair blowing loose around his face. 'And my brother will not be going without at Caerllion, believe me.'

His serious face seemed to pucker for a moment. Thinking about past Old Soul's Nights, perhaps? Back when he wasn't out of favour with Artwr.

'You have been guarding that single pot for some time, Yvain,' Gwalchafad said, sinking down beside him, reminding him that surveillance went two ways. 'Is Trellech's mead as displeasing to your tastes as its women appear to be? Or have the ancestors brought me an old friend with new tastes as an Old Souls gift?'

He steeled himself against the urge to take a large swig from his cup—or to bend some woman over a bale—just to prove his friend wrong, but Gwalchafad had toyed with the minds of his friends for all the winters of their youth, and resisting his ploys was the fastest way to best him. Ultimately, Gwalchafad took as much pleasure from losing his battles as his more famous brother did from winning them.

More, perhaps, because finding a better mind was so rare for him.

Eifion snugged the bowl more firmly in his grasp but did not drink from it. 'The night is long, friend. If I am to be standing at the end of it I need to take care now.'

And if he was to be able to spot the right moment to take advantage of then he could not be clouded by fermented sweet-stuffs.

Gwalchafad grunted and eased himself back against the timber walls of the long-hall with great show. 'You have grown soft.'

Better he believe that.

'What does Gwalchmai do for the Chieftain now?' Eifion asked after moments.

'Anything Artwr asks.' Gwalchafad shrugged, happy to be led to a new discussion. 'He is the high Chieftain's Second. Greatly adored. Much the favourite. A brother, almost, since Artwr lost Cai.'

Lost? It was a battle not to scoff. The Pendragon drove his brother's glorious reputation into the dirt with his furious vengeance.

'Gwalchmai is named *Gauwain* in Artwr's great hall,' Gwalchafad went on.

Eifion took a sip of the excellent mead. *Closed sheath?* 'I cannot believe the boy I remember has trouble finding any sheath more than willing to open for him.'

Gwalchafad snorted. 'Because his sword is so often employed in Artwr's name, it rarely requires its own sheath.'

'From nephew to brother,' Eifion observed. Then he took a risk. 'Gwalchmai might well remember what care Artwr takes of his brothers.'

Far too many winters had passed for news of Cai's 'death'—and the supposed treachery that led to it—to have remained only in the north, but that was compassion, not judgement, on Gwalchafad's face.

'I was saddened to hear of Cai's passing. He was a great warrior.'

The greatest. Who else did people imagine raised a young Artwr to be the leader he was—Cynyr fucking Forkbeard? That man was skilled in nothing but treachery and death.

Eifion raised his draught in sad salute. It was the first honest thing he had done since arriving at the stronghold. 'To Cai.'

They both swallowed deeply.

'Why are you here, Yvain?' Gwalchafad turned suddenly sharp eyes to him. 'Truly?'

He should have guessed that his friend wasn't fooled by his paltry excuse. He turned to face him front-on.

'Would you return to Artwr's hall? If you could once again be welcomed there?'

Gwalchafad's eyes glowed, but he did not answer. He regarded Eifion steadily. Still, the fact that he remained seated meant he was interested.

'If you could bring something to him,' he went on. 'Something that would transform this war with the Angles. Something that might earn back Artwr's favour.'

The man's shoulders stiffened. 'Such a transformative *something* might be better spent earning *your* favour back with the Chieftain. No?'

So Gwalchafad knew more than he'd said. That shouldn't be a surprise, but if others suspected that he was of such interest to Artwr then his very presence here at the stronghold was riskier than he'd imagined.

'It cannot be me,' Eifion murmured. 'Would you accept the risk if the rewards were great enough?'

His friend skipped right over the *reward* part. 'Risk? What exactly would I be bringing him?'

'A...weapon,' Eifion confessed broadly.

'Artwr seems to have a surfeit of talented swords already. Growing out of stones and burbling up from the most mysterious lakes.'

Which meant he believed neither tale. 'No sword, Gwalchafad. Something rarer.'

An old whore strode up to them, her massive breasts bared despite the cold and thrust them out in such a way that they jiggled enticingly for both men in the flickering firelight. Gwalchafad turned his gaze away, bored, but the whore took no offence. She simply turned her wears to Eifion. He reached into his pocket as though they were full of coin and gave her his second-to-last one.

'Dance for us.'

The woman blinked. 'Dance, sir?'

'And…touch yourself,' he improvised.

She looked to the most senior man in the stronghold and Gwalchafad just shrugged. 'He's from the North.'

He might have said *'he's taken a blow to the head'*. The woman nodded with such understanding.

'Not here,' Eifion commanded. 'Back a little where we can see you…. Back…'

While a dancing, touching whore was holding court before them, no-one else would interrupt their conversation, but he didn't want her overhearing, either. 'Just there. Yes. Now be sure to give us the coin's full worth.'

The whore would know to the moment how much half-naked dancing an old coin of the Empire was worth. She began to move to the rhythm of the drum and lyre being played across the yarden, clumsily, awkwardly, her arms and her cold-mottled breasts swinging in opposition to each other. For a moment neither man could speak thanks to the spectacle but soon enough, Gwalchafad picked up the conversation where it had been interrupted and, as Eifion might have expected, he'd used the time to think.

'Artwr has sent men out to the furthest corners of this land in search of his rarities,' Gwalchafad murmured. 'Yet none returned with anything of particular value. Why would I risk myself for your…trinket?'

Eifion leaned in again and locked eyes on his as meaningfully as he could. 'Because it is not a trinket.'

Curiosity blazed in Gwalchafad's gaze, and strategy, and a healthy dose of suspicion. 'I think I would need to know more in order to decide the risk for myself.'

Eifion held his gaze. Negotiating was Gwalchafad's purpose, now, but even Thanes could be swayed by iron will. 'I need your commitment first.'

His friend's face hardened in a way that Eifion had never seen. The reward of a life close to Artwr? Eifion thanked the gods for the life he'd had instead, no matter its challenges.

'Perhaps you would like me to jiggle my udders before you like this whore?' Gwalchafad gritted. 'Until you are satisfied I can be trusted.'

'You would do no different,' he urged. 'And you will understand when you…understand.'

The ridiculousness of it struck Gwalchafad first. The granite expression eased into a scornful one. Then something that was almost a smile. Though it scarcely disarmed him. 'Words still not your gift, Yvain?'

'Never were,' he acknowledged. As long as he was getting what he needed he wouldn't begrudge Gwalchafad the odd home strike. The Creil would go with Gwalchafad, Gwalchafad would go to Artwr, and then, all being well, Artwr would be so consumed with his powerful new weapon he wouldn't be quite so fixated on capturing another dragon for his stronghold.

Gwalchafad's mind worked busily behind shadowy brown eyes.

'We are friends, Eifion,' he said, leaning in close, his words short puffs of mist, 'and so I will curb my natural inclination to have my men-at-arms toss you in our bolt-house for this insolence in my brother's own stronghold, and I will, instead, consider the circumstances of your arrival.'

He shifted and resettled. 'You risk much coming this close to Caerllion, given which warrior you served last time anyone heard of you and given what he let slip from his grasp back then.' His eyes grew steely. 'Yet—*given which warrior you served last time anyone heard of you*—I have a seeping sense as to the value of this…*not-trinket* of which you bring news.'

The oblivious whore stumbled against the fog her spinning had given her but managed a deep and theatrical bow before she tucked her breasts somewhat back into her wears, popped the coin in between them, and hurried off to find someone else to dance for.

'And given that seeping sense,' Gwalchafad finished, ignoring her departure entirely, 'I am prepared to commit to hearing you out, at least, and to doing whatever I can to help you. But if it endangers me or my brother beyond reason, then you will understand when I ask you to ride on with your trinket and put someone else's life in peril.'

Eifion studied his dark features before agreeing. 'Good enough.'

'But not tonight.' Gwalchafad sat back against the wall. 'Tonight we welcome our ancestors back with music and drink, we don't embroil them in political schemes. We shall meet on this matter when the sun is high.'

He pushed himself onto his feet and went to move away but then turned back. 'Now, for Gods' sake, will you fuck something?'

XXII

Whore

TRUTH BE TOLD, Eifion had never felt less like a fuck in his long life, and only half of it was concern for this scheme he was undertaking. There were any number of women here within the chilly stronghold who would gladly wrap around the cock of a clean, sober, *warm* warrior—with coin or without—but the idea of putting it anywhere else after it had been inside Gwanaelle…

Ever again…

He glanced up at the dancing whore who stood, peering back at him from the shadows. She tilted her head curiously. Hoping for another coin of the Empire perhaps?

'Back for a touch this time, warrior?' she said when he stood and crossed to her. She freed her breasts again in anticipation. Up close she was not quite as old as her manner had suggested. 'You can suck one, if you like. Without charge. Happy to have them warmed by a talented tongue.'

He held up his last coin. Silver this time; the one he'd been saving.

'Will this get me into the shadows with you?' he urged, nodding to a place tucked away behind a stack of straw around behind a storehouse.

Her eyes bulged the way a dead man's did. 'My love, that will get you into *my* shadow several times over.'

'None of that,' he murmured, taking her by her cold-ravaged hand and leading her toward the straw. 'But I will require another performance.'

'Whoever would have thought my dancing would ever be quite so sought after…'

'No,' he chuckled. 'I think there's been enough dancing.'

He led the woman into the gloom behind the straw. 'Now kneel, please.'

Whether he was the first man ever to give her a please or a thank you or whether she was simply taken aback at his sudden change of heart she knelt before him even as her face crumpled into a guise of confusion. The ample curve of her skirted arse and her wool-covered ankles poked out in the fire's lingering light for all to see while the rest of her—and all of him—disappeared into the straw stack's shadow.

'Now what?' she frowned up at him.

'Now just...jiggle a bit. So it looks like you're...'

She peered up at him. 'You gave me an old silver noggin to just *look like* I'm sucking on your pipe?'

'Yes. Please.'

'Why don't I just suck it, then? Since I'm down here'n all?'

'Thank you. No.'

'*Thank you, no.*' She gaped. 'Are all you Northlings this touched?'

'You've just earned a whole night's pay without once getting your skirts dirty. Perhaps fewer questions would be wise.'

She started to rise. 'I think perhaps *more* questions would be—'

'Stay.' Eifion pressed down on her shoulder. 'I may be the only man here who isn't looking for...this...tonight, but I can't let them know that.'

She looked like she wanted to argue, but then her expression cleared. 'Oh! I thought you were just talking to him.'

Eifion blinked. 'Who?'

'His Thaneship. I wondered why he were glowering so much while I was dancing. Right you are, one false pipe-job coming up. Though no doubt its him you'd rather be tooting on it. Imagine away, warrior. Close yer eyes if it helps.'

'Wait,' Eifion said. 'You're talking about Gwalchafad ap Gwyar?'

'Who else? He's the most famous around these parts known for his...pipery.'

The whore seemed inordinately pleased with her own wit.

'What do you know of it? Of him?'

'Oh, I know plenty about himself,' she snorted.

'Such as?'

Caution flooded her face. 'What's he to you, first?'

'We were friends, as boys. I've not seen him for a score of winters. Trying to get a sense of him. What do you hear from your...fellows?'

The whore began a slow rocking motion in and out of the light, and just clasped either side of his hips for balance. 'Well, I hear nothing first-hand from the women, of course...'

Of course.

'But I hear plenty from the men we take coin from. He's a nasty one, that. Cold and clever. Always looking for the advantage in everything.'

'You describe half the men of Artwr's court. They're trained to find the advantage.'

She glared up at him. 'He's not just ruthless. More'n one man he's betrayed. Gone back on his word. To be honest we're all grateful that he prefers his entertainment pucked rather than furrowed so none of us have had to be victim to him.'

Faithless. Ruthless. The man she described was not the boy he'd known. The man she described sounded more like his brother had been. 'Ruined by his older brother perhaps?'

'Oh, *Gauwain* we do know about first-hand and in much detail. Strong, loyal-to-the-death to Artwr, a pleasure to look upon. Golden-tongued, that one, and a pleasure to lay with, though I can't say that one from my own personal doings,' she grumbled.

No, something told him Gwalchmai wouldn't lower himself to a whore of this standard.

'Not arrogant? Not self-absorbed?'

The bobbing continued. 'Yes to all of that, from what I've heard, but that describes most of the warring men in Cymry. Yet not where it counts. He's stuck with his brother through it all, and that takes quite a serve of character given what his Thaneship done.'

'Simply for being over-fond of his fellow warriors?'

That scarcely required much courage on Gwalchmai's part. His brother was scarcely the first—or the last—to prefer the hard, tight fit of a man.

The whore snorted. 'For killin' their own mother dead.'

Eifion's cry was almost as high as the whore's as he dragged her up to her feet. 'What?'

'Back all those winters when he still sat in Artrw's hall,' she babbled, and it seemed to Eifion that her voice softened, smoothed out a little in her fluster. 'You must know the tale. All the Bards were singing it.' But as he just stared at her and she realised she was not in peril after all, she obliged him with fulsome detail. 'Because his mother was bending over for that young warrior, Lamorak.'

Eifion shook his head to understand. 'Why would a son care who his widow mother was rutting?'

'Widow at the hands of Lamorak's sire, winters past,' she explained as if he were the most delightfully simple fellow she'd ever met, 'and so Gwalchafad lopped off the Lady Gwyar's head for the insult against his father.' She glanced around her, then leaned in closer. 'Or so the Bards sang.'

Did she know that her rough, country accent had fallen quite away in her distraction?

'And you think not?'

'Her *maids* thought not and told such to any who ask in whispered voice. The Lady Gwyar was seeking the bloodprice for the murder of her husband, they say—a son for a husband—and she made bait of herself so her own flesh could catch them at it in some half disguised place and Lamorak be dispatched in righteous defence of a mother's honour.' She took a much needed breath and her face crumpled. 'But the wrong son was baited when he waylaid the messenger, and Gwyar was not expecting quiet Gwalchafad's vengeance to be equally against *her*. He lopped off her head with one stroke and Lamorak's still-hard member with the backward pass, 'til the young warrior succumbed to his own spurts.'

Gods, if ever cock-sucking fell out of favour, this whore could grow fat on her story weaving.

He sagged back against the stacked straw. 'Artwr banished Gwalchafad for exacting a bloodprice, merely? The law of the land? Why?'

Artwr himself had exacted it many a time.

The whore cursed and her roughness returned. 'Is everyone in the North as dim as you? Artwr banished him for killing his *sister*. Half, anyway, and, yes, he then would have struck him dead by the bloodprice if not for his brother-lord's forswearing.'

'Gwalchmai recalled him here, instead? Made him Thane?'

'No-one in Artwr's hall was going to stand next to a man—fight by him—who is so inconstant when roused. No doubt my Lord thought this to be a place and role his brother couldn't find further trouble.'

'But he does?'

'He punishes everyone for Artwr cutting short his glorious progress at court. He just goes about it differently. Sneaky-like. Worser.'

Eifion stared at her.

'How do you know all this?' And more rightly, 'Why tell me?'

The whore's expression grew shrewd. 'The *how* is the same way that you warriors know all about the habits of your enemy right down to when and where they shit. We gather it because our lives depend on it if you snatch the wrong man's coin.'

'And the *why*...' She frowned up at him, her reddened eyes haunted. 'That's harder to tell, except that you've been generous with your coin and civil to a whore which is more than any of us have seen in this stronghold for winter on winter. You call both lords by the names their poor headless mother gave them, yet you are never before seen in Trellech and cannot know what either man has become. If your dirty old silver isn't to buy a warm rest for your cock tonight then let it buy you something more useful, warrior-traveller. Let it buy my most serious warning about your boyhood friend.'

And that was when he knew...

He'd trusted the wrong brother.

The Hag Feast

NYNEVE SPLUTTERED against the unfamiliar sensation in her mouth. 'It burns like the Searing.'

'*Warms*, Nyneve. That is what it is for.'

'And Men drink this for…pleasure?'

'In vast quantity…'

She took another sip, to test it again. 'It is horrible.'

'Tell me that again after you've finished the whole cup. *Aqua vitae* the red cloaks knew it as. The water of life.'

Nyneve snorted in the darkness, lit only by their fire. 'This is not water, Bleheris.'

'In the crowded cities and courts where the water running in their streams and wells can harbour death, *this* is what people drink to preserve their health.'

She sipped again and found her tongue did not protest the taste quite as strongly as it first had. 'It does not taste healthy.'

It tasted at once bitter and sweet, and a little like fire, and quite a lot like the putrid brew that animal skins were prepared in.

'Fills the belly as meat does, stifles the thirst as truly as water and eases discourse between enemies. It is like an everyday magic.'

'And Men honour their ancestors with this at the…Hag Feast?'

Eifion and Gwanaelle had both been raised in the way of Christ and so she knew it as Old Souls Night, but the Myrddyn—perhaps *y Ddraig*—knew it in the language of the old Gods.

'The departed souls return but once a winter to enjoy the pleasures of the flesh again.' His eyes grazed over her when he said "flesh". 'This night. Who are we to deny them one of their favourites?'

Bleheris tossed back the contents of his bowl, unconcerned, and then refilled it from the skin he'd brought from his shelter. What else had he been secreting in there?

'I cannot guess what importance this ritual of Men has for *y Ddraig,*' she said.

'It has none,' Bleheris admitted, 'beyond being one of four nights in the entire Sun's March where a young, un-Ascended dragonling might find her way into the sole company of a man not known to her without difficulty. *The* man she needs to father all her future offspring. That makes it a crucial night for *y Ddraig.*'

Her eyes immediately went to the snow-capped tree line of their clearing. Expecting some handsome young man to step out from the darkness and begin his seduction.

Disappointingly, none came.

'Come on!' Nyneve called out into the night, downing a mouthful of the burning drink as she did. 'Don't be afraid. We have fire and comfort and...' *a Myrddyn to instruct them* '...and Aqua Vitae!'

Her bowl sloshed as she raised it in salute to the darkness, but still the tree line stood undisturbed. She turned back to Bleheris and shrugged. 'Another time, perhaps?'

'You are a child,' he tutted. 'Am I misled about you having reached your fortenyear?'

His criticism stung. 'What else am I to say to such a ridiculous notion? I do not see a host of suitors readying themselves to...storm my stronghold. Do you?'

Her own wit sat smugly in her gut.

'You do not need a host. You simply need one.'

The right one, he added straight into her mind. Then, when she just blinked at him. *Oh, use your wits, girl... Why else am I come?*

Storm sky blazed at her out of eyes framed with creases and silver but still she was slow to understand. 'You came to teach.'

I come to seed, he gritted. I teach since you have the wit to be taught.

'Seed?' The unfamiliar idea rattled in her mind, yet somehow she knew what it meant, and the way he spoke... As if he'd done it before.

'No—'

'It is a quick thing, Nyneve.'

'No! You are...old!'

'And you are foolish. The best Aurochs have fathered many generations.'

'I do not love you,' she grasped, remembering Gwanaelle's descriptions of the intense connection between Melangell and Cai who rutted as often as beasts.

'You are not required to,' he scoffed. 'There is no faster way of tarnishing love than to diminish it with this act.'

Her mind moved slower, fettered by the rich distillation but she eventually grasped the most important part of Bleheris' revelation. Truth puffed out of her.

'Myrddyns are dragons un-Ascended!'

Rare and long-lived and with such powers...

'How else could we speak with *y Ddraig*? Or presume to speak for them.'

'You have the power of the Ancient Ones?'

'Some of them. Like this brandy, distilled down to a smaller, more powerful set of talents.'

For the moment, she set aside the fact that Bleheris had come here to bed her, and that he would not be leaving without that accomplished. It was easier to be unafraid if she kept her interest fixed to matter-of-fact things.

'You can speak into the minds of *y Ddraig*. You have their Sight. What else?'

'Thrall, which I can use in different ways.'

'What ways?'

'I can make a Man forget me the moment they turn their back.' He looked up. 'I can persuade him to climb to the top of that cascade. To jump off, if I want to.'

'Have you ever wanted to?'

His answer was not to answer. 'I can ease his mind when he is in chaos. Or change it when he is fixed on his path. Persuasion. Distraction. Reassurance.'

Like he had on Mother.

'Are you using any of those on me?' Would he use it to get between her thighs?

'No. They do not influence *y Ddraig*. Only the weak mind of Men.'

She felt around inside for the lie but found none. Still, she felt there was danger here somewhere. 'I am not yet *y Ddraig*.'

'You are dragon enough. I cannot influence you by thrall, Nyneve.'

'Can you divine the truth the way I can?'

His eyebrow rose and she remembered she had not yet told him of that talent. 'Not unsolicited. Unless the Sight has shown me the truth.'

There was a kind of comfort in knowing that, eventually, she would have the same powers as Bleheris, and more. That his Cunning would be like a child to hers once she had Ascended, but she needed more than comfort against the threat of his violation. She needed power, and she needed it now.

Deep, silent breath filled her. 'So you are indeed a deformed kind of dragon, then.'

The darkening in his eyes was the only clue that she had angered him, and she remembered that he'd had three-score years to master his abilities while hers were yet as unformed as the day she'd tumbled out of her crust. Yet, if she could see his anger at her slight, how great must it truly be? She swelled a little with the power.

'Arrogance,' he muttered. '*Y Ddraig's* least enviable quality.'

Perhaps, but it was a dagger against him—no matter how it trembled—when a moment ago she'd had none.

'Fortunate for you, Bleheris, that such fresh, tight furrows part on your command.' How naive must they have been, those foolish half-girls. 'For such a worn tool.'

'I could convince a servant of God to part her legs for me with the lift of one brow. You imagine I go to all this trouble for my own pleasure? If I had my choice of the women in this valley, believe that it would not be you, Nyneve. I do as I must. As will you.'

She crossed her arms. 'Who says I must?'

'You will not anger me with your petulance, child.'

Strange then that his eyes still swirled darkly. 'And you will not *have me*, old man.'

Power rushed through her then, raw and heady. Scarcely the first time she had defied someone, but the first time she'd done it with the power of *y Ddraig* behind her.

His lips thinned into a smile. 'Will I not?'

'Not unless you force me.' She glanced at the half-drunk bowl in her hands and recognised it for what it was. It stained the snow like blood as she upended it. 'Or coerce me with your fermented fruits.'

'Half the lords of this land were conceived through coercion, Nyneve, and the other half through force. You imagine me above either act? Have you forgotten how *y Ddraig* are usually raised?'

As beasts. Never spoken to, never held. Raised like wild creatures. She looked into Bleheris' face and searched there for the lie, but she only found truth.

'Mating you will not be quite so perilous but it will be just as hasty.'

She was proud enough to feel the sting of that insult. 'I do not wish it.'

'Your consent is not required.'

Eifion gone. Gwanaelle gone. No-one left to defend her, save herself. How much of that was Bleheris' doing?

'And if I do not wish to Ascend?'

Laughter cracked across the clearing like a branch-fall. 'Do you think it a choice?'

'It is *my* choice.'

'It has already begun, ignorant child. What use your choice then?'

His eyes fell to the place on her hands that the dry, cracked skin emerged from under her cloak of furs. Despite Gwanaelle's slatherings. Despite the eel's grease...'

She lifted her horror back to him. 'You said you didn't know what it was.'

'I am Myrddyn. I see further than the horizon into our past and our future. There is not much I do not know or could not for simply asking.'

'And so what is it?'

'It is Ascension.'

Her eyes fell again. Had it truly started?

It started winters ago, Nyneve. With what you call the Searing.

She forgot to protest his intrusion in her mind. How do I stop it?

It cannot be stopped, once started.

'I did not start it!' she cried, pushing to her feet.

'A part of you did. The part that has waited patiently all this time. The part that burns to unfurl its wings in the light. The part that yearns to plough this land with burrows for its offspring.'

No... No!

'And yours?' she snorted.

His anger returned. 'I do not do this because I want to, Nyneve. If choice was not denied me, then I would choose a woman—round of hips and sturdy of frame—and not some half-child who might snap under my very weight.'

Truth. This was no choice for Bleheris.

'Then don't do it. Simply refuse.'

'It is not simple, girl. I burn, just as you do, until I have fulfilled my part of nature.'

She blinked at him. 'What? With pain?'

'I Sear, too.'

The pronouncement was so unexpected it stole the strength from her legs. She sank back down onto the log by the fire. A fire, it seems, neither of them really needed.

'But it is not so bad,' she urged him. 'It can be endured. As I have.'

'You have had but a taste, Nyneve. I have seen un-Ascended dragons writhing in the earth with their pain. Screaming with it. Daily.'

The image was all too easy to imagine.

'But it is easing, so—'

'It is not. I am taking it from you.'

If he is taking it, he can give it back...

Disappointment streamed into Bleheris' eyes. 'You listen too much to the man you call father. I take it to spare you, foolish child, not to threaten you with.'

But could he take it away or did he simply take it on himself? Heap it onto his own pain.

The tiniest trace of gratitude sprung to life. 'Why would you do that?'

'Because you are different, Nyneve. You are...a person. With thoughts and feelings and conversation. I could not watch you twist in torsion, and it is a short enough time until you Ascend. I hoped you would have enough of Man's reason to simply consent.'

It hit her then, a flesh memory of Bleheris—either shared or stolen into her mind—of him circling a half-naked, half-wild young girl as she twisted in the grass, sobbing. Her muscles were taut and stringy, her face misshapen with pain. She writhed and he circled until she was almost too weak to move. It wasn't until the wave of searing passed and the bunched muscles in her exhausted body eased that Bleheris moved in, calmly turned the almost unconscious girl to her back, fumbled at his furs for a moment, knelt, then covered the girl's weakened body with his own and began moving against her, within her. Until it was done. The girl did not protest. The girl did not fight.

But she did not consent.

And a Morwyn Ddraig stood as quiet witness to the rape of her charge on the edge of the trees with a careful nothing on her face.

Bleheris' voice came to her quietly. 'It is how it is done, Nyneve. One moment of pain to end a lifetime...'

'I will not be doing *that*.' Passion flowed through her. She was still in that girl's body, she could still feel the impact of that moment she stopped fighting. The shame and self-loathing. As the girl would, forever.

'You must.'

She spun on him like the wild dragonling she'd seen in the vision. 'Or what?'

'Or you will never reproduce.'

'So be it, then.'

His head bowed. 'You cannot understand...'

'Understand what?

'The Searing is a herald of your Ascension,' he began, 'but that is not its primary purpose. The Searing is nature's drive, its urge, to create someone in your own image. To ensure the continuation of dragon-kind, and it will not stop until you have fulfilled your purpose.'

Nyneve felt around within for the familiar burn she had lived with for so long. It was there, as it always was, simmering and stinging, burning from the inside out. Tolerable enough to live with as she had this long, but then Bleheris said he was taking it for her.

How bad would it be if he was not?

'There is one,' she breathed, 'old and hoary you said. She laid no eggs, and so did not mate...'

'And she lives, alone and ferocious, far from here quite mad from a century of pain, and will do for a hundred years yet, poor creature. She has since begged me to seed her but I cannot. It can only happen before Ascension.'

'Then I will not ascend.' It had started as a childish response to his pressure but the idea took form and root in her mind. 'I will stay as I am. I will endure.'

'That is not possible.'

'You said Eifion and Gwanaelle living in harmony with *y Ddraig* was impossible... Just because you have not—'

'You could be the greatest of your breed,' he barked. 'More powerful and cunning than the world has ever seen. Man's instincts with a dragon's heritage. Conceive of it, Nyneve!'

Isn't that exactly what Artwr Pendragon wanted to be? Man...with the power of *y Ddraig*, and look what he had done in the name of that ambition. 'Not if I do not wish it!'

'You will tear your way out of that skin, Nyneve, if you fight yourself. Ascension cannot be stopped.'

Her mind spun with denial even as her blood told her it was true. 'And my ascension will begin as soon as we are...you are...done?'

'It is a step, merely. It will happen whether or not we do this, but it is part of the trigger, yes.'

'I cannot Ascend until Eifion and my mother are returned. I must be able to farewell them.' Before she wanted to eat them.

'They will not be back until the thaw, Nyneve.'

She pressed to her feet and loomed over him. 'Then you will wait, Cunning Man. I *will* get my farewell.'

Conveniently, it also gave her time to think of a solution.

'Nyneve. Do not force my hand.'

She did not like the use of his word 'force'. It reminded her too much of the vision she'd just witnessed.

He leaned in closer, as if to help her understand him. 'I will not endure your Searing as well as my own all winter. I cannot.'

'Then return what's mine to me, Bleheris. I will manage it.'

'You do not know what you ask, girl.'

'Nonetheless, it is mine to bear. I will have it back.'

Pewter eyes regarded her. 'I will return it in part. Then more. Then more. You might not survive a sudden return all at once.'

The longer he took the better for her. 'That is acceptable.'

Gods, she sounded like some highborn thing...

You are *highborn, Nyneve. Grown from Ancient seed. There is no higher in this land.*

She sank back onto the log near him, but not close. The closeness they had forged was now gone. How could she trust a man who sought to violate her and turn her, unwilling, into a beast? Bleheris was not here to teach her out of the goodness of his heart, he was here because he was that rare male creature that grew, un-Ascended, from a dragon egg. He forced himself onto creatures too pained and too ill-equipped to protest because that was what he was born to do, and when he wasn't, he travelled the land singing songs of the mythical Myrddyn—of *y Ddraig* in the form of Men—mingling amongst the most powerful in the land and composing his own stories, while all along…

…he was one of them.

XXIV

Mousehole

EIFION PEERED through the darkness to the place behind a stack of barrels where he'd seen a watchman disappear and not return earlier. Wherever that led, it was out of this very public yarden.

Good enough.

'How long will that silver keep you here in the shadows?' he murmured, now peering through the gaps in the packed straw at the ongoing feast while the whore resumed bobbing about his waist. Fortunate she wasn't doing true service to his cock or all that talking would have dried her mouth beyond comfort.

She curled her fists in the wears at his hips. 'Most of the night, warrior, if that be yer fancy.'

He paused, looked down. 'I am no warrior...'

Her snort would have been a gag had he really been going at her mouth. 'You carried your sword as one when you rode up to the stronghold.'

That gave him pause. 'You saw me?'

'Not I. News of a travelling man with iron always excites us because where there is iron there is very often silver. Nothing travels so swift as whore-talk. You and your sword were first seen lurking around the three ancients.'

If they'd seen him at the Stones—yet he'd not seen them—what else did they see...just after?

And if he was seen by whores, who else might have witnessed the Creil's hiding place?

In that moment, despite his own best efforts and convincing himself he could still salvage something of his plan, it became too dangerous to continue. He would know the anger and frustrated effort later but, for now, he kept his focus fixed on an unseen departure. He would ride far away and regroup.

'I'm going to step away, and I'd like you to stay here and continue this deceit.'

'On my knees, without pause? I'm not young like I used to be…'

'Stand, then. Just appear in and out of the shadows, so that you can be seen but I cannot. Their minds will do the rest.'

'If you are not here, you will not chance being seen,' the woman muttered.

He stole a final glance through the straw. 'I would not have that known until the last possible moment. Will you count five score and then flounce off with much disturbance?'

Her weathered face brightened. 'Oh, flouncing be a sure speciality of mine, warrior. And disturbance.'

But before he left her, he paused. 'What is your name, woman?'

The confusion and then small distress he saw in her eyes in the moment it took her to answer made him wonder if she did not remember because no-one had asked her in so long.

'Angharad. I suppose there is no sense in asking after yours?'

'I hope you understand that I cannot tell.' Her eyes narrowed, and so he took her hand and raised it, turning it at the last moment to the place where the skin was least marred by a life hard-lived. 'But they sometimes know me as Yvain.'

Her eyebrow shot up. 'Do they just? There's a story there. One that I sense I'll be quite sorry not to have discovered for myself.'

'Thank you, generous Angharad.' He pressed his lips on her under-wrist for a moment and felt the flutter of her life against them. 'You have likely saved my life this night. Farewell.'

As he stole toward the shadowed barrels, he wondered how dire a Thane had to be that even the whores divulged all against him to utter strangers. He paused at the edge of the shadows, listened out for voices beyond and then casually stepped out and around, risking the far reach of the all-fire's glow for just a step or two, keeping his face casually averted, before ducking in behind the stack. Beyond it, the edge of the great-hall finished short of the stronghold wall and created a man-sized crevice, well-trod judging by the firm earth and absence of grasses, and Eifion pressed down its length until he found a disguised breach in the stronghold's timber uprights mid-way along the edge of the great-hall where a man could barely pass. He squeezed through into the tangled bracken that secreted the breach from the outer-side.

Here was a mouse-hole intended for use by informed mice only.

All of Trellech unfolded before him—clusters of smoke-puffing, straw-roofed dwellings in misshapen circles, not ordered and efficient rows like Artwr's camps and towns—while most of its security still celebrated with mead behind the wall he'd just squeezed through. He should melt away into the night, down the furthest side of this rise, down into the trees then wait days before returning under cover of dark for the Creil, but if he was not going to conduct this dangerous bargain at all then he needed to get back to his valley—back to Gwanaelle and Nyneve—as quickly as possible.

And he wasn't going to do that on two feet.

Cai's mare was not accommodated within the stronghold's walls but rather barred-in on its outer-side with the other pack horses. He needed to move quickly to liberate it while attention was still so firmly on the strongholds yarden. Inside, he'd taken note of where the sentries were posted high on the stronghold walls but he couldn't see them from here and so dashing across into the thick foliage was a risk. The first of many to come. He lingered for a five-score count, waiting for the whore's disturbance to draw those eagle eyes for the heartbeats he needed to make his run, but either she failed him or Lord Gwalchmai's armsmen were too well trained to react to any ruse. In the end, he had no choice but to simply continue his mouse-like dart across the cleared space between stronghold and wood and then tumble headlong into the thick growth on the hillside, laying as flat as safety would allow once there.

Working his way around the steep slope to the far side of the stronghold was an exercise in agony for the muscles low in his legs but he pushed through the frosty bracken, cursing every crack and snap, until he drew level with the horse-yarden. At least half the horses held within were the same brown as his own, but only one was tall enough to carry the long legs of Cai ap Cynyr. Her head stood at least that much again atop the others.

It took no time to break enough thongs to loosen and then quietly lower two timbers on the edge of the hillside then crawl like the fox he hoped any watchman would assume he was until he drew up at the legs of Cai's mare. Her height, and his, meant that he could stand at her flank and lead her, his fist full of her frost-crisped neck-locks, toward the edge of the yard without being seen from the stronghold should any eyes be drawn by the disrupted whiffling of the sleepy horses.

At the edge, he looped over his shoulder one of a score of lengths of corded flax coiled there before tugging her by the neck-locks into the trees.

He led her into the wood as it fell away, found a place within the protection of the trees that she could stand with some confidence, then twisted and looped the flax into a head harness. Even the mare seemed happier to have it on when he was done. He nudged her slightly ahead of him, down the slope and held onto the tufts of hair on her neck for balance. A horse—unlike a man—made a lot more noise stepping through the woods, but this horse—unlike this half-addled man—was far surer picking its way down the hillside. At the bottom, he took a moment before emerging from the trees to tighten the corded flax and toss it back over the mare's head. It wasn't leathers and mouth-irons but it would be enough, at least, to get away from this place.

She stood patiently as he readied to scramble up onto her back— too cold and stiff for his usual ease, but he took a moment to stop, to breathe, to plan the next stage of his flight—away from the stronghold, away from the little village, away from the Creil's resting place. With his foraged coins spent and his food and wears all still captive inside the stronghold—except that already on his back or in his belly—he would have to turn thief again, find more villages, steal some mouth irons, head leathers and a back pad in one, more furs for the road in the next, whatever food the Gods would deliver of him in the third. Yet he had his sword, his horse, and the equal gifts of darkness and Gwalchafad's ignorance.

Those were worth more than any full belly.

The mare shied away just as he tightened his fist around her neck-locks, but, as he swung his leg to mount her, furious fists dragged him back down and something knocked him so hard from behind that his eyes near exploded from his skull.

The mare screamed.

Then all was dark.

XXV

Noble

A WEAVER-WOMAN at the first village they went to begged an hour of Cai's time taking an axe to her winter woodpile in return for stitching Gwanaelle into Melangell's cloak so that she could spare her fists the arduous task of taking turns poking out into the cold to hold it together. In the next village, she'd managed not to weep as she traded her mother's brooch to a village smith rich with ambition for every coin he had in his possession and three quality mounts that he, himself, hastily traded a box full of smelted mouth-bits and ornate bridles to secure. He'd been suspicious of Gwanaelle's tale of robber-men on the road who stole their fine belongings and previous mounts, particularly given the giant standing just back from her, but—perhaps also because of him—he did not challenge the lie. At the village a day further south, she'd surrendered some coin for travelling supplies and bags of winter-feed which they bundled over the back of the spare horse who looked entirely offended to be thus reduced to a pack-mount and she entrusted the rest of the coin to her massive protector who glared at anyone who so much as looked at her askance.

'Are you trying to be remembered?' she muttered after one particularly withering glare.

Cai didn't so much as turn his focus off the road. 'This was your deceit, Gwanaelle, I merely play my part.'

'So you're a Bard now, are you?' Again she tried to bring Bleheris' name to tongue but could not. 'Just try to be a little less...striking.'

'As you—with your flaming hair and startling eyes—are managing so beautifully?'

She tugged her cloak up more firmly over her braided hair. Cai was right. Neither of them was doing a particularly good job of disappearing into the snow thickened world. The only thing in their favour was that every night that passed sent another family indoors, not to emerge until Thaw two moons from now. The roads and the villages grew quieter and quieter every step they took.

'You play the noble quite well,' Cai murmured, a little further on. 'It suits you.'

Just because Melangell had intuited the details of her past did not mean she had shared them with Cai, no matter how great the love between her two friends was. Melangell's ability to hold a confidence was nearly as great as Eifion's, but sharing the comforts of her past would only lead him to question what had led him to first find her— torn and bedraggled—running from his Lord's hunt all those winters ago, and how would she refuse his question if he voiced it, this man who had done so much for all of them? Better ridden around the subject the way they'd passed wide around Cai's old stronghold.

'It only has to last until we find Eifion, then we can trade everything again and return to our valleys as paupers,' she murmured.

'Perhaps we should keep the horses?'

'To graze our valleys to dust? Grow idle from lack of use?' Or to become a meal for a confused dragonling should Nyneve begin her transformation...? 'If anything, we should keep the coin.'

Twelve hooves plodded onwards, almost silent in the deepening snow, but their snorts and the jangling of the wrought bits in their mouth let any around to hear know they were passing. So far, none had been robber-men or, if they had, none had the lack of sense to take on a warrior of Cai's stature.

'Something I've been wondering,' Cai started a little further along. 'Why now?'

She turned to him and slowed a little so he could ride alongside. 'What?'

'In all this time he could have taken the pieces of the Creil to Artwr... Why now?'

Other than as an excuse to leave their valley? Her mind turned to Bleheris but—as always—she could not bring him to lip. She tried a number of different ways to work her way around to it until one was allowed.

'It is Nyneve's fortenyear,' she murmured.

His eyebrows raised. 'Has it been that long?'

'It has.'

'Has she grown any sense yet?'

It was easy to smile. 'She has not.'

'And is she still…'

Burning? 'Yes. She is still plagued by the searing, and by something new, now. The perishing of her skin.'

'And what has that to do with the Creil?'

Again she hunted for words that could form. 'I do not know. Perhaps he worries for her now that she is grown. Things could…change…without warning. Perhaps he's planning for the future.'

'That sounds like Eifion. Ever the strategist.'

'How is the sanctuary?' she asked for something less arduous to her mind.

'Full,' he muttered below his cloak. 'And starting to draw attention.'

'From who?'

'From Brychwel's enemies. From those who imagine despoiling a sanctuary full of virgins to be equal parts sport and insult.'

'For men just like Brychwel, you mean?' His silence was all the answer she needed. Cai well knew how branded the memory of that day was in her mind. It had taken her winters to fully forgive his part in it. 'What happens to them when they come?'

'*Divine retribution* or so the stories say. Some decompose on the spot, some are swallowed into the ground whole.'

She well remembered how the sap from the ancient yew trees had ruined Artwr's soldiers when he'd first sent them to root out Melangell. Some did look like corpses dug from the earth by the end of the short battle.

'And does it? Swallow them whole?'

'Eventually.' He grinned. 'With a little aid from my sword.'

As always, people's fear of the mysteries of Melangell's valley was the greatest protection her sanctuary could enjoy. Not counting one of Cymry's greatest warriors and a proficient Morwyn Ddraig. The only protection their valley had was Eifion.

The thought brought her gaze back to the snow-buried track ahead, and the sparkle the river ahead managed in the dim winter light where it had not yet frozen completely over.

'The Gwyr,' Cai murmured. 'We'll find a ford and cross. Not far now.'

X X V I

Bolt-house

'WHAT DID YOU imagine, Eifion? That I would put a long-absent friend ahead of my brother? Of my Chieftain? Of myself?'

Gwalchafad's voice came to him as splinters of pain. Their light pierced the darkness that had taken him. The slivers flickered and danced as clumsily as the whore had and he slipped one hand around to feel for the loose bone fragments at the back of his head. None, just a mighty skull-knot where he'd been clubbed into unconsciousness.

'Angharad,' he groaned, realising. She had betrayed him to Gwalchafad just as she had betrayed the Thane to him. What else should he have expected of someone reduced to whoring—she sold whatever had a value. It was how she survived. He did not begrudge her that.

'What?'

'The whore.'

Impatience stained Gwalchafad's already tight voice. 'What care I for whores?'

He did not betray any awareness and Eifion's wits had cleared enough to realise that the woman may yet have kept his faith. He would not repay that with a death sentence.

He touched the skull-knot again and winced. 'My wits are...addled.'

'You should not have fled, Eifion. Then I would not have had to...send for you.'

'I was your guest.' Yet, still, he'd squeezed out the mouse hole on some instinct.

Gwalchafad's pale face thinned in a tight smile. 'You still are.'

Eifion rolled onto his side and peered around the small space through crusted eyes. All the fresh straw in Brython could not disguise the stench of old urine and recent death in it. No stable.

'A guest? In your bolt-house?'

'You should not have fled,' he repeated, as if one thing explained the other.

'What has become of you, Gwalchafad? We were friends once.'

'Do you deceive all your friends, so, *Yvain*?'

'What deceit? I came to you for your help.'

'I was in Artwr's court when his brother disappeared—'

'Died.'

'—and you missing with him as far as any knew.' Suspicion stained Gwalchafad's narrowed gaze.

'I've been in the North. Gone, but scarcely missing. Ask any of the—'

'Where did you go?'

He meant '*you and Cai*', of course. Eifion did not pretend to misunderstand. 'Cai and I parted ways five winters before his death. I rode away from his stronghold at Crug Eryr while he was still there.'

The strategy to a solid deceit was to tell what truths you could.

'And where were you, after?'

'Ranging the north. On my Lord's business.'

'Yet you did not ride south to re-join the high Chieftain when your Lord *died*? Why?'

Considering Gwalchafad had spent twelve long winters away from the authority of Caerllion his manner was unpleasantly demanding.

Eifion took a deep breath. 'The north is full of prospects. I found them to my liking. My Lord Cai had pledged that I was released from service on his death.'

A lie but a necessary one. He had been pledged to Cai until death—by his own choice. Now he was pledged to a woman and a dragonling. The thought of admitting it almost made him smile.

Gwalchafad's eyes narrowed. 'Which means you are here on Cai ap Cynyr's business even now.'

Every deceit he'd ever perpetrated, every nuanced deception young Nyneve had ever committed on him… He poured it all into his words, now, as if Gwalchmai's suspicion was a startling, revolutionary idea. An utter confusion. 'You believe Cai is not dead?'

'What I suspect about Cai,' Gwalchafad murmured, easing up off his perch and crossing his legs before settling again, as though for a stay, 'is of less import than what I suspect about you.'

Staring would be easier if his eyes were not as scratchy as his wears from lack of water.

But Gwalchafad was not concerned by his comfort. 'Tell me of this…*not*-trinket.'

'Trinket?' he hedged.

'Your reason for seeking out my brother.'

'Release me and we may speak of it like men.'

'When you have your own bolt-house, Yvain, perhaps then you will be in a position to make demands. Until then, I act for my brother and my brother acts for the high Chieftain. So consider this order comes from your Lord, Artwr.'

Straw dust from the floor flew off his cheek as he puffed out his scorn. 'You act for yourself. Let us at least be honest, now, as we were as boys.'

But Gwalchafad would have none of it. 'Speak! Of this gift that will win me back into Artwr's company.'

He pushed to sitting. 'He must be of prodigious cock, whichever warrior it is you battle so dishonourably to return to.

Gwalchafad's wide nostrils flared and his wispy hair swished about his face. 'The weapon, Eifion—rarer than a sword, you said. That will transform the endless war with the Angles. Speak of it now.'

'I doubt presenting even that to Artwr will make amends for killing his sister.'

Fury flared behind controlled eyes. 'You seek to best me in a war of words, Yvain? You, who was near mute as a boy. Have at it, then. Come on, say what you will. Let us see whose wit remains sharpest.'

Yes. Bound and without his iron he only had words to wield, but he was not going to be at advantage while the Thane was still calm. He therefore soaked his words in disdain. 'She was your mother, Gwalchafad. Where was your honour?'

'She was a whore!' he snorted. 'First, bending back for the man who murdered her bonded husband, and later bending forwards for his handsome, valiant son.'

'And what is it to you who a widow grants between her thighs? Did she concern herself with where you put *your* cock?'

Ice blue pierced him. 'Everyone knew of Loth's sons. Conceited, handsome Agravane. Heroic, charming Gwalchmai. Who was young Gwalchafad but the weak little brother who carried after them endlessly when they were young and arbitrated their disputes when they were older? Who was Gwalchafad if not an appendage of Gwalchmai's, more firmly fixed at his feet than his own shadow. Yet Lamorak saw who I was. He, alone, saw what I craved above all else and helped me to become a warrior in Artwr's court. He trained me in secret, grew my skill and I grew to love him for it.'

'Yet, your reward to him was death—'

'My good *mother* killed Lamorak.' Spittle flew. 'I was just her sword-arm.'

Eifion's gaze lifted. Genuine pause. 'She drew you into some scheme?'

'It was the Pendragon's court, Eifion. Where lives were made and lost on the diligent delivery of a message by a maidservant. How could it be that I just *happened* upon a messenger searching for my brother who was lax enough to blurt her charge to the first person to ask of it? How would a wife who had survived the devious machinations of King Loth and his treacherous court—who had even bested her most re-known half-brother—make such a child's error as to let a message of that kind be simply *mis*delivered?'

Eifion sagged back against the wall. The battering had not completely robbed him of his wits. 'She doubted Gwalchmai to complete the task.'

'Not his courage, and not his right—God knows. No doubt, she would have preferred my brother to invoke the bloodprice—righteous *Gauwain* with his flashing swords and lofty morals—but she knew that he would first seek counsel of his Lord and that Artwr would keep peace with Lamorak's father at all costs, else he already would have sought retribution, himself, for the killing of mine.'

Of all Loth's sons... Gwyar did not need the valiant one, she did not need the righteous one.

She needed the unstable one.

'If she believed one son wouldn't do it...' Eifion murmured. *Then she made sure that the other would.*

Gwalchafad tossed his head and his narrow eyes glinted. 'What mother ever knew her son better, eh? She used us both. She used that wavering maidservant. She used weak Lamorak.'

'So you exacted the blood price from him? This friend you swear to have held in such regard.'

'I went there to protect Lamorak from my brothers lest mine was not the only messenger charged.' His head sagged. 'I wasn't expecting to find *her* there. Nor her whore thighs around his ears.'

'So you killed them both with a sword soaked in passion?' Gwalchafad never had been able to think clearly while overcome.

'Lamorak I killed in blind fury.' His gaze hardened. 'Mother, no. *Her* I killed very much with intent. For all her treacheries but this latest one, especially, that was against me.'

Blind fury? Then the truth soaked through him... The bolt room swirled as much as if he'd been drinking all night.

'Lamorak was *mine*, Eifion. The only thing I'd ever had for myself.'

Love. How blind of him not to realise sooner, and of his mother not to have seen it when choosing a son to manipulate into killing a man she could rightfully not. A mistake she paid for dearly.

'Her own death must have come as quite a surprise.'

'It truly did, I think. So defeated... Even as I hacked away at her neck.'

Gwalchafad stared into the shadowed corner of the room, his face twisted like a yew branch, as though the whole thing happened right there, right now, before him. Scarcely the noble and swift dance of Ylfael that Cai had taught his warriors when removing head from shoulders on a blood-debt. So either Lamorak hadn't taught him all that well, after all, or it was Gwalchafad's choice to do it with a handed blade.

Looking at his old friend now, he suspected it was the latter.

'Sadly, Lamorak preferred the stink of an old lady's flapping furrow over the delightful strangle of a warrior's puck and I was bested by the biggest of all whores. My mother.'

'Why confess all this, Gwalchafad?' Eifion finally whispered.

Though, really, he already knew.

'Because you and I were like brothers once...'

Crazed eyes finally came back to him. He reached out and squeezed Eifion's shoulder gently, like he was commiserating on some shared loss.

'…and because you are going to die.'

XXVII

Searing

'WHY DO YOU study me so?' Nyneve snapped at Bleheris as they sank down to rest the following noon. Even with the Myrddyn's cunning arts to encourage a hare to simply walk into his hands, eating was now exhausting where once it had thrilled her. 'During labour, during rest, your eyes always watching. I imagine you peer into my mind when I sleep.'

Did he hope to wear down her resistance through persistence?

'You intrigue me, Nyneve. You are so…different to the others.'

When Bleheris said "different", she heard "broken". Could she not even be a beast-in-waiting satisfactorily?

'A bundle of firsts,' he murmured, his eyes narrowed and piercing.

'And the first to Ascend when she is ready!' she announced.

His smile was not amused. Yet it was not unkind as he spoke simply. 'You will be ready.'

'You are so certain, Bleheris. What if I continue to proceed…abnormally? How can you know what I will do?'

He studied her. 'It is possible, I suppose. Yet unlikely.'

'How arrogant you have grown. Knowing so much. Knowing all.'

'I never professed to know all, Child,' he glared. 'But I have seen a good deal more than Men, and the sight gives me more. My Myrddyn's training gives me more. One hundred winters on this earth gives me more.'

Whilst she had lived only a fortenyear in this one valley. With only two people for company.

'If I Ascended,' she chanced, 'would I learn as much as you?'

Knowing eyes turned up to her. 'You already know it.'

No. She did not. She was as that honey-miser grub, but she was not about to admit it. 'Hardly an incentive to Ascend, then.'

'*Y Ddraig* carry the knowledge of all their kind passed down through the generations, as well as the ability to See anything else they might wish to know, but they do not have the same concerns as a Myrddyn, they do not wish to know the kinds of things that I might. Their concerns are…as insular as they are.'

'Where is it kept, all that knowledge?'

'When you were as Creil you knew it all. Your experiences of the world may have been muted within your crust but they piled in on top of every experience your forebears had in their time. That knowledge will return to you on Ascension.'

'Like a prize?'

'It is why *y Ddraig* go into immediate sequester. To come to terms with everything they suddenly know.'

Then again most *y Ddraig* have been raised as little more than beasts, the moment of Ascension is enlightenment indeed. 'Perhaps I will digest it more easily given my upbringing.'

Bleheris considered her, that light of intrigue live in his silver eyes.

'Perhaps.' Before she could gloat much about having had Bleheris' measure just this once, he stood to return to his labours, and left her with a parting shot. 'But I am delighted to hear that you are growing more used to the idea of Ascending.'

Nyneve glared at his back, certain that he could still see it no matter the direction of his gaze. Relying on it, even.

Yet, no, she was not growing 'used' to anything, but the knowledge of all the world… Places beyond the sea, beyond the forests. Places of sand and places of ice. People and creatures such as she'd never seen… They couldn't help but be seductive.

If only they did not come at such cost.

Eifion's departure and then her mother's… She had been pleasantly surprised, at first, to discover how much of what they had taught her had remained fixed in her mind once they were gone— where to find the best roots for the pot, which creatures to kill and which to leave for a future meal, how to make best use of the furs and sinews and claws not eaten—but she was not nearly ready to live without them for long. Longer than it took for Eifion to complete his task and Gwanaelle to ensure he returned safely from it. All those lessons and endless repetition from both of them had taken root, no matter how she had railed from them, and now they were flowering in the winter of her need.

Yet before there was railing and resentment at being cloistered here much as the virgins in Melangell's sanctuary, there was happiness. She remembered it. Happiness and love and energetic bursts around the valley floor that had first seemed so very big to her. Eifion and Gwanaelle had swathed her in love the way they later swathed her searing skin in mud.

The way she now swathed it with oils where it perished more every day.

Her fingers brushed over the cracked crust on her wrists and flakes broke free and fluttered down to litter the snow. Perhaps the cold was only making the cracking worse. Yet, the cold was only outward, inside she burned as fiercely as ever. Moreso, it seemed, since she took her fierce stance against Ascension. Was that Bleheris returning her curse to her as he had promised—little by little? It was now too cold to wade naked into the waterfall pool and the water cascading down would freeze over any day now. And besides...who would slathe her body in soothing mud? Bleheris? He was just as likely to take advantage of her nakedness to accomplish his foul task.

So she eased the Searing as best she could accomplish alone, long after Bleheris had retired behind the skins of his shelter for the night, behind her own, rolling naked in the rapidly piling up snow. It melted as fast as she writhed but it did at least ease the burn for a short while, and there was no shortage of snow.

It was only 'a little' of what Bleheris had taken for her. To spare her, he'd said.

No longer. What else was to come?

Would she ache? Would she scream? Would she, too, gouge chunks of flaking flesh from her limbs to ease an itch that took her mind? What had happened to the dragonling in her vision that made lying quiescent beneath a rutting old man as he pushed his hardened flesh into her the better choice than enduring Ascension's heralds?

And more important perhaps...

How soon would it come?

~

Ever in her head, Bleheris seemed to know just when to return a little more of the suffering he'd been taking for her. It did come in the form of an ache and it came just as Nyneve lay her head down to sleep. Like the toothworm that burrowed its dark-stained chamber into her tooth, once, and had to be bored out by Eifion with a block and pin. Chip, chip, chip—as she'd gagged and wept. Gwanaelle had plied her with wyrmwood and nettle before he'd started, and then packed the worm's excavated chamber tight with a mix of ground barley, ochre and comb-wax but none of it had done anything to remove the awful memory from her mind.

And they never had found the worm, but at least it had never returned.

Now the pain of that memory returned, three-fold, spreading its ache everywhere a bone grew until she felt heavy and exhausted from hosting them.

Yet it was only the second of Ascension's heralds.

She curled into a tiny ball, the stretching bringing a moment's relief from the deep, strained ache—a giant standing on her bones— but no sooner did the ache pass than it made way for the Searing that hadn't stopped and she'd stretch out straight again to try and release some of the heat. Rolling in snow made her bone-ache worse, but not doing it made the burn inside thrive.

She was in misery either way, and alone. No Eifion to lend her his strength, no Gwanaelle to give her a mother's comfort. All she could do was curl up and rock herself into a half-lucid state—like the mystics of old—and wait for the heat and the ache and the pure self-sorrow to pass.

They never did.

Rise brought the itch. It started as the weakling sun felt out with its pale fingers into the morning, as a prickle in that same cracked skin she was trying not to pick at, then grew to a tingling and then to an all out tormented itch. The chunks of flesh she'd seen the dragonling in her vision gouging out were the only thing that kept her from taking to the driest patches with her own fingernails, but she rummaged out her mother's scratchiest shift of nettle and goat hair and donned that so that every move she took would rasp against her tormented flesh in the place of fingers. It didn't help her dangling limbs but it seemed to help the core of her body, yet it was only then that she realised that the itch wasn't always coming from outside her body, much of it was inside. As if the very sinews that gave her shape were, themselves, inflamed and cross.

Impatient almost.

She grew silent as she concentrated on enduring the suffering she knew Bleheris had returned intentionally and he did not press her for her attention. The day passed in that way, Bleheris watching her from across the clearing—always watching—and when he returned from the trees around their clearing with some creature, she didn't even bother to heat over the fire. Eating a hare dripping-raw seemed to ease the Searing a little and so she did.

Yet nothing eased it for long.

And still he said nothing.

She crawled back into her shelter before the sun had even reached the far hills, exhausted by her focus, tormented by the three screaming pains, as miserable and as suffering as she had ever been in her life. The tears she shed didn't help, but at least they didn't hurt, and she even rubbed them into her skin in case they already held the magic of *y Ddraig*. Perhaps she could convince herself through thrall that she was not in pain.

She could not. Neither did licking bring about any miraculous remedy.

There was nothing for it but to lie here, enduring. Enduring and weeping. She wept for herself and for the loss of all the freedoms she hadn't even realised she had. She wept for the future that now felt as inevitable as death. She wept for her mother and father—Eifion, Gwanaelle—because they were not here with her, because they were in danger, and finally she wept for her real mother and father—whoever they were—because they had created this whole situation by not being stronger. By not standing against their very natures. Either one of them could have prevented her suffering if they had just stood firm against the urge.

Yet could she stand for long? Within this suffering?

Perhaps, like the un-loved, un-touched, half-wild creature in her vision who had endured this for so many se'nnights before it drove her mad, but she had been raised on a pasture of love and kindness, and she was edging closer to madness after only a day and a night.

She would endure. If she could. Maybe Bleheris had returned it all now, maybe there was no more to come and maybe she would grow used to the pain.

And if she could not…? Then she always had death.

Surely this pain could not follow her there.

XXVIII

Torment

A LIFETIME AGO, when he was as slight as Nyneve and first learning how to manage a sword well, he'd tumbled into the spring that ran fast through their training field and the sword-master had made him stay there all day as punishment for his clod-footedness. At first, it was funny, then it grew cold, then uncomfortable as his skin swelled and bunched from the immersion. By the time the sun was low on the horizon even his innards had started hurting. His legs had never again shaken as badly as they had that long day when finally he'd been allowed to clamber out. He almost couldn't do it unaided.

Just from rushing water.

That day was a feast-dance on this one.

Since the sun first rose, he'd been sunk up to his neck, swine-bound, in water drawn from the river nearby. The frigid water had been startling enough but it soon eased to match the little warmth of the room and—after a fashion—had even begun to feel comfortable. They'd striped his face in a brew of sour milk and honey and then forced him to drink the rest.

Wasting two of the most valuable foods in the stronghold on torture?

Gwalchafad wants to keep you alive as long as he can. That's what he'd first believed, anyway.

With his hands bound to his feet, he had no option but to sit, knees splayed, awkwardly bent forward in his cauldron, straining to keep his mouth above water. Sometimes he'd give the muscles of his neck rest and let his chin lower, just a little, breathing through his nose. Or he'd stretch his lungs with air and then lower his whole face below the water to ease the torsion of his shoulders and help ease the insane, unscratchable itches where the gadflies of summer's-end—drawn by the honey and heat of his face—had bitten him into a pocked mess. Yet, all that would do was re-wet the milk-honey brew where it had hardened and make it all the more attractive for the bloodthirsty little scuts once he lifted his face again.

No-one had gagged him, but the armed watchmen would have cut his tongue out if he'd used it and—this deep inside Gwalchafad's stronghold—what was the point of calling for help that would never come? And so he sat from mist-rise until disappearance; strained, frozen, his back screaming, half-leaning against the side of the cauldron for relief, clenching his bowel against the inevitable, determined to endure whatever punishment they found for him.

The door to the bolt-house opened and Gwalchafad stepped in from the rain and nodded once at his man who surrendered his sword and left the cell. The water splashing down onto the muddy yarden outside didn't make it any easier for Eifion to master his howling bladder.

'*Yvain*,' Gwlachafad said, sitting, and resting the sword casually against the cauldron's edge. Eifion knew it at once; he'd been looking at it for winters...

The sword from his vision.

Eifion tipped his head back in the cold water and let it rest on the back edge of the timber cauldron so that he could see his enemy and keep that sword in his periphery. All this time the only comfort he'd taken from his vision was that he didn't recognise the blade in his own hand.

So what was this? His destiny delivered up by a madman? Or was the throat in his vision Gwalchafad's? It was pale and feminine enough. And with that hair...

Gods, let it be so.

'You were prepared to *give* me the weapon just one night before this one.' Gwalchafad said. 'Why, now, do you keep its secrets?'

Why *didn't* he just surrender the Creil pieces? It wouldn't save his own life but the shards would still end up with Artwr as Gwalchafad tried to win back his Lord's favour—probably more convincingly— and then Artwr might well be so distracted by their magic he would halt awhile his endless searching for *y Ddraig*.

He would be dead, but Nyneve and Gwanaelle might live.

And yet... This Gwalchafad was not the young man he remembered from their training days. *This* Gwalchafad had grown into a man who could kill his mother and his love without pause or—apparently—much regret. Who ran a stronghold with a spiked glove. This Gwalchafad was just as likely to use the Creil for his own ends and hold Artwr prisoner with the secrets it offered, and while Eifion no longer owed his loyalty to the man he'd once raised sword for, he did still trust Artwr more than the man standing over his swollen body right now.

Everything Artwr did he at least did for protection of Cymry.

Gwalchafad protected only one person...

'I have changed my mind,' Eifion croaked. Better no man ever found the Creil shards than this man.

'Then I must change it back, I suppose.'

'I am not afraid of death.' He shrugged at the water all around him. 'And this drenching has not weakened my resolve.'

Though it was certainly weakening the cords in his back.

'Oh, but we are barely started,' Gwalchafad laughed.

He reached across the tub and braced a hand there, lowering his gaze until it was level with Eifion's. 'You have seen what water does to the skin of a dead body?'

Eifion just glared.

'It does the same to a live one. Except you're still cloaked within it to enjoy the sensation. For instance—'

He plunged is free arm into the cauldron, of a sudden, between Eifion's splayed legs and wrapped his fist around the water-wrinkled cock he found there, all the while holding his friend's hard gaze.

'—if I returned after sunset on the morrow to do this,' he drew his fist just once up the foreshortened length of Eifion's cock, even as he twisted and lurched against the contact, 'your skin would likely come loose, and the more firmly I do it...' He did, and Eifion froze, refusing to give him further satisfaction. '...the more entirely it will come away. Like the fat off a hide in the tanners' tubs.'

He tugged the length of the thickening penis in his hand, and dropped his voice, almost to the intimate tone of a lover as he pushed and pulled his fist up and down Eifion's flesh.

'The longer you swill in here,' he murmured, 'the more of your skin will come away—first the outer, but then some of the inner, then your water-logged sinews—until this tub floats with chunks of your flesh like some grisly pottage.'

The image was nowhere near as horrific as the threat of his cock hardening further under Gwalchafad's touch. His movement was so restricted, short of closing his eyes—which he would not do lest Gwalchafad think it was a sign of weakness or, worse, pleasure—all Eifion could do to look away from his tormentor's keen attention was slide his stare over Gwalchafad's shoulder as he bobbed up and down with the movement of his arm.

Ignoring the man and focusing on a splintered piece of timber on the wall. Mastering his body's response.

Giving him nothing.

But Gwalchafad was too much the tyrant to accept nothing.

'Of course, once your skin starts coming away, the same horseflies that have turned your face into their meat will start laying eggs in the crevices, and the maggots that hatch out will munch you open, and once we've shoved enough sour milk-honey down your throat, the shit starts to run no matter how disciplined you believe your bowels, and then you're sitting here soaking your open maggot-wounds in a stew of your own skin, shit and seed.' He continued pumping and Eifion continued struggling against his flesh's involuntary response. 'It won't be long before the rest of your body starts failing.'

Gwalchafad fell silent for moments, concentrating on his filthy handiwork and watching Eifion's face for any hint of weakness.

He knew from fucks past that his whole body got involved when he cast his seed; it was a military formation that needed several flanking forces to achieve, and right now, all his forces were either numb or screaming with the pain of being immersed and bound for so long, and his fiery vengeance was far too busy plotting ways to kill Gwalchafad to be stirred by his whore's touch.

No matter how practiced.

Gwalchafad's top lip sprang with sweat as he gave himself fully over to the task, fingers fanning out on the downward stroke to tease the codpair now tucked up so tightly seeking his body's protection. It took all of Eifion's concentration not to let his unknowing flesh respond to the firm milking.

He would not even give him a flinch.

'Your sword has grown blunt from disuse, *Yvain...*'

'Perhaps your talent has,' he gritted, fixing his gaze on a broken splinter on the timbers of the bolt-house wall over Gwalchafad's shoulder. The only time he would ever meet his old friend's eyes again would be as he drove a blade into his throat. 'Or perhaps you have at last met your better.'

The pumping paused, the fist tightened, and he released his breath on a long, angry hiss, but there was something else there, too. Something older. Something sadder. 'That would be cruel fate, indeed. To have known him all along...'

He straightened, releasing Eifion's punished cock and scattering water droplets as he shook his hand dry.

'Someone once lasted a whole fortennight in this tub,' Gwalchafad finally said. 'He was barely more than muscle hanging loose on bone when he finally succumbed to his suffering and whimpers. He certainly was no longer a man to any that looked in.'

He leaned in close, right up hard against Eifion's ear. 'Or...you can tell me what you have and where it is waiting and I'll have the guards cut your throat straight across right now. A merciful end.'

He leaned so close, Eifion shrank from the caress of his breath even as his icy skin craved the little warmth. It crossed his mind to wonder whether a man could die from having his nose bitten clean through, but before he could turn thought to action, Gwalchafad pushed to his feet and peered down on the sorry spectacle of a naked, pickled man dissolving in his own juices.

'Your choice.'

XXIX

Surrender

'THE WORST OF the pain is you growing a second heart, Nyneve. You will need one heart to power each of your mighty wings.'

Bleheris put his hand over hers where she lay in her shelter and pressed it against her breast where her heart beat with powerful fury, then dragged her hand to the other side and pressed there, too. Something beat there, something new and bird-like.

She snatched her hand out from under his but he did not remove it, lingering on her breast. Squeezing gently.

You can end it all, Nyneve. It will take but moments.

'No!' The denial was almost lost in the piled furs beneath her as she writhed and rolled against Bleheris' intrusion into her suffering and the logic of his words.

I do not want it any more than you do but it must happen. Far less intimate having me in your body than in your mind and you have grown used to that.

'Get out!' Of her shelter. Of her mind.

And it is not as bad as this. It is not as bad as death.

She had no patience for his sense or his presence. For all she knew it was *Bleheris* doing this to her, some scheme the ageing Myrddyn employed wherever he went, convincing gullible maidens that they were unique, that they needed to mate with him to unlock what was special about them. Squeezing himself with a sigh into their child's parts as they spread wide to accommodate him. Warriors took what they wanted at sword-point, Bards had to charm their way in.

Look into your heart, Nyneve, you know everything I have told you is true. Eifion and Gwanaelle know what you are, where you came from. They were there. Or have I manufactured that as well?

She pressed her hands so hard onto her ears she thought her skull might crack. 'You might. Who knows what you can do with your thrall.'

But beneath all the pain she knew the instinct inside her that could divine truth from deceit had never once called his tale a lie, but the need to hurt him burned within her almost as fiercely as the Searing.

'You are an old man, Bleheris, and unworthy of me, and any offspring I might have.'

With that, everything stopped.

The Searing, the tormented itch, the bending bones. It was like plunging her face underwater until the sounds of the valley were suddenly…silent. The end of the pain was somehow worse than experiencing it, as though she had forgotten already how it felt not to have it. Suffering and relief left her on a hacking sob.

'I am worthy of none of you,' Bleheris murmured, his silver eyes downcast. 'I understand that. Yet I have a drive, too, and pain. Most importantly, I have purpose. *This* is why I exist.'

When they came up again his gaze was wretched.

'It does not please me to brutalise creatures that, to me, are holy. Creatures that were my mother once. My sisters. I spend a fortenyear preparing for brief moments of violence that, to me, are akin to the foulest deeds of the basest beast-rutters in the most remote villages. That the creatures come in the form of human women is no particular comfort to me because they are so dirty and damaged by the time I find them. Yet nature does, as one small kindness, at least make the business fast.'

She didn't need to enter his head to know his pain. In fact, she almost couldn't. It was too intense in there, and as much as she didn't want to feel any kind of empathy for this man, she could not help the word that sang through the silence of her body.

Truth.

He placed a hand gently on her ankle. 'A fast moment of intrusion, Nyneve, and then the worst of your pain will be gone. Forever.'

This was like her tooth. Eifion had made the quickest work he could of chipping out the worm's burrow and—while it had been excruciating—it was at least over quickly, and the worm had never returned to make a new home.

There is no toothworm, Nyneve. It is only a weakness of one tooth's crust to the honey and breads that you eat that creates the rot.

No worm? That simple truth stopped her whirling thoughts cold. Eifion, Gwanaelle, Melangell, Cai… They all knew of the toothworm. Believed in it as surely as they believed in their Gods. How many things in this world would she just…know when she was Ascended? How many mysteries would have an answer and how many sage pieces of wisdom would she be able to impart? *Nyneve*… The girl that no-one had ever listened to. Nyneve the child.

Nyneve the *Ancient One.*

Impossible not to find that, at least, alluring.

'It will be fast?'

His whole body changed then, grew taught and keen. Still old but not quite as…offensive. 'As fast as I can accomplish it.'

'And it won't hurt?'

'Nothing like the Searing. I will take particular care with you.'

'Why?'

He tipped his head and ashen hair fell around it. 'Because you are *a person*, Nyneve. Because we have spoken and eaten together and shared our stories, and because I am not the monster you believe.'

'Then what are you?'

'I am a Herald, I suppose. My arrival means it is time for you to fulfil your purpose.'

To Ascend.

She blinked at Bleheris and wallowed in the absence of pains new and old. She did not want to leave her mother. Or her father. She did not want to leave this valley forever yet neither did she want to remain in it for as long. What adventures awaited over the rim of the valley, in the uplands filled with magical beasts? What secrets? What mysteries?

Everyone leaves their valley, Nyneve. Now it is your time.

'Promise me you will not let me hurt my mother or father,' she whispered. 'When it happens. Give me your vow.'

His clouded eyes grew steady. 'I so vow.'

'Then do it.' She threw herself back onto the furs. 'Quickly.'

Bleheris fumbled his way closer toward her in the small space, loosening his trews and tugging his own furs up. Nyneve squeezed her eyes shut, not at all ready to see the instrument of her violation. She'd seen Eifion without his wears—many times—so the make of a man was not a complete mystery, but she was not about to replace that safe memory with an image of wiry silver hairs and a member as wrinkled as his face.

'Part your legs... Let me closer.'

'Don't speak,' she barked. 'I don't want to hear it.' The grunting from her vision was bad enough.

He acquiesced—why wouldn't he now that he was getting what he wanted?—and so she had to endure the rasp of his fingers as he pushed her dress up and the nettle shift beneath it. Now that he had taken the itching from her, the nettle became almost unbearable, especially as Bleheris lowered himself onto her more fully and flattened it against her.

She lay rigid beneath him, but let him nudge her thighs away from each other and tried to forget that she was now naked and exposed to an old man, but his fingers would not let her forget as he fumbled them into place and parted her with one hand while pressing into her with the other.

Immediately she was someone else.

Somewhere else.

Sometime else.

Still laid out in furs but they were finer and softer and more fragrant than any she'd ever lain on. Nearby a fire crackled and its warmth cocooned her even as she lay open to the air from the waist down, and the man pressing down on her wasn't some old stranger. Feelings of love suffused her, of safety, and she curled into the sensation to escape what was happening to her in her own shelter, but as the fingers in her vision pressed in and out of her body as Bleheris' did in the real world, the vision-man began to speak. Words of praise, words of comfort, and she waited for the love she could feel to swell, but it did not, as the fingers set about their work, all she knew was confusion, and the beginnings of shame, and fear.

'Better you learn this from me, my love,' the voice murmured, hot against her ear. 'Better it be done with love, gently than at the fumbling of some half-man you barely know.'

She tried to press up, to protest but Bleheris used his weight to keep her down, the man in the vision used a splayed hand pressed hard onto her flat chest.

'Let me teach you, child'

'Father...'

Bleheris paused as Nyneve spoke at the same time as the vision voice.

Gwanaelle! She knew her mother's voice instantly. Those were her mother's fine furs she could feel, her mother's fire keeping them both warm, and that was her mother's own father preparing her body for his violation.

'Stop...'

She pushed at Bleheris as Gwanaelle pushed at her father. Small, ineffectual hands. The shame of what he was doing, what she was allowing, swamped in where sense should have been.

'Relax...'

Gods, the very same words from both men. The very same croon.

'Stop!'

The vision ended and Nyneve opened her eyes to find Bleheris half-tumbled out of the shelter where she'd pushed him in the blindness of her vision, his wears as out of place as his astonishment. Somewhere deep in her mind she wondered if she was the only person ever to have physically hurt the Myrddyn. Fury filled his gaze.

And then the Sight returned. Another vision, a darker one, impossibly awful.

Gwanaelle, torn and bloodied, arms and legs shattered and twisted impossibly. As if dropped from some great height by a creature. Eifion crippled with despair, cringing back in terror from something as it tore into his wears with flashing talons.

Realisation shattered. Cringing back from *her.*

Truth.

'You gave me your vow!' she cried as Bleheris surged back into the shelter. She kicked out with her legs and, again, threw him out of the shelter with her new power. Every sinew in her little body coiled up tighter with the horror of what she had seen. Of what she would do to the people she loved.

'Nyneve!' his fury roared. 'I *will* seed you! I must!'

'You will not!'

The shame and horror of living the violation Gwanaelle felt at her father's hands slammed headlong into the terror of what she would do to the people she loved if she Ascended. She looked again at the tableau the flash vision had seared into her mind. Gwanaelle dead and bloodied, her throat severed near clean through, proud, brave Eifion reduced to a cowering animal, scrambling backwards from what she would become. Terror live in his despair-filled eyes. A bloodied blade in his hand.

She scrabbled to her feet, better to defend herself. 'I will not Ascend.'

'You will. Regardless of what happens here today, but you will be barren and lonely for age after age after age.'

'I will be alone regardless,' she snarled, realising. 'Whether or not I produce heirs will not change that.'

She thought again of the hoary old dragon Bleheris had mentioned who had Ascended without being seeded. How had she resisted the Searing? But she had not... she had gone quite mad with the—

'So be it!' Bleheris sneered, and with the wave of a hand returned all of Ascensions heralds to her. Everything she had endured overnight and more. Every part he had been taking for her until now.

She screamed and doubled over with the sudden, returned agony.

Bleheris took his opportunity and knelt behind her, reaching in under her shift with one hand as he twisted his other in her hair. 'Perhaps this is how it is ever supposed to be.'

The memory of the dragonling in her vision returned and she twisted with all her might away from his hold and onto her back, leaving her legs free to kick out and defend herself.

A new energy came from somewhere, more powerful even than her many pains, and she fought him until he realised the truth of her passion.

'Ascension is making you strong,' he panted, old beyond his years. 'It is starting.'

'Then it will happen without you,' she pledged. If she was going to tear anyone apart let it be this man.

He crawled back across the shelter, pressed to a crouch and blazed anger in her direction. Yet in there somewhere was concern. 'This will kill you, Nyneve. No-one has ever resisted Ascension.'

Her reply was more snarl than speech. 'Then I will be the first.'

Doubt made his words tremble and she knew that if ever there was a dragonling to refuse Ascension, she was the one. 'I will not help you. I will not spare you your pain and I will not give up. I will find another way to help you Ascend.'

Her chest heaved with the effort of not ripping his throat out. Right now, she felt like she could actually do it.

'But I will not seed you. I, too, can bare the pain and it will go away for me as soon as you have Ascended, but you… You will live with it for the rest of your long, long life whether or not you Ascend. Your Man-like form will not be able to survive it for long and so either you will finally relent or you will tear yourself apart. Your *y Ddraig* form will be able to endure it forever, but you will feel every, agonising moment.' He sneered so close in her face she felt his spit sizzle against her skin. 'And I will visit you every winter to gloat as you slowly go mad from despair.'

She bent double, then. Crippled beneath the pain. Beneath the vengeful image of herself alone and miserable for such a long life. But she managed a little spirit, still. 'You give up so easily, Old Man?'

'It is not surrender,' he panted, 'it is sense. You are an aberration amongst your kind. Better you were raised by wolves in this valley than by Men. Who can know what offspring of yours would become? It is better for all that the aberration dies with you.'

Who can know? *He* could; with one look. He was Myrddyn.

She realised then. He had looked, he had seen. And whatever he saw frightened him.

Power, raw and satisfying billowed up deep inside her gut and it grew bigger and faster and more furious as it swelled within her and barrelled ever upwards towards the light, until it burst from her lips on a scream such as she'd only heard in her vision of the beasts above the waterfall. Fulsome and terrifying and deadly in its focus.

Instinctively she knew it should be filled with the fire that blazed within her, but the terrifying screech was enough.

Bleheris' skin paled to the same colour as his hair and he stumbled backward out of the shelter, truly terrified for maybe the first time in his life. His legs failed him and he scrambled backwards in the snow until she could no longer see him through the flaps of her shelter, and then she let herself fall first to her knees and then onto her side on the furs, exhausted but exalted, the pain lessened for having been so violently expelled through her fragile, human throat, but lessened nonetheless.

Euphoria swilled through her—the thought that there was one way, at least, to keep the pain at bay without allowing her transformation. The thought that *she* now held the power. She well believed that the

Myrddyn wouldn't try to force her again—to save his own skin—and that he would do nothing to spare her any pain of the looming Ascension, and she well believed that he would set his considerable mind firmly on the task of finding a different way to trigger her Ascension.

But he wouldn't do it today, and he wouldn't do it this se'nnight, and by the time he had discovered how, Eifion and Gwanaelle would be back and she would have her family as well as her heritage to help protect her. They could return to Melangell and see what she knew. She could surround herself with people who would help her *not* fulfil this purpose.

She would be as a Myrddyn—*y Ddraig* in human form.

And she would be eternal.

And so, despite the weakness of her body, despite the pathetic position she lay in quite unable to right herself, she reached out with her mind and pressed a thought straight into Bleheris' the moment she felt the swampy softness of his.

Welcome to a new age, old man!

X X X

Death

THE FIRST TIME Eifion's gut twisted, deep in the night, he knew that Gwalchafad's taunts were more than just a tool to stoke a fire of terror within a victim. They were truth. Honey and milk on their own would sustain a man under normal conditions but forced, together, down his throat... Gut-twist had quickly led to gut-spurt and seeping a fetid slime between your thighs was bad enough when marching or riding but when you were submerged in a sea of your own decaying body it simply added to the horror of Gwalchafad's torment.

Until the filth came, he'd reduced himself by still dunking his face into the flesh-and-piss-soup to keep the flies at bay. Surely nothing on his lips could make him sicker than the death that would eventually seep in through his sores. For a moment, he thought he had his escape because though his skin swelled horribly it also flexed, formless and utterly senseless, beneath the leather ties, but no matter which way he strained, all it did was tear more numbed, pale flesh open on his ankles, and where did he hope to go if he tumbled from this cauldron to feet that could not stand him up.

Three nights had come and gone by his reckoning and, each mistrise, one of Gwalchafad's watchmen would ask him if he was ready to reveal his secrets and—when he wasn't—the man would force-feed him more death and leave him in comparative darkness with only the streaks of morning light creeping through the ill-fit wall timbers of the bolt-house. In the dim light, he'd watched the skin he thought he knew so well—every mark, every spot, every scar—turn white as death, swell up and start sloughing away on what little tide his pathetic attempts at movement caused in the water.

And then he'd just stopped looking down.

Because seeing his death did nothing to change it.

Waves of stupor came over him first, then a lingering belly-sickness—though thanks to the gut-spurt, he had nothing to gag up into the putrid mix—and then the most violent of tremors as the sweating sickness took hold. On the fourth morning came the head-lolling visions and when Gwalchafad's watchman came in just after mistrise, a weave pressed against his nose against the stench, he didn't ask him for his secrets and he didn't fill his throat with honey-brew. He just backed out again and left him be.

That was when he knew he had bested Gwalchafad.

But also that he was dead.

Still, days had passed since been able to feel any one specific pain, the sweating-sickness ensured he was almost warm, and his visions were both engaging and filled the long, lonely day of darkness until yet another night came. His long-dead mother crouched by his bed and gently stroked his head, her breath warm and sweet against his fly-bitten flesh. He buried himself deep in the first girl he'd ever laid with and sighed at the relief of one small part of him being warm, if not quite dry. He clashed swords with a younger Cai in a field—hale, healthy, nimble—and would have bested him had a vision of Gwanaelle not appeared at the foot of his cauldron and distracted him, her blue eyes round-wide with horror then flooding over with tears at the sight of him. Real enough to touch one last time if only he could master any part of him to do more than just bob there, rotting. Ghost enough to croak her name aloud in the moment before she vanished. And then the whore from Old Soul's night, dancing around him from left to right, her enormous breasts jiggling, trying to draw his gaze off Gwanaelle's soft beauty. Failing.

He knew the scream of rough hands on open flesh—though could not issue one—and the added agony of a cheap cloak thrown over him for final insult. But the last thought that was born in his addled mind was that he had also bested the Creil—he would die without murdering any that he loved. Without bleeding the essence from Gwanaelle's sweet flesh.

And after everything he'd done and seen in his time in this life, that was a satisfying enough way to end it.

Part III

XXXI

Retrieved

BOTH FORTENNIGHTS of *Smoke* passed before Eifion so much as murmured in his insensible state. Gwanaelle had grown used to his new, butchered, aspect and she hated it less and less as her hatred of the man who had perpetrated it grew and grew with every passing day.

When they'd finally arrived, she and Cai had skirted around the edge of bustling Trellech unseen by the stronghold's watchmen. But not by its vigilant whores, here or in all the villages they'd travelled. They were ever the first to greet a pair of travellers late in the season. Two had welcomed them almost immediately: one, sturdy and ample enough to bear even Cai's massive weight, and the other with hands as soft and small as a bird who pledged herself to the gentlest carnal care of a noblewoman, should that be of interest. It almost was after days on horseback. Gwanaelle thought she would happily endure any awkward intimacy in return for a soft matting to lay on for one night. But they'd handed over coin, instead, for information and the older, ample whore had cast them a curious look before taking them back to her place of business to tell what she knew.

As it transpired, she knew rather a lot.

Before another day had passed, the whore was urging her to keep her head as they each hefted one of Eifion's rotting shoulders over their own and lurched with him out of the bolt-house, the skin of his swollen feet peeling off as they dragged him across the snow. Angharad's stern words were the only thing that got Gwanaelle moving again as she'd stood transfixed and horrified at what little of Eifion they'd managed to find in the bolt-house after a se'nnight of Gwalchafad's brutality.

The other whores were not at all pleased that Cai had lopped off the heads of the stationed watchmen while they still had their mouths wrapped around their fusty, midnight cocks. But, either worse things happened regularly to whores or they took one look at Eifion's sloughing flesh and decided they were grateful for the comparative reprieve of a dead-cock twixt their lips, because they recovered from their ire quickly and helped scurry the group away into the woods under the comparative darkness of the new moon.

Since then, they had been nothing but accommodating to Gwanaelle's little party of runaways—and not just to their coin—hiding them in a tiny winter cellar in the whore-house and running interference whenever any came too close. Cai was impossible to disguise for long in such a small village—and too big in such a small room—and so Gwanaelle anxiously sent him off just one night into Eifion's sequester to steal his own mare back and then make what winter-shelter he could deep in the woods where he could keep to his privacy. And she…? Well, she became a whore, as far as any in the ramshackle dwelling were concerned. She surrendered her finery in a great show of reluctance, as though it was a brand new hardship, and returned to the kind of shabby wears she'd become so used to this past near-score of winters, in order that she blend in like a pale hare against the snow.

It was the time of *Plenty* and anyone with sense was tucked safely into their little houses, gobbling down anything that would not survive the whole of winter yet—still—a few men each day found their way to the whore-house where a resident fiery-haired noblewoman would have drawn attention. As it was, they kept her hair dulled with a mix of wax and dirt dug from the cellar and, for the most part, they kept her out of sight below the floor.

Gwanaelle stood and flexed her stiff shoulders. She was no Cai, but even she could barely stand straight in the tiny, windowless place.

When all had left the house, the whores lifted aside the straw matting used as a soft bed for their fucking and laid open the cellar's hatch and an unconscious Eifion breathed his first fresh air in hours. When customers were afoot they laid it back on and Gwanaelle could only sit, blushing, right below it as one of the women who had been so kind to her was ploughed into it again and again for a scraping of grain or a gnarled tin coin.

Still, as long as there was fucking above, it meant it wasn't one of the local Lord's men conducting a furious raid to find Eifion. Those early days of *Smoke* were the scariest. Eventually, though, the Lord must have accepted that Eifion had—somehow—escaped far away, for just one day after Eifion's horse also disappeared, the raids stopped. Or perhaps they only moved their search further afield?

In which case they were now Cai's problem.

A throaty murmur brought her eyes around in the dim light. These days, Eifion rested more deeply. Not the fitful, pained starts between delirious bouts when they'd first brought him here—butchered and stewed raw—but actual proper sleep. Healing hour after healing hour. Still only moments of consciousness but where that had first distressed her she now saw it as a blessing. Not only was he being spared the agony of his recovery but he was spared the endless, excruciating days and nights without end in this tiny, dank space.

And a sleep-murmur—while not speech—meant that he could still at least use his chords. One less salve to apply.

If the whores had been curious as to how a noble-woman knew so much about the pickings of the woods, they never said so. Angharad watched at her side like the most eager of students—or like someone ravenous for a way out of whoredom—and teaching her helped to pass the interminable fortennights below the hatch. Together they prepared an unction of swine-grease stamped in with staunch-grass and lathed it straight on to the weeping, open gouges in Eifion's flesh after they'd first laid him carefully onto Gwanaelle's new cloak—the finest weave any of them could find in this place. Staunch-grass was not her first choice—the stink of it was scarcely better than Eifion's own rotting flesh—but it was the best they could do on the sharp edge of winter. She scraped what little winter-moss she could from the corners of the dark cellar and packed that into the wounds as well and laid the whole lot over with a sticky press of weavers-web. The whores already kept Foxglove in their house—useful for ending unwanted quickenings—and, in small, regular pinches, it strengthened and slowed the press of blood against Eifion's butchered flesh. They eased bitter Wormwood down his throat—oh, how he'd fought them even in his delirium—to act as salve to his abused stomach and to help him fall into the kind of sleep he needed to heal, and pressed a wad of willow-bark between his teeth where it served to prevent his tongue from falling back into his throat and where it soaked in the waters of his mouth and slowly released what he needed to ease some of his pain.

They could not burn the bay leaves—even the whores used that one to help them sleep—because its distinctive smell lingered long after it was extinguished—even during the time of *Smoke*—but once Eifion's flesh had healed enough that it was no longer hanging from his bones, they bathed him twice a day instead in boiled bay to take away the anguish of his sinews re-growing and help ease the crippling twist of those that had endured.

And all of it, at all times, was done with water from the same spring Bleheris had directed Eifion to. The dragon-burrow she assumed he'd hidden the pieces of Creil in, though she'd not bothered to look. The whores grizzled as bitterly as the cold air outside at having to go to such a distant well with a pail in each hand, and so Gwanaelle had adopted that as her particular responsibility, taking the opportunity to get out of the cellar. Their complaints had stopped as they saw the warrior slowly—surely—returning from beyond the dead. His skin healing over if not quite filling back out.

Instead, they began to look at Annais' spring in rather more admiring terms.

'My skin has never been so clear,' said one.

'It burned as I pissed, afore,' whispered another. 'Until I started drinking from Eifion's fresh pail. Now…nothing!'

'I've been sluicing it on my furrow. Fresh as bloody rosemary now, I tell you.'

Even as they approached the bitterest and stillest se'nnights of the year—*Silence*—the women of the whorehouse now scrabbled for the privilege to brave the frozen land and fetch the water every second day. Which suited Gwanaelle because she grew less and less inclined to leave Eifion in case he chose that moment to wake.

He would not find himself alone if she could help it.

'I miss you,' Gwanaelle murmured to his grey, closed lids.

His face had fared best of the torture he'd endured because it hadn't been below the water. The strange bites and marks had taken their time to heal, but heal they eventually had and the few pocks and scars left were nothing on what still lingered below the soft weave draped over his healing flesh. Entire chunks were now absent on his limbs and torso, like he had survived the skin-rot, and where they were not, the flesh was an angry kind of red as it grew back in.

When she looked at Eifion's face only it was almost possible to forget the horrors he had endured while she and Cai had plodded ever southwards, taking their time to protect their own lives. Had they plodded too long? Should they have run their horses until they could not stumble another step? Had they preserved their own lives at the expense of Eifion's? Should they have stormed the stronghold rather than talk their eventual way around to Angharad's enclave of whores? For the first fortennight, she had feared so.

She curled her fingers around the two smallest on one of his hands—the ones with the least wounded flesh—and held on there, repeating the simple vow.

'I miss you.'

Miss. Because she could not say *love.* Not aloud. Not even with him oblivious in fever.

He never answered her murmurs; she did not require it. Sometimes she sat and spoke for half the day to his insensible form because it made her feel better. Closer. She told him things she'd never spoken of before—inconsequential things about her childhood, her thoughts, her opinions—simply so that he had something to grasp. He may not return her love but he knew her voice like he knew his own, and she wanted him to have *something* to climb on back to life when his body was ready.

'I understand them now, Eifion.' She lowered her voice to a bare murmur and leaned in closer to him lest she be overheard. 'These whores. All whores, really. I have blamed them for the longest time. For having you. For taking you away from me, but these are no creatures of greed or sin. They are entirely made from compassion. From patience and acceptance. Even in their own misery. I have heard them speak of the men that come here—the arrogant watchmen that treat them so poorly, the old herdsmen who fumble and stammer through it all, the young boys on their fortenyear—never with contempt or disdain. They understand them.

'They know the burning frustrations of trained fighters who rarely get to use their swords, watching the comings and goings through their Lord's gate. Keeping honed their swords for a battle they will never see. The deep shame of that. The need to purge that shame somehow.

'They are kind with the forten-boys laying for the first time with a woman, and they have that one opportunity to teach them how to behave with respect.' Days later and the lesson would be subsumed as they rutted their way through the village maids like prideful little beasts, but the lesson could not ever be un-learned and perhaps, the good whores imagined, it would be remembered when they were grown, when they were finally men. And perhaps some other woman would benefit from their careful patience, now.

'They are kind, even, to the goat-herds who slide into them stinking of the beasts that they share the fields with. Men with wives they do not see but three times a year, men with nothing but time and silence to contemplate. Men whose closest friends are goats.'

She sank her head. 'They do not judge others as I have judged their kind, Eifion. I am shamed by the generosity and care they have shown you.' And herself. Not one of them had ever pressed her for details of their origins or the great excitement of a *woman* coming to rescue a *warrior*. 'At enormous risk to themselves.'

'And so I see why you go to them. I might never truly accept it, but I do understand it. They offer you their silent acceptance when all I have offered you on the matter is my judgement. Like some fisher's wife. I am truly sorry.'

A tear grew too fullsome even to roll down her cheek, tumbling instead off the ledge of her cheekbone and splashing onto Eifion's healing face.

'I will do better, Eifion. Just come back to me and I will be grateful for the gift of your friendship, your company and your protection and I will not be greedy for more.'

Within her own careful clutch, Eifion's smallest finger twitched and then tried to curl around hers, but found itself too weak.

Her heart began to pound. The effort was enough. The effort meant that he could hear her, understand her. The effort meant they had not only kept his body alive but they had brought his mind safely through his ordeal, too.

She leaned in, keenly. 'Eifion? Do not try to move. You are in a safe place and I am here with you. It is mid-winter, we cannot leave this place yet for fortennights and so there is no rush to heal. Take your time. There is no rush,' she repeated.

Yet he would not settle. The balls of his eyes flicked and rolled behind their lids and he seemed more agitated than confusion would cause, but she sought to reassure him, regardless.

'The Creil is safe in its nest. Cai is here, hidden, waiting to protect us as we fly back to the valleys. We have horses and coins. Nyneve is in the care of Bleheris. All is truly well, I promise.'

But the twitching did not cease and his fingers joined in, as if eager for a blade to circle around, and Gwanaelle wondered who was in his dreams that he so badly wanted to run through.

XXXII

Truce

ALL THE LONG winter had given Nyneve and Bleheris plenty of opportunity to declare a careful, distrustful truce. He had never again attempted to take her by force or by seduction, but he had withdrawn his protection—returning her Searing completely—and he had withdrawn the thing she valued more.

His conversation.

No teaching. No tales. Not so much as a greeting.

He retreated to the edge of the valley when she was around and barred his mind from her, watching her warily. Planning his next strategy, probably. This must be what it was like for a dragonling in the care of a Morwyn Ddraig. Surviving, but little else.

She may have been *alive* but she was *alone*, despite the Myrddyn's presence.

If nothing else, it had taught her to be self-reliant and resilient. She had perfected the release of the awful tension that built up in her body through throat-stripping roars thrice-daily, by thrashing and tearing at things with the torn nails of her fingers which was strangely abating, by channelling the energy into bursts of climbing on what little of the waterfall's face was still climbable. Her fear of falling was nothing compared to the fear she held that the Searing would not stop until it had completely subsumed her.

The fear she held that she wouldn't be able to resist Ascension after all.

That the Myrddyn would be proved right.

But roaring helped, clawing helped, exertion helped, and in her better moments she got an idea of how she could live this way forever; she would grow used to the management, the pain. She *could* endure.

And then the Myrddyn would be proved wrong.

And that was the fire-stoke she needed to keep going.

She'd given up, now, on oiling her skin. It helped, but not much, and the flaking did not progress much beyond a certain point if she left it and so she did leave it and now was one big flake. Conveniently, it made her even more unattractive to Bleheris and so she felt somehow safer with her scaly coat on. It was hard to ignore the way the skin of her hands was pulling back as it dried and toughened, creating claws out of her damaged nails, but as soon as Gwanaelle returned with Eifion they would set to work easing all her sufferings.

She stretched out with her mind, far beyond this valley, toward the nothingness she knew as 'south'. She could not find Eifion at all in the darkness although she got very subtle, very random flashes of Gwanaelle. So one of them, at least, was still alive. On her fortenyear she would have raged that it was her mother who yet lived and not Eifion, but a lot had passed since that day and even Gwanaelle's arms would be a blessing around her now—fractured though their relationship was.

But if these past fortennights had shown her anything it was that *alive* and *living* were not necessarily the same thing. Just because Gwanaelle yet breathed did not mean that she was well. Or that she was returning.

Nyneve turned and glared towards the Myrddyn in the trees at the edge of the clearing.

'Watch away, old man,' she called with her voice since he had long closed his mind to her. 'Watch away.'

X X X I I I

Frost

'HE IS ASKING for you,' Angharad announced the moment Gwanaelle staggered back in from the freeze with her single cauldron of water.

It was too cold now to risk the slow walk weighted down by a pail in each hand so, instead, she went at both mistrise and rest, hurrying more quickly with the burden of just a single pail. Nonetheless, her lungs burned as surely as her bound feet despite her haste, but she would not die from the discomfort, and Eifion still needed the Creil's healing waters even though he was now awake, talking and managing to eat a little every day.

She surrendered her burden to Angharad and hurried down into the gloom of the carved out cellar, the frost on her wears cracking off and tumbling around her.

'Gwanaelle.'

'You are sitting up!'

'Angharad helped me,' he croaked. 'I am tired of staring up at the timbers of the whorehouse floor.'

'The earthen walls are so much more interesting.'

'Less like a grave, this way.'

He wanted to smile but some of the sinews required for even that simple thing were tethered in the part of his neck that was worst affected by his torture. He could manage a half-grimace but nothing more. Gods how she mourned his beautiful smile. It had always filled her with such confidence. But it had gone the way of so much of his once-strong body—hollow and frail.

'I want you to return,' he croaked. 'Go back to Nyneve.'

Everything in her tightened. 'I am sure you do.'

'She needs you.'

'You need me.'

'I have Angharad. The whores will continue my recovery. Your coins will yet buy me fortennights of their protection. Find Cai and have him escort you back to the valley.'

'While you seek your retribution on the man who did this?' Blinking was easily achieved with what sinews he yet had. 'You think I do not know what acts of revenge fill your dreams? What it means when your hands twitch and curl in your sleep? Cai will return when you and I are ready, both, to ride north to our valley. Together.' She glared. 'Directly.'

'I must face him, Gwanaelle.'

Gwalchafad. She had heard so much about the man that had caused this suffering, and she wanted vengeance on him almost as much. Eifion was a warrior first and foremost. Denying him would be foolishness. 'Not until you are strong.'

'Look at what he has done to me,' he gritted.

'Failed to kill you, you mean?'

He threw back the large weave covering his naked body. 'I am ruined, Gwanaelle.'

Still beautiful to her. There was now no small part of it that she did not know. Yet she still secretly hungered for it despite the angry welts and deep gouges. 'Do you hope to shock me with your tortured flesh, Eifion? Who do you think has been coaxing all those new sinews back to strength one by one?'

His brown eyes dropped to shadow. 'It must have disgusted you.'

'It broke my heart, but never disgust.'

'I will have vengeance for these gobs of flesh missing from my body.'

'I know, but I will not leave you to do it alone, and neither will Cai.'

Silence fell, until he eventually asked, 'How does he?'

'His complaints are as bitter as the air whenever we meet, but he endures. Winter is turning now, and he knows the time for action will come soon enough. He is ready.'

'And the Creil...?'

'Still safe as far as I am aware.' She was finally able to ask the question foremost in her mind. 'Why were you giving it to Artwr? After everything we had done to keep it from him.'

'He is losing this war against the Invaders, the Creil's remains might help him. I believe they still offer visions though not as readily as we knew.' He paused as his tongue arranged itself for yet more speech after such long silence. 'Despite everything, I do not wish to see Artwr or our lands fall to the Angles.'

He paused long enough to wet his mouth and throat from the scoop of well water Gwanaelle pressed against his lips.

'And while he is distracted with its visions,' he finally gasped, 'he might suspend his search for an actual dragon.'

She'd heard the stories. The warriors going out on great quests just as Cai and Eifion had all those winters ago. To all corners of Brython. A most unholy quest in the name of the God she'd been reared on. They had brought their Chieftain any number of powerful relics stained with the blood of his own people but nothing to rival the dragon he lost in the destruction of his stronghold at Caerwent.

His creature.

Nyneve's mother.

Would this truly stop Artwr from hunting Nyneve? 'I will stay, and Cai will stay, and we will leave—together—when you are ready.'

Which meant both *well* and *avenged*.

A floorboard above them creaked loudly.

'I don't mean to lurk,' Angharad called down from beyond the hatchway. 'Nor to have listened, but do I understand aright that you have something that is greatly desired by our Chieftain?'

Gwanaelle and Eifion both turned their dismay up to the light then glanced at each other.

'You do,' she said, simply. Carefully. After everything the whore had done for Eifion, she would not reward it with her mistrust.

'And will that thing bring danger onto this house?'

Eifion's shoulders sagged. 'It could. If it were discovered.'

'And might it change the direction of this warfare with the Angles? This...*something*?'

'Aye, it might.'

Angharad leaned over the cellar opening, a dark shadow against the light. 'And would Artwr punish any who have kept it from him?'

Eifion gritted. 'Almost certainly.'

Angharad eased her bulk down into the tiny cellar, treading carefully on each rickety step. 'Then would it not be a great satisfaction to have it number amongst the possessions of Gwalchafad ap Gwyar?'

Eifion froze… 'I had not wanted to give him such a powerful tool. Ever. What he could do with it…'

Gwanaelle had worked alongside Angharad all winter long and grown a good understanding of the direction—and the sharpedge—of the woman's mind. 'Yet, it would be satisfying indeed were it *discovered* there…'

Eifion began to see the wit in her words. 'Are you proposing hiding it amongst his possessions, Angharad?'

'I might be.'

'You do not know what it is we discuss. It could be the size of a horse.'

'Then we secrete it within his stables, warrior.'

Whether because Angharad had not made one move to know what the Creil was or because Eifion had simply grown tired of keeping its secrets, Gwanaelle noted the very moment he decided to trust her. 'And how would Artwr hear about this cache of treachery?'

'From his bonded wife.'

'The Lady Gwenhwyfar? We can no more get information to the Chieftain's lady than we can get the Creil to Artwr himself. We are fugitives.'

'Perhaps *you* cannot…'

Eifion pushed himself straighter with some pain. 'Who could?'

'A woman who knew her when she was younger. A woman who met her needs and groomed her beautiful hair 'til it shone.'

Gwanaelle gasped. 'You are kin to Gwenhwyfar's maid-servant?'

Angharad stared hard. 'I *was* Gwenhwyfar's maid-servant. Before she married Artwr. For six winters.'

Warriors were trained to digest information and recover their composure quickly it seemed, for while Gwanaelle was still rocking from how close to Artwr they had somehow come once again, Eifion was onto another question.

'And what grudge do you owe Gwalchafad ap Gwyar?'

'Everything he has done to the people of Trellech is reason enough to want him brought low before his Chieftain.'

Eifion's gaze narrowed. 'But this will not be low. This will be death. Treason. Why do you wish that on your Lord's brother?'

Dismay struck her eyes.

'Confess Angharad. If we are to trust you with our greatest secret.'

'Because *I* was the messenger, warrior. His mother's messenger, made complicit in her death and Lamorak's, and when he'd finished separating them from their heads, Gwalchafad ap Gwyar made it his business to see me punished as well for giving in to his coercion. Banished. Here to Trellech for my part in the whole mess. With no position.'

'To his own stronghold?'

'It brings him pleasure every day to see just how low I have been brung. He fairly recommends me to those lords and warriors of his acquaintance who visit, especially the brutal ones. That pleases him especially.'

'He made you a whore...' Eifion murmured.

Companions to a Queen did not come from any but the very best families. Gwanaelle crossed and took Angharad's hand—woman of blood to woman of blood, not that either of them looked much like it anymore—and murmured.

'And you would make him a traitor.'

X X X I V

Deceit

THERE WAS NO-ONE else to do it. Angharad had ridden off on one of the quality horses, accompanied by Cai for safety, squeezed into Gwanaelle's purchased finery, to take a message to her once-mistress, the Chieftain's bonded wife. She rode out wide to avoid the returning party of Trellech's Lord after wintering with Artwr. Gwalchmai rode in a flurry of lesser warriors, armsmen and bannermen which—even for him—was excessive.

Then again Gwalchafad was nothing like the boy he remembered. Why would Gwalchmai be?

But the festivities of his return were the perfect opportunity to get into the stronghold and disguise the Creil where it could later be found. The very first thing Gwalchmai would call for would be a clutch of whores to wipe off the weariness of travelling.

Not only would he or Cai make a very average whore but both their faces were far too recognisable to emerge anywhere near Trellech's stronghold, and his own muscles were so wasted yet, he could barely lift a sword, let alone use it with any force.

Gwanaelle truly was the only one suited to the task.

Not that any man would believe her a whore if he looked at her long.

It did not sit with him well to be the most passive part of any plot and so he'd worked for a se'nnight straight to build the strength he needed to first rise, then walk, climb out of the hatch and set foot in the fresh air. He did it at night, of course, to satisfy Gwanaelle's anxiety and to ensure that Angharad's kindness was not repaid by capture for aiding an escape. Until finally he limped toward the stones, then the circle of trees around Annais' well, and he sunk himself once again into the healing waters to retrieve the Creil.

Angharad blazed with curiosity but did not ask to see the Creil and she certainly did not try to touch it. Not after Gwanaelle sombrely confessed what it was that she would be carrying in her message. She gave the large leather fold very wide berth and watched it constantly whenever she had cause to be in their cellar.

And now she was gone. A messenger once more... Yet perhaps this message might undo the harm of the last.

'You know what to do?' Eifion asked as a small, dark-haired whore and a taller pale-haired one plumped and tucked and pinched Gwanaelle's flesh until it flushed with colour. Far too much flesh, far too readily displayed for his comfort, but there was no question she could pass as one of them as they entered the stronghold.

'Enter with our friends,' she said arranging her own flesh more to her satisfaction, 'then steal away, secrete our package in the location described by Angharad, then secrete myself until the festivities are waning.'

Then leave. With haste. 'And what else?'

Her pretty eyes rolled. 'Do not grow curious. Do not try to make better on the plan.'

He curled his fingers around her soft wrist. Some part of him felt like a filthy leper touching the mother of Christ, but Gwanaelle did not so much as flinch, she just met his eyes seriously. 'Come back safe to me, Gwanaelle.'

Was he corrupt for playing on the feelings he knew she had for him? Or was he justified in fashioning a weapon from whatever was at hand?

Her confidence soaked into him. 'I am as Angharad, delivering a message, merely.'

Yes. A deadly message if she was caught. 'This entire plot fails if Gwalchafad catches on to what we are doing.'

'He will not. Not because of me.' She looked at the two women. 'Sisters, are we prepared?'

They nodded and Gwanaelle stepped back amongst their number. Eifion released his breath slowly. She would stand out in any such crowd, let alone one as lascivious as Gwalchmai's was reported to be. She bent gracefully, lifted the weave-wrapped Creil shards into her arms and watched as the whores all did the same with bundles of whatever they could get their hands on. One such parcel would stand out, if everyone had one…

'I will return to you, Eifion,' she murmured and then pressed her lips briefly to his cheek. Right near the corner of his mouth. Right over one of his pock scars. As though they were nothing to her.

And then she was gone.

And he was left with nothing to do but pace the back room of the empty whorehouse as they made their way up to the stronghold.

'As soon as this is done…' he told himself. Promised himself.

Because if he'd been stronger and less set on vengeance, then he and Cai and Gwanaelle would be riding north right now, ahead of thaw, returning to Nyneve. Had his arrogance—his conceit—put Gwanaelle in danger?

He might as well have put that sword to her throat just as he'd seen in the Creil's vision.

The little dark-haired whore burst back into the room, as pale as the snow kicked up on her cloak but with stains of terror in her cheeks.

'Gwanaelle sent me,' she panted. 'I only have a moment. Lord Gwalchmai has come.'

'Good. He was expected.'

The girl was young and clearly had a flare for the dramatic. Not what you'd expect in a whore…

'You do not understand, sir,' she urged, her little fists curled in cloak, dark eyes peering up. 'He is not come alone.'

A nauseous feeling akin to the decay of his stomach after days in Gwalchafad's piss stew came over him in the face of the girl's trepidation.

'The King is here,' the girl squeaked. '*Artwr is here.*'

XXXV

Artwr

WALKING INTO the stronghold was easier flanked by the women she'd come to know over winter, yet still Gwanaelle trembled with every step. Despite the frost, each of the whores paused at the gates to the stronghold and shrugged off their cloaks to carry them bundled in their arms the way that Gwanaelle carried the Creil pieces bound up in hers. In that way, her burden went unremarked. The watchmen assumed they were merely displaying their assets to their best for their returned Lord Gwalchmai and his illustrious guest, never realising they were in fact accomplice to treachery.

The presence of a new, flame-haired whore drew more attention than Gwanaelle would have liked, even disguised as she was by walking midst her sisters, but every man knew that the whores had not been assembled for them—least not first choice—and so the group passed unmolested deeper into the heart of the stronghold.

Eifion had described the outer yarden, and how to locate the mousehole to the outside but his access within the stronghold had been limited and so she had to rely on the whores to direct her within it. As they passed into the long-hall, one of them first caught her eye and then directed it with purpose toward the far end of the hall.

Gwalchafad's chamber.

'Welcome home, brother,' a man who could only be Gwalchafad said from near the fire, loud and extra pompous. 'Everything is in readiness.'

Gwanaelle craned her neck to see but warriors, arms-men and watchmen alike all milled between her and the glimpse that she sought. Still, a crowd would make it easier for her to step away.

'I would expect no less,' another voice said.

'Gwalchmai,' one of the whores whispered and then readjusted her breasts to flattering advantage.

After a moment of murmured silence, the voice continued, extra loud. 'Your Lord and mine, Chieftain and protector of all Cymry, Artwr, pen Dragon.'

The assembly began a rousing chant of warrior cries and their heads turned as someone—Artwr presumably—moved along the front of the group, greeting his servants.

'Can you see?' one whore murmured.

'Nothing but warrior arse,' another grumbled.

'Then to purpose,' Gwanaelle said over the chanting.

As sheep they began shuffling back, a small flock buffeted by the assembly, but really doing their own share of nudging through all the wet fur and leather, until they lingered near the opening that led to Gwalchafad's chamber. There they stopped, on the sheer face of their own treachery, and Gwanaelle knew they had done all they could.

The rest was up to her.

'I have been in the East for two long winters,' Artwr's voice intoned from beyond the screen of men, 'holding the Angles back at the old Roman circus. For now, they are held.'

A rousing cheer and cacophony of upthrust swords and shield pounding provided the cover Gwanaelle needed to simply step back into the shadows beyond the opening. If there was a guard on the far-side too disciplined to have drifted into the long-hall to see his King, she would play the novice, overwhelmed by the ferocity of the crowd, seeking a moment from her inevitable violation this day.

What she would do then, she was not quite sure.

But as she eased back into the shadows, and yet further back, she discovered that none in Gwalchmai's stronghold was disciplined enough to withstand the lure of Artwr the King and so she turned and counted her way along the long hall, past opening after opening.

Being women, none of her sisters had been invited to Gwalchafad's own chamber but—being whores—they had done service in most every other room in the stronghold at one point or another. Foodstores, chambers, stairhalls... And so they had been able to draw a map of the fortification and identify most of the spaces in it. Except for two.

One was the Gwalchmai's treasury. The other was his brother's personal chamber.

Either one would do for her purpose except that Eifion had suspected the man—and Thane—he remembered would know to a pile what was in his brother's treasury but he hazarded the man would have little idea what lay below his own bed.

And so she came to the first of the chambers on the map gouged into the snow and took a deep breath before stepping within.

Chamber or treasury…?

Air puffed out of her on a soft hiss.

Chamber.

Without pause, Gwanaelle crossed straight to the straw matting Gwalchafad rested his head on and laid down her burden. Then she took up the summer-cloak draped over a nearby hook and laid it out before transferring the fractured contents of her own into Gwalchafad's and re-bundling the Creil. Something fae made her apologise to it, under her breath, for placing it into the hands of someone so unworthy, and something yet more dangerous made her touch it, palm down, right before she folded the quality weave over on itself. As ever it had, she saw her mother, a brief glimpse of her despair at sending her own daughter away to uncertainty and, as ever it had, the sight brought her strength as well as comfort, but it took all the strength she had to give the Creil away, knowing she would never again enjoy one of its visions, and duck down to shove it far to the back of the wooden supports that kept Gwalchafad's matting from the earthen floor.

That will teach you to be too good for a straw mat like your fellows...

Once that was done, there was nothing left to do but throw on her cloak and scurry like a mouse to the gnawed hole Eifion had described and make her way back to the whorehouse. Back to him. Yet, as she re-traced her path, the rousing cheers suddenly ceased and with it her footsteps and her very breath.

Artwr was speaking. Low and passionate. Entreating. Seducing…

This was the high Chieftain of all of Cymry. The *King* of the Brythons—those that were left after the Empire withdrew but before the invaders came from across the sea. One of the most powerful and charismatic men in all the land.

Yet enemy of *y Ddraig*.

Should she not learn something of this man that would take Nyneve into bondage and use her cruelly for her magic? A glimpse at least so she knew who to fear? Perhaps it would help to put a face to the man who had wrought their lives for all these years.

She paused on the stairhall. Right, to the yarden, Eifion's mousehole and freedom. The other way to the long-hall, the whores and Artwr's passionate speech.

Do not try to improve on the plan, Gwanaelle...

She could leave, her task completed, and earn Eifion's relief as well as his gratitude, and by the time the hue and cry went out over the discovery of the Creil they would be far from this place. Or she could stay, glimpse Artwr with her own eyes—accomplish what Eifion himself never had—and perhaps earn a measure of her love's esteem as well.

If she could not have his heart, she would have his respect.

She turned left.

~

The whores had been gathered up by the time she slid back into the long-hall, but not so far that she could not scurry to rejoin the shelter of their number. Several of her sisters looked alarmed to see her slide back in amongst their flock but kept their heads and their focus as they were squired through the champing armsmen toward Gwalchmai and the front of the assembly. Once there, Artwr's Guard stepped up first, moving through them and examining them like so much meat as they purported to check them over for an assassin's blade. Gwanaelle ignored the Guard's roaming, intrusive hands and stared instead at the men who were ignoring them—Gwalchafad, Gwalchmai and their King, Artwr. Though which was which she could not readily say.

Two were Lot's sons, from the north-most reaches of Cymry like her mother and so those must be them; the taller man with a warrior's bearing and with travel-worn, blade-hacked hair the same colour as her own, and a paler man beside him, clean-shaved of face, long, clean locks and not a stitch of his wears out of place.

Ranging warrior, Gwalchmai, and his stronghold-bound brother, Gwalchafad.

Her eyes moved to the left. Which made *that man* Artwr.

Finished speaking now, the high Chieftain stretched back in the largest seat in the long-hall, seemingly at rest, his own battle-wears worn but not shabby. If he had seen any battle action, he hadn't seen it in those leathers. At least, not recently. Perhaps the King liked to remind people every moment that he was a warrior first and a King second? Or perhaps he was riding to battle as soon as he left Trellech?

Or riding off to seek a dragon?

His face was as weathered as his leathers, his nose crooked where it had been broke in some skirmish or another, but it did not diminish him. Largely because a person would be too busy being drawn into those blazing, hooded eyes to much concern themselves with the condition of his nose. Bearded, like most warriors, as carefully crafted as the rest of his warrior appearance. This man was five years Cai's junior, she knew, but you would not know that from his appearance. Every crease in his face told a tale, and most of them spoke of hardship, loss and pain.

Yet all men would whore their mothers out to be King.

'Bring them,' Gwalchafad called.

Still Artwr and Gwalchmai ignored the flesh-for-sale, even as they were paraded right before their stations. At least that is how it seemed to Gwanaelle, but the whores surrounding her knew better; they stood tall, slightly turned, ribs pushed out. Anything to earn advantage. This was a *King*, she had to remember, and Kings brought rewards, but she'd seen Artwr now and could describe him to any who asked and so she was no longer interested in remaining in this company as the men picked over the women like ravens on a corpse. She shrugged her cloak more fully around her and kept her face averted.

'This assembly lacks lustre indeed when even the whores are disinterested,' a loud voice said, and she was too afraid to look to see which man it was that slurred—King, Lord or Thane. 'I think this one has somewhere else to be, Gwalchmai.'

King, then.

A sharp little elbow in the ribs brought her gaze back to the men at the head of the hall, though she was careful to fix it at a cluster of buckles on Artwr's chest and not on his own regard.

'I do not, sire.'

The feminine gasps all around her reminded her that women of low birth never spoke directly to nobles. Certainly not in public and without being specifically addressed. She should have just dropped her head as they now did. Like dogs fearing retribution.

Artwr's not quite steady gaze crackled the air and Gwalchafad stood more tensely beside his brother. Afraid of the slight, perhaps, and how that would reflect on him?

'Yet, there stand you, eyeing the door and dressed already in your travelling cloak.' It was only then that Gwanaelle remembered her sisters had removed their cloaks on entering the stronghold as part of their deceit whereas she had donned hers in readiness for the mousehole. 'Perhaps you have heard of my exploits on the battle-field...and off. My reputation frightens you.'

She studied those buckles as if they held the answers to the world's greatest questions.

'Or are your mysteries so great you choose not to reveal them immediately? Is that part of your tease, girl?'

Still she held her tongue. It just seemed safer.

'And now she is mute. Gwalchmai, tell me, are her talents as rare as her manner would suggest?'

'I do not know her, Lord. I cannot say.'

Behind Gwalchmai, his Thane brother seemed to realise that *he* did not know her either. The man who knew *all* about his stronghold. His eyes narrowed.

'By the Sword, that is singular enough in my Second,' Artwr said. 'I thought you'd ploughed every furrow from here to Caerllion.'

Gwalchmai laughed which gave his men permission to do so. Some of the danger leaked from the room at the sound, but not much.

'I would be happy to act as scout, Lord, and report back on her...terrain.'

'No doubt.' Artwr pushed to sitting. 'Step up, girl.'

One of Artwr's Guard grabbed her by the arm and propelled her through the whores the short distance to the foot of Artwr's seat. As though she could not make the journey unaided. Or would not. Fear twisted at the coils of her guts as her clever plan to get a glimpse of the King suddenly became so very dangerous. This was far closer than she had hoped. Close enough to feel the heat pumping off him even amid the swill of so much male lust, but she did not raise her eyes.

'Cloak,' he said, mildly, and those rough hands divested her of its warmth and what modesty it had provided over her exposed flesh.

'Built like a whore,' he observed standing and circling Gwanaelle slowly.

Heat flamed up her cheeks to be so rudely assessed in front of an entire assembly. One man seemed particularly amused by the entertainment. Gwalchafad ap Gwyar. She stole a glance at the man who had hurt Eifion so very badly, who had sought to take his life. At the man who would be traitor.

Artwr stripped off one hide glove and tossed it to his Guard then forked Gwanaelle's hair out of its modest twist so that it fell loose and wild around her shoulders. Flaming. 'Yet she does not speak like a whore, or compose herself like a whore.'

He placed the gloved hand on her belly and pulled it back towards his chest whilst using the un-gloved one to press her shoulders forward until her barely covered cleavage projected like any of the women-for-coin around her. Artwr circled fully around her, drawing his hand to her chin, lifting her face, and he began to speak, but then she lifted her gaze to boldly hold his and the words died on his lips.

His fingers dropped.

He stepped back a half-pace.

In the corner of her vision, she saw Gwalchmai frown and Gwalchafad beside him blazed dangerous curiosity at her. A stranger in his stronghold, standing just a blade's width from the highest power in the land. Never mind that she had breasts; all the better to secrete a weapon amongst. He was not going to take his focus from her for a moment.

'You have her eyes,' Artwr whispered, captivated, his meady breath eddying around her.

She risked a response. 'My Lord?'

He stepped in closer, private. 'Gwenhwyfar's. My bonded woman. You have the same eyes as she. The selfsame.'

His wonder and closeness was at once terrifying and captivating. Like standing before a wolf. Or, yes, a dragon. Yet she found enough sense to speak. 'They are the eyes of my family, Lord.'

'I was not aware that Gwenhwyfar had any whores in her family,' he said, a dangerous edge to his words.

Had she just insulted the Queen? Terror made her bumble onwards. 'What family would tell you if she did?'

Silence stole three breaths from her, then Artwr tipped back his head and barked a relaxed laugh.

'Truth.' But then he turned and faced the assembly again and decreed, 'This woman is no whore!'

Gwanaelle's legs near buckled at the exposure. Had she been discovered so easily? Immediately, she saw that Eifion and Cai would both die in the attempt to recover her and everything any of them had done would be for nothing. Melangell and her virgins left without defence, Nyneve left without a family. Without protection.

All because she wanted to assuage some curiosity about a King.

Stupid woman. Stupid, stupid...

'She with eyes such as the honourable Gwenhwyfar will not be passed around a stronghold like so much mead. Tonight, she will stand for my good wife who winters yet in Caerllion. None here shall know her.'

Gwanaelle worked hard not to sigh her relief. Instead, she said what a bold whore might, though she said it in the mumble of a frightened woman which was much easier to achieve, convincingly. 'My Lord, I must earn—'

He barked again. 'She demands compensation! Spoken like a wife, indeed.'

The assembly laughed along and Gwanaelle caught the astonished stares of her sisters. Had they never seen boldness, or just never to a King?

Artwr examined his hands for their adornment and plucked a ring off his smallest finger. It fit only the largest of hers. 'There. Now you are paid for all the cock you will not service this night.' He stepped closer, dropped his voice and raised her hand to the light. 'Or any other. Gwenhwyfar's eyes should never be scorched by the perversions a whore beholds.'

The ring on her thumb glinted a pale sheen.

'Cymry's finest gold,' he murmured. 'Gouged from the hills west of here. Enough to plough you any path you wish to follow until you are too old to walk it. You need never choose whoring again.'

That brought her gaze back up. 'You think it a choice, my Lord? Show me one woman here assembled who wouldn't rather some other occupation.'

He snorted. 'Look at them. They are so proud—'

'There is a kind of man who favours his whores broken, Lord. They do not wish to draw the eye of such here assembled.'

The colour of earth beneath Artwr's long lashes streaked over with darkness. 'Aye, I know the man of which you speak...'

Did he recognise him in this room? Or in himself?

'I will not hoard this shiny favour like some dragon,' she decided. 'I will share it amongst us all.'

His eyes swung back to her. 'And what do you know of *y Ddraig*, woman?'

'Little,' she lied. Yet it was also not a lie. 'But their greed is widely known.'

His face twisted then, darkened again and she lost him in some long forgotten memory aided by whatever Gwalchmai's aids kept refilling in his cup. 'Greed? No. Never that. Exacting, perhaps,' he went on, as though she hadn't spoken. 'Biding. Possessed of power and wisdom equally. A great and enduring foe, but they do not collect trinkets for their own sake.'

Her words were barely breaths. 'You describe yourself, Lord.'

That brought his round gaze back around to her. Had he never considered the similarities?

'I trust that a King is also kindness and compassion...' he said. 'When the moment is right.'

'Surely dragons have that, too. If only we could know their hearts.'

Two forks formed between his dark, slanted brows and, in his cups, he drifted away from her, deep into thought. Yet as she turned to step away his voice brought her back.

'Woman! If you will not keep the ring, then at least take your part of it and use it to find a place of God. Where you can be lifted up once again, restored to Grace.'

It had been so long since she had spoken with the faith of her childhood. Would God even recognise her?

'At least that, then?' he slurred. 'Could you find your way to such a place?'

A place of safety? Of sanctuary? 'I think I know such a place, my Lord.'

'Then go, Gwenhwyfar. To God with you.'

Then he let her go, step back down and move through the assembly as the whores did. The warriors and armsmen parted like sword-cut skin before her—the taint and shine of a King's word gouging the very path he had spoken of. Every one of them peered with curiosity at her face, wondering what it was that the King found there, but none was foolish enough or cocksure enough to step in her path.

All but one, that is.

At the heavy doors, Gwalchafad ap Gwyar waited for her, his hand outstretched.

'You surely did not believe you would get to keep it, little stranger-whore?'

No, but she wasn't ready to simply hand it over, either. Not to him. She lifted her chin, and closed her fist. 'It was a gift. To me.'

He took her fist and began to pry her fingers open. 'You are only here at all by *my* good Grace.'

If she had remained with her family, grown to become a noble woman with soft skin and fine bones, there was no way she could have withstood the pressure of his twisting fingers. As it was, he grew confounded by the strength of her work-toughened fingers.

'And are *you* not here by your King's good grace?' she smirked as he tugged with no result. 'Or should I say his *bad* graces?'

Dark fury stained his pale face. 'Surrender the ring, whore.'

'I will not.' Her entire lifetime of toil amongst earth and rock had prepared her for this one moment of defiance. 'You will have to break my fingers to retrieve it. In full view of your watchmen.'

His snort had no impact below the frustration of his gouging. 'You imagine any would step to the aid of a whore?'

'Not at all, but they will all witness their Thane's weakness.'

The pressure of his man's fingers was almost too much for her own and any moment one was going to splinter, but she forced the pain away in favour of staring hard into the eyes of the man who had wished Eifion dead. Around her, the struggle began to draw attention and the witnesses to Gwalchafad's shortcomings mounded. He stepped in closer, put his shoulder to the effort, twisting her wrist painfully. It screamed and burned yet, she only clenched tighter, feeling the ring's edges bite into her flesh as her nails did.

'Perhaps if you swung a blade instead of a coin-purse, your wrist would have more strength,' she sneered, loud. 'I cannot imagine how you find the strength to even pump a man's cock, Lord.'

Somewhere, someone laughed, but she passed with the protection of a King through his hall.

'Fuck!' Gwalchafad's curse spattered on her face and she stumbled back as he released her arm of a sudden. 'Take it then, desperate slut, but do not return to this stronghold again or I will cut that hand from your arm with my bluntest blade.'

She stepped right up into his face where none but he could hear. 'I have no interest in lingering in the stronghold of a traitor, Gwalchafad ap Gwyar.'

His frown, then, was genuine. 'I am no traitor.'

Gwanaelle put every hint of breeding she had into the imperious lift of her brow and reminded herself very much of a certain young Ancient One. 'Are you so certain?'

And then she pushed past him, out the door that the watchmen opened without request and straight into the hallway she had trod earlier. The clouds would have barely brushed past the moon in the short time since she had last scampered here, yet that woman and this one were almost different creatures. With no pause she turned back towards Gwalchafad's chambers, marched straight in, dove down under his bedding and exposed the Creil pieces within its cloak. Then, into the centre, she placed Artwr's ring, before bundling everything back up again and replacing it into its shadowed corner.

Then she strode back out, as though this were her own chamber in her own stronghold, turned right where she had previously turned left, and stepped out into the night. Those few mingling out of doors looked at her with curiosity but no suspicion as she strode past them toward the stacked straw Eifion had described. By the time any thought to wonder why she had not returned, she would be back in the whorehouse, tucked in their little cellar.

And by the time Gwalchafad was dragged before Artwr to account for his secret possession of one of the relics he'd dedicated his entire life to finding— Artwr's *holy* Creil—he would also stand accused of stealing the property of the King, a gift given to the whore who'd stood protected by Artwr's own proclamation. A whore who had disappeared not long after a very public struggle with Trellech's Thane.

And when Gwalchafad looked down on that ring he would know *exactly* whose face his death wore, and in whose name.

X X X V I

North

GWANAELLE RODE behind Eifion not only to spell the mount that had run Angharad to Caerllion and back in a day but also to ensure the still healing warrior did not tumble off when he tired, which he would do much sooner than either of them. The two of them sat alongside Cai on his mount atop Highpoint, the river tumbling down behind them and the bustling village of Trellech at the feet of its stronghold in the distance before them. From here, they could see the comings and goings as Trellech awoke from the feast and remembered they were hosting a King and they could see the south road, a churned, dark streak against the diminishing snow.

'You know where to knock should you find yourself in our town again,' Angharad said, stretching up to curl her firm hand around Gwanaelle's shoulder.

'Forgive my baldness if I say I plan never to return to Trellech again.' Then, before the woman could retract her hand she pressed all the coin she could spare into it. 'It is not a King's ring, I'm afraid, but it is enough for food for a whole travelling party from now until the end of Thaw.'

Angharad curled her fingers around the coin gratefully. 'And where will we be travelling?'

Gwanaelle bent and tucked a piece of parchment into Angharad's ample cleavage. 'I have drawn this. It is not good but it should aid you. If you need to leave... If you simply *want* to...come to this valley in the north. I will be there, as will Eifion. You can live there with us or I can take you somewhere else—a place of refuge where women are required to do nothing more than work hard and live in peace. You will find a friend's welcome in either valley, for what you have done for Eifion here. You all will. Please tell them.'

Angharad began weeping then and her blubs were only interrupted by Cai's alert as a score of tiny dark riders came thundering along the distant road from the South.

'Gwenhwyfar's personal guard.' Cai guessed. 'And one of them a messenger.'

'That's my girl,' Angharad murmured under her breath.

The riders did not abate until they were practically atop the stronghold and then they only skidded to a dramatic halt even as the watchmen on its walls began to scurry in panic like so many ants.

Eifion turned their mount away, toward the river.

'You do not wish to witness your vengeance?' Gwanaelle murmured against his shoulder.

'I do, of course, but had I not put my own desire for revenge ahead of all else we would be safely on our way back to Nyneve by now and you would never have found yourself in such peril as befell you last night. In the clutches of Artwr.' He sagged back into her. 'I am done with vengeance.'

Cai turned to follow them as Angharad began the long trudge back down to the town and they were no more than halfway down the river-slope when bells began pealing in the distance behind them.

'You may have risked us all, Gwanaelle,' Cai murmured, ignoring the import of those bells. 'By revealing your name. Our location.'

'Angharad risked more,' Gwanaelle said. 'By revealing her shame. Who she was. Who she now is. Besides, your valley has not truly been a secret for many winters. Look how steadily those in need come.'

Cai grunted.

'Besides, I trust her. How many times could she have profited from us and did not.'

'True enough,' Eifion said. 'It is done, now. Let us face the road north and get home to Nyneve as quickly as we can.'

~

As with all journeys, the return was faster than its pair. With a third horse riderless, they were able to ride further, longer and so it was the weary little group plodded into Melangell's valley just two nights later.

A little shape threw herself into Cai's arms as soon as he dismounted.

'Lifebringer...' he murmured, swallowing her in his embrace. Lifting her easily and turning around and around. Curling her into him.

Gwanaelle had to look away from such affection. Witnessing the expression of their bond caused such an ache in her chest.

Cai turned as soon as he'd finished kissing his woman and faced them. Eifion reached his forearm out and his Lord clapped it firm.

'Thank you, Cai, for your part in my salvation.'

'I did very little, Second,' he grunted. 'Spare me from ever knowing the limpness of cock that I felt sitting in that cave in the woods with three farting horses all through Silence and Frost. Poking my head out like some hare to see what was happening in the world.'

'You brought Gwanaelle safely South,' Eifion said. 'You fought me out of that bolt-house. You made ready our escape. You protected Angharad with her message for the Queen.'

'Then why do I feel so impotent?'

'Because you are a warrior still and warriors do not sit idle on their hands.' They still gripped each other, these two men who had each learned so much about impotence. 'Yet you have my gratitude whether or not you want it. I yet live to protect Nyneve and Gwanaelle thanks in part to you. I will not forget.'

'We are getting too old for such intrigues,' Cai muttered. 'Perhaps it would be better if we did forget.'

He turned away, before returning to their side. 'I forget myself. Here. To replace the ones you lost.'

Eifion stared at the blade in Cai's hands, his stomach turning to stone.

'I took it from the guard in your bolt-house. You will need it.'

His face twisted quizzically at Eifion's refusal to reach for the blade and so he buckled it, himself, to their mount's leathers.

'Let me treat your flesh, Eifion,' Melangell begged as he did. She had been staring at the ruins of his throat and chest since Cai placed her feet back on the earth. Wondering what was below the veil of his wears, no doubt.

'I have been in good hands,' he murmured, distracted by the ominous blade at his thigh. 'A dozen eager attendants. Two healers. All that can be done has been done, Melangell.'

She let her dismay fall, again, on the scarred twists she could see at his chest. 'I am so sorry.'

'Do not be,' Gwanaelle spoke up. 'He yet breathes. He yet walks. He is not ruined.'

Her words were confident, immediate, full of truth. Yet he'd never heard emptier.

He was ruined. Even for her.

'Will you not rest the night with us?' Melangell entreated.

'We ride for Nyneve,' he gritted. 'She has been alone long enough.'

Still...? She and Eifion had been able to speak of the Myrddyn when they were alone in the cellar; she had almost forgotten the magic that thickened their tongues and dulled their senses when they tried to speak Bleheris' name in the company of others.

'She will be quite changed,' Melangell said, not quite lightly.

Would they ride back into their valley to find it ravaged by a dragon? Find it absent of Nyneve and Bleheris both? Or would they tread foot into their clearing and see their girl running towards them, excitement on her pale face and a stream of complaints on her tongue?

'How I will welcome her grievances,' Gwanaelle mumbled as Eifion turned their horse for the path to the uplands. Quality mounts were too scarce. After days at his back she had no compunction at curling her arms around his hips and leaning into his strength. Resting there.

And if he did, he did not say.

'As will I,' Eifion's voice rumbled against her cheek.

'That we have been gone too long.'

'That we have not brought her a keepsake.'

'That Bleheris has become a bore.'

Oh, would it were so. That nothing had changed in their little valley and everything could return to its usual state. As though they had never left. Though they would always have Eifion's tortured flesh as a reminder, and she would always be as changed inwardly as he was outwardly.

Eifion kicked the mare to an amble and turned their back to the sunset.

XXXVII

Reckoning

THEY COME, Nyneve. It had been so long since Bleheris had entered her head, his unexpected intrusion caused her to twitch in her furs. Just when she thought her ruined body was incapable of feeling anything but the blinding agony of the Searing. His presence was a gentle stroke by comparison.

A caress.

She had been having visions for se'nnights now, but never anything useful. Never a happy glimpse of her mother, riding alongside Eifion. Just...strangers. A fattish woman, riding like the wind accompanied by a shrouded warrior. A sneering, flame-haired man kneeling before another as his own brother lifted an executioner's blade. A tormented man with streaks of silver, all in leather lying, sleepless, staring at the timber ceiling of a stronghold. Nothing to help her believe that Eifion and Gwanaelle were returning to her. Yet here they were. After so long.

She was not about to greet them like this.

She pushed herself to her knees and forced her sinews into the position that was most comfortable, on fours like a beast, back arched and elongated. Everything hurt least this way and it also opened her throat for the purge she could feel coming. The howl that took the edge off the pain, long enough to greet her returned parents. The sensation burbled and grew in her belly, like the worst kind of ague, it billowed and rose the way her stomach did when she ate something rancid, but it gave voice to the scream that would, ultimately, ease her a little. No matter how much it burned in the build up. She would not have her parents see her crippled and weeping, and she would not have them see her do this—what she was becoming regardless of her intent—and so she forced it now, hot and acid and not quite ready until it tumbled up her throat, over her tongue and out into the air as a harrowing cry.

A roar.

It went on for long moments, squeezing her lungs dry of air, and then echoed across the silent clearing as soon as it was done. There were no creatures to burst from the undergrowth, to flutter up and into the sky, to scrabble up the rocky edges of the valley. Any living thing with sense had long since cleared out of this valley.

Given what resided within it.

Her chest heaved and she writhed still on all fours, easing the crippling twist of her flesh, loosening the parts that had grown so tight. The cry helped her to endure but it was pure suffering while it happened.

Yet it was done, now, and she could greet the people she loved without a rictus of agony on her face, and upright. Both a blessing.

A horse burst into the clearing through the trees, wild-eyed and forced, and Eifion leapt off long before it had stumbled to a halt, drawing a blade from his side. Gwanaelle clung to the beast's pad until it slowed and then she, too, slid off.

Her first thought was that the horse looked entirely delicious. It's blood up and surging, it's eyes wild. The stuff that gave it what it needed to survive surging through its blood, making its meat more delectable. She was so tired of hare and moorfowl.

But she pushed that thought away—it didn't belong in the heart of a girl—and began to run toward her parents as best as her pain would allow.

Eifion surveyed the clearing, found no risk and staggered to his knees, arms outstretched.

Running into them was the most natural thing in the world.

'Nyneve...'

Eifion breathed it against her ear and she felt more like one of Man's kind than she had in fortennights. Gwanaelle skidded to her knees beside them and threw her arms around them both, and as they closed around her she thought that maybe she could do this—resist— if she could do it in the arms of people who loved her. If they never let her go.

'You are come,' she murmured weakly. 'You are come.'

Her mother pushed back and forked her hands up the sides of her face, examining closely. Gods knew what she would see there. 'What is wrong?'

'We heard a beast—'

Nyneve sagged down, onto her side and lay against Eifion. He shifted to accommodate her and she felt rather than saw his wince, but he did not protest. 'It was nothing. I will explain later.'

Gwanaelle searched the clearing. 'Where is Bleheris? Tell me he did not abandon you.'

Nyneve reached out with her mind, searching. 'He is in the cave. He has watched you come.'

Both their gazes went to the cascade. Water streamed down around the frozen falls as it melted, all but obscuring the entrance to the cave they had first used that lay behind it.

'Why is he not with you?' Gwanaelle asked.

'We do not... We have not spoken in some time.' Her parents shared an anxious look across her head. 'It was better for me this way.'

'What has he done?' Eifion gritted.

'Nothing. I am well.' Or she would be, now that those who loved her were back.

Gwanaelle pressed lips to her hair. 'You are as fire. When was the last time you slathered?'

'I have been so tired...'

Soft hands scraped along the flakes of her skin, but it was not Gwanaelle who spoke. 'And your skin...?'

That's right. Eifion had left before her skin began drying and flaking. 'It has grown no worse.'

But since ever she'd known him, Eifion's hands had been work-roughened. She forced strength into her flesh and pushed up to look at his hands. They were pink and soft and hairless. Like the kits of the hares she sometimes pulled from their burrows. She tipped her face up to his and now noticed the pocks on his jaw, on his forehead, the scarred flesh around his throat. She scrambled to kneeling and tugged at the clasp of his cloak, then at the wears around his neck and tugged them down, away. Everything below his neck looked as raw and new as his hands and there were welts and dips where once he'd had strong, firm muscle. Nothing was whole anymore.

She turned her dismay to her mother. 'What happened? You were supposed to look after him!'

Her pale skin blanched further, but she did not drop her head the way she usually did. 'I got there as fast as I could. I acted as fast as I could, and he healed as fast as *he* could.'

She was already scrabbling more, exposing Eifion's skin. He did not fight her hands but he did fight her blame. 'This was done to me by a man, Nyneve. Gwanaelle is responsible only for keeping me alive and helping me heal.'

'A man?' she shrieked, a kind of panic overtaking her. How could she not have *seen* this? 'What man?'

'It no longer matters, if he is not yet dead he very soon will be executed.'

Executed. Like the kneeling man in her vision. 'This man... Did he have hair like Mother's?'

Eifion's eyes softened as they looked over her head. 'Nothing like it except in hue.'

'He is dead,' she murmured. 'At the hand of his brother, I think. Another one with red hair.'

Her parents glanced at each other and she thought she felt them both sag. She matched it, letting Eifion bat away her hands and right his wears, then gently push her to sitting and himself to his feet.

'And you are well?' he checked again. 'You have been safe?'

What could she tell them? What could she say?

No. You made me prey for a lech and left me vulnerable to his power.

'I am well.'

'Bleheris!' Gwanaelle called.

'He will not come. He does not come when I am out.'

Curiosity blazed in her blue eyes. 'Did he teach you?'

'For some time, yes.'

'But now he does not speak to you?'

'Out of my head or in it.'

'And the Searing?'

'Worse.'

'And your—'

'I will tell you all, Mother. Soon.' She turned to Eifion. 'But first I want to hear everything that happened since you left me. Why I felt your fear, and what happened to you.'

~

The telling took much of the day with Nyneve's constant questions. Gwanaelle watched her try and hide the pain she was in, as if either of them would fail to see it in the careful way she moved or the slowness of her reactions. Or the darkness below her eyes.

'Beheading was too good for him,' Nyneve had spat when the tale was spent. 'I would have torn him to pieces bit by bit, as he did you.'

'A man like that...' Eifion had started '...death is no real punishment. He needed to be shamed and belittled.'

'And then beheaded.'

He laughed and hugged Nyneve close. 'And then beheaded.'

Then—though she tried to avoid it—it was Nyneve's turn to speak of the fortennights that had passed, and what had passed between Dragonling and Myrddyn. Gwanaelle had to restrain Eifion from running up to that cave and running him through as Nyneve got to the point in the tale where Bleheris forced himself on her.

'Think, Eifion!' she urged, practically laying atop him to prevent his hasty action. Weakened as he still was, she managed it. 'He could have blocked those words from her mouth with ease if he was not prepared for our reaction.'

'His thrall does not work on me,' Nyneve cut in.

'Then from our ears then. Or make us forget it the moment your words are done. We have passed fortennights being unable to speak of him and growing befuddled whenever we try. He would have no difficulties barring that part of your tale from us if he so chose.'

Nyneve frowned. 'Why would he not protect himself?'

'Because he does not need to. He can hurt us or stop us at any time. He could make Eifion turn his sword on himself if he so chose.'

How had they never realised before just how dangerous a Myrddyn could be?

'He has magic and cunning, Nyneve,' Eifion added.

'Better,' a croaky voice said right behind them, 'I have reason.'

Eifion spun, on instinct, and hurled himself toward the Myrddyn but then he slowed, stopped and danced a ridiculous jig instead. Flushed fury suffused his face even as he did so.

'Sit!' Bleheris commanded and dancing Eifion jigged back to his log and sank down onto it. Gasping from the pain.

'She is a child to you, Gwanaelle, venerated to you, Eifion. To herself she is a woman grown, but to me she is *my people.* You can no more judge us for the manner we conduct ourselves then reproach the fox for its scavenging or the wolf for its violence. It is the way of *y Ddraig* that they must be seeded before Ascending if they are to continue their line, else they remain barren for the entire era of their lives. And that task must be undertaken by a Myrddyn. I recognise that she does not wish it to be so but the reality is that she will be in agony until she ascends and then if she has not been seeded when she does, she will continue to suffer after Ascension.'

He glanced at Nyneve. 'I have removed myself from her these past fortennights in order that she fully understand the solitude and pain that she has ahead of her, and because I do not wish to frighten her further, but perhaps you can help her see sense where I could not.'

'I will see my own sense or not without help from others,' she bristled and the words were the first hint that *their* Nyneve was still in there.

Eifion was still struggling against Bleheris' thrall and so could not yet speak, so Gwanaelle cut to the crux of the issue.

'There must be another Myrddyn?' Gwanaelle said. 'Someone younger?'

'Mother!'

'I do not wish to see you suffer, Nyneve, and it is a quick, meaningless thing.' The whores of Trellech had taught her some of that, and Eifion the rest.

He glowered up at her from within Bleheris' thrall.

'It must be a Myrddyn born far from where the Creil was first deposited, so that he can be no kin to *y Ddraig.*'

'This is a wide land, Bleheris,' she pointed out, reasonably. 'You could travel to the east—'

'Mother! You will not entertain this idea.'

'You will suffer in pain for an age if you Ascend without being...' She looked to Bleheris for the term.

'Seeded.'

'I have no intention of Ascending,' Nyneve bit back. 'I do not wish to assume my dragon form.'

Eifion had struggled free of the thrall but the effort weakened his already tiring flesh. 'Is it possible?' he panted. 'To resist?'

'Nothing I have seen here is possible.' Bleheris glowered at Nyneve. 'She has found...ways...of keeping the suffering at bay, but, no, Eifion, I do not believe that it is possible to resist forever. She will succumb. Either pain or madness will weaken her and she will allow it.'

'I will not.'

'You are afraid,' he barked. 'Like a child. You have suppressed your true nature and dressed like Man and now you do not wish to be anything other.'

'What is wrong with Man?' Gwanaelle asked in defence of her kind.

'There is not enough sunlight left in this day for me to elucidate on that, but—in essence—there is nothing wrong with being Man if that's what you were born to, but Nyneve is *y Ddraig*. She does not belong here.'

'This is my home!'

'Nyneve,' Gwanaelle was fast to placate, 'you do not have to leave this place.'

Although even as she said it she remembered that she'd invited a whore-house full of refugees into their valley. Drawn them a map. What chance of keeping a grown dragon secret then, even in the cave behind the cascade.

'Then *you* must leave,' Bleheris said. 'Man and *y Ddraig* sharing one little valley. It cannot work.'

'The way I could not possibly have lived here with people, growing up?' Nyneve hissed. 'You speak with such certainty but you know so little about me. About us. This family.'

He turned to face her. 'When you Ascend you will come into such powers that you can not comprehend.'

'And I will master it!' she cried.

'You will. After ten winters or so, and by then all that will be left of this valley are some scorched stumps and the bones of those you love ground to dust.'

Despair streaked across her angry gaze.

'Nyneve,' Eifion finally murmured. 'What do you want?'

'I do not want to change,' she pleaded. 'I do not want to leave this valley and I do not want to leave you, Eifion.'

Gwanaelle winced only a little for the thoughtless cruelty of this girl.

'Then it shall be so. Like everything else in your life, we will work it out as things arise.'

'She hungers for your horse,' Bleheris announced, happily. 'There's something you'll need to *work out* quite soon.'

Nyneve gasped at his speed to humiliate.

'Then she shall have it,' Eifion said, without hesitation. 'If that is what she truly wishes. What care we for a horse over our own daughter?'

Those riven eyes filled with tears at Eifion's unhesitating acceptance. The love she felt for that man... Gwanaelle knew that love so very well. She recognised it because she shared it.

'I do not *want* to eat it,' Nyneve entreated. 'But I do hunger for it. I cannot help it.'

'Then we will get you a horse of your own. Something old off the uplands.'

Nyneve sighed. 'There are none there, they have all been picked off by another Ddraig.'

Gwanaelle gasped. Had Bleheris let her leave the valley after all? 'How do you know this?'

Nyneve's pretty face crumpled as she concentrated. 'I do not know. It is just...truth.'

'She is right,' Bleheris announced. 'But there is no dragon up there picking its teeth even now with a horse's rib. That Ddraig has not flown these skies for some fifty winters. It's ancestors used to roam those uplands when they were still forested, swam the great lakes that are no longer there. The horses do not return out of fear.'

'So Nyneve sees what has been as well as what is?'

'Or what will be. Yes. That is a talent of *y Ddraig*.'

'And how can she know which she is seeing? Past, present or future?'

'Do you imagine being a dragon is all slaughter and free-flight from sunrise until set? She has an age in which to develop her skill. Hone it like one of your swords, Eifion. She will work hard once she has Ascended.'

Nyneve opened her mouth to protest, once again.

'But she has the talent now,' Gwanaelle pointed out. 'She does not need to Ascend to perfect it.'

Nyneve turned her astonishment in Gwanaelle's direction. Had she never felt backed by her own mother before?

Bleheris grew dangerously still. 'The power she has now is nothing compared to her magic after Ascension.'

'But it is enough for her,' Eifion said. 'Sight is a useful tool on its own. Perhaps she does not need any more.'

His eyes darkened. Had he truly expected them to be allies against their own daughter?

'Bleheris,' she said, 'this is a family matter. We need to discuss it. Alone. Will you please leave us?'

Nyneve's mouth gaped unattractively.

Bleheris grew a dark kind of red. 'She is *my* kin. Not yours. No matter what you think. She will tear apart the first living things she sees when she Ascends and if you are still here then, it will be your bones she feasts on instead of some horse.'

Eifion stood and moved behind Nyneve, resting his hands on her shoulders. From there, he stared Bleheris down. 'Again. What care we for our own lives over our daughter's?'

Bleheris trembled with the rage he could no longer disguise and stalked off, back toward the cave.

Across from her, Nyneve slid her hands up to curl around Eifion's and she tipped her head back against his hip in a sight that was so heartbreakingly familiar, but then her eyes lifted, found Gwanaelle's and hung there—in confusion—instead of flitting off and avoiding her.

It felt like the first honest moment of communication they'd had in winters.

~

'Nyneve,' her mother called from across the clearing. 'Will you step into my shelter a moment?'

How many nights had she curled up in there, drowning in her mother's lingering smell after she had gone after Eifion? Then the following night in her father's. She had contemplated dragging their furs into her own shelter but somehow that seemed just too…

Weak.

She took her time crossing the clearing and then ducked and entered where Gwanaelle had left the flap raised for her. As she entered, she saw her mother glance up at Bleheris' cave. She turned to follow the direction of her gaze and saw Eifion hefting himself up the well-worn stones to its entrance.

'I need to ask you something,' her mother said, bringing her focus back around to her. She placed a hand on each of her shoulders and positioned her exactly within the shelter. Her back to one of its hide walls. 'Can you bar Bleheris? From your mind? From your witness?'

'I...yes...' she stammered. 'I think so.'

'Do it now, then.'

It took Nyneve a moment to realise Gwanaelle was serious. She was waiting. She dropped her lashes and closed down every opening into her mind. If Bleheris began pressing—or battering—she would know it.

'Is it done?'

She nodded, almost afraid that speech would draw the Myrddyn's attention.

'Then look...'

Gwanaelle took her shoulders once again, turned her, and stood back in silence. The taut rear of her mother's shelter was like parchment onto which she had rendered such a wonder... Likenesses of each of them. Like a tale captured on hide. A handsome man, a wild-haired woman, a young girl, a bent over old Bard. Even her riven eyes were captured in coal, and over there, a dragon. Quite like the ones she had seen in her dream. Was that the animal Gwanaelle remembered from the battle in Melangell's valley? Her dragon mother? Nyneve stepped up closer and studied the shapes, admired them. A little of the darkness smudged off on her fingers when she brushed it.

'Coal from the fires,' her mother said, anxious.

Distantly, she could hear shouting but it was not powerful enough to drag her eyes from this wonder.Nyneve gazed over the images but then stopped when she looked down at the feet of the mighty dragon. There lay the handsome man, the wild-haired women, impaled on the claws of the dragon. She turned her dismay to her mother.

'Keep looking,' she begged.

Nyneve turned back and studied the next wall. There were likenesses of all the things that she could do—all the things that she *did* do—to keep Ascension at bay. The slathering, the eels, the roaring, the snow, and it showed likeness after likeness of Eifion and

Gwanaelle embracing the charcoal Nyneve in their thin arms. Safekeeping her.

'If the Myrddyn uses his thrall against us,' her mother whispered as though that would help if Bleheris wanted to listen in, 'if we forget to always help you in *not* Ascending, I will have this to look at every morning and every night. A story in likenesses. A reminder of what you fear and a reminder of what we can do to help you. Bleheris will never come in here and he cannot imagine we have done this.'

'How *did* you do it?' Nyneve breathed.

'I fashioned a map for some...friends...in Trellech,' she admitted, 'and found I had a talent for it. This seemed like one way to best the Cunning Man.'

Nyneve spun and faced her mother. 'Is this what you have been doing these past days?'

'It has taken me longer than I thought.'

Outside, the shouting grew louder. 'What is that?'

'That is Eifion keeping the Myrddyn busy so that we might have this conversation without him knowing.'

'What are they shouting about?'

Gwanaelle smiled. 'Anything he could think of.'

It was impossible not to laugh and impossible that she *could* laugh after all this time and pain, and that she could feel so close to her mother. How long had it been since she felt close?

'I saw,' Nyneve confessed.

'Saw what?'

'What he did to you.'

Gwanaelle took a half step back. 'Who?'

'Your father.'

She tried to remain brave, Nyneve watched her mother's struggle, but she could not. She sagged down onto her furs and dropped her head. 'I am sorry.'

Sorry? 'For me?'

'That you had to see such things.'

'I am sorry for you, Mother! That he—'

'Do not be. I survived it.'

Nyneve sank down next to her, though it pained her to arrange her sinews so. 'How did you?'

'My own mother. She gave me a pack of supplies, set me off in the direction of an Abbey, a place of God. A place of safety.'

Not '*she protected me*'.

Not '*she put a sword through him*'.

Only '*she sent me away*'.

Nyneve sagged. Had her life of love and security been more exceptional than she knew? 'Did you find the place of God?'

'Better. I found Melangell.' She smiled. 'If I ever drew near the Abbey, I did not know it. I wandered lost for fortennights. Running much of the time. Used all my food, wore my shoes clean through.'

'Yet you said it is an easy thing. To be violated.'

Her eyes grew clouded with grief.

'I said it was quick, and meaningless the way Bleheris proposed it. I did not say it would be easy.'

They fell to silence.

'I do not want to hurt you,' Nyneve finally murmured.

'You will not. Bleheris just says that to frighten you into compliance.'

'I have seen that, too,' she said in a tiny voice. 'You, a bloody pulp laying still in a pool of your own blood, and me pressing Eifion back into the earth and…shredding his wears. Or his skin… I cannot tell.'

Gwanaelle turned to stare. She grasped not the horrible details of her own death but the awful images in her daughter's head. 'This is the kind of thing you see? What kind of a gift is that then?'

'You are not afraid?'

'Of you? Never. Of Bleheris, always.'

'But if I—'

'If it happens then Eifion and I both have led full and happy lives caring for you, Nyneve. If we become the first meal of a desperate and starving dragon, then we will be happy to do it if it helps you change into your powerful self. If it helps you grow strong. Remember Melangell's stories of the old Morwyn Ddraigs?'

She had not. Not until just then. 'They wandered out into the heart of *y Ddraig's* territory when it was time to die. Gave themselves as a meal.'

Her mother's smile was brave. 'It is a fine tradition of your kind, then.'

Nyneve struggled against the surge of warmth. After so long being in opposition to her mother. 'How are you not afraid?'

'I have seen a lot this winter. Death is not the worst thing that can happen to a person.' Gwanaelle curled her arms around her from the back. 'And because it is a trifling point. You do not plan to Ascend, and Eifion and I are going to help you with that in any way we can.'

She pressed to her feet. 'Just try and eat us without your dragon's claws, I dare you.'

XXXVIII

Broken

'BLEHERIS?' Gwanaelle called up to the cave's opening 'Are you there?'

The old man stepped into the gaping maw of the rock and peered down at her in silence. Looking utterly defeated. 'What do you want, Gwanaelle?'

He had not emerged for a se'nnight, withdrawing from them all as much as from Nyneve. She wondered if Bleheris was too ashamed of his actions while they were gone to mingle with them. Nyneve thought he simply watched them with his mind from the comfort of his furs. Eifion was certain that he *was* coming down, walking amongst them and then wiping it from their very memories. The very thought was unsettling. He could do anything and they might never know. She could only draw so much on her shelter walls as a remembrance.

'The passages are open at last,' she called. 'Eifion and Nyneve have gone to hunt boar.'

He tipped his head. 'And you wish me gone from this valley?'

A well-mannered woman would deny it. She pressed upward, closer to his cave. 'Is there any reason for you to stay?'

He hissed but she knew his frustration was not with her. When she arrived at his side he turned to her, urgency live in his silver eyes. 'She must Ascend, Gwanaelle. You do not know what you condemn her to if she does not.'

'I think she does know, Bleheris. Yet it remains her choice. No one can make her do anything she does not wish.'

'Is that what you believe?'

'Your thrall does not work on her.'

'No. It does not, but it works on you.'

She lifted a single brow. 'Have you not been trying to wipe her reluctance from our minds? I can almost feel your frustration.'

'It is curious how you are resisting, but then, there is so much about Nyneve that I cannot predict. She was not raised as other Ddraigs.'

'She was raised with love.'

His eyes dropped, defeated. 'Yes, and that, ultimately, will be her salvation.'

Perhaps he finally understood. 'I'm sorry, Bleheris. You came so far for her. To help her. Only to discover she did not want your help.'

'Why did you take the dragonling up, Gwanaelle? All those winters ago? Why not just leave her to the care of someone else?'

She frowned. 'I had to. It was…my purpose.'

Bleheris lifted his gaze, stroked his knuckles across her cheek. 'You are so very kind, Gwanaelle, and quite beautiful in a wild sort of way. Had I but stumbled into this valley and found only you all those fortennights ago...' He sighed. 'I would have gladly given you what Eifion will not. A man could happily grow old and die between those strong thighs.'

Humiliation washed through her that he should know her secret shame but she refused to give him the satisfaction of seeing it. She twisted her face free of his touch.

'Ah, there it is. That new defiance you returned with from Trellech. It flames most becomingly in your cheeks, and you will need the fortitude, beautiful Gwanaelle. It will sustain you.'

'Through what?'

He paused a moment, poised on the blade's edge of some decision and then he spoke. 'Through this.'

One moment she stood with Bleheris at the lip to the cave she and Eifion had raised Nyneve in, a hard climb up the waterfall, and the next she was weightless, staring in confusion as the cave-mouth simply vanished and she was staring instead at grey sky. But that thought had barely entered her mind when it was forced violently out of it again on the rocks of the pool below. The twigs of her limbs and spine snapped and cracked like thawing ice and she lay frozen in the melt, broken limbs outstretched at awkward angles, unable to move, unable to cry, unable to do anything other than gasp for a breath she could not find.

The sky began to swirl and darken before, finally, her body managed to compose itself enough to suck in some air.

How many moments had she lain there gasping before Bleheris appeared above her, a dark shadow against the sky?

'Do not struggle, beautiful Gwanaelle. It will not hurt for long. She is a complicated girl,' he murmured, 'but she loves you. You are her mother.'

And love, ultimately, would be her salvation.

She knew then what the Myrddyn had done—how he had forced Nyneve to his will—but she could not rail at him, could not speak, could only gurgle. Yet Bleheris had no difficulties understanding her.

'I had to,' he shrugged, echoing her words from just moments before. 'It is my purpose.'

And then he turned, hoisted his pack onto his shoulders and simply walked out of view, leaving her broken, half-drowned and almost senseless at the base of the waterfall.

~

Gwanaelle drifted in and out of sense while tracking the sun's excruciating arc across the heavens and watching the clouds float serenely across the sky, oblivious to the pain of the poor, broken woman below. It felt like a se'nnight she lay there before she heard the muted thud of two sets of feet running towards her across the valley floor and Nyneve's scream; before Eifion skidded to her side in the water and struggled to find a single place to gently lift her that didn't cause her to whimper in agony. He barked some commands to Nyneve, the girl too insensible to comprehend them, before he left her for the time it took to strike Nyneve across the face, gain her attention and command her again. His words made no sense to Gwanaelle. They were garbled, another tongue almost, yet they must have held meaning for Nyneve because she returned and worked with her father in the icy water to lift her mother's twisted legs onto a large fur and then tugged the rest of the fur as Eifion eased her up.

Gwanaelle choked on her own tears as the pain grew greater than the numbness of the icy water, but it did shock her into a kind of awakeness.

'I don't understand,' Nyneve kept crying. 'This is not what I saw.'

Nonetheless, it was what they had. She spent a moment trying to get her tongue and lips coordinated enough to make the shape necessary for a 'B' and then abandoned the effort as fruitless because of her shattered jaw. Who else could have done this? Who else was absent the camp for the first time since the onset of winter? It made no difference to her death who had broken her so badly. They would guess soon enough.

But as Eifion carefully lifted the corners of the saturated fur closest to her head and Nyneve took those near her feet, and they struggled her up the slope to their shelters, she took a moment to study the people she loved. Nyneve's ashen, tear-streaked face staring at her in horror. Eifion's strong, reliable back—those shoulders she'd always loved regardless of how pocked and gouged they now were—if the jerks of their movement caused her heart to fracture free then she was happy to go in the presence of those she loved best. Not everyone got that gift.

But then Nyneve stumbled and dropped one side of her burden on a horrified cry and the pain of crashing down onto the ground stole even that from her.

And everything was darkness.

X X X I X

Sacrifice

'SHE CANNOT LIVE. The damage is too great.' Her father laid a gentle hand on her shuddering shoulder.

'Her infusions?' Nyneve wheezed through her own mucus. 'Her unctions?'

'No, Nyneve. I am sorry.'

'How can you be so calm?' she roared. 'Or sure?'

'Because I have seen a lot of death. It is an old and recognisable enemy.'

She slapped her hands onto the scars around his neck. 'But she saved you and you were just as bad. You cannot just…surrender her.'

'Her bones are in shards. Pickings cannot mend those. There are too many and bone does not heal as flesh does. She is suffering.'

He glanced at his sword, propped up against the shelter wall right below the charcoal likeness of Gwanaelle. Horror filled her heart. 'No…'

'Nyneve—'

'No!'

She could number the times she had seen Eifion angry in just one fist, but she saw it now, anger boiled up and swamped his tenuous control. 'Would you have her linger in misery just so that a child does not need to face the truth?'

She turned her stinging eyes up to him in appeal. 'I would have her be *whole* again.'

His voice was as heavy as the rocks that had broken her mother to pieces. It ached with acceptance. 'That cannot happen.'

'But I have not finished telling her…things.'

Eifion sagged. 'Then, tell her now. As I will.'

Before it is too late. That is what she heard with her heart, though not what he said with his tongue. Yet that little voice inside of her said...

Truth.

Eifion was going to end Gwanaelle's suffering. Because he loved her too well to let her linger. She sobbed and then flung herself forward, scraping at her own wet cheeks with her hands and then smearing it onto Gwanaelle's broken body. She leaned over her and let her tears tumble directly onto the places on her mother's face where her flesh was split open. Licking it where it was bloodied. Kissing where it was not.

'Then let me heal her...'

'She is dying, Nyneve. Your kisses cannot change that.'

'I am *y Ddraig.*'

'You are not. You do not have their magic. You wept enough over my scars to have worked a miracle if such a thing were possible.'

She rocked back and forth where she sat, eyes frantically darting around the room, falling on Gwanaelle's charcoal likenesses. On the Myrddyn. Though that is not where her mind strayed.

Then her head snapped up. 'I will find Bleheris...'

'Good, then I can kill him.'

'He can heal her.'

'He *did* this to her, Nyneve. Why would he now help her?'

'Because I will agree to the Seeding, in return for his help. That is what he wants.'

A flash of hope birthed in her father's tormented gaze, but then it d again. 'No. Gwanaelle would not want that in her name.'

'It is not her choice to make. I am a woman grown and I will make my own choices. Give Mother foxglove. Protect her from pain with the sleep of the dead while I chase him. Make him return.'

'He is a Myrddyn. You cannot *make* him do anything.'

She pressed to her feet and stood tall over them both. Taller and stronger than she felt. 'You would be surprised what I can do. Just keep her alive until I can return to her with the magic of the Ancients. Please,' she begged. 'For me.'

He groaned and dropped his head. 'Foxglove, then, but you may not find him, Nyneve. He is probably long gone by now.'

Her voice was somehow both triumphant and meek. 'I can try.'

~

Where are you, old man?

She reached out further with her mind as if she could see for herself his hiding place, but even as she did she made her way, determined, toward the cave where he'd passed the last fortennights.

The cave he had tossed—or thralled—her mother out of.

Gone, he finally volunteered. *Far from your accursed valley.*

Why her? She was nothing but kind to you.

I did not do this, he mumbled.

No? Then who?

You, Nyneve. Your conceit and pride have killed her.

The truth roared through her, dragging knives as it went. Eifion was not going to get an opportunity to kill the Cunning Man because, if ever she saw the Myrddyn again, she was going to rip him apart with her bare hands and crush his skull between her palms. Such was her fury and loathing.

You will return! she demanded.

I am too far away to be of any use.

I will...allow the seeding.

It was not a laugh but it was like one. *Too late, child. Besides, I warned you that your mother's line would end with you. I will not perpetuate this...wrong.*

Her guts twisted up on themselves. One mother given her life already, and now a second in her name. It was intolerable. Besides, what if he only said that to maintain power over her. He was nothing if not motivated by power.

I will lay there and not make one single sound as you poke around as you wish! As often as you wish.

She will not last that long, Bleheris said, simply.

Truth.

'Then I will find you and I will tear every piece of flesh from your body while you watch and you scream,' she roared, aloud.

It felt better to roar. To snarl.

To promise vengeance.

You certainly may try, he said, all calmness. *Once you have buried your mother.*

Broiling despair threatened to blind her, and he was the last one that she wanted watching her breakdown. He'd seen more than enough of her tears.

Or you might use it, he spoke again. This time all tension. *To save her.*

'I do not have any magic. You said so yourself.'

But you do, Nyneve. Perhaps the greatest magic known. If only you would accept the inevitable. If only you would ask.

He fell to silence and so did she. Asking wasn't as simple as just forming the words. Asking was a kind of surrender. It made a mockery of everything she had done until this day in resisting Ascension; all her suffering. *Asking* weakened her.

Yet it might save her mother.

Somewhere deep down inside, a suspicion raised its gnarled head and blinked in the sudden light and she forced her secret thoughts down to that pit with it, where Bleheris' magic could not follow. What if the Myrddyn spoke truth about the offspring he feared so much? What if she *was* to mother a new breed of dragon—with the wisdom and magic of the ancients and the dominance of Man? What if her line was a danger not to *y Ddraig* but to him.

Truth.

The stunning realisation weakened her limbs.

She would Ascend unseeded if she transformed now and would be mother to no line, miraculous or otherwise. Yet she dare not wait as Gwanaelle lay dying. All she could do was hold Bleheris' secret fear to her chest and put it aside for another day—some future day—when she could use it against him to seek her vengeance. One challenge at a time. Only one creature was powerful enough bring a human back from the edge of death. And only one creature was powerful enough to shove a Myrddyn, screaming, over it.

And she was not yet either creature.

But she could be.

Tell me, she murmured. And, then, when he did not...

Please.

~

It was so obvious.

Her blood was magic. The waters of her mouth were magic. Her tears were magic. Every part of an Ascended Ddraig had some magic, it seemed. She did not need the half-magic of a Man-shaped dragon when she could help her mother herself. Save her, herself.

Ascension.

And all the power that it wrought.

Her dragon mother had healed Melangell's torn feet with the quick slathe of her tongue across them. How many times had she made Gwanaelle retell that story since Bleheris had come? They were shredded on the rocks until the Ddraig licked them. Surely her mother's battered body would mend with regular swathing from a newly Ascended Ddraig? Bleheris promised her that her magic would never be so concentrated and raw as those first days after Ascension.

If only Eifion could keep Gwanaelle alive until it was managed.

The frosty, earthy air of the cave beckoned and she stumbled inside, purposefully not looking down to where they'd found her mother. Where Bleheris had tossed her with such absent care. It was exactly as he'd left it, even the firecoals still glowed a little. She fell to her knees and turned her thoughts inward, searching, seeking out the knowledge that she needed. Bleheris the Teacher had told her how Ascension progressed but he'd never told her how it *began,* how she might commence it in the absence of a Seeding to make it start. What should she do? Just lie here and…wait? She did…for moments. Willing it. Yet nothing changed. If anything, she was more comfortable now than she had been all winter now that she had decided to Ascend. She barely Seared.

Frowning, she looked to where Bleheris' abandoned fire still glowed red, his furs still lay out. Surely the Searing had some purpose beyond driving young girls to madness. Was heat what she needed?

Truth.

She scrabbled over to the coals and tossed two more thick branches onto it from the small mound Bleheris had stacked up and worried them to flame, then she curled herself tight in his left-behind skins, rolling close enough to the fire to singe the fur. The stink of burning animal filled the cave but the heat soaked into her skin immediately. She twisted against the discomfort but did not roll away.

Ascension was not likely to be a comfortable thing. How could it be?

'I will heal you, Mother.' She gasped through the heat and growing sweat. 'With my mouth-waters. With my blood. With whatever I have. I will give you my human life as you gave yours for me.'

The driest patches of her skin felt like they were going to split from the roasting, but she endured.

While her mother could…she would.

X L

Proven

HE DID NOT want to leave Gwanaelle for the time it would take to get more Foxglove from her stores within the oak-hollow at the end of the valley. She had slept—the sleep of the dead Nyneve had called it—for a day and a night on what little he had found in this very shelter, but it was not enough to keep her comfortable.

Thus, she now stirred with pain where before she had lain pale and quiet. Her flushed face twisted, as though trying to shake free of some fugue.

'Sleep,' Eifion pressed against her injured skin where it would hurt her the least. He'd packed the gaping wounds with staunchgrass, sealed them over with weaver-web and gently wiped her face clean of blood. That was all he knew how. About as useful as calling out into a wild storm.

But his voice and touch seemed to sooth her, he ventured she almost turned into both, and so he murmured again. Nothing of consequence. Reassurance. A pledge that he would not leave her side.

'Nyneve has gone for Bleheris. She believes that he will help.' The twitch of one eyebrow was his only sign that she had heard him. 'She seeks to bargain with him for his healing. I have allowed it because I am weak,' he confessed. 'And I sought any other way out than what I fear I must. I do not think I have the strength.'

One of her swollen, black fingers seemed to dance for a moment, like it wanted to stroke him, then fell back to rest.

His voice grew thick. 'But if I must send you away from me to ease your pain then I will do it. I will find the strength. For you.'

He stroked a length of soft hair made crisp by the dried blood coating it. Shame washed through him at the leap of hope he'd allowed. That he would consider letting a man like Bleheris climb atop of the child they'd raised, violate her, even for her mother's sake.

That he would put the burden of that on a young girl rather than find the strength in himself. Gwanaelle would never, ever forgive him even should she regain her life.

But to *save* that life... He'd learned to live with her love, without ever being able to touch her. He could learn to live with her hate.

Because she would be alive to feel it.

A fat tear splashed onto Gwanaelle's cheek and it took Eifion a moment to notice that it was his, but, where it splashed, her skin twitched at the sensation. Then again, and again as it rolled closer to the corner of her mouth.

'Gwanaelle?' Had the Foxglove retreated enough to let her climb back to awareness?

'Can you hear me?' He shuffled closer. 'I am here.'

It took a moment, but she first frowned through her swellings and then her lips began to move.

He wet his fingers with water from the self-same pool she'd tumbled into and traced them across her parched lips. Then he let some more trickle down past her teeth. Perhaps her tongue was the only flesh in her body not swollen or battered from her fall, it eagerly sought more water.

'Slowly...'

Her lips trembled as she tried to shape them for speech.

'Bleheris?' he asked, watching her trying to fashion the shape for the start of his name. 'He did this. We know. Nyneve had a vision when we were hunting. Him standing over you. We returned as fast as we could.'

She took a moment to let his words become sense. Then her lips moved again.

En...En...

Was she struggling to say his name? Nyneve's?

'She has gone after Bleheris—'

Her frown this time was immediate. He sucked back his words. When she did finally manage a croaked speech, all the hope he didn't realise he'd fostered since she began to stir, fizzled around him in the little shelter.

End me.

His heart filled with stone. 'I cannot, Gwanaelle. Not until all else is tried. I gave Nyneve my vow.'

'Myrddyn—' she croaked.

'He is gone. Nyneve is gone after him.'

He would repeat himself forever if it helped her to come to terms with her shattered body. Tears streamed down her face while her lips moved again.

'Trap?' he guessed. 'For Nyneve?'

Her swollen eyes rolled to the charcoal likeness of an Ascended Nyneve on the wall. He followed the direction of her pained stare and let the words swill all around him as the images on the hide did.

Bleheris. Trap. Dragon.

'Gods!' It came to him like a vision. As clear and as horrible. 'He did this to you, to force Nyneve into Ascending?'

The tears flowed faster, choking the speech she could barely manage as they gathered in her throat.

'End…me,' she gurgled. 'Please.'

All he could do was stare. Gwanaelle wanted to die—not because of her own pain—but because Bleheris had used her to force Nyneve to his will.

'Save…her.'

Her last word was his name, on a puff of pain. A plea. Gwanaelle wanted to die so that Nyneve had no cause to Ascend. Or to be violated.

'I will,' he croaked. Ending his own life as surely as hers. 'If I must, I will.'

He knew he must. Yet he wasn't letting her go to the Otherworld without knowing what she had been to him.

He bent lower, hot and hard against her ear so none but she and God would hear. 'You were my life, Gwanaelle. I have been yours since Cai first chased you into Melangell's yew circle. If I had been less of a coward, I would have returned your affection in full force, every day, no matter what my vision showed me, so that you could bask in the sunshine of my love as long as you lived. You deserved at least that.'

Another croak. Too little. Far too late. He would take that pitiful sound to his own grave. 'Instead, I pushed you back. Over and over. For fear of what loving you might mean, and now here we are…'

He leaned across without taking his other hand from her face—nor his eyes from hers—and gently unsheathed his blade. The one from

Trellech. The one Cai had liberated when they killed the watchmen. The one from his vision. It hissed in the quiet of the shelter.

'When Nyneve returns with Bleheris I will take his head off and bury him under a pile of the stones he threw you on where nothing further will come from him, but you...' He stroked her crusty hair back away from her throat with unsteady fingers. 'We will place a beech seed under your tongue so it will grow as golden and blazing as your hair and warm us through winter as your presence did. I will protect Nyneve until she no longer needs me and we will remember you every single morning as your favourite light peeks over the valley-ridge.'

Silent tears streamed down her face and she turned her eyes away from his blade, up to his. Clinging there.

'Hold onto me, Gwanaelle,' he softly ordered. 'Let the softness I have longed to show you be the last thing you behold.'

She did; gratitude, fear and love filling them in equal measure. All the love she had never been able to express. Eifion clung to that as he drew his sharpedge along her jaw from ear to chin with a wildly trembling hand, fulfilling the Creil's promise. The pain of it would be no worse than her broken body but it would take her a moment to surrender. Her body fought the loss of its own lifeblood, lurching more than someone with shards for bones should be able, but then was still, the eyes that had clung to his now lifeless.

And she was gone.

Eifion tossed the blade away and fell forward over his love; protecting her far, far too late.

X L I

Ascension

SHE HAD long-since tossed Bleheris' furs aside and his fire had long-since exhausted itself but, now, Nyneve lay wrapped as snugly as she had for a century in the Creil. This time she did not resent it; this time she was there by her own intention. The dry, scaly patches on her skin had first spread across the rest, overcoming much of her body and then she had been plagued by a thirst so great that she had struggled down to the waterfall pool and nearly drained it dry. Her body, swollen almost unrecognisably by so much water, had split through scaly skin in patches, and then the fine hairs on her body had begun to grow and weave, forming a firm sheath around her, becoming thicker and pressing her more airlessly tight within it at much the same rate that a weaver spun their web. She'd panicked at first, twisting against the pressure on her lungs which made every inward breath a bit harder for every outward one she took until, eventually, she tried not to breath much at all; just shallow little huffs.

The absence of air first made her weak, then very sleepy and she'd lost track of how long she'd lain here.

The whole time she had just one thought in her head.

Save Mother... Save Mother...

If she could get to her within a half-day of Ascending, her magic might be powerful enough to heal her broken bones and seal her torn flesh.

Within the hug of her flesh sheath, parts of her started changing, moving independently of her own will. Between one moment and the next she'd get the uncomfortable sensation that something was in there *with* her. Like...worms... Tickling and wiggling their way through the tightest of spaces. Seething. But there was no Searing, there was no pain.

Until there was.

It came on the second day. A pressure so powerful and complete that she felt sure her bones would snap from the bending, one after the other, leaving her as weak and formless as her mother. A few muffled cracks made her wonder if some had, in fact, fractured from the pressure, but her bonds were so tight she could not tell. She wriggled what she could of her fingers—*still fingers*—and her toes—*still toes*—and she flexed any sinew that wasn't too compressed to move. They felt like her own sinews and yet…not, somehow. Then the pain returned and the bones seemed to reform, realign, to strengthen again into something strong enough to hold up a body.

She knew the moment her second heart started to function. It quickened deep in her chest and beat out of time to its twin at first—which is how she came to notice it—before catching her body's rhythm and slipping into pattern. Then it thrummed in time with its fellow and she felt its power surge through her body. The magic of a second heart. It was then that her back began to twitch and she realised how hunched over she had grown within her prison sheath. Not the kind of hunched that grew painful with the passage of time, the kind of hunched that felt…right. Natural.

'Gods! Nyneve!'

She first heard Eifion's voice as a quiet, muffled thing but he began clawing at her sheath with his bare hands, tearing at the silk-skin mix and trying to give her some air.

'What have you done?'

It was only when she tried to speak that she realised she no longer had the talent. Her tongue and teeth had changed—one shrinking, one sharpening—and whatever lips she had once had were now numb. Or gone. Yet speaking with her mind was second-nature now and so it was easy to shout a warning to him.

Stop!

He flew back across the cave a short distance then gathered himself up and crouched, warrior-ready, assessing. She could see him without eyes. Was that part of the magic of Ascension?

He crawled back to her side. 'Oh my sweet girl, what have you done?'

I have saved her for us both, she thought, proudly, and wished for just one more moment of speech so that she could say those words to her father. To the man she'd only ever wanted to make proud.

'Foolish, foolish girl...'

Disappointment washed through her. How could he not be happy at her choice? She had *saved* Gwanaelle...

He plucked at her sheath, not urgently but with concern, discovering its makeup, feeling her form within, reeling back when some part of her curled and vibrated against the pleasure of his touch.

'Can you hear me?' he whispered to the quiet cave. 'Nyneve, do you live? Please tell me you live.'

She could not, but she could show him. She concentrated inwards and thought as strongly and clearly as she could.

I love you.

Eifion gasped and pressed a hand to his chest. 'I felt that. Was that you?'

Well, it wasn't God! Frustration broiled within her. She had spoken to Bleheris with such little difficulty yet Eifion was as insensible as a newborn.

He sagged back against the cave floor. 'I was going to come after you, track you, but your tracks only led here...'

He was going to leave Gwanaelle? To follow her?

He sighed. 'In my heart that I would have done it, too—in a moment, if I had such magic in my own blood—but, Gods, how I wish you had waited.'

Waited? While her mother suffered? His greatest love?

And in that moment, she saw with blazing clarity what it was that had caused such tension between them these past few winters. She wanted her Father's love; all of it. She was as greedy for it as the Dragon she was finally becoming. Yet Eifion had a whole part of himself that she could not touch; the part that was locked up safe for Gwanaelle.

That always had been.

'Nyneve.' Sorrow leached off him. Strong enough to smell. Almost to taste. He stroked the length of her cocoon. 'You did not want this...'

I want her to live. More than anything.

'And now I have lost you both.'

Within the heat of her humid little sheath, icicles formed.

No...

'She is dead, Nyneve. She is at peace.'

No!

This time he flew clear across the cave, almost to the door. Almost over the very edge that had killed her mother. A furious grief formed deep in her gut and burned to be outted. She twisted and raged against it, rending her skin-sheath in places. Cold air rushed in where the rends were and she had her first moments of liberty in two days. She flexed the first limb she could twist free, and gouged her toes against the dirt to get purchase. They clawed deep into it and held her steady. Her writhing became moans and then frustrated snarls as she struggled against the clingy sheath, but then her snarls became yowls and she realised that it was her lungs making the monstrous squall.

Outside, Eifion scrabbled back from the edge, beyond the protection of the massive boulders at the cave's lip and watched.

Her head tore free of the sheath and she saw for the first time through the sensitive eyes of *y Ddraig*. The darkened cave proved no difficulty, she could see into its furthest corners. Outside the cave, on its lip, she could see well past a cowering Eifion, over their clearing, and right into the branches of the trees on the far side where birds curled their knuckles nervously without knowing why. Everything was so...clear. So close. How had she not noticed how poor her sight was before? She turned to look at her leg and saw only a massive, shimmery thing, glinting different hues of blue, scaled like a fish yet armoured like a shield. Greater than her own leg but nowhere near as big as the dragons in her dream. Just as lustrous as they had been, though.

So, *y Ddraig* must grow like any other creature. By her reckoning she was the size of a horse. How long before she was as big as her dream dragons?

She tossed her heavy head back and flexed her shoulders, splitting the sheath down her bony spine, ripping her way out of it until it hung, tangled around the lumped masses at her back.

Wings!

They flopped there, wet, curled and crumpled—useless!—and had no strength to break free of the flesh sheath she had sloughed nearly completely away.

But she could worry about them later. Feet had served her well enough for a fortenyear.

She lurched upright and struggled to balance there. Her massive legs had a new joint in them—was that one of the cracks she had heard?—and they let her new bulk sit comfortably on them like springs, but her first steps sent her tumbling chin-first onto the earthen floor of the cave as she tripped over her elongated feet. Coals and ash went flying as she slid across the cold fire. Her short arms—forelegs now, she supposed—were mostly useless in terms of righting herself but they gave her the start she needed to haul herself back up again.

Her mercy dash to her mother was scarcely going to be a picture of dignity.

She staggered, she wobbled—if she tumbled over the edge she would not be able to save herself from the rocks below—but she made it to the cave's mouth and turned toward the rocky incline she'd used to climb up here when she was still a girl. She'd made this descent scores and scores of time and she knew every footfall as well as the skin on her hand.

Although there was nothing familiar about *that* now, either.

'Nyneve…'

Instinct, pure and simple, made her turn and roar a warning to Eifion. She had no idea what her body could do yet—she had a tail slashing around behind her that seemed to have a will of its own determined to over-balance her—but she didn't want to hurt her father while she found out. He paled and retreated. Time enough for apologies later. She turned and continued her path downwards. Making the climb with nimble, human feet was one thing, making it with the deformed, clawed feet of *y Ddraig* was quite another. No wonder they flew everywhere. Stones went tumbling down into the pool below and cascaded ahead of her as she rode the landslide as best she could. Those useless wings were slowly filling with life, unfurling, flush with blood, but remained nothing but a hindrance to her right now. Yet, she made it to the bottom and the flat, grassed valley floor she knew so well where it took no time with her greater steps to lurch over to Gwanaelle's shelter. Eifion ran behind her, his hand on his sword. Her keen eyes saw his fingers flexing on the hilt from their new position high on her skull.

That truth nearly killed her: her own father was afraid of her.

She skidded to a halt at the opening to the shelter; half because she was uncertain of what she would find inside, and half because she simply couldn't fit through the opening. Those stumpy forelegs finally came in useful. She shredded the hide and tore herself a horse-sized entrance, effectively bringing Gwanaelle out into the open air.

There she lay, laid out like a princess, broken and battered as she'd last seen her but bruised horribly now, and sticky with her own blood, but Eifion had composed her so she had dignity in death.

Her dragon vision went straight to the fresh blade wound across her throat.

'Nyneve—'

She spun on Eifion as he ran towards her and roared her pain, flushing woodland creatures out of their hides as far as the next valley. He skidded mid-sprint and changed direction just as she coughed up her first flame. Or would have if her body had been working fully yet. As it was, it was a vulgar kind of belch that nonetheless communicated her dismay and disgust at what he had done.

You took her life?

While she had given up hers to save it.

'She begged me,' Eifion called from behind the log that was his refuge. The fire-side log that had been a seat for countless meals and rest times when she was human. 'Bleheris did this to her in order to force you to Ascend. She wanted you free to choose.'

Truth.

A hatred for the Myrddyn both deep and pure surged through her. He might have been her own kind, but he was well and truly marked. Whatever it took, she would find him and she would make him pay for what he had done to them all. Had he not come, Eifion never would have left the valley and he never would have fallen foul of the warriors in the South and returned home so disfigured. Had he not come, Gwanaelle never would have lain there, broken. Had he not come, a young dragonling never would have been seduced by the beauty and magic of her people.

The tiniest voice of reason knew that, alone, was not a reason to hate him, but she could hate him for attempting to violate her and she could absolutely hate him for tearing apart her family. No doubt he would spout a score of reasons that he was not a bad man but she would always know the truth. He was the worst kind of man. Worse than Man himself.

She spun back to the lifeless form that was Gwanaelle and let her legs fold her to the ground whereupon she immediately began to slather her mother with her long, thick tongue, curling it around her broken limbs, streaking it across her bare flesh. She tasted of violence and sorrow, and of death.

But she did not change.

Even the mouth-waters of *y Ddraig* could not help now.

The silken skin-sheath suddenly became an unbearable annoyance as it dangled from one of her horns in the corner of her vastly widened vision and she twisted and spun to try and shake it loose. Gods, why could she not be free of it now it had served its purpose and transformed her?

'I can help you,' Eifion called out from behind his log. 'Do you need it, Nyneve? Will it help her?'

Truth.

Nyneve's head came up, then looked back toward her wings, her hearts pounding. The sheath could help? Why not, since it still pulsed with the magic of *y Ddraig*? She turned back to Eifion and nodded, except that to him it clearly looked far more fearful than a simple nod because he cowered behind his log once again. She raged both at his human incompetence and to see him so belittled as he ducked completely away. It took everything she had to calm herself, lower herself as flat as she could and make no sudden moves so that Eifion could peer above the log, ease his way across the clearing and move closer to her side.

Still that cursed hand twitched on the sword.

Had it not done enough damage this day?

'Easy... Easy...'

He spoke to her exactly as he spoke to the deer and boars he wrestled just before he delivered the swift blade to their heart, but the small hands of Man were nothing if not nimble and he had some success first loosing the sheath from the tangle of her spine-horns and wings and then, as he grew bolder, shimmying it down toward her unpredictable tail taking care not to rend it. She pushed back up onto her legs before he reached the dangerous tail and he stumbled back out of the way, leaving her to curl around and take the sheath carefully in her mouth. Her sharpening teeth were next to useless but it turns out she had not lost her lips entirely, they had just grown thin and long with her snout.

She lay the sloughed skin over Gwanaelle like a shroud and spent some time tucking it around and below, pressing it with her mighty nose, and eventually rolling her mother twice until she was as thoroughly swathed as she, herself, had been. Just nowhere near as suffocated. Although, did it matter if she was not breathing? If the transformative power of the sheath was enough to restore her mother to life, then it certainly would come to matter.

Truth.

'What have you done?' Eifion asked from a safe distance. She turned at the sound of his voice and he stumbled back a little, then caught himself and stepped bravely forward again.

Too late, Father. I have seen it.

'Is that a burial shroud?'

No! Gods, would he kill Gwanaelle a second time by burying her?

She crouched low, tucking down below her shoulders and snarling right at him, baring those needle teeth for him to consider.

'I should leave her?'

She sheathed the teeth, stood a little taller. He understood.

'I will leave her. How long?'

What did he want her to do, stamp the ground three times? She swung her head to look at her Mother's shroud then back to her father and did the best imitation of a shrug that she could do with her uncooperative new body. It was enough.

'I suppose this is very new to both of us,' he sighed.

'Will she be healed?' he wondered, aloud, and Nyneve wouldn't have answered even if she could have. Because she simply did not know. What if Gwanaelle, too, was transformed into a dragon? Then what?

Was it horribly selfish to hold some tiny measure of hope for that because it would mean she would have company?

It was a kind of agony to be able to understand the language of Men yet no longer speak it. Other Ddraigs were raised in virtual isolation, and so living the life of a hermit would be no great challenge for them.

How lonely might she be?

'Will she be scarred?' he continued, gently stroking his hands across the silken sheath as he had done with her. 'Will her flesh be as monstrous as mine?'

That brought Nyneve's head around. The waters of her mouth might be wasted on her mother but perhaps they could still do some good for her father. She pushed to her feet.

He flinched again but, this time, he did not stumble away from her. *Progress, Father...*

She took a moment to decide how best to approach this then decided that the best strategy was a fast one. She sprung, knocking Eifion to his back and pinning him down with the weight of her belly on his legs and her forearms on his shoulders. Peeling his wears away with her new claws was difficult enough without his twisted struggling, and so they tore more than she would have liked. Who would mend them for him? No Gwanaelle, no Nyneve; his own stitching would be poor indeed. But as she peeled, her vision fortennights ago was proven.

Not attacking. *Saving...*

'Nyneve!'

She laid him virtually bare and then set to work with her large tongue. A faster exercise for a Ddraig fully-grown, certainly, but once he realised her intent he eased his struggle and let her swathe every exposed inch of him, rolling as Gwanaelle had so she could attend to his back as well where the worse of the gouged flesh was.

Gods, he was delicious. Her own skin seemed to tighten as her newborn's hunger made itself known. She'd always liked her meat uncooked but never had a desire for it living before. She began to chuff as she lathed, filling her massive snout with the scent of him, trembling with the desire to just clamp her teeth into this thick flesh.

'Nyneve...'

It took more strength than she thought she had to stop, withdraw, back away a score of paces and let Eifion struggle back upright. He tucked his torn wears around himself in the still-cold air and stared down at his flesh.

Nothing. At least not so soon. But it would heal far better than any of her mother's salves.

Truth.

He retrieved his sword, stumbled over to Gwanaelle and dropped down next to her, then lay panting as her guardian.

Nyneve found the only patch of sunlight in the valley with her keen eyes, lurched over to it and sat herself down in its subtle warmth. Immediately her wings began to tremor happily and she thought how much better they would feel dried of the cocoon's sticky moisture. She concentrated on them and felt them stir, rise, and they unfurled a little to dry in the sunlight.

At last, she could rest.

They had been through an ordeal these past days, all of them.

Gwanaelle and all her broken bones lay suspended in her sheath. Eifion slumped, one arm draped across her, sleeping for the first time in nights of vigilance.

And, so, Nyneve rested, too. Enjoying the way the weak, returning sun soaked into the shimmering blue of her scales, the way it energised her as much as any bloodied beast, letting her new body recover from the trials of Ascension. Her eyelids felt heavier as a dragon than they'd been as a girl and they longed to close, so she let them, for just a moment, and felt the tickle of her thick lashes on the rough scales of her snout. How odd that such tough hide should be so sensitive to the kiss of eyelashes. She opened them again and let them flutter closed just to enjoy the sensation.

But, as she did, she caught a glimpse off to one side, lurking in the distant tree line of the clearing, of a man, robed in grey and with a pack slung over his shoulder, watching her. Nodding. As if satisfied.

Bleheris.

She sucked in a mighty breath to roar her hatred of him but as she turned to better focus on him she found nothing lining the clearing but trees. She grappled out with her mind, hunting for him but found nothing but silence.

Yet she was certain of what she had seen.

Flee, Cunning Man, she said to the silence. *For when I catch you, you will wish you had never lived.*

X L I I

Rise

HOW DEEP DID someone have to sleep to wake feeling like they were born anew?

Gwanaelle stirred and remembered too late the horrors she had endured at Bleheris' hand. She prepared for the screams of pain to come, but there were none in the darkness. It was only as she frowned that she felt the rough rub on her face of...something...and the pressure all around her. She shifted and found that she almost could not.

Gods, had she been buried still alive? Had Eifion interred her in the manner of her birth-kin, wrapped in the shroud of her cloak rather than laid out for the earth to reclaim? Had he not checked that her heart had truly stopped? The panic of instinct made her twist and lurch against the bindings and immediately the pressure lifted.

'Gwanaelle?' he murmured sleepily from right atop her.

She thrashed, not pausing to wonder how she could manage it with barely an entire bone left in her body, and gasped for air that she could not find.

'Gwanaelle!'

It took only a moment for Eifion to claw his way into the shroud, not near her mouth but close enough that she could wrench her face sideways and suck in the cold fresh air. The heady mead of two strong lungs filled with life. Had the air in their valley always tasted this sweet? Or had she, indeed, died and this was the passage to the Otherworld? Either way she practically lapped at it.

'I will help you.'

He could not work fast while sobbing and Gwanaelle wondered that she'd never ever seen him weep before. Not strong Eifion. Tears ravaged his face as her eyes grew used to the light after so long in the dark. Though she could not say how long it had been.

He took up his blade and began sawing at her bindings and in that moment she remembered it—the cold sting of its blade on her throat, the warm torrent of her blood fleeing her body. Yet...she lived. How? But as she tried to speak, he was reaching into the shroud and wrapping his strong, smooth arms around her. Pulling. The shroud came away and tumbled aside and she was free.

And naked. In Eifion's arms.

Yet he seemed not to care. He hauled her up against his chest where they sagged together on the floor and buried his nose in her matted hair.

'You are restored,' he croaked against her ear. 'You are come back to me.'

Had she been gone? But then his choice of phrase struck her. 'Nyneve!'

Eifion held her tighter, closer. 'It is done, Gwanaelle.'

'No!'

'She chose it. To help both of us. It is done.'

Nyneve Ascended. Forced into it by the Myrddyn. 'Not for me.'

'For us both. Look...'

He leaned back and it took her a moment to notice any different. Even after his torture he had always looked the same to her. Beautiful. Her still bloodied fingers came up to his jaw. 'Your face...'

'All of me, Gwanaelle. I am restored, too.'

She scrabbled at his wears and examined the flesh of his chest where it had been furrowed with wedges of rotted away flesh, covered over with thick, knotted scars. The best they had been able to do in the cellar of the whorehouse. Most of his body had been left like that. Now, though, his flesh was more even. Imperfect, still, yet no more scarred than if he had fought a recent battle.

'You are healed?'

'We both are.'

'Why did you not end me, Eifion? You gave me your vow.'

He took her fingers in his large ones and traced them across her throat where she now wore a torc of disrupted flesh. The only part of her not to have healed. 'I cut you from ear to chin, Gwanaelle. She brought you back. Or at least...this did.'

She pushed to sitting and her gaze followed his hands to the sodden sheath lying inert on the ground. 'From the Otherworld?'

'This was what changed her into *y Ddraig*. She wrapped you in it while it was still full of the magic of Ascension. You are restored.'

She remembered laying in the pool at the bottom of the valley's mighty cascade, staring at the sky, counting her broken bones, trying to get a sense of her wounds. Now, she squeezed her own limbs, poked at her ribs. In her arms and legs she could feel only broad lumps where her breaks had been. Scores of them.

She looked up, around. 'I am in your shelter.'

'Yours was destroyed, I brought you here to be safe, but you are never leaving it again.' His dark eyes blazed at her. 'Do you remember what I said right before I...'

Her lashes fluttered. She remembered being in such pain, and she remembered the sting of his blade, but between that... Not words, just a feeling. Just... happiness. Which made no sense if she was about to die. It could not be real.

'I am sorry.'

He rubbed the forks between her brows away with his thumb. 'Do not be. I have reason to say it again.'

Yet then he seemed to falter, undecided.

'For as long as we live, Gwanaelle ferch Eiludd, wherever we go, I will protect you. Protect and love you. With my body. With my soul. As you deserve to be loved. So many winters ago the Creil showed me a vision, showed me my blade on your throat and I have been running from it ever since, but now that vision is spent and I no longer have anything to fear from loving you, from laying with you as befits a woman of your grace and beauty. As befits my bonded woman.'

Life surged through her blood, anew.

'You... You wish to bind with me?'

'It is already done. I cannot think of a more solemn binding than for us both to have been transformed together by our magical daughter.'

She stretched up toward his lips and he easily met her halfway. This kiss was not as forbidden as the last they had shared, not as desperate, but it blazed and broiled and endured as long as their love had. Eifion scooped her up into his arms again and simply held and held and held. It was some time before either of them were willing to surrender the embrace.

'Nyneve...?' Gwanaelle finally mumbled.

'She is still here, though I do not know how long for. Her Ascension was a se'nnight ago—'

She had slept in that airless thing for seven nights?

'She will need me...'

'She is ravenous, from sunrise until set, and has frightened away most of the creatures of this valley. I do not think that it can sustain us all as she grows.'

Gwanaelle looked up at him. 'She cannot leave.'

'If she does not, I believe we will have to. There will be nothing to eat within a day's ride of a waked dragon.'

'Then we will eat grasses. Plants. Like during the Darkness.'

'You need to see her to understand.' He eased her out of his lap and pressed to his feet then reached for her hand to lend her his balance. 'Every day she is less and less the girl we knew and more and more a dragon. I dare not even get close now. She dares not. She has been sleeping in the cave.'

Gwanaelle forced steadiness to her shaky feet and stepped behind him as he cleared the way for her to leave the shelter. She stepped out into the bright sunlight.

The roar that accompanied that emergence frightened her badly enough to cling to Eifion's side. He slipped an arm around her and pulled her close.

Far across the clearing thrashed a beast perhaps one-third the size of the one she had first seen in the battle of Dragon's Rest. This one was blue-hued where its mother had been red. It hunkered low and locked its gaze on them while that tail swished behind like an angry cur.

'Nyneve?'

Eifion held her back with a firm hand on her shoulder. 'She knows us, I believe, but she struggles against her new instincts. Do not get too close.'

The dragon lifted its snout, remembered that her mother had been dead just a few nights ago, and offered a strange mewling sound from deep in its throat. Until that moment it had been hard to imagine how this creature could possibly be the girl she had known. Gwanaelle shrugged free of Eifion's hold and took a small step forward. Then another. Then two. Dragon-Nyneve watched her come, narrowed her riven eyes. She was too newly restored to be able to master her sinews to run if Nyneve chose to attack, but she had to hope that any creature who had gone to such pains to save her life would not choose so casually to end it again.

'You are much changed, daughter,' Gwanaelle called. 'But I would know you anywhere by your eyes. They are as beautiful now as they were when last I looked into them.'

The mewling eased, became a half-purr.

So, there was no more speech for the girl who liked so much to have her say. What an absence for them all.

'You have restored my life, Nyneve. Thank you. I hate what it has cost you, but I cannot say that I am not happy to be in this world a little longer.'

Dragon-Nyneve stepped in and her size meant that it brought her closer than ten of Gwanaelle's, but there was no malice in it even as she strained, obviously, against the instinct to swallow her whole.

'Eifion says if you continue to grow so fast you will have to find more food than this valley can offer.' She studied those neatly recumbent wings. 'Can you fly?'

Nyneve stood, unfurled, and began to flap. A storm-like breeze whipped up and bits of dirt and grasses flew wildly around her as the dragonling lifted off the ground like an injured bird. Not high, and not far but...up, but then she slammed back down onto the ground and roared in frustration. The sound was terrifying, but a mother's compassion was deep.

'Like any sinew,' Gwanaelle reassured, loud, to distract Nyneve from her self-pity, 'you will have to grow those that support your wings. Strengthen them. Do you think child Eifion could lift a mighty sword the first time he tried? It is the kind of strength that will only come through use. You need room to practise.'

Nyneve lifted her snout and looked up at the highest edges of the valley.

Gwanaelle took the opportunity to move closer. Dangerously close. She stepped well within striking distance. Nyneve peered down at her, her eyes suspicious slits, but then Gwanaelle did nothing worse to her than place a hand on her shimmering hide. It was like oil on armour under her touch.

'It breaks my heart, Nyneve, but I think you need to leave this valley. At least to hunt. There is not enough food for you here.' Nor for them, but Nyneve as a girl had always been self-interested. There was no reason to assume Nyneve as a dragon would have new interests. It was part of who she was. Part of *y Ddraig*. 'But how, if you cannot fly out?'

The sight of a shame-faced dragon, head hung, was thrilling in its absurdity. Her hand curled into the blue scales. Riven eyes went to the waterfall.

Gwanaelle realised. 'You never finished your climb.'

Nyneve's intent gaze flicked past her and she knew that Eifion was approaching. He joined her.

'Some birds pick their way over rocks,' he said, 'when they could as easily fly. Perhaps you can, too—?'

'I have known the uncomfortable bottom of that cascade,' Gwanaelle broke in. 'Do not try it until you believe your wings can at least stem your fall.'

Nyneve's flesh trembled from the force of being so close to prey. Gwanaelle did not want her to suffer so.

'You will not eat us,' she reassured her daughter, and believed in her heart that was true. 'But you are as newly made as I am. Your body does not know that yet. Go, Nyneve. Travel long. Find something bigger and slower in the upland moors to feast on.'

An aurock. A horse. A boar. A family of goats.

'Once your wings are fully strong you will be able to return here as often as you like, and we will await you.'

Enormous, glistening eyes passed from mother to father.

'You are *y Ddraig*, now,' Eifion said. 'And a woman grown. Our job is done. You will always be our Nyneve and we will always love you.'

'But your future does not lie with us,' Gwanaelle added sadly. 'Get to the uplands where you can stretch your wings and build them. Hunt. Learn. Come back to us a giant, accomplished creature and show us what you have become.'

Nyneve dropped her snout to the earth and they were both able to curl their bodies around it in farewell. As she sat back up, her snout paused at Gwanaelle's belly, and she chuffed in a mighty breath.

Riven eyes widened.

'I could hear another presence within your shroud,' Gwanaelle said. 'Tiny and pattering beats between my own. You have saved more than just your mother this day.'

Eifion stared. 'The shroud has…made you with child?'

Gwanaelle had never imagined she would laugh again. 'I believe we have you to thank for it, Eifion ap Gwilim.'

He practically fell into her embrace and then scrabbled to be more gentle with her. She curled into his strength.

Something about that changed Nyneve. She stood, stepped back, withdrew. As though she knew that their responsibilities now lay with *another* child. One who needed them far more than she now did.

Her gaze went to the cascade.

'We will always be here, Nyneve. Waiting for your return.'

But if the dragon heard her, there was no sign.

Her riven eyes were fixed firmly on the horizon.

Uplands

HER FORESHORTENED little forelimbs were not much use for climbing except that the curved talons on the end of each knuckle was spectacular for gripping around the large rocks comprising the face of the cascade she'd lived below her whole life. Nyneve knew this climb almost as she knew the pathways and pockets within their valley. At least, she knew it as far as the toad-shaped stone. The upper limit of her previous climbs.

Now, she clung to that stone with her scythe-like claws and drew her bi-fold legs up under her for another push. Far below, Gwanaelle and Eifion watched her progress. She could feel her mother's fear for her, but several times when she'd nearly fallen her wings had heaved madly and created enough lift to steady her against the sheer rock-face. Now, all of them believed she was not going to plummet to her death, but a tumble was most definitely still a possibility and the higher she went, the more injurious a tumble could be.

She pushed against the stones at her feet and her legs lurched her awkwardly upwards, her wings and tail both providing added purchase. At their full stretch, her legs were long and so each push— exhausting though it was—raised her significantly toward the top that she had seen in her dream. The one where her charred flesh had come away on the sharp rocks and she'd cowered away from the beasts waiting and resting in the great lakes at the top.

Now, she *was* one of those beasts. Albeit a small one, and she had a vast amount of growing to do in her first year, and a vast amount of growth required an even greater amount of nutrition.

Her mother was right in this—she would not find enough food in their valley to fuel such growth.

But Gwanaelle was wrong about something else. She had no idea how hard it had been for her to crouch, quiescent, as two people moved about at her feet—hugged her!—when all she wanted to do was gobble them up. It took every shred of willpower she had not to do more than lay there and look.

Gods, how tasty Man smelled.

So she could not come back, not as long as her parents lived there, and certainly not if there was to be a child.

The damage she could do…

The lip of the waterfall grew closer as she shoved her way toward the top notch of the cascade's stony spine. Once she passed that threshold, there was no going back. To Eifion. To her mother. Not until she had learnt how to control that part of her that was more beast than woman, the part of her that wanted to consume everything that breathed in that valley. The part of her that wanted to kill.

The late-Rise sun warmed her back but where, in the past, it had caused sweat to trickle down between her small breasts, now it simply soaked into her hide and gave her more strength to undertake this arduous climb. Near the top, she paused, rested, ashamed that the magnificent beasts waiting there for her would see her so pathetic and lumbering. Unable to fly, crawling like an ant along the earth.

She reached out with her mind and felt for them but found only silence. So they were not yet aware of her coming. *He* wasn't… The one with the voice that could insinuate itself straight into her mind the way the Myrddyn had. The one who had spoken to her. The one who said he would wait for her. How much harder would this be if she did not have a strange kind of friend waiting for her up on the moorlands; if she was doing this completely by herself.

When she was ready, she used her legs to push and her weak wings to haul herself up over the cascade's lip as proficiently as she was able, until all of her tumbled up into the waters where they gathered before spilling the great height down over the edge of the rocks, but as she lay there, panting, she lifted her head and saw nothing of the world in her dream.

No stands of wood.

No deep, sparkling lake.

No dragons. Anywhere.

No….*him.*

Just a trio of determined streams coming together off the bland moor into one larger one that fed the cascade tumbling down to the valley floor. To Eifion and Gwanaelle's world. The world that was no longer hers. She pressed up onto dragony elbows and peered down her snout at the days and days of nothing but flat uplands that she could see all around her.

And she immediately knew what loneliness was.

EPILOGUE

She is going to need you.

She does not need anyone, Master.

Bleheris glanced at his acolyte. They did not waste energy with speech when together, not when their minds would serve so very well. They had not done so since that first day by the entrance to the Otherworld. Since *their* first day.

So she will have the world believe, but she is wrong, Lailoken.

The younger man stared deep into the fire, but Bleheris knew what it was that held his focus tight-fist. The Ddraig, Nyneve, lurching her way across the moors. Finally amid the kind of space she needed to perfect the synchronicity of her sinews; to feed and to grow into her new body.

Finally out of that cursed, aberrant valley.

She bested you, Master.

She has Ascended, has she not?

Lailoken shrank away from the anger he sent, then, deep into his mind. Yet he did not rush to apologise. They had known each other far too long.

Un-seeded. What purpose will she have now?

None, usually. A barren dragon lumbered about, bothering swine-herds and picking off wild creatures for an age until it got too old and too lazy to hunt for the food that would sustain it. Then it *became* the food, feeding the earth and the forest that would grow from it, but that was a regular *Ddraig,* raised as a wildling and with intelligence for only dragon things.

Nyneve was raised in love. Raised by Man to be one of them, with his cunning and his awareness of the world. None knew what would come of that kind of unnatural mating. Nor what else she could do.

Lailoken tipped his head. *Yet, you still say she will need me?*

More than any of us can know. Someone needs to guide her. She is dangerous, whether or not she could ever reproduce.

In the fire's eye Nyneve came crashing down on her first attempt to scoop up a stray moor-goat in her claws. She roared her frustration and finally gave forth a decent plume of fire. The fleeing goat exploded to flame and fell, dead, onto to the short grasses. Bleheris smiled. Nyneve hated her meat any other way than raw.

Why must it be me, Master?

Because I must make my way south, Bleheris said. *To Artwr. He seeks an interpreter for his Holy Creil. Someone to teach him in its use…*

Nyneve pounced on the goat and tore it to pieces as they watched, sobbing in a fashion unseemly for *y Ddraig,* yet she still ate every goaty morsel, so rapacious was her need.

…and because she will not have me.

Lailoken looked up at him, finally, a half-smile on his hairless face.

That surprises you, old man? I should have gone. She might have accepted me more readily.

Ah, the arrogance of youth.

'You will have your chance, boy,' he said, aloud. 'And a far greater challenge it will be. Let's see how you fare before you crow too heartily.'

When will I go?

'Not for winters. She has a lot of raging and weeping yet to do before she is brought low enough to accept your help. Besides, I have need of you for something else, first.'

Lailoken looked back at the fire and his eyes softened.

Bad enough watching them suffer when they are barely sentient, this will be a difficult few winters.

'Do not grow attached, Lailoken. She is *y Ddraig*; the first of many that will be your responsibility as Myrddyn.'

Lailoken considered Nyneve in the flames long and deep, but then he dutifully looked up and murmured.

'Yes, Master.'

~ * ~

Also by Gwendolyn Beynon

If you enjoyed *Ascension* please drop me a line or leave a review where you bought it. Reviews help other readers discover great books and I'm hugely appreciative of anyone who takes the time to share their thoughts online.

I'm working now on *Myrddyn,* the third book in the *y Ddraig* series due the start of 2017.

Afterword

THE ORIGINS OF GWANAELLE

Much like Melangell from Book 1 of *y Ddraig* ('Sacrifice'), I modelled the character of Gwanaelle on another Welsh saint, St Winefride (or *Gwenfrewi* in Welsh). As the 7th century tradition goes, Gwenfrewi was the beautiful, pious and only daughter of an important ecclesiastical noble family living in the North of modern day Wales, much desired by Caradog, the son of the local chieftain. One day, so the story goes, Caradog ravished Gwenfrewi, who escaped and fled to the safety of her Uncle Bueno's nearby church. Enraged by her rejection, Caradog pursued her, caught her up just as she arrived at the church and lopped off her head in vengeance, whereupon her blood spilled on the ground and a flowing well sprung up out of nowhere. Her pious Uncle cursed Caradog (who was promptly swallowed whole by the earth) and then reattached her head by sprinkling it liberally with the healing waters of the holy well.

Today, that same well still bubbles forth in *Treffynnon* in northern Wales and it is the most visited holy shrine in Britain. Before the middle ages, the town was known as Llanwenfrewey (Gwenfrewi's enclosure) and going back as far as 795, the town was referenced by the English as *Haliwel*, or Holywell as it is still known today in English, showing that already it was regarded as a spiritually sacred place. Some twenty chapters of 'miracles' have been performed in or around its waters since she was believed to have lived in the early years of the 7th century.

It is a sensitive thing to take one of Britain's most revered spiritual figures and bend them to my fictional will and so I opted to recast Gwenfrewi as Gwanaelle ap Eiludd and the ravisher she flees as her father. Later, her violent death happens not at the hands of a Prince but at the hands of someone just as powerful, Bleheris. Rather than a trickle of holy, healing waters restoring life to Gwenfrewi (and her head to her body), I had first the slathering tongue of *y Ddraig* and then its snug, transformative cocoon bring her back to life.

GWALCHMAI AND GWALCHAFAD

Gwalchmai (*Gwalch = Hawk, Mai = May*) is a warrior who features centrally in *The Mabinogion*—a cycle of Welsh oral tradition believed to date back to around the 6th century but not captured in writing until the 18th century. But he is also a figure from the Welsh Arthurian tradition and believed to be cognate with 'Sir Gawain' of the English tradition. In the Welsh, Gwalchmai (Gawain) is second son to King Loth and younger brother to another familiar Arthurian name, Agarafane (Agravain). He is also older brother to Gwlachafad (who is known in English Arthurian tradition as *Gaheris* [French, *Gaheriet]*) and Gareth. Gwalchmai stands in place of Lancelot as Artwr's closest and most trusted advisor.

Courtesy of the similarity of his name, Gwalchafad is also sometimes connected with the (later) Galahad figure (who was, traditionally, Lancelot's ill-begotten but handsome and perfect son). Galahad was the excruciatingly honorable warrior who achieved the Holy Grail for Arthur and then gave his own life escorting it back to heaven. Bringing Arthur the grail is about the only element I have taken from Galahad's tradition in *Ascension*. I was much more interested in the grittier, more vengeful Gaheris who was believed to be the secret lover of the dashing, one-handed Sir Bedwyr (Bedivere) and who beheaded his own mother and got himself exiled by Arthur. Now THAT is a character!

In Malory's *La Morte d'Arthur* which is a 15th century compilation of older, oral Arthurian tales, Arthur's half-sister Morganna (*Gwyar* in Welsh) sleeps with the man who killed her husband, Lot, in battle and then also sleeps with his handsome son, Lamorak. For insulting his father's memory, Gaheris lops off her head and then the brothers set off to punish Lamorak who has fled. It was too tempting to merge Bedivere and Lamorak to give Malory's tale a twist and also to recast Gwyar as something altogether more hardened and clever than a woman of vaguely loose morals. She truly would have needed to be to survive the conniving King Lot.

MYRDDYN/MERLIN

Two 'Merlins' have come up through the ancient literature of Briton. They were *Merlin Emrys* and *Merlin Wyllt*. Of the former, 12th century scribe Geoffrey of Monmouth first names him *Merlin*. Geoffrey translated into Latin a 9th century Welsh tale about a boy sought as sacrifice to restore a King's crumbling stronghold and changes the boy's name from *Ambrosious Aurelianis* to *Merlin Emrys* a name familiar to most modern fans of Arthuriana. (*Emrys* sounds in Welsh a *"Air-m-brus"* and so it is not difficult to see how it could have morphed in an oral tradition from or into *Ambros[ious]*.) Monmouth makes Merlin a seer and he is able to save the stronghold (and his life) by revealing and releasing two skirmishing dragons below the foundations (said to symbolize the Welsh and the Angle/Saxons).

Later in his writing life, Geoffrey returned to mysterious Merlin and dedicated an entire book to him (the *Vita Merlini*), including the origin tale of that boy with no father. In it, *Emrys* is the son of a woman who is ravished by an Otherworldly figure (an Incubus) who vanishes back into the night leaving her pregnant. She is branded a whore and, while still pregnant, sentenced for execution. A holy man and bard named *Bleheris* (Blaidd) intervenes and has the execution stayed until the innocent child is born (he later becomes Emrys' mentor). The fatherless boy has unnaturally fast growth (of a kind often found in Welsh legend) such that he is able to defend his mother at just three years of age and she is freed of her crime.

There is another Merlin, known simultaneously in Scots and Welsh (and possibly Irish) oral tradition. It names Merlin as one of the three famous bards of Briton (along with Anierin &

Taliesin) and cites a hideous battle in 573AD in which Merlin goes quite mad following the carnage and flees into the Caledon woods to live as a wild-man. Hence his name in Welsh, *Myrddin Wyllt*. In Scots it is Lailocen. He retreats into seclusion for years with only a pig for company until, one day, his sanity is restored except for the enduring ability as a seer.

It is these diverse stories that first gave me the idea that Myrddyn is not a name but a title/position, and that a number of men could be a Myrddyn through time. It also introduced me to Bleheris as the mentor of Lailoken.

TRELLECH

The tiny village of Trellech is so named because of the three megaliths erected at its heart— now known as Harold's Stones. *(Tre = town, llech = stones)* which, if you believe some, are angled to reflect the course of underground water supplies that reputedly serviced nine natural wells. Today, it sits quietly on a high plain between two large valleys but in the 13th century it was allegedly a bustling centre of activity with more going on than in contemporary Cardiff or Chepstow. Recently, archeologists have been able to support this with evidence, having uncovered the foundations of a significant medieval township in a farmer's field just outside Trellech township (purchased, on a hunch, by an archaeology student who mortgaged his parents' home to secure the finance).

ABOUT THE AUTHOR

Australian author, Gwendolyn Beynon, comes from a long line of storytellers of Welsh and Cornish stock. She grew up reading fantasy and romance but the '*y Ddraig*' series is her first foray into writing fantasy and historical fiction. The idea for '*y Ddraig*' came while on a pilgrimage to Wales where she was visiting holy wells and ancient yew trees. She grew captivated with the way that the ancient stories of Welsh literature, myth and history still co-exist comfortably in contemporary Cymru, and by the atmosphere of mystery that still exists around much of Wales' natural space.

An Arts graduate from Curtin University (with double-majors in Film and Theatre Arts), Gwen has worked in communications all her life. She sold her first book in 2008 and has been writing for a living with her hounds at her feet and Celtic music as a backdrop ever since.

www.yDdraig.com.au | gwen@yDdraig.com.au